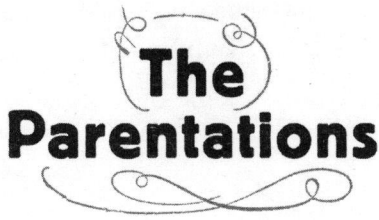

The
Parentations

Praise for *The Parentations*

'Mayfield's delightfully rich and uncanny novel, *The Parentations*, manages to be pacy and addictive, while simultaneously asking profound questions about life and death. Quite unlike anything I've ever read before.'

Ben Fergusson, author of *The Spring of Kasper Meier* and *The Other Hoffmann Sister*

'*The Parentations* has all the twists, richness and atmosphere of a dark Dickensian epic but with a tale that casts its net over two centuries. It's rare for a debut novel to have this much ambition and flair but what Kate Mayfield promises in *The Parentations* she delivers in spades.'

Jason Hewitt, author of *The Dynamite Room* and *Devastation Road*

'A strange and marvellous tale of death and long, long life from a startling imagination. A joy to read.'

Michael Ridpath, author of the *Fire and Ice* crime series and *Amnesia*

'*The Parentations* turns the epic on its head. It is a family drama splashed across the decades, with a changing and shifting London rendered in exquisite detail. The research is gripping and the ambition breathtaking, and the journey this story takes you on is quite unlike any other I've experienced.'

Lloyd Shepherd, author of *The English Monster*, *Savage Magic*, *The Detective and the Devil* and *The Poisoned Island*

'*The Parentations* is a story told on an epic scale, taking the reader from the wilds of 18th century Iceland to present day Camden Town, and which is as much about the nature of love as it is about the nature of evil. Kate Mayfield weaves her uncanny tale with rich historical detail, creating an atmospheric read which is vivid and compelling.'

Sophia Tobin, author of *The Silversmith's Wife*, *The Widow's Confession* and *The Vanishing*

'Reminiscent of both Carr's *Alienist* and Norfolk's *John Saturnall's Feast*, this debut novel is utterly compelling – acute plotting, vivid characters and writing so accomplished that Mayfield has you by the throat from the very start.'

Kate Colquhoun, author of *Mr Briggs' Hat* and *Did She Kill Him?*

'So inventive and unexpected and original.'

Sally Magnusson, broadcaster, presenter and author of *Where Memories Go* and *The Sealwoman's Gift*

'A shadowy crawl through the caverns of London's murk-filled past. Clovis Fowler is the most magnificent monster. In her Mayfield has created a dastardly villain easily able to outwit Hannibal Lecter or take on Moriaty if the whim so took her. *The Parentations* is a masterful work, by turns thrilling, beautiful, revolting, sexy, moving and downright nasty. Mayfield's prose glitters like icy stalactites illuminating the lesser-explored corners of the human (and inhuman) condition. Perfectly and sweetly chilling.'

Syd Moore, author of *Strange Magic*

'A hugely impressive novel – I loved it.'

William Ryan, author of *The Constant Soldier* and the *Captain Korolev* crime series

'An ambitious, wildly imaginative masterpiece.'

Isabel Costello, host of The Literary Sofa, and author of *Paris Mon Amour*

'*The Parentations* is beautiful, innovative and atmospheric. I was completely captivated.'

Anna Mazzola, author of *The Unseeing*

'Epic. Gothic. Magic. Somebody better snap up the film rights.'

Jane Harris, author of *Sugar Money*, *Gillespie and I* and *The Observations*

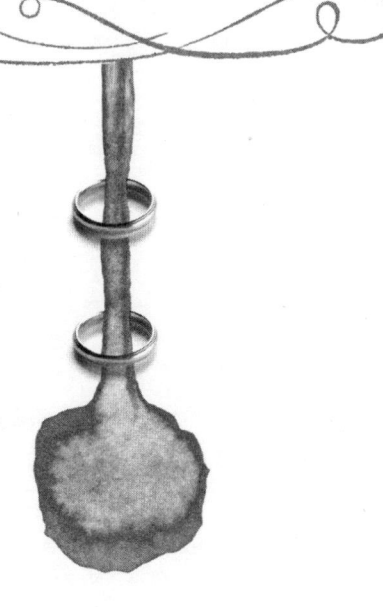

The
Parentations

Kate Mayfield

A Point Blank Book

First published in Great Britain and Australia by Point Blank,
an imprint of Oneworld Publications, 2018

ISBN 978-1-78607-242-9 (hardback)
ISBN 978-1-78607-243-6 (export paperback)
ISBN 978-1-78607-244-3 (eBook)

Typeset in Janson MT 11.5/15 pt by
Palimpsest Book Production Limited, Falkirk, Stirlingshire
Printed and bound in Great Britain by Clays Ltd, St Ives plc

This is a work of fiction. While, as in all fiction, the literary perceptions
and insights are based on experience, all names, characters, places,
and incidents either are products of the author's imagination
or are used fictitiously.

Oneworld Publications
10 Bloomsbury Street
London WC1B 3SR
United Kingdom

Stay up to date with the latest books,
special offers, and exclusive content from
Oneworld with our newsletter

Sign up on our website
oneworld-publications.com

MIX
Paper from
responsible sources
FSC
www.fsc.org
FSC® C018072

For Malcolm.

And for the two sisters of Marylebone
In Memoriam

Four thousand, fourteen thousand years, might give us pause, but four hundred years is nothing in the life of our race, and does not allow room for any measurable change.

E.M. Forster

Death. It is in the very air of London. It is stacked in charnel layers under the streets, it dances in whispers through the churchyards and falls into step with young and old alike, in whips of gritty breezes. Old kings, young whores and secret piles of children's bones lie beneath the pavement.

Death is the law that rules every living thing. Until one remarkable day, when death turns its head for a perfect second; when, after nature's foul breath is cleansed, a crevice is formed. A phenomenon breaks through the fissure to cast off the caul of death's darkness.

In the absence of death, true darkness emerges.

LONDON
2015

CHAPTER ONE

In the winter, when the low veil of cloud forms against the rooftops of London, there is little difference between night and day. The past and present may become confused under the charcoal sky, swirling together in a sudden gust of wind, until finally, they both die down, entwined in the fine soot that coats the city.

It is but noon, yet candlelight illuminates the rooms of Lawless House as if it were midnight. The macilent fingers of the sisters Fitzgerald pinch tapers that bring the candles sputtering to life, throwing light on this day, December 17th, to mark the afternoon's ritual of hope.

'Shall we turn on the lights?' asks Verity. The taper, still burning in her hand, casts a soft hint of warmth to her face and catches the rose gold chain that rests around her neck.

'No, no. Let's do as we've always done.'

Her sister Constance moves to the fireplace where the embers spit final sparks. She lays her hand on a thick cloth and wraps it around the handle of the fire shovel that has been resting near the flames for hours, red-hot and ready for her task. She lifts it like a beacon and strides into the kitchen.

It has taken two days to make the stew: pottage they once called it. Three bowls steam with a fusion of Jerusalem artichokes, almonds, milk, bread and a partridge, all of which Constance has pounded, sieved, minced and coaxed into a thick soup. She raises the shovel and carefully places the blade directly on top of the stew, toasting it without disturbing the delicate pastry that forms a rim around the pale blue china bowl. Twice more she brings the shovel down on the remaining servings. She beams with satisfaction and then, with a little flick of her fingers, garnishes the bowls with pomegranate kernels and pistachios.

It is the only day of the year upon which the sisters Fitzgerald lay three places at their table. It is another gesture of hope. Their spines ripple with just a fraction, just a tinge of excitement containing the whole of the past year's anticipation.

They eat in silence. Earlier, Verity had thrown eucalyptus leaves on the fire, along with frankincense and sandalwood. The exotic aroma lingers still. Neither has an appetite, but they eat for strength for what may happen later. Or what may not.

Verity clears the table while Constance climbs the winding stone stairs to the first floor to draw two baths. She sits on the side of the claw-footed bath while her hands seek the perfect temperature and her memory stretches to something cold and shocking, a time when water was never hot enough. 'A little more heat,' she says aloud. Her bathroom, austere in its lack of adornment is nevertheless comfortable; cosy with thick cotton rugs and heavily lined sea-green silk drapes that fall in a thick puddle to the floor. She opens them to reveal a view of the garden.

The second bathroom down the hall is slightly larger. Silver pots full of potions and lotions shoot shards of silver light through the room, crowding the small table by the window. A strand of beads hangs from a shelf littered with Mercury glass bottles from which peacock feathers shoot up and fan out. A decoration dangles from the beads in the form of death's head, a skull carved from lava stone from Mount Vesuvius.

As always when she enters Verity's holy retreat, Constance balks under the eyes of the saints that bear down upon her. She opens the taps fully in an effort to drown her claustrophobia with the sound of rushing water. Around her, Anthony of Padua, Felicity of Rome,

Adjutor of Vernon, saints protected by vapour-proof glass, hang in gilt frames, resisting the rising steam.

Constance hears Verity making her way up the stairs. They glance at each other as they pass in the corridor, and for a second or two it seems that all of their long lives, each moment, is contained and met in the invisible space between their brilliant blue eyes.

The sisters close their doors, undress, and sink into the water, each surrendering to their private reverie of the afternoon's possibilities. A train's distant, low rumble disturbs the familiar ticks and clicks, groans and creaks that Lawless House has developed over its years.

Verity adds a few drops of oil to the water, closes her eyes under the gazes of the saints and in a quick anxious burst, chants a prayer of her own invention.

'May he still be alive. May he be safe. May he find us today.'

Later, the sisters are seated at their tables in the dressing room when Constance notices that Verity's hands tremble as she makes an effort to pin her hair. Gently, she takes the pins from Verity.

'I always expect that I won't remember how to pin your hair in exactly the right way.'

'You do it perfectly. I'm going to cut it all off soon. It's easier when ... you know.'

Constance looks at her sister's reflection in the mirror.

'No hiding today,' she says, gathering Verity's hair and twisting it into a long, silver tress. 'No disguises.'

'No.' Verity rubs a hint of colour onto her cheeks. 'The only disguise we wear today is—' She stops and turns to her sister. 'I wear blue and you wear lavender, his favourites. So that he might recognize us in a crowd, he used to say. Do you remember?'

They speak these words as if they were new thoughts, as if they'd not spoken them many times before.

'Of course,' Constance whispers.

'He cried out from his dreams in this house. *"Auntie Connie! Auntie*

Very!" No one had ever called you Connie before. He couldn't pronounce my name and shouted in his little voice, *"Very! Very!"* And he was so cross with us when we laughed at him.'

The sisters are brought to silence with a memory that is older than they dare say.

Constance is the first to break the spell by reaching for the necklace she wears, one that is similar to her sister's. Searching by habit, she grasps a golden fede ring that dangles from the delicate chain. She checks that the ring is secure.

Verity, too, fingers her own necklace with an impatient twirl.

The day the boy proudly presented the sisters with the rings, he bore their kisses of thanks with patience.

'So that we'll always find each other,' he'd said, producing a third ring, one that he also wore on a chain around his neck.

They had thought it an odd thing to say, and were amused that he was so delighted by his own chain, which he kept tucked underneath his shirt. Perhaps it was a premonition of what would take place shortly after his plump little hands proudly presented the gifts.

The sisters rarely leave the house together any more; staggering their departures makes them less noticeable. But today is different and they allow the indulgence this afternoon. The sky darkens, though it is but half past two. Verity chooses a pair of sunglasses with round-shaped lenses, similar to a pair she wore when the boy was still theirs.

The air is sharp and a quick wind hits them like a sheet of ice. It's a perfect excuse to wear their long capes without fretting about unwanted attention. After all, this is Camden Town, and nowhere else in London, nor in all of the United Kingdom does costuming reach such soaring heights. It's only one day, they reason, and their only risk-taking of the year. For if their boy appears at the meeting place, they are determined to make it impossible for him not to recognize them. They are resolved that he will set his eyes upon their long, blue and lavender cloaks, he will catch sight of their necklaces with his rings shining in the dull winter light, and look into their faces, and he will know them.

Constance waits for the sound of the front gate to click into place before they turn their backs to Lawless House. The weeping willow shed late this year; its tiny yellow leaves look like eyelashes that create a carpet on the pavement.

'Oh good great God, the streets are throbbing,' says Constance as they turn the corner onto one of the main thoroughfares.

'And it's only Wednesday.' Verity replies.

'Christmas shoppers.'

Their long capes swirl in a breeze that carries discarded sheets of newspapers and the invisible grit of the high street. The sisters reach the pulsing intersection, where one of Camden Town Station's resident buskers plays a cheesy, pop rendition of 'White Christmas'. People surge from the Underground in droves; pulled by the gigantic magnet of the market, they make an orderly migration to the stalls.

The sisters, immune to the market's force, turn their anxious faces south to one of London's secret gardens, nestling off the high street. They arrive at the gates of St Martin's Gardens gripped in anticipation.

They aren't even sure he's still alive. They'd tossed around ideas about him so often and for so many years that they'd created a shared fantasy about the kind of man he might have become. He might still be a boy, they reasoned. They considered, too, that he might be dead. They have no way of knowing.

CHAPTER TWO

Clovis Fowler's eyes race across a sheet of paper. The longer she reads, the stronger her fury builds. She tosses the letter on the table.

'Willa!' She bellows.

Nothing.

'Finn!'

Sheathed in a long black dress, she stands like a proud raven in her gleaming white kitchen. She gathers and twists her burnt-red hair that flows in a thick wavy mass, and secures it with a wide clip, then begins a swift search through her house.

On the top floor in the converted attic, her boot heels clip across the wooden floor of Willa's room. She surveys her employee's space. Once littered with charms and tokens, the room is now home to bolts of fabric and a small sewing table. Shelving holds remnants of old lace, a pair of Victorian ladies' boots and boxes of buttons and trimmings. An original Mary Quant fits snugly to the form of a tattered dressmaker's mannequin. Her single bed is neatly made.

Clovis feels the quiet of being high above this south-east corner of London. Her glance falls towards the small window tucked into the eaves as a steel-grey cloud passes. In a rare moment, her expression is unguarded and her thoughts ride that dark cloud to the green and blue shimmering skies of her birth country. But this indulgence passes in an instant and her face returns to its more familiar mask, steely like the cloud, and she walks out of the room, satisfied that Willa is out for a while.

'Finn!' She calls from the landing.

Clovis moves quickly down the stairs. She jets around the house, stalking the rooms for a sign of her husband. She won't allow him to trick her again. Satisfied that neither Willa and Finn are in the main house, she takes the stairs again to her bedroom on the first floor and quickly enters her compact walk-in wardrobe. There, behind the shelving, is a small concealed compartment. She enters the code. When the door pops open she snatches a silver chain belt, places it around her waist and then reaches back into the compartment for the chatelaine.

She fastens the chatelaine to one of the links in her belt. Six delicate chains hang from the chatelaine's clip. Suspended from five of the chains, keys of various shapes and sizes jingle against each other. It is the sixth chain that she grasps tightly for a moment. Attached to it is a glass phial filled with a fluorescent greenish-blue liquid. She closes the compartment and changes the code.

Downstairs again, she dashes to the back of the house, puts her ear to a door, raps and waits. Satisfied, she uses one of the keys to unlock the door and steps into an anteroom. Here, another heavy wooden door leads to Finn's workroom. This, the oldest section of the house, is in stark contrast to the modernized rooms in the front.

The windows in this vast space are without order and sit nonsensically high near the ceiling. Only a few beacons of light shoot down into the room, inhibited by towers of furniture that look like great, tall monsters rapidly gaining strength in the darkening December afternoon. Clovis flips the switch, casting shadowy light from a carnival of lamps, chandeliers, lanterns and shades onto a sea of furniture mania.

At first glance the warehouse-sized room seems to be a wonderland of junk – a madman's stash, from decades of collecting. An educated and experienced eye would declare no such thing. Treasures. Haphazard in their presentation, but nonetheless treasures of beauty, rare and priceless, occupy this corner of Bermondsey.

Clovis keeps a mental inventory of each and every item: where they are placed, when they arrived, and what they are worth. She locks the door and heads directly to the middle of the room where a grouping of seventeenth-century wardrobes dwarf the delicate Victorian birdcages piled on tables beside them. Hidden behind a six-legged Portuguese wardrobe, a smaller oak tack cupboard seems unimportant in the company of more ornate pieces. But a certain precocious young prince had carved his name inside it and therefore rendered it practically impossible to price. Clovis gives it a light pat. One day Finn will sell it for an enormous sum.

The cupboard doors open with a faint creak. Kneeling down, she removes a thin plank that covers a false bottom and carefully retrieves a wooden box. Clovis places the box on a nearby table and opens the lock with another of her five keys. Her eyes greedily fixate on three rows of phials, neatly nestled and protected in their felt-lined home. Intricate leather fastenings hold the glass vessels in place. She counts – not because she doesn't already know the number – but because now the number is more important than it ever has been.

She moves amongst the jumble of furniture – a marble dining table here, a few gramophone cabinets there – considering in which of her several hiding places she'll place the box this time. Not satisfied, she makes an abrupt turn and leaves the vast space in darkness once again.

A low, moaning wind is whipping up, foretelling a cold night. As she passes the kitchen table she grabs the letter and then takes the box upstairs to her office. Just as she sets it down on her desk, she hears the harsh melody of keys at the front door. Quickly now she retrieves a screwdriver from her desk drawer and kneels down to an unused electrical socket, which she unscrews. The phials are gleaming more brilliantly with light than before: the liquid appears alive, as if it's moving up and down in the glass. Clovis breathes more deeply as she places each phial into the specially padded space in the wall behind the socket. She keeps a cautious eye on the door while her fingers probe. Her lips part as she reaches deep into the recess of the wall until all twenty-one phials are secure. After she replaces the fixture, the empty box is stored in a small Burmese chest beneath her desk. There's a knock at her office door.

'I'm home,' Willa announces through the door.

'Good. Light a fire downstairs.'

'Yes. I will as soon as I . . .'

'Now.'

Behind the door, the girl closes her eyes for a moment before she speaks again.

'All right.'

Clovis sends two texts, each with the same message:

Come home. Urgent.

CHAPTER THREE

A gormless drunk sleeps it off in St Martin's Gardens, oblivious to how many bones he lounges upon. His head rests against one of the tree-eating gravestones that cluster around the north wall in the green space that was once Camden Town's cemetery.

The sun that never appeared is setting now somewhere behind a wall of cloud. It was either going to be the sisters' brightest day of the year, or the darkest. Constance blows into her hands and stamps her feet in a futile effort to create warmth. Verity stands frozen. Hidden behind her dark glasses, her eyes are further deadened by the realization that another year's mountain of hope has evaporated, just like that.

It takes exactly four minutes to walk the paved path that marks the perimeter of the gardens. Sometimes they walk it together, but more often Verity begins at the Camden Street gate and Constance at the Pratt Street entrance where the black iron fencing encloses a few graves. Chest tombs covered in moss rise above the ground and stand surrounded by long grass and overgrowth.

Constance strolls past the almshouses that once offered shelter to forty-two poor women of the parish of St Martin-in-the-Fields. Verity walks in the opposite direction of her sister by the north wall. She is familiar with each gravestone, many so worn and old that the inscriptions have faded completely away, as if erased by a severe hand.

The sisters wait. For an hour they pace, they sit on the edge of the bench and feel their hearts in their throats whenever anyone enters the gardens. They perch, ready to fly to him. They search the faces each time in such earnest, and each time they are deflated when in return they are dismissed and ignored.

Another half hour passes. With moist eyes and handkerchiefs, veils of dull undisguised grief cover their faces and accompany their slow steps back to the gates. They had entered them so hopefully, but now they lumber.

Their heads remain lowered until they reach the edge of the gardens where the gravestones look as if they recede into the brick wall. Constance removes a bundle from her bag. She places a small bunch of wild Scottish December heather, tied together with a black tartan bow, at the base of the stone that reads: *In Loving Memory of Beatrice 'Bertie' MacFarlane. Died 1844.* The wild heather's purple blush against the pale, grey stone brings warmth to the lonely corner.

'Dear Bertie,' Constance says.

Verity crosses herself.

Dusk is finished; it is fully dark. Verity pulls her sister away, towards the gates, but Constance looks back once more. She notices a movement in the dark, a man, and for an instant her breath quickens and she reaches for Verity. But no, it is only the awakened drunk who comes towards them, looking stunned that he's still alive.

In Camden Town's evening rush hour, the snaking cars bounce light on the eclectic mix of architecture. Drivers poke their heads out of their windows with impatience, buses groan with the weight of their passengers. The sisters bend to the mighty power of London's workforce in a silent daze, each inhabiting their disappointment and the knowledge that they will fret through the coming year.

A bitter wind carries the scent of a cocktail of restaurant foods. The music of a violin rises above the traffic. The sisters reach the corner, where at Camden Town Station, the DJ with the disconcerting plastic grandpa mask has been replaced by a group of professional carollers. The haunting words and melody of 'Coventry

Carol' and the dark voice of the violin cuts through the sisters today like no other.

Constance feels Verity begin to crumble beside her. She clasps her arm firmly and pulls her up.

'Hold up, sister, hold up. We're almost home.'

Verity regains her balance and steps quickly away from the music; she can bear no more.

Their blue and lavender capes sweep around the corner, leaving the road that curves towards the Regent's Park and its beautiful landscape, which tonight seems miles away instead of a few metres. They pass the pub and the former coach house, then survey the street that Lawless House occupies, once again wary of being seen together. The middle of the crescent fans out, which affords them an ounce of privacy.

Verity taps in the passcode beside the black gate and they slip in and wait to hear the click that secures them. Constance is particular about her keys and the one she needs now is already in her hand. Shaking with exhaustion, she heaves a great sigh of relief when the door swings open and they are safely inside.

The strong scent of their earlier fire has lingered, and greets them now as they unwrap their scarves and throw their capes on the hooks in the entry hall. They have no need or desire to speak. Weighted as they are by their disappointment, they trudge up the stairs. Three flights they climb, winding up the anomaly that is a tower – such was the folly of its architect. On the top floor they enter the room that is completely round and that was christened the Tower Room on the first day they moved in.

The night jumps out at the sisters from the windows. The clouds have lifted to reveal a view of the brick railway bridge, sparkling clearly against the naked trees and the light from a sliver of moon.

Verity sits on the edge of the bed from where their boy once dreamed. She pats the duvet, then strokes it, then pats it again with nervous fingers.

'Will you stop that!' Constance stands at the window with her arms crossed.

Shocked at the impatience in her sister's voice, Verity jumps and clasps her hands in her lap like a scolded child.

'I'm sorry.' Constance goes to her at once and sits beside her.

There's not enough space in the Tower Room for the grief. For most of the year they keep it at bay, but rather than observe the day he was taken from them as a memorial or anniversary, it is this day of the year, this date on the calendar, the hope of an anticipated reunion, that is the hardest. It begins full of hope and ends with the trembling shadows of the sisters against the pale, grey wall of the turret.

The metallic sound of the letterbox attached to their front gate shatters their mourning. It's too late for the post. Verity darts to the window just as a man in a black hat rushes away.

'It's him. There must be a message, or another delivery.' She hastens down the stairs with Constance close behind her. The sisters look right and left as they make an effort to catch a glimpse of their messenger. He is called Benedikt and that is all they know of him.

Verity retrieves the post from the letterbox with a shaky countenance and a glance at Constance, whose form is outlined in a dark night sky.

'Here,' she says. 'You open it.'

Since the boy's absence, along with a package they receive once a year, the man in the black hat sometimes delivers parchment-coloured envelopes. These are little crumbs of hope in letter form. The sisters are keen that the letters may contain an inkling of information about their boy, and surely, they surmise, the messenger must know something of value to them. Yet no such information had been forthcoming.

'Come, Constance. Let's go back inside and read it by the fire.'

They shiver as the wind scatters winter's remaining leaves around their feet and they close their door to the thick sound of a quiet

December night. The temperature has dropped. Constance is glad to engage her mind and body to the task of starting another fire. Verity watches her, knowing that it isn't just that the temperature has dipped, but because tonight, sleep seems far away, and the fire's light offers comfort and protection from the hours before sunrise when their thoughts turn darkest.

The black-inked handwriting stares out at them from the page. The words this time are different from any other message from their unknown benefactor. Constance always considered these missives as a surrender of logic, but tonight's message has the potential to change everything. She reads aloud to Verity:

Greetings,

Please read this only as a word of caution and not as a cause for panic.

'Well that's a fine way to begin,' Verity interrupts.

Very soon you will receive your regular supply of phials. I must make you aware that the source of the contents of the phials shows signs of decreasing its output. We have never encountered this previously and are not sure if, or when, it will revert to its former production level. You are in no immediate danger; however, we are not completely without a heightened sense of awareness of the situation and . . .

CHAPTER FOUR

. . . therefore, I urge you to take great care handling and administering the liquid. To spill even a drop would be wasteful, not to say dangerous. Be assured we are constantly monitoring the situation. You will be informed of any and all new developments regarding this issue.

A reminder that to hinder, delay or subvert Benedikt – in any way – is not permissible. Any such behaviour will instigate a review of your circumstances. This again is for your safety as well as necessary for Benedikt to perform his tasks to the best of his ability.

'And then the usual reminder to keep the letterbox empty so that there's no problem receiving the next delivery.' Clovis Fowler carefully folds the letter, holding her small audience rapt.

The three people seated around her fall into their own private musings. Booming silence thickens the room. A wave of fear passes over Willa's face and tears well up, despite her efforts to control them. The young man sitting opposite her, his leg draped over one of the cushioned arms of his chair, instinctively moves to comfort Willa, but Clovis, who leans against the mantelpiece, adjusts her position slightly, implying her disapproval. He settles back in the chair and turns away from Clovis.

'Rafe,' Clovis says to the young man. 'Everything your father and I do is for your safety. I don't perceive or accept any real danger in this message. So there's no need to worry.'

Finn Fowler stands by an arched window with his arms folded. It's barely noticeable that his jaw tightens while his face remains passive. His wife's chatelaine mocks him, and the keys hanging from its chains sing a terrible chorus whenever she moves.

'But that's not true, is it Clovis?' Rafe picks at a thread in the leather cushion.

'It is true.'

He stands and faces her. They have the same auburn hair, the same high cheekbones and full lips, but all similarities end there. Rafe's glare pierces the reproachful, examining regard of the woman he refuses to call 'Mother'.

'It's a caution to be more careful. Nothing more,' Clovis says.

'And what if it's not?' A hint of panic cracks Rafe's voice.

'Are we going to die?' Willa asks.

'No one's going to die.' Clovis remains steady.

Rafe observes how small and delicate Willa looks. He notices she seeks solace from the white jade token that she fingers in her pocket and he winces at the memory.

'How many phials do we have left?' Finn finds his voice.

Clovis considers her response; normally she wouldn't bother to answer him, but she needs to quash the rising panic that threatens to fill the room.

'We have enough for now. And there's Mockett to consider. Perhaps now you'll be more appreciative of the efforts I've insisted he makes on our behalf.' The hint of an accent floats softly through her speech, her voice remains steady.

How remarkable it is that Clovis appears unmoved. Her earlier private annoyance with the letter has evaporated. No – what Clovis feels is quite the opposite of fear. A satisfaction flows through her like the warmed whisky and honey her husband once prepared for her when she first arrived in this country, its burning sensation, trickling down her throat in sweet heat. Tonight she smells their fear and senses their unease. They each revealed their hand this evening. How badly they want to live! After all their bravado, all their efforts to convince her otherwise, they still crave life.

Remarkably, the Fowler household seems a typical one, and, in a way, they have fashioned their own quotidian lives. The house, though not a grand property, affords privacy and even a small measure of clout.

The street itself is quite dull considering its central London location. Magdalen Street supports no businesses, no convenience stores, not even a cafe or pub. As a key holder street, the people who walk its pavement do so only if they live in it. Each morning the residents disperse into the neighbouring streets anonymously, rushing to purchase their coffee on busier thoroughfares. Pasty-faced bankers and young, trendy professionals, a scattering of the semi-retired who live out their last few years in east London before they retire to Kent – all these share the buildings of Magdalen.

It was an accident of fate that the Fowlers discovered this property, one that affords them a semblance of seclusion. When they first arrived in Bermondsey it was a god forsaken place, but Magdalen is a safe street now – as safe as any can be. Its transient nature is a boon to them, but that too was down to luck and not careful planning. No one asks questions of a familial nature in this corner of Bermondsey. No one asks questions at all, unless they're lost tourists searching for what remains of the antique market.

This evening, behind the doors of Number 9 Magdalen Street, they speak aloud of phials and death. Each of them wants nothing more than to disperse, to retreat to their own private space, where they can discard their masks and allow this latest news to sink in properly.

They wait until Clovis leaves the room before they stir, then they watch her climb the stairs and hear her steps clipping down the hall to her office. Finn motions to Rafe and Willa to remain quiet, pointing upstairs, until he hears her office door close.

Clovis locks the door then pauses a moment with her back against its wide wooden frame. No, this can't wait until tomorrow, she thinks. She removes the chatelaine and returns it to the safe. Standing at the window that offers a view of the back of the property, where the rooftop of Finn's workroom hides beneath the snarled empty limbs of a tree, she searches on her phone for a name in her speed-dial listing.

'Hello, Clovis.' Owen Mockett makes an effort to disguise his irritation.

'I'm coming by.'

'Now?'

'It's urgent.'

Mockett closes his eyes, summoning patience.

'Of course. The letter. I'll see you shortly.'

Downstairs, before she leaves, Clovis turns to the three people whose lives are entwined with hers, who, when they look at her, cannot conceal their impatience for her to go. The way the blood rushes to Finn's face when he spots the car keys in her hand seals the coldness she feels.

Seated in her car, she's certain they will search the house as they always do whenever she's out. They will not find the phials. A splinter of a smile crosses her face. Clovis drives away secure and undaunted by the letter's news.

She steers slowly through the portal of the Rotherhithe Tunnel. It's like a claustrophobic carnival ride, this narrow road under the Thames, demanding the constant negotiation of oncoming vehicles that pass only inches away. She takes the sharp bend where it goes under the riverbed and presses the horn in frustration.

She checks the time with a conceited smile, knowing that Finn has already begun to search his workroom. Five minutes later, when she pulls up to a single-storey warehouse on Copenhagen Place, she is just as confident that Willa and Rafe will be riffling through every inch of her office. Their predictability bores her.

When Owen Mockett sees Clovis's car on the security monitor

he takes a deep breath and releases the gate. He stands by while she parks, and waits for her request for entry into the building. Once inside, she strides through the corridor with such supreme confidence that Mockett withers a bit inside. He dreads the sight of her, and yet he cannot look away. She doesn't bother to press the second intercom, but instead waits until she hears the lock turn over – she knows he's watching. She and Finn had argued bitterly about placing a security camera outside their house. She was for it but he insisted that it would attract attention and would look sorely out of place when no other house on their short street had one. She had allowed him this little victory.

The lab is spotless. The lighting is low tonight, relegated to one corner of the room where Mockett's most powerful microscope is set. A row of small, glass sample-jars topped with black thermoset caps sit on the work counter, pristinely labelled. Clovis chooses one, holds it up to the light and turns to Mockett, who stands near, worrying a coin in his trouser pocket.

'Rafe's?'

'Yes.' He nods.

'Sometimes . . .' Clovis slides into the chair at Mockett's desk and places her elbows on top of his papers, steepling her hands.

'Sometimes, Mockett, I think your passion to reach our goal is not as great as mine – as once it was.'

'Oh it is, I assure you, it is. But, as you know, I need to stay on top of the cosmetics or we lose funding.'

'Yes, so you remind me whenever you've made no progress. But I haven't driven to Limehouse on a freezing night to talk about that. I'm here about the letter. I'm taking your extra phials. You can keep two for your own use and one for experimentation.'

'One? But, what about the project? I won't be able to continue much longer with only one phial.'

'Yes,' she snaps. 'You will. Until production is back to normal. Prepare them, please.'

Mockett stares at her. The first time Mockett saw Clovis Fowler he had been stunned by the image of her, the way her beauty commanded attention. It had been a blustery night; a strange tint of pink was cast against the grey, overcast sky, as though the heavens intended to complement her flaming hair. Mockett remembered the moment she turned her deep amber eyes on him, and how astonished he was by the way they perfectly matched the colour of her hair. She unsettled him then, as she does now.

'Mockett.'

The sheer threat she enforces with a single word from her sensuous mouth discomfits him. As much as he hates these encounters, he simply enjoys looking at her. Though she is as polished as any, there's still a quality to her that looks as if she belongs in the wild, and he often thinks of her as she was then, when it all began. The way she drank everything in. How hungry she was for the city, how she never shrank from the people, whose customs were so foreign to her. She took quickly to the utterly unique life on the Thames and wholly inhabited this country and its ways. How proud she was to sweep into his place of business with a command of the language. How she held sway over his wife. She turned heads, customers nodded when she entered. He remembers too when she first began to change and sometimes wondered what he'd missed, how he didn't see it coming. Then the baby arrived, and it was clear to him that its presence seemed to repulse her, until ... How very long ago that was.

'Owen, for God's sake. Stop leering at me.'

He flinches when she uses his given name.

He carefully wraps nine phials with Styrofoam sheets and places them into bubble pouches, then into a velvet pocket.

'Can I offer you something? A drink of some kind?' He feels he has to ask.

'No. I'll be on my way.' She flashes a smile lacking any genuineness and waits for him to open the door.

'Less cosmetics, more science, Mockett.'

'It's only a matter of time, Clovis.'

She stops abruptly at the door, and with her back to him says, 'How ridiculous you sound.'

He returns to the security screens to make certain that she's seated in her car. Her legs swing into the front seat and then she pauses to look up at the camera. He recoils from it, forgetting for a moment that she can't see him. He grabs his phone and waits for Finn to answer.

'She's on her way.'

'Got it. Thanks, Owen.'

Mockett leans back on his work counter for a moment. He thinks about what will happen the day Clovis discovers that he's no longer keeping his agreement with her. Would it be so bad? She still needs me, he reasons.

He sets the alarms and walks through the dark laboratory, then enters another section of the building in which he'd built a large flat. It makes him feel more secure to sleep on the premises. He opens the fridge, places his hands on a cold beer and mutters to himself that he'll be sorry tomorrow. Her visit has left him anxious, so tonight, at this moment, he doesn't care about tomorrow.

CHAPTER FIVE

Clovis arrives home to muffled stirrings: the faint purr of Willa's sewing machine, Finn's monotonous tinkering in his workroom. She pauses like an animal hunting in the dark. There is one missing – Rafe has left them again. The empty space in the house holds the residue of his presence.

After the additional phials are hidden with the others in the wall, she changes into a pair of black cashmere lounge pants and a long, flowing silk shirt the colour of a steel smokestack. A pair of velvet slippers cushion her steps back downstairs to the kitchen, where she fills a crystal bowl with mineral water. Holding a white linen cloth under the bowl, she carries it into the sitting room.

In the corner of the room, against the wall nearest the window, is a rare mahogany stand and oblong case. Clovis places the bowl of water on a short shelf built into the stand. Her movements are focused, as if she were performing a ritual. She steps to the other side of the room to retrieve a decorative box from a shelf, opens it and pours a small mound of a white substance into a small silver tray that rests beside the box. This tray she places beside the mineral water.

Clovis grasps the thin brass handles positioned on the side of the wooden case and opens the lid. The glow from the flames in the fireplace bounces off the row of glass bowls that are encased in their coffin-like home. Thirty-seven bowls in diminishing sizes and fitted with cork through the bottoms, are attached to an iron rod. The bowls, which lie on their sides, fit inside one another, nesting without touching, their rims painted in candy-coloured shades of pale yellow, pinkish-red, green and blue. The glass armonica, one of only three originals that exist in Britain, is her treasure.

She dampens her fingers in the bowl of water and then tips them into the tray of fine, silky chalk. Perched on a leather-cushioned stool, she steps on the foot treadle that turns the wheel attached to the rod. With her hands poised above the bowls, the pad of one of her middle fingers lightly rubs a glass rim. A clear, rich tone fills the room. Skilfully, she adds another tone that melds with the first, until gradually she builds a haunting melody. The melancholic music floats through the house, the instrument's timbre wholly its own.

Within minutes of hearing the first ethereal notes, Willa appears in the doorway of the sitting room in an ankle length white cotton nightgown. One hand grasps the doorframe, as if she's unsure if she should cross its threshold. Broken chords rise from the armonica and Willa's eyelids flutter then suddenly droop.

Clovis moistens her fingers again and continues to play.

'Sit down, Willa.'

Willa obeys.

Clovis, who has clearly dominated this strange instrument, plays languidly now, and in response Willa's head falls to her chin, heavy and exhausted. Single notes in a pointed melody further mesmerize her until she slumps and her head lolls back.

Barely touching a single bowl, Clovis creates a distant bell-like tone that drifts and fades, leaving only a faint vibration clinging in the air until the note eventually dies.

Clovis pauses in the ensuing silence, then slowly swivels on the stool to face Willa.

'Keep your eyes closed, Willa.'

The girl seems peaceful sitting in her old fashioned gown, her tawny hair resting on her shoulders. She resembles a vintage doll, the perfection of her pouting mouth and black lashes is such that they appear painted on her face.

Clovis places a chair directly in front of Willa and sits. After a moment of observation, she raises her hand and passes it over the crown of Willa's head moving it over her face, and then follows with a downward movement over the front of her body. Using stroking gestures, she repeats this path over and over again remaining within a hair's breadth of touching Willa's body. Ten minutes pass before Clovis lowers her hand.

'Willa, can you hear me?'

'Yes, mistress.'

'How did you spend the evening?'

'I searched the house, mistress. Me and Mr Fowler and Rafe did, mistress.'

The young woman's voice is less mature, with a cadence lacking its usual conversational delivery. Willa has reverted to a time long past, a time when she spoke with her head bowed, her eyes on the tips of her worn boots.

'And did you find what you were searching for?'

'No, mistress.'

'Where did you look?'

'There weren't much time, mistress.'

Clovis bristles. That's no answer.

'Willa?'

'Yes, mistress.'

'Where did you look?'

'Most places we could think of, mistress. Mr Fowler, he searched his workroom, in a few pieces of the furniture, all he had time for. The young Mr Fowler, he looked in his room and in the kitchen. I looked in your working room, mistress.'

Clovis pauses.

'How did you enter my ... working room, Willa?' she asks.

'Mr Fowler had a locksmith in, told him we lost all the keys, and had one made.'

'How long has Mr Fowler had a key?'

'About a month, mistress.'

'Willa, when you hear the music again, you will wake, and you will not remember our conversation. Do you understand?'

'Yes, mistress.'

Clovis positions herself on the stool, dampens her fingers, dips them into the chalk tray and begins the first notes of a more cheerful melody. Willa wakes to the tune of lilting phrases that resemble a child's music box. She blinks, and then becomes aware that she sits on the sofa. A blush crawls up her face, for she realizes to what she has been subjected. A sickness fills her stomach for she has no idea what private matters she may have divulged. It has happened again.

A creak in the floorboard announces Finn, who is leaning against the doorframe, his arms folded.

'You may go now,' Clovis tells Willa.

Finn steps aside to allow Willa to pass, and the girl skims out with her head lowered, aching to get away. Quickly, and almost imperceptibly, she taps the edge of the doorframe three times before she retreats.

What passes now between husband and wife is unspoken. Finn remains in the doorway watching Clovis as she closes the case of the armonica and gathers the water bowl and chalk tray. She moves towards him, and for one elongated moment Finn stands in her way. Their eyes meet, and he steps back, allowing her to pass. Her unctuous, rich perfume sweeps past him, her thick hair faintly brushes the side of his face. Weakened, he returns to his workroom where in the air of his odd collections and the snaking lines of furniture, he breathes deeply and returns to his senses.

He walks further through the maze to the conservatory where a spit of heat prevents the glass from frosting in the small hours of the morning. Certain that it dries his soul, Finn despises the parching heat of the rattling radiator.

He retrieves fresh linen from his most valuable French armoire. It is a soothing chore he performs in the conservatory, the unlikely home for his immense nineteenth-century opium bed. Willa always offers to change the linen, but she has enough to do, and he feels rather possessive of this one space that is solely his.

From here he counts the stars of winter and marks the Synodic Cycle. He believes that trade and markets move in a circular direction rather than up and down. When the new moon reaches its waxing crescent he begins calculating his next big sale, and when the moon wanes, any transaction that is not complete must wait until it waxes again. He's never lost a client using this method, though they are sometimes perplexed by his refusal to rush through an agreement on their behalf that would, in the end, handsomely line his pockets. He waits like a patient lover, following the lunar calendar for the right moment to woo, to approach, to fondle, to mount.

On the nights when the moon passes through the earth's umbral shadow he makes important decisions, like the one he made – he forgets what year it was, but quite a long time past – when he moved out of his marriage bed.

A few years ago, when life and death were imperfectly balanced, he made another vital decision. It was the night of the longest lunar eclipse in more than a decade. On the 16th of June 2011, the shadow began to fall at nine o'clock in the evening. The moon passed very deeply into the darker umbra, making it an especially Cimmerian and long eclipse. The cloud coverage that evening obstructed the view, but Finn waited patiently until an hour later, when the clouds shifted for a few moments and there, like a wise counsellor over the conservatory roof, a blood-red moon burst into view. He had been filling his pipe, which he then let slip from his hand, the tobacco falling in flecks on his lap. His upward gaze swollen and fixed towards the crimson globe, he felt its magnetic pull, much in the same way he still feels the power of the Thames tide at London Bridge.

On that midsummer night when the clouds once again curtained the remainder of the eclipse, his decision was resolute. He left the opium bed and stole upstairs, knocked gently on first Willa's door, and then Rafe's. He'd asked Rafe to sleep at home that night, certain that after such an auspicious event he would know how to advise them.

They closed their doors quietly and stepped lightly across the landing and downstairs, following Finn to his workroom. Rafe guided Willa through the rows of furniture with a light hand on her back.

Willa and Rafe waited silently that night while Finn paced up and down between a marble dining table and a stack of portmanteaus. Regardless of the sticky night air, Finn had closed the windows for complete privacy. Their faces were damp and shiny. For a moment he wavered. Is suicide really suicide when they'd lived this long? He struggled to find words that would appeal to whatever inkling of desire they had left in them to remain alive.

'Here it is,' he said. 'We cannot do it. It's not the right time. As long as there is any hope, we remain as we are.'

Willa let out a sigh of weary relief, weary regret. And Rafe – Finn could never look at Rafe without a welling of remorse – Rafe seemed resigned and just nodded.

They weren't going to die on June the 16th, the night of the total lunar eclipse. Instead, Willa and Rafe would go back to their rooms and Finn would crawl back into his private house of a bed.

Clovis had already returned to her bedroom by the time Rafe and Willa made their way back upstairs. She had been aware that the three were coming to a decision that evening. It wasn't the first time. Society always debated whether or not the act of suicide was cowardly or brave. Finn, Rafe and Willa were weak in her eyes. Their consideration of such an act was preposterous anyway, because they couldn't achieve it without her, and she'd never give her consent. But it was amusing to watch them play with the idea. She took a drink of water from the carafe on her bedside table, opened the window, and climbed back into bed. Content with the results of her eavesdropping, she slept deeply and without dreams.

Now Finn is stirred from his memory of that night by the sound of a few drunken men singing in the most appalling off-key fashion, a raucous ringing through Tooley Street. The streets leading to Tower Bridge are filled with the Christmas-party office throngs that spill onto the side streets at this time of year.

December 17th – a night on which the moon is a slice of yellow in the sky, when all those in this house are still alive and each of their hearts thump with a power that is against every rule of the universe.

CHAPTER SIX

*. . . Any such behaviour will instigate a review of your circumstances.
This, again, is for your safety, and is necessary for Benedikt to perform
his duties to the best of his ability.*

*Please remember to maintain your letterbox to ensure safe delivery of
future communication.*

It's signed, as usual,

Regards, S.

Constance folds the letter and places it in the large writing slope
that sits on her desk. The box is filled with letters, and the handwriting is that of the person they know only as 'S' – the man who
seems to act as an overseer of some sort.

'What in the world does this "S" person think we would do to
hinder Benedikt? We've never even seen the man! Not really – just
a glimpse of his coat-tails, or a peek at the top of his hat. He's a
phantom, for the love of God.'

'You forget, sister. I've seen him.' Constance motions for Verity
to sit beside her in one of the two armchairs by the fire. 'But only
for a flicker of a moment, and I would not recognize him if he walked
into this room.'

'Ah, yes, so you have.'

Verity goes quiet with the sting of a bitter memory. The sisters
had fought that day.

'We should discuss the contents of the letter.' Constance pokes a sizzling log.

'Well, there's nothing to be done but wait.'

'You know I don't like to wait around for something to happen. I think we should have a plan in place.'

'How many do we have left?'

'Three each.'

'That's fine, then. Four drops a year, and by the time we use the last phial, why, there's sure to be more!' Verity is unusually positive. 'And there's the new delivery that is promised in the letter.' She grasps her sister's hand. 'Now, let's toast a few slices of that lovely bread and not worry about it tonight. The day has been mournful enough.'

'All right, Verity.' Constance is not convinced but humours her sister. 'You know, I've a strong urge for the old toasting tongs. I'll go fetch the bread and butter, you make the ... Oh ... Oh, no.'

Constance grasps the edge of the mantelpiece. Once she's secure, she stands perfectly still, though the room still spins. She tries to gain her balance but the dizzy spell overcomes her.

'Verity, it's coming.'

'All right, sister, I've got you.'

Verity leads Constance to the chair and then streaks into the kitchen. She fills the kettle, flips the switch, and twirls around to the opposite counter, where a large bowl of lemons form a yellow mound. Just as the water begins to heat up, she juices half a lemon into a glass, and heads back to Constance with the lemon water.

The tart liquid settles her sister's stomach, but a frown of worry clouds Constance's face.

'I don't like leaving you like this. It's not fair that you'll be on your own after today's disappointment, and that blasted letter as well.'

'Never mind.' Verity masks her disappointment. 'I'll be fine. Let's make sure you eat something. We'll have that toast now.'

With the nausea subsiding, Constance finds she's once more steady on her feet. The sisters continue to make preparations for their small feast, fetching and carrying to prepare a table by the fire. A tray of butter and jam is brought, the kettle is on again, and the china is laid. Their shoes lie on the floor beside their chairs, a quilted throw casually drapes the table. The hour is late.

'I can't believe it's been six months already.' Constance says. 'No, it hasn't. It was only five months ago. I remember . . . it was July. We were in the garden and . . .'

Bang! A terrible crash of iron meeting stone rings out.

'Verity?'

Verity has dropped the toasting tongs onto the marble tiles surrounding the fireplace. Her head reels back, her arms reach out searching for the chair's support.

'No. Not you as well?' Constance untangles her legs, and kneels beside her sister. She lays the back of her hand on Verity's forehead.

'Just a bit warm. Do you need lemon water?'

'Yes, please. Just a little. I can't believe this is happening. Both of us. The timing is off.' Verity closes her eyes.

'There now. Wait until it passes, then we'll decide what to do.'

The sisters discovered quite by chance that warm lemon water relieves the symptoms that are a prelude to their condition. The dizziness and nausea are acute, though thankfully brief. They can only guess that the fresh lemon juice neutralizes the acidity in their bodies.

Constance sits on the edge of her chair, turning the old toaster tongs as thick-cut bread darkens to golden-brown in the basket.

'I love the smell of toast on a fire.'

Verity feels steadier now. Now that they've both recovered from the warning symptoms of what is to come, they sit quietly, the shadows of their profiles drawn sharply against the wall. The day's events are no less daunting and they weigh heavily upon the sisters.

A chunky bit of strawberry oozes from the side of Verity's mouth, which she lops off with her tongue, noting a hint of vanilla. She greedily dips the silver spoon in for more of the thick jam.

Fortified by the strong tea, Constance broaches the subject that resides as a fixture between them.

'Perhaps it is time, sister,' she says.

'Time for what?'

Three pairs of floor-to-ceiling French doors stretch across the far wall, each opening onto a large crescent-shaped Juliet balcony. Drawn to the view in the glow of the garden's security light, Constance fastens her gaze upon the seemingly endless rope swing that hangs from a massive, bare London plane. She mentally places the boy in its seat and hears his bubbly laughter and his commanding screams of 'higher, higher'. The picture vanishes; the velvet night whispers his absence.

'Time for what?' Verity repeats as she butters another slice.

Constance turns to her, charging the space between them with her meaning.

'Oh.'

Verity dabs her mouth with her napkin and brushes crumbs from her lap before she sidles up to Constance who has wrapped her arms around herself, and welcoming Verity beside her, she slips her arm around her sister's waist. Their temples touch while outside snow-flakes begin to swirl in a breeze that sways the ferns and contrasting foliage. The tongues of the great marble sea serpents on the patio collect the precipitation in icy patches.

'Perhaps the letter is a sign that our circumstances are moving towards a natural end. I'm just suggesting that we consider moving it up a bit in the calendar . . . to exercise the control we have.'

'But Constance, you've always insisted, even when times were at their darkest, that as long as there was a sliver of hope, as long as there was no proof of his death, that we would not . . .'

'It's a damnable decision.'

'Please, can we talk about it again when we wake?'

'Of course. We should prepare the house now, we've only a short time left.'

Snow clings to the ground of the three-tiered garden; its appearance conjures the picture of a deep woodland. Constance closes the shutters while Verity stacks the dishes on the tray. The fire is almost at its end, but Constance banks it as a precaution and places the screen in front of it. Verity scribbles a note, places it in an envelope and waves it at Constance.

'For Benedikt.'

Without bothering to throw on her coat, she scurries outside to the letterbox and drops it in.

Between them they perform a number of chores that secure the house, checking and double-checking that alarms are set, lights are off, curtains and shutters are closed. The thermostat is set to twenty degrees centigrade.

Once they're ready, Verity makes a note of the day and time. She pauses in her note-taking.

'I don't want to sleep alone, not when we're both going to be under. The Tower Room?' she asks.

Constance nods.

Verity climbs the stairs to the child's room where she drags the mattress from his bed onto the middle of the floor. Constance joins her and pulls out the futon from one of the bespoke cupboards built into the circular room. The futon conjures another memory of the occasions when they would sleep on the floor while their boy tossed in fits and woke in the middle of the night from nightmares. Lawless House swells with memories of him.

After they build their makeshift sleeping arrangements with cushions and quilting, Verity places a bowl of dried lavender on a shelf near where their heads will lie.

Each sister still wears her necklace and phials, which they remove now.

'Where? Where should we hide them – there's usually no need.'

A strange moon-faced mechanical man stares at them from a shelf on the other side of the room. Their boy had been fascinated by automatons, and had just begun a collection when he was taken from them. Constance places their phials inside the compartment of the round wooden platform on which it stands.

The sisters fall back on the mattresses in sighs, relieved the day is finally over and that their preparations are complete. Sighs turn to gaping yawns and now a deep weariness overcomes them. They lie, side by side, facing each other. The mattresses point their four corners into the circular room. Speaking softly with one another, as they did when they talked late into the night as young girls, their eyes become incredibly heavy.

And then, Verity is gone.

Constance still has a few more minutes before she too, will be lost to the long sleep. Her gaze remains on Verity, whose long silver hair fans out behind her. Only once before had the sleep overtaken them at the same time. It is just as unnerving now as it was then. She thinks again of the letter, and wonders if they are strong enough to live with the fear of their supply dwindling. Lastly, before her body commands her to fall into oblivion, the face of the boy appears, and now, lying on her back, one arm at rest upon her forehead, she reaches out to touch it. His face fades as she closes her eyes and turns on her side to face her sister again.

Their bodies curve like parentheses, mirroring the walls of the room. For two weeks they will sleep in an undisturbed half-death. They will have no sense of adjusting their positions, though their bodies will move and stretch in a variety of scenes. Dreams will not crowd their slumber. Time will pass without the call to relieve themselves, nor will their bodies sense hunger or thirst – all functions that normally poke through the nights to remind them they are still alive will be absent for fourteen days.

The snowfall has ceased and the evergreens no longer bend from thrusts of wind. The nocturnal animals that feed upon the garden have completed their evening business. The train tracks lie empty. A cowl of stillness descends upon Lawless House. The sisters Fitzgerald will not wake again until a new year rises.

ICELAND
1783

CHAPTER SEVEN

It is the latter part of May and the spring has been mild.

The insides of Stefán Hilmarsson's calves and thighs ache, even though his horse maintains a smooth gait. His roan Glossi is a good *tölter* and Stefán hopes to break his journey at one of his southernmost farms before nightfall – if the skies remain clear. Tethered to Glossi is another horse, a black, silver-maned mare, Vinda – both horses have scrambled through the bogs and over rocks and whenever they come to dry, smooth ground they dart forward into the tölt at an explosive speed.

Anxious to be home again after a week of travelling, Stefán makes his last official journey as magistrate. He has had enough of governing and longs to retreat from the responsibility. The crown of Denmark holds the monopoly on all trading and though he was one of few who lobbied for an open economy, it has come to nothing and only made him unpopular in Copenhagen.

His tenant farmers, men, women and children, split the skin of their fingers and ruin their eyes to produce the coarse, dense woollen fabric, the *wadmal* they illegally trade with the British. He allows it, and indeed secures his own trade agreements with forbidden ships and their countries. He relishes slipping through Copenhagen's mighty grasp – but only for the right price. The foreigners' ships transport the wadmal to Ireland, Scotland and England where its durability is prized. Whenever the English translator complains of the inclement British weather in his patchy, laboured speech, Stefán laughs outright because the translator has never wintered in Iceland, where horses and sheep drop down dead on account of the cold.

This wadmal, that is their life source, and the uncountable hours of tending the sheep, the endless winter days and nights of weaving and knitting, makes people touchy. Many of his farmers would rather be fishing. The truth is, they are all part-time fishermen, and the Crown continues to isolate and monopolize them, though they give their lives for a net of cod. All do what they must for one reason – to hold a begging, starving hand up to keep death at bay.

Glossi and Vinda are slow to navigate the black steaming mud pots. Sulphur suffuses the air. Stefán's mind wanders to the English again. Each year they make an effort to push up the prices. Their ships will be near the coast now; they may have already arrived if the winds have allowed it. Last year the foreigners complained about rotten stockfish. They whined that there was black sand in the wool; the mittens and socks were badly knitted, they'd said. In turn, the tenants accused the British of trading tainted grain laced with mites, and they railed against seawater in the wine.

These headaches, cultivated by a pack of bickering traders and constant negotiation, are one of the reasons he will soon relinquish his position. Surely, he thinks, it is not the best use of his law degree.

The tenants of one of his three farms welcome him this evening. He requests a simple meal of a little cheese and dried fish. He sleeps and rises early, eager to be on his way to the coast.

When he has ridden for thirty minutes and the rhythm of the pace is well set, the earth begins to tremble. The horses stop short, and for what seems like minutes instead of seconds, Stefán and the horses are suspended in fear, standing perfectly still while the whole of the ground undulates beneath them. He's experienced it many times and yet it is still disorienting. The helpless feeling of the earth moving underfoot and the terrifying abrupt way it takes them unaware, with no warning whatsoever. It is not the first time in his life he feels this complete helplessness. It will not be the last.

It is the first week of June and despite a few ground trembling moments, it is with a light heart, and a feeling of happy anticipation that Stefán and his horses proceed ever closer to the sea. His only son is due back soon from Copenhagen where he has been at his studies. Stefán has been counting the months, eager to see Pétur again. The whole family yearns to be surrounded once more in his jovial presence. The void he left when he departed was never filled, because there is no person, no place, nothing at all that can equal Pétur.

A soft wind blows the scent of fresh, fragrant herbs, and the beards of green pastures shimmer, dressed as they are in wild flowers. The mild winter has blessed them with healthy livestock, a welcome change. June's breeze brings the news from Skálholt that even the bishop's cattle are reported to be sleek and strong. The hand of fate seemed for once to point towards a fruitful summer and an abundant harvest.

Stefán breathes in deeply, relishing the faintest whiff of salt that infuses the air. His favourite part of the journey lies just ahead. To the east the dirty, ancient ice of a glacier is juxtaposed against the verdant green fields. The pale blue ice formations are sculpted by nature, that greatest of artists, and sink down a hundred feet to form dangerous crevasses.

As vast as the eastern glacier is, several miles north from where Stefán rides there is another. No other glacier in the world is as large, or as beautiful. Its majestic white body descends to black sands; hot streams erupt from banks of ice. The massive glacier has many tongues, each with their own names and characteristics. Today one of these tongues struggles more than the others within its contrasting complexion, a forceful interplay of volcanoes beneath the ice.

Stefán stops to admire the glacier and the largest mountain in the country that presides over the deepest lake. He continues at a comfortable pace between these two wonders thinking about the possibility of a happier Christmas this year.

But the trading season will not begin this summer. The inhabitants of this demanding land stand on the back of a giant, slumbering beast. The monstrous beast under the ice cap is beginning to wake. For just as Glossi and Vinda's hooves plod into the path of the next farm, another violent shake of the earth brings Glossi down and Stefán with him, his legs still hugging the horse's ribs as he hits the ground hard.

Afraid to move, and not sure if he can, Stefán lies watching his hands rise and fall with Glossi's breath. Vinda is frozen like one of the glacial ice sculptures. The earth is still and the air is quiet, too quiet; only Glossi's whimper disturbs it. The horse is frightened but manages to stand, offering up a groan and a grunt. He nudges his owner.

The monster below the ice returns to its fretful slumber.

Stefán rolls slowly onto his back. His right side is sore and throbbing. Disorientated, he turns his head and gasps from this perspective.

'What in hell?'

A blue skein of mist floats just above the ground.

Everyone from elder to toddler is familiar with the queer, coloured lights in the skies and the blues and greens that hover over their glacial mountains, but this pale blue fog that skims the ground is something entirely different.

Carefully he rises to discover he is able to stand and walk, and is grateful for it. Anxious to determine how Glossi and Vinda fare, the fog swallows them into a shadowy blur. The air is death-like. As suddenly as the earth had shaken them, the eerie stillness that follows forces him to halt in a speechless and untrusting pause.

Despite his attempts to ignore it, a feeling of dread has dogged Stefán's journey and it washes over him now in a cold sweat. He knows that these increasingly violent series of earthquakes precede the possibility of something much, much worse.

*   *   *

It is Whit Sunday, June the 8th.

The clear sky and calm weather is a hateful tease. Pillars of smoke rise to the sky from the hills north of the coast, and a thick, black cloud rolls south against the wind. The cloud begins its swift descent upon the coastal plane.

For a moment Stefán is suspended in a stupor as he gapes at the black heavens. Then the wind blows the cloud mass towards him so quickly it is only a few moments before the first layer of grit rains down upon his head.

Complete darkness envelopes him so that he cannot make out his own hands in front of his face. A looming, smoky blanket of haze obscures the sun and the sky. The cloud showers down sand and ash an inch in thickness. It continues to rush south against the wind until the whole district is blanketed in darkness.

The cloud splits for a hair's breadth of a moment only to reveal the appearance of fresh cones of smoke rising from the lowland hills. Stefán covers his nose and mouth with his neckerchief and helplessly watches the cloud increasing in size.

Another passel of earthquakes shakes the terrain. Stefán is overcome by a sense that there is something different about this cloud, this rain of ash, these tremors.

Weary with fear for his family, and with a sick feeling beginning to crawl up his throat, he's unable to keep to his feet. Before the angry earth can throw him again, he falls to the ground.

The beast awakes. A mighty and absolutely ruthless, meaningless force heaves and struggles and bursts.

God seems to have deserted them.

The sun neither rises, nor sets.

These last two nights when Stefán beds down in the traveller huts it is with an anxious foreboding, and when the dark ekes out an even blacker existence, his fears oppress him, ghost-like.

A tremendous roar awakens him on the morning of the 12th of June. Laki finally finds its voice. Yet it screams not from its centre – it is not the volcanic mountain that speaks – instead, it screams from its side, a twenty-five-mile-long fissure underneath the glacier, from which a huge current of lava bursts and begins its awful, terrifying flow. Stefán quakes with it.

Flames burst into the air from the schism. Burning fountains of molten rock shoot up, up and up – thousands of feet high, and releasing hell on earth. The sky is painted with fire. Streaming, crashing lava rushes down the hills and threatens the low country leaving Stefán to imagine the desolation it has surely poured down upon the pastures and homes north of them, spreading its red-hot flood.

He hears shouts – the first people he has encountered on this leg of his journey. He is stupefied to see a smattering of men and women rushing towards him. What in the world are they doing here? Have these people abandoned their livestock, their livelihood? The motley group arrive gibbering; they have been running since morning. Shouting in the gaps of crashes of thunder, they circulate breathless stories of the lava flowing in such a wide mass that it looks like a giant bolt of cloth being unrolled upon anything in its wake.

Stefán asks each of them about his farm. Do they know if its people are safe?

No, they do not know. They come from the north.

The farmers report that the great river Skaftá north of them, that only days ago had been swollen with late spring's clear water, is now fetid and filled with gravel and dust.

'By the end of the day ...' A farmer spits ash, '... the Skaftá disappeared. It is gone.'

When the thunder finally ceases, an eerie whistling sound fills the silence. One of the men nods.

'It is the Medalland's old lava fields. They burn again. The air trapped in their cavities makes that sound. It is bleeding ghosts.'

CHAPTER EIGHT

It is the 13th of June. The waves pound furiously on the black volcanic sand. Stefán has been here before – when the sun cast a golden sheen on the basalt, infusing it with warmth. Today, in the sun's absence, this shore littered with lava rocks is as dull and lifeless as a phantom's kingdom.

His stomach knots with anxiety as he draws closer to the shore where the natural chiaroscuro of the scene appears before him like an etching. There on the black sand and clinging to a smoky fog, a schooner has run aground, split down the middle.

Empty barrels, their rims encrusted with the precious and expensive salt they once held, float in and out of the tide. As he draws closer a horrific tableau paints a beach littered with bodies. The shore's tiny, black pebbles are embedded in the men's bare chests. No. He sees they are not pebbles at all, but coffee beans studded into their lifeless skin. Shards from wooden planks protrude from limbs and stomachs. Everything is covered in black ash.

Stefán stumbles, searching through the haze. The wreckage continues on down the beach. A young man's purple face looks up to the hidden sun; his head rests on the rock that split his skull. Stefán is almost delirious with joy – it isn't Pétur's face.

He wipes the ash from his face without thinking. Moving faster now, he combs the shore. Then he stumbles and falls next to the body of a young man whose mouth is open and filled with sand. Stefán focuses on the hair, then the face. A sand crab crawls out of his son's mouth.

Stefán retches into the sea.

The great magistrate lifts his son in his arms and with his knees shaking and his body sinking into the sand, he carries him away from the shipwreck, away from the crashing, horrible sea.

Stefán sits in this corner by the sea and nurses a low moan that gradually builds into a rage. It is said that once, during the crashing of rocks and sharp snaps of thunder, while the lava flowed in its hot fury, there were those in the low country who heard a wail that transcended nature. It echoed through the hills from the beach that became a graveyard. Stefán is unaware that it is he who owns this moment of grief, for he is lost to the pain of it.

Somehow, though he is spent, he wraps the body of his son in a vagabond shroud of sailcloth, linen and cotton remnants he scavenges from a wooden box that was no doubt meant for the wealthiest in the country. He binds the makeshift shroud, which he fashions like an envelope, with straps removed from his packsaddle. Gently, gently, he drapes his swaddled son over Vinda's back.

He is anxious to be away from this place of death and walks Glossi, and Vinda with her awful load, away from the beach. The boy's body undulates with each step forward.

A new wave of fear rises and lodges in his throat. The kittiwakes, auks and skuas – where are they? The cliffs are empty, there are no winged scavengers preying upon the wreckage. The fulmars should be out at sea circling the fishing boats, feeding off their discards. Something is wrong. Never could Stefán fathom that he is on the precipice of the fury the subglacial volcano has wrought.

He thought the eruption would be confined to the north – everyone in the south thought the same. But he was wrong, they were all wrong. In the midst of heat and haze he is struck by a raging thirst, which grows like a thorny vine with each crack of thunder. Neither he, nor his horses have taken water since morning and suddenly nothing is more important than finding it. He follows the path his horses' hooves made in the sand only hours ago that lead to a large stream on the route home, which he should have reached by now. But there is no stream, and the path that was previously so clearly laid has come to an unexpected end, swept away, leaving no trace.

Another path appears that leads away from the beach to a sudden change in landscape from sand to grass, then to a brilliant green moss that grows over stones. This area is marshy, boggy, with large rock formations jutting out from the steaming ground. Stefán almost weeps when Glossi's upper lip curls and he pricks up his ears.

'Good, good. Water? Do you hear it? Do you smell it? Where is it?'

He allows his horses to lead the way until he hears it, too. A grouping of surface springs and underground hot boiling pools are just ahead of him. A small waterfall gurgles. The benevolence of precious, precious water.

The overall symmetry looks completely normal, yet here in this marshy spot of wetlands the air is too still. The ducks should be moulting, the fulmars nesting, and in their absence the land lies eerily empty and far too quiet. When Stefán lifts his son's stiff body from Vinda's back she makes a hoarse grunt that echoes. As gently as he tries to place the shrouded body on the ground, it thumps. Never was there an obscener sound.

Stefán directs the horses to the pools, but they will not drink. One of the water sources is the same colour as the pale blue ground mist. He looks closer. The water teems with insects he doesn't recognize; dark-red flying insects, and yellow-and-black striped pests swimming, long and thick on the surface. He recoils from the sight of it.

The other streams and pools emit a strong sulphurous odour. Stefán dips his fingers in to find it tepid, and the taste sour and bitter. Undrinkable.

Glossi turns his head towards the small waterfall.

'All right, you be the guide. We'll try to drink from this waterfall.' But Glossi inches forward and past the waterfall. Another pool

of water shimmers almost completely hidden from view. An iridescent, green hue skims the surface of the pool. Stefán is so thirsty
and impatient to reach the traveller's hut that he doesn't care about
the water's green glow and takes a quick sniff. Relieved to find it
odourless, he touches the surface with his fingertips to gauge its
temperature and then licks his fingers. Finding the water pleasant
and with no aftertaste, he drinks a small mouthful. Glossi drinks
beside him, while Vinda shies away and turns instead to the run-off
from the waterfall, where she drinks greedily.

Stefán fills his travelling cup when he hears something rustling
behind him. Startled by a swishing sound, he drops the cup and
breathes heavily as he strains to hear it again. He senses someone
watches him.

'Do not be alarmed.' A voice comes from the rocks.

'Show yourself.'

'I do not take commands.'

Nevertheless, a man steps out from a large, craggy rock formation
where he had crouched unseen. Rising to his full height, Stefán
staggers at the sight of him. An elderly man, taller than any he had
ever seen, towers over him.

'Drink no more from the green pool today. Only two drops must
be taken after the long sleep that will come twice yearly. Two drops.
Any more than that, you will die. But you must ingest the two drops.
You will understand. Tell no one of this place. Follow me.'

'What . . .'

'I entertain no questions. Come.'

Stefán looks back to where his son lies.

'He will come to no harm.'

Stefán takes four steps for the giant's one stride. He cannot make
out in which direction they tread, the fog is too thick. The great
man stops and raises his arm. Like a wraith he points to turf-covered
burial mounds. The green-carpeted humps are too numerous to
count and the thick air disguises how far the area extends.

'They died so that you might live. For most, the sacrifice was their choice. These dead provided our knowledge. Two drops.'

He turns and leads Stefán back to the pool.

'Fill your flask. Mark this place in your memory. You will come here again to replenish and store the pool's liquid.' He points to the ground. 'Beneath your feet lies something foul and aberrant, full of death – and yet it brings life. When nature has its way it is inexplicable. But the pool will not bring your son back. Remember this in the future when you think on this day.'

At the mention of his son, Stefán's grief renews like the sky's black smoke.

'How did you know who . . .?'

The mountainous man lumbers away until the rocks hide him once more.

Stefán turns back to the pool. He cannot drink another drop anyway; his thirst is queerly sated. His once parched lips are soft and moist. When he steps away from the pool he hears the same rustling, like clothing brushing against the rock. He stands motionless, waiting. Now there is only thunder.

'Let's be on our way,' he says to his dead son.

CHAPTER NINE

1785

The rain pelts down. Stefán can almost hear the clouds grumbling as they sweep past his view as he stands at his front door shaking off the wet. He removes his shoes, turns off the long hall to the kitchen and there tosses more turf on the fire until it spits flames. Coffee first, and then he inhales a bowl of fish, its sweet taste made bitter by his loneliness.

The pounding of the rain ceases, leaving in its absence the quiet that he hates. In the sleeping room he removes a stack of papers from his wife's trunk and returns to the kitchen's fire where he prefers to sit these days.

He reads the pages again, though he knows them by heart. The curled edges of the paper fold in on each other. The reading is tortuous and comforting.

Entry, Late June 1783

People arrive each day having fled areas just north of us, almost mad from what they have lost; they are humbled by their new poverty. Those of us by the coast and the low country miraculously survive, but the fear that our land will finally succumb to the screams of the volcano seeps into our bones.

Entry, 20th July

We are jubilant these last few days. Finally, we feel safe from the lava's course. Our livestock is well. Our hay is dry. My sulphur stores are safe.

We celebrate as if it is Christmas. Other survivors are welcome to the farm to dance and sing and share the food we managed to save through my wife's clever management.

Entry, 27th July

The gaiety that surrounded us last week is eroded. A tenant came rushing through the farmstead shouting that the livestock has turned colour, their snouts and hooves are a queer sickly yellow.

I am certain that a poison falls from the sky. Some toxic mist permeates the hay and the grasslands. Vegetation withers and burns. I walk across my pastures to find the grass so brittle it turns to powder under my feet.

Entry, early October

The monster still erupts. Our daughters are terribly sick.

Entry, end October

The flesh falls from our horses. The sheep are swollen with tumours. Their skin rots. One lamb was born with the claws of a predatory bird instead of cloven hooves. To see such sights – my daughters are terrified.

By some miracle Glossi is still healthy. He never fails even though he eats much contaminated hay. Amongst the diseased and deformed animals, many men wonder that Glossi is the freak.

Entry, February 1784

Laki stands quiet. She has exhausted the beast within her.

Entry, July 1784

It has been a full twelve months since the first eruption, the plains of the Skaftá remain so hot that they cannot be crossed, steam and smoke still rise from it.

The disaster is only beginning.

I do not know why I am still alive.

There is no food, no water that is not poisoned.

My wife is dead. My daughters are dead. Everyone on my farmstead and those on my other holdings – they are all dead.

Their bodies became bloated, the insides of their mouths and their gums swelled and cracked. Little Mara's tongue festered and fell off. Everyone was plagued with complete hair loss.

The whole country, what is left of it, is on its knees. Copenhagen threatens to evacuate the island.

And yet, I live. Glossi, still lives.

Stefán folds the papers and holds them to his chest, and then in one swift movement he tosses them into the fire.

For the second time this year he is suddenly light-headed. He moves away from the fire, first thinking the heat has made him dizzy, but then he remembers the last time, when he became drowsy ... the way he feels now.

He crawls to bed and within seconds the heaviness leaves him powerless and he sleeps. He is given the death he craves – for fourteen days and nights.

When he wakes he takes two drops from the phial, eats, and packs his things. He can wait no longer. With a forced calm he folds his clothes, rolls his stockings and wipes his shoes.

Stefán rides Glossi to the coast where he will seek the giant by the rocks near the pool. His heart is as empty as his home, his spirit hollow. His rage foments a decision. He will either take his place in the mounds of the dead, or he will find a good reason to stay alive.

LONDON
1783

CHAPTER TEN

'All the world is in Limehouse,' Averil Lawless announces.

Tall, in the way a London plane reaches to the heavens surpassing others, the woman in the towering hat cuts a striking figure through the streets and narrow alleys that bustle with all of humanity.

Found in this maritime community, this gateway to the world, in the eastern end of London are the sailors, the ropemen, the coal heavers, the lumpers, the lightermen, the sugar bakers, the shipwrights, and those on their miserable journey to the place of their execution. Dotted amongst the sailmakers, the chandlers, the potters, the merchants, the watermen and the oyster-sellers stand a smattering of rich landowners, who would rather throw themselves into the bubbling stew of the river than live too far from the source of their wealth.

The Japanese sailor and the Malay pass side by side with the Scandinavian and the Russian. There is little difficulty in finding the Persian, the Egyptian, or even the South Sea Islander. They all rub shoulders with the pirates, the bawdy women, thugs, smugglers, the hard-working labourers and the downtrodden. The smell of tar and rope is everywhere, and yet they do not mix with the frying oil and the burning fat, nor share their pungency with the smoke from industry or the cottage fires. Each odour saturates and overpowers, claims its particular victim, and moves on with the breeze.

Averil grasps a hand of each of her two daughters and elbows her way through the bevy of people on the approach to the Duke Shore Stairs.

'Do not remove them!' Averil Lawless commands of Verity in her most formidable voice, which is very nearly as formidable as her bearing.

'But I cannot see, Mammy!' her youngest pleads.

'Do not remove your spectacles.'

It is, indeed, dark. It was so dark at dawn that when the maid-servant opened the door to a sharp rap there was nothing but a blank space on the doorstep. Then a scrawny hand protruding from the sleeve of a black coat gave the young maid a start when it appeared out of the mist. Pale, thin fingers presented new chapel tickets and without a word, after the tickets were accepted, the hand disappeared.

'It were like a ghost hand, ma'am,' she said as she handed the new tickets to her mistress.

Earlier this morning, when Averil heard Mass, she prayed to St Ignatius for guidance on all her decisions, as she does each day. The Lawless family make up only a handful of Catholics in Limehouse and they keep their secret close; papists on the inside, they are Protestants in public. The doorkeeper at the small mass house checked her ticket and then locked them in and guarded the door. The embassy chapels, the penny houses, none are truly safe. Since the Catholic laws had relaxed, hearing Mass had become even more dangerous.

Her twelve-year-old daughter adjusts the frames of forged iron that sit awkwardly at her temples and Averil bends down and holds the girl's face in her hands. Two oval, glass lenses the colour of a dark, blue sea meet her gaze. Averil silently curses the condition that has plagued her daughter's eyes since birth. Her youngest has suffered cold-water baths, fever therapy, herb-filled gauzes boiled in milk, and tinctures of belladonna drops, but the inflammation disease is stubbornly recurrent, leaving Verity's sight weakened and sensitive to light.

'The air is full of dirt today. You must protect your eyes,' Averil says more gently.

As they wait at the Duke Shore Stairs to board the next wherry that will carry them upriver, the water rushes up almost to their shoes. The girls clasp hands, excited at the prospects of the day. The breadth and expanse of the Thames lifts their hearts. The busy port, the scores of moored barges and the glorious ship masts that pass in an endless queue stir the dreams of man, woman and child, and reminds all who lay eyes on this sight that London is the port of the world. The girls realize, because they have been told time and again how fortunate they are to be allowed these special excursions and patiently, but breathlessly, await their turn to board.

The clang of hammers hitting iron, the plonk of heavy-footed men carrying wooden planks, the foreign tongues, and cries of hawkers forge a mariner's opera, and underneath it all is the incessant ticking of the clocks, the timekeepers of the seafarers.

There is, however, something queer in the air today.

The motley passengers are uncommonly subdued when greeted by the abnormal fog. This is not the damp, cool, slushy fog to which they are accustomed, but a dry one that sits heavily with blasting heat and leaves the cobblestones greasy.

Averil and her daughters congregate with others who stand waiting by the lapping water of the Thames to hear their destinations shouted, 'This way for London Bridge!' 'Anyone for Westminster?' But the ships' bells and horns, and the cries of the watermen are heard in a muffled monotone, playing second fiddle to the overbearing heat and increasing darkness. The river is empty of waterfowl.

Quiet comments gurgle and skip across the landing.

'There has never been a hotter, more stifling June.'

'There have never been as many wasps as there are this summer.'

Averil Lawless despises both heat and wasps. In fact, it is so desperately quiet, even for this noisy river-hugging community, that she thinks perhaps she should listen to the nagging voice entreating her to take her daughters home, to carry out her appointment another day.

The pointed bow of a bright red wherry appears in the uncommon gloom. Then another. And another. So fierce is the competition that the watermen are yelping at each other to make way. A ship's horn sounds out and a small boat's bell clangs. As if the river's life sings her to her senses, Averil glances at her eager daughters and calculates. 'No, we will attend. The fog will lift and my mind will be at ease once this day is over.'

Constance and Verity Lawless remain quiet and still, leaving the fidgeting to the children and impatient adults who race past them on faster boats with sails. Their father helped them to understand that it is not how fast one travels, but how well. The wherry is clean and the seats are cushioned in leather. They understand too that the trading empire of the Thames affords them privileges, if not their very existence. Francis and Averil Lawless have impressed upon their daughters the concept of the consequences of a single moment, and there is no better teacher than the river's majesty and its demand for respect for its waters, which can easily bring violence and ruin as well as wealth and peace. Today, the watermen expertly steer and manoeuvre through the traffic in the yellow fog. The air grows ever warmer.

When the wherry reaches the stairs at Temple wharf, Constance and Verity are pink-cheeked and damp with heat. Averil holds her daughters' warm palms as they make their way up the stairs. Covered in a fine dust, they have never felt so parched. The midday sun hides above the dry fog that now hovers depressingly ever closer to the ground.

The unusual absence of the breeze from the riverbank sends a shiver up Averil's spine, which feels wrong in the heat. Never has there been such placidity in these gardens. It seems that no one strolls along the gravel pathways until, suddenly, out of the haze, men robed in black silk appear, floating past, like deflated, grim angels without gusts to enhance their flight. The view of the river appears and disappears with slices of brown vapour that stream by. An unwanted guest imprisons the Thames.

Like a great swan with her cygnets, Averil leads the girls to the appointed meeting place by the black mulberry tree. The stone bench is empty today and the girls seize it and collapse on its rough seat.

Mr George Fitzgerald arrives with a young man who appears to be a complete model of him, a younger, trim and meticulously groomed version. But what is this? Behind the mirror image of the second Mr Fitzgerald is a third version, noticeably similar, and noticeably different.

Constance and Verity rise to their feet in the company of what appears to be an overwhelming quantity of Fitzgeraldness. Striking forms with straight backs and rising chests are presented in a physically perfect descending order: Mr George Fitzgerald, forty years of age, a long-standing family friend with whom they are of course already acquainted, William Fitzgerald, son of George, aged sixteen, and his brother Sterling Fitzgerald, fourteen; all of whom are most devotedly at their service.

Mrs Lawless and the young ladies are informed that there are more, indeed several more male Fitzgeralds from whence they came, and all with an enthusiastic regard for the law. Each Fitzgerald is taking private tuition, for in all truth, not much instruction in the area of the law is on offer to young men of the Inns of Court, most of whom are called to the Bar by way of their charm and privilege.

Constance and Verity find it difficult to be at ease in their presence, as if a military stance might be required of them as well. They look to their mother for a clue to this gathering, but Averil makes no effort to enlighten them and stands perfectly at ease, waiting — only her eyes betray her, they dance from one Fitzgerald to another, yet always return to the sheaf of papers George Fitzgerald carries under his arms in addition to a small leather box. Then the toe of her shoe begins an almost unperceivable tap, tap, tap.

Gently, Fitzgerald the elder speaks. 'It is dastardly warm out today and you must be eager to conclude our business.'

'Well, yes, George, exactly that,' she says.

'Perhaps the young gentlemen might entertain your daughters for a moment. There's a fascinating rookery just down the path, well within our sight, even in this ghastly fog.'

Sterling Fitzgerald has taken it upon himself to become somewhat of an expert on the rook and its behaviour. With his arms folded in an instructional stance, he leads the way.

'The Temple Gardens rookery is quiet today, but their cawing can be deafening. There must be at least thirty nests in this tree.'

'I am not sure that the young ladies are interested ...' William is apologetic, particularly to Constance, who smiles queerly.

'Oh, but we are, aren't we Constance? I am interested in all sorts of birds.' Verity encourages Sterling Fitzgerald, whose forelock falls forward at the attention of such a fascinating person, a female, no less, who has him thinking that blue-shaded spectacles must be the most interesting outlook from which to view the world.

Constance glances back at their mother just as George Fitzgerald produces a quill from his compact writing nécessaire. Her mother looks terribly intense as she holds sheets of paper close to her face, and for this, too, the fog can be blamed. The attorney seems to have created a makeshift office in which their mother now positions the quill and writes upon the sheets of paper, the feather crossing the page like a slender young ghost.

William Fitzgerald notices that Constance's attention has swayed from the business of rooks to the business of her mother's mysterious legal matters.

'A poet once stated ...' William clears his throat. '"It is apt that the rook should be associated with the law courts, it being a grave, legal bird, both in its coats and habits. They are renowned for their intelligence and cunning."'

When Constance turns back to William and smiles at his attempt to entertain her, he feels a foreign, but not unpleasant sensation, something new that demands to be fed again.

The girls observe Averil as she makes her way towards them. For a moment they gaze upon her not as their mother, but as a woman of the world. Her whole being emits a brighter mood after her meeting with George Fitzgerald. Constance takes in a sharp breath at how regal she looks, her red, silk taffeta gown shimmers in the dull light. Her hair survived the brutality of the wigs she once wore and is still as black as jet and piled high in the latest fashion, her elegant hat sits at exactly the right angle. The shadow of tension present on her face this morning is erased. Her face seems somehow wider, her eyes more relaxed, and a contentment that she cannot contain brings a sparkle to her laughter. Constance has spent hours studying her mother's face – she notices every nuance.

Verity hopes that one day she will resemble her mother. They share the same blue eyes and aquiline nose, but Verity doubts her own carriage will be as elegant, or her stride as confident, as the woman gliding towards her now. She doubts, too, whether she will ever be as clever as her mother, because even their father drones on about 'their mammy's infinite wisdom' and she has never before heard any man speak so highly of a female.

It is the sisters' last image of Averil Lawless before the rooks fly.

Torches are lit in the Gardens as if it were two o'clock on a January afternoon and not four o'clock in high summer. Verity can see but a few feet in front of her. The trio of Fitzgeralds escorts them towards the river stairs.

When they stroll past the sycamore, the rooks that have silently nested all afternoon now stir from within the recesses of the branches, and the tree comes alive with their calls. Their cawing begins in single cries as if they speak to one another with urgent messages. They grow noisier, and as the party passes close by, the rookery screeches in a wild chorus accented by a high-pitched falsetto call. A swift flourish of flapping wings sounds like thunder when they take to the sky. All lift their heads as a sheet of black rises above them. Exclamations percolate through the Gardens when the parliament of rooks wing in unison towards the river, cutting through the haze with its dipping flight. The black-robed men of law congregate on the grounds to stare in amazement as their avian mirror images move skyward. Visitors to the Temple Gardens point upwards, bumping into each other as they follow the frenetic wingbeats of the colony.

Averil holds on to her hat, for what reason she does not know, perhaps in fear of a rook swooping down on her head. William and Sterling look quizzically at each other, their jaws dropping until their mouths gape.

'What about that then, Sterling? There is no known record of this rookery behaving in this fashion!' William whispers.

'"No, none at all.' Sterling quotes: "'They do not desert their nests in this way unless . . .'" He falters and looks at his brother alarmed.

'"Unless the abandonment is a prelude to battering one of their own to death, or . . .'" William pauses. "'They are known to depart en masse preceding a human death.'"

'Come now, girls. Quickly, please.' Averil orders.

'Mammy, I cannot see. Please go slower.' Verity pleads.

Truth be known, Averil is completely perplexed that the day progresses and still, this blasted strange haze burdens them.

'I cannot see either, Mammy. It will be worse for Verity.' Constance says.

George Fitzgerald looks out over the Thames to another distraction – hundreds of lanterns and torches light the Thames. There is a ripple of confusion flowing through the gathering crowd at Temple stairs. Men shout at the watermen to stop for them, only to be met with foul and loudmouthed banter in return.

Hopeful passengers crowd the steps in a tangle, volleying insults at each other, while confused passengers alight from the boats trying to press pass the growing numbers who wish to embark. Order has been lost to the June darkness. Feet fight for limited space on the seven or eight stairs that lead down to the river and it is difficult to determine how many steps already lie beneath the rising tide.

Perhaps it is the heat, or they are nest drifting; whatever the reason, the wasps are in some strange flight behaviour and their nuisance contributes another edge to the growing danger. Hands that clasped other hands now release to swat the pests. Among these irritable and frightened people, Verity feels a panic so great that it threatens to clench her lungs and never let go. She has lost her mother's hand and cannot find it again. She fails to think that she could simply remove her spectacles to see more clearly, but instead blindly reaches for her mother's hand, her arm, anything. Constance is near but cannot reach her mother or sister. Finally, with her arm stretched out across a barrister's chest, Constance holds fast to Verity's shoulder. The sisters work their way over to their mother whose hat they can just make out at the edge of the stairs.

Averil recognizes the tops of her daughters' heads inching towards her. 'Be careful, girls!' she calls out to them. 'Stay together!'

A wasp flies across Averil's face, then two, and now a swarm of wasps circle her head. She swats at them. Averil feels her foot on the edge of the step and in trying to find a secure place she loses her balance. Bile rises up to her throat – the taste of fear shoots through her watering glands. She pivots and falls backwards into the water, arms outstretched, her eyes bulging with terror. Her hat flies off before her frame hits the indecently black Thames. Hairpins shoot out from her head like thin spears. Hanks of hair unravel. Faecal matter hits her face.

'Mammy! Mammy!' Constance's young arms reach out, her fingers splayed. 'Here, Mammy, here!'

Averil's view of her daughter's desperate flailing arms, aching to pull her out, fades as she chokes. Sharp pains pierce her lungs. Her limbs are so quickly paralyzed by the shock of the cold water that she cannot sustain herself. Her exquisite red, silk dress swells up like a flame in the cruel water that robs her of her dignity, her modesty.

The sisters watch helplessly as their mother's body sinks into the hungry river. Averil spins in a treacherous journey beneath the surface of the water. Sucked down by dangerous currents and hidden tides, Constance and Verity gasp at how quickly their mother has gone under. The river grants them one gift – when she sinks deeper, the girls cannot see the sharp-boned carcasses that shred their mother's skin, or her distorted limbs slapped by splintered planks of a mangled sloop.

There is no further attempt to rescue her, no one willing to jump into the awful water. Offering an oar is a blind, thankless effort. There is a shortage on bravery. Though it might have been any one of them, the river has left its dark, blood-red stain upon Averil Lawless.

The girls are bonded to the river stairs like statues. Dangerously close to the edge, they stare down, unbelieving, into their mother's destiny. Then a flicker of a movement when Verity's fingers stretch to meet Constance's hand.

They cannot find their voices. Someone is speaking to them, muffled sounds erupt from a large animated woman, a stranger, whose mouth moves quickly, froth settling around her lips. The sisters look away from her and turn back to the river, searching, fully expecting their mother to rise, drenched, but alive.

'Miss Lawless.' George Fitzgerald, shaken though he is, parts the sea of people on the stairs to reach Constane and Verity, with a force unexpected from so slight a man.

'Miss Lawless,' he calls again to Constance.

The sisters turn to him in unison, but their stare is blank.

'Make way. Make way,' William calls out.

Sterling is close behind his brother. The three Fitzgeralds form a protective cluster around the girls.

Verity, without any adherence to the danger of it, falls to her knees right where she stands on the stone step. She crosses herself, looks through her lenses to the wild, restless clouds that she cannot see and folds her hands in prayer.

'I pray to St Adjutor. Take your place in a boat and row to this spot. Say prayers here and sprinkle holy water. Grant Mammy the serenity to swim and help her to rise from the river Thames. I pray you perform this miracle as you have done before.'

Constance grasps her sister's hands and lifts her up.

The expressions on the faces that surround them, which had only moments ago been struck with horror and pity, now frown on them. The first murmurings are faint, whispers of 'papists'. And then louder, 'They are Catholics.' Verity trembles, and Constance notices herself quiver, too, and cannot stop it. She recognizes the Fitzgerald boy and his brother, and there, too is the older Fitzgerald. Strangely, Constance cannot remember their names. She feels surrounded by their wool, and their clothing feels hot; she is hot. The woollen clothes try to take her away. But she will not go, instead she turns stubbornly back to the river and peers as deeply into it as is possible, and now she lets loose a wail from the very bottom of her being. All who gather at the river stairs and even the Fitzgeralds step back; only Verity stays beside her, holding her hand.

Averil Lawless may sink to the bottom of the Thames where her body will join the graveyard made of the thick, ancient mud. She may be delivered to shore by a swift current, or she may be buffeted by boats, or further assaulted by seagulls. Averil may take the curve of the U-bend and appear with a host of other victims at Dead Man's Stairs in Wapping where the tide tends to deliver the recently drowned. Or, one day soon, she may be found floating near her own home in the dusky waters at Limehouse. The currents of the Thames are ruled by something powerful; they may take her out to sea where she will ride beneath the ships that sail off to new and old worlds. It is impossible to know her course.

The news of the drowning travels swiftly. It ripples up Temple stairs, through the Inner Courts, and in its tragedy, spills out of Temple into Fleet Street.

The sisters' gazes remain focused on the river. Lanterns have been placed behind them on the ground. In their glow, Verity rests her head on Constance's shoulder.

George Fitzgerald has sent both carriage and boat for Francis Lawless. In this weather, there is no guessing which will reach him first, or how long it might take his dear friend to arrive. And still, the sisters stand on the river stairs.

'Would you like to come with us to chambers? You will be more comfortable while we await your father,' he asks the girls.

'Constance and I will not move from this place until Mammy returns,' Verity says.

'My dear Verity . . . Constance . . .' George hesitantly takes their hands.

The girls do not avert their gaze from the water.

'Your beautiful mother is not coming back. The Thames has taken her. She is with God now.'

Verity's chest rises as she takes a deep breath and finally turns to look into George Fitzgerald's kind face. Constance, too, cuts her eyes to the man who smells of ink and parchment. This mention of God has sparked life from the girls.

'Why?' Constance asks. 'Why did God take her from us? Why would he do that?'

'Darling girl, your mother fell. It was a terrible, terrible accident.'

'Might God give her back to us?'

'No,' George says softly. 'She is dead and with Him now.'

'But if God is truly God, then is it not within his power to return her to us?'

George thinks very carefully before he replies.

'I do not know. I simply do not know.'

'Thank you for your honesty.'

Constance takes hold of her sister's shoulders and turns her. Then, with gentle hands, she lifts Verity's spectacles from her face. Verity squints, and Constance passes her hands over Verity's eyes to close them.

'Shhh,' she says to her younger sister. 'Shhh.'

Constance leans in and kisses Verity's pink eyelids.

'We are motherless now, Verity. With your pitiable eyes, look to me for our future.'

William and Sterling had remained nearby during the whole ghastly affair, and both are shaken to such a degree that their blotched and tear-stained faces pulse with heat. William squirms in frustration for not knowing how, but desperately wanting, to be more useful. He has fetched cool drinks, handkerchiefs, and stayed alert to any miraculous news of sightings, or the discovery of a body floating in nearby water. But the black-hearted Thames released no such secrets.

When Francis Lawless arrives his pallor is grey, and there is something behind his eyes that threatens madness if he does not learn to live with his loss. The sight of his daughters seems to stabilize him, and finally they turn from the stairs and run to his outstretched arms and sink into them.

'I cannot thank you enough, George, for the care you have shown my daughters today. I shall never forget it.'

'I am so very sorry, Francis. My dearest and most loyal friend. Wretched, wretched day. I would like to help you in any way, please do call upon me. If it is any consolation, your wife's affairs are in order,' George tells him.

'The girls are protected then?'

'Yes.' George shakes his head in sad disbelief. 'Only moments before the accident.'

'Well, that is some small relief. Thank you. I really must get them home now.'

What remains of the broken Lawless family sways to and fro in the coach until they are swallowed by a dim twilight.

ICELAND
1830

CHAPTER ELEVEN

The sun gleams on the glaciers to the south and to the east. Jón Eymundsson and Elísabet Ingólfsdóttir hear the waterfall crashing down, though they are miles from it. Each plod of their horses' hooves brings them closer to its thundering roar. The spray looks like thick smoke from where they ride. The curlews wing overhead, moving south, the white bog cotton slants in the wind.

The path is rough with tremendous ruts, full of holes and stones, but their sure-footed horses pull ahead as if to defy each patch of ragged earth. Their load is lighter now; two days ago their carrying horses bore the weight of Elísabet's knitting and weaving work. Every piece was sold or traded giving them a heady sense of relief and pleasure at their luck that the merchant sailors had survived another journey from England.

When they arrived at the trading settlement, Elísabet faced the hard stares of the men whose wives were at home with their children. Thus far in her marriage of five years, she has been unable to produce a child, and for this she blames herself. Each month that passes brings an unspoken sorrow to her, and a burden to her husband. How will they survive the future of their old age without the help of sons and daughters?

Jón never mentions the night he found her in the traveller's shelter, bleeding, almost to her death. On that day, returning home from a long walk, she felt the beginnings of her loss. She did not know the pain of childbirth, but surely it was not as painful as this. Her breathing became heavy, laboured from fright. There was a seat in the shelter, a bench-like seat made from the vertebra of a whale, and someone had left a coverlet of three folds of wadmal. She threw it on the cramped earthen floor and knelt down on all fours. After what seemed hours, a horrifically slow pace set, gravity won and the bloody mass fell from her. The baby she held in her hand, a sac with a complete foetus inside it, was conceived before she met Jón. The blood flowed on. Dusk fell as her blood seeped under the crude door. She'd never felt so cold. Then, hope. She heard hiking steps, plodding along. They stop. Through the crack of the door, a woman's skirts. But Elísabet is fevered now and cannot trust the vision, for Koldís is not due home until tomorrow. Yet, with her face resting on the frozen floor, the tips of the boots stay in her sight.

'Help. Help me.'

The skirts remain still.

'Please. Help me.'

The shadow in the crack of the door disappears. It was then that Elísabet knew she was going to die, as her mother had; bleeding to death after expelling her baby. It was just before full dark that Jón noticed the dark, wet blood soaking the ground as he passed the shelter.

Elísabet draws up on her saddle, her face lifts to the bracing air. A return to the trading settlement always reminds her of this for it was here that the waves had washed up the English ship that carried her misery.

The skies were clear two days ago when their horses entered the seaside camp. The ships' sails billowed above the sand and shared the same breeze that carried the pungent scent of trade. There are but three months of harvest and trade, and these must be worthwhile or starvation and death come as surely as the sun sets in a purple glow.

The camp trading was brisk, and the temporary makeshift settlement throbbed with the day's work. The island's livelihood was piled on slabs of lava rock – Icelandic fish for barter.

Jón worked near Elísabet as he always does, ready to enforce respect. The English sailors and traders are too free with their eyes. Not an innocent grunt of admiration, nor compliments on her beauty will go unchecked. The older women gravitate to her, drawn by her warmth, they admire her knitting and weaving work.

On this late August day, on their journey home, they venture off the sand path to explore a suitable place for their second meal of the day. Walking along a rough pathway of high ferns, bilberry plants and a few birches, they veer towards the rushing of a small waterfall that plays against the sound of murmuring springs.

Elísabet tears off chunks of sweet bread that she had baked at home in the hot springs. She unwraps fresh angelica stems spread with butter. Earlier in the day the trade of two pairs of mittens procured pork and stale beer. The meat is salty and though the beer is good, it is not enough to quench their thirst.

'We did well. Thank you for working so hard,' Jón says, as he moves towards the hiss of bubbling water.

'It comes easy to me.' She would like to say more, to tell him that when she knits, her busy hands and the clicking of the needles quieten her mind. She wishes to confide that with each row she weaves, her worries cease, if only for a few moments, and that a terrible and inexplicable sense of foreboding is released and evaporates. Knitting satisfies, like a dusting of sugar after the shock of something bitter.

Several small pools ripple where they stand. Two are washing springs, the water a perfect temperature for laundry and bathing. Clouds of smoke rise above hissing streams. The waterfall, set within a rock formation, trickles down to form a pool. Elísabet unwraps horn cups while Jón tests the bubbling water, letting it run through his fingers. He notices another pool hidden behind the waterfall.

'Look, Elísabet.'

He kneels beside a small pool full of queer, green-coloured, slightly iridescent water. He tests the temperature with his hand. Tepid.

'It smells fine.' He cups his hands and drinks.

Elísabet kneels beside him and scoops up two palms full.

'It's thicker than spring water. Strange.' She sips. 'It tastes cleaner than it looks.'

'I feel as though I drank a whole pail of it,' Jón says.

'Yes, so do I.'

Sated, they suddenly feel forced to sit, desperate with an overwhelming urge to sleep. Jón tries to stand up, but he cannot.

'Elísabet?'

She has fallen back on the blanket. He shakes her but she doesn't wake. It is an effort for him to focus on her chest, to make certain that it still rises and falls, because now he too is groggy and collapses beside her.

Jón and Elísabet do not stir at the sound of Stefán's approaching footsteps. Many things register at once as his attention darts back and forth from the pool of water to the couple, who look as if they might be dead. The pool is full again. He surveys the surround to make certain no one else is about and then fills one of the wooden barrels he carries.

Only when his two barrels are full does he kneel down to more closely observe the couple. Their breathing is shallow and faint, but they still live. *Two more*, he thinks. He sits on the ground next to them, patiently waiting. She is stunning, beautiful in an earthy way. Her face appears chiselled from some flawless white stone, with dark streaks of brow and lashes accenting her milky skin. A plaited thick rope of hair, the colour of roasted coffee beans has been blown across her mouth. Her black, woven tail-cap lies next to her, its long tassel spread in silky threads.

The man is red-haired. A massive spray of freckles covers his face and hands and gives him a boyish look as he sleeps unawares. He and Stefán wear the same sort of breeches and stockings, both black. Jón's dark blue vest rises with his breath.

Stefán moves away so as not to frighten the couple when they wake. He hopes it is soon; he must persuade them to return to the farm with him. The Watcher has not appeared and perhaps will not show himself today. He closes his eyes to help him concentrate on the task at hand – how to tell them what has happened, what has changed for them both. It is the most difficult and dangerous of beginnings. It always is.

Jón wakes first. Disoriented, he rolls slowly away from Elísabet. It takes him a moment to notice his surroundings and then finally to register Stefán, who raises his hands in surrender.

'Greetings. I came upon you almost one hour ago.'

'Why are you still here?' Jón moves in front of Elísabet, blocking Stefán's view of her. 'Why do you stay?' he asks again.

'Please, I mean you no harm. I must speak with both of you. Something has happened.'

'Jón?' Elísabet, still drowsy, sits up and peers over Jón's shoulder.

'It's all right, Elísabet. This man ...' Jón now addresses Stefán, 'I saw no signs that we are trespassing. I hope ...'

'No, no, nothing like that ...' Stefán assures him. 'Though I'd like to know how you've discovered this area.'

'Our horses rest on the path over ... well, I'm not sure now. I don't see them.'

'I rode past them, they're just ahead and safe. Did you see anyone else here? Anyone at all?'

'No. Why?'

'It would be better if we could speak somewhere else, would you follow me to my farm? It is near and you are welcome to have coffee with me.'

Jón and Elísabet see no reason not to trust this man. It is the custom to offer hospitality to travellers. They have done the same for many.

Stefán glances once more at the pool beneath the waterfall. 'Did you drink from any of the pools?' he asks, though he knows the answer.

'Yes,' Elísabet says. 'The one behind the waterfall.'

'Ah, yes.' Stefán nods, revealing nothing in his expression. 'How much did you drink?' He knows the answer to this as well.

'That's an odd question.' Jón looks up at him as they gather their belongings.

'Yes. I agree . . . it is. And it is why I need to speak with you.'

'Have we drunk from a poisoned pool?' Elísabet smiles, but then feels awkward when the man doesn't respond. There's something odd and heavy in his pause.

Stefán places the two barrels on either side of his horse, checking that the lids are secure.

'Why don't you ride Glossi? Your husband and I will walk alongside. We'll collect your horses,' he offers.

An hour later they arrive at what appears an ordinary scene, a farm like any other of the scattered settlements throughout the country. The one-storey group of buildings gives it the appearance of being the humblest of villages, if indeed such things exist, but there are no villages, no towns, except the single street of Reykjavík to the east.

Here, on this farm, the earth is domed with turf huts that look like fresh mounds of graves waiting for their headstones. Sheep and cows, horses and ducks encroach upon the living quarters as they meander through the breaks in the low stone walls. Fermenting shark hangs dark and shiny outdoors.

Elísabet has the feeling she's being watched. Dark pathways run crookedly between the sod-covered huts, one of which hides a man she catches peering out at her. Then a woman appears, then another, until slowly, and disturbingly, the people come out of hiding. Jón and Elísabet glance at each other, their brows knitted. The people follow their movement with unblinking stares, offering no greeting, or friendly wave. Stefán nods at the people and they recede back to their various corners. There is an absence of laughing children, and also missing are women of childbearing age. In fact, Elísabet notes, in the short glimpse she had of these people, they all look older than those of the normal family-run farm. Where are the young, hired help, why aren't they working alongside the older and middle-aged people?

Stefán leads them inside his house through a dim, narrow passageway; its walls are composed of lava rock, the intervening spaces stuffed with moss and earth. Bridles, hanging herbs, outer clothing, a saddle, these protrude from pegs thrust into the crevices. Sweet-smelling turf burns in the fire and marries with the rich aroma of an earlier coffee-roasting session, the remnants of which linger in the common room. Jón and Elísabet glance at one another; these signs of luxury register immediately. This is not a poor peasant hut where one is greeted with the unpleasant fumes of smouldering fish bones that choke the visitor, and the stench of farm animals that sleep just a room away. Stefán had thrown a large handful of dried herbs on the fire earlier in the day. It is a friendly and inviting welcome. But for all the luxury, Elísabet senses Jón's body tensing beside her. He overworks his jaw as he is wont to do when nervous.

The common room is neat and clean, and there is no evidence of any other inhabitants, save a pair of knitting needles and wool that lie on a driftwood bench to suggest perhaps a woman might live here, though it is common during the endless winter nights that many men also knit, spin or weave. Tightly packed on shelves of lava rock, books line a wall.

Stefán emerges from the kitchen carrying a tray laden with a small plate of sweetmeats, a coffee pot, cups and saucers. Elísabet wonders at this somewhat formal note to a farmer's hospitality, but the coffee is strong and reviving and produces a familiar sharp lift in their senses.

'How long have you farmed here?' Jón asks.

'A long time. A very long time.' Stefán replies.

Rain begins to thump down upon the brushwood and turf roof. Stefán glances at the small round window hole.

'Fog. No rush to take up the rest of your journey I hope.'

'No,' says Jón. 'We had planned to pass the night north of here in a traveller's hut where we have stayed before.'

The rituals have been performed and still the man fails to enlighten them after his seemingly pressing need to speak to them. They look at Stefán expectantly through an awkward silence. He sits on top of a wooden chest with his back against the wainscoted wall. Again they notice the luxury of this feature in a farmer's home. Wood is scarce.

Stefán notes their anxiousness, and that he can no longer evade his duty.

'Jón, Elísabet, how old are you?'

Jón laughs nervously. 'I don't understand ...'

Elísabet places her hand on Jón's.

'Jón is twenty-nine. I am twenty-eight,' she says.

A weak, half-smile crosses Stefán's face and he nods. The youngest, he thinks, the youngest of them all.

'What I am about to tell you will sound fantastical.'

They nod, wide-eyed, more than ready for the mystery to end.

'The legends we are taught ... the stories we tell children ... that elves, trolls, dead spirits and the supernatural are inherent in our culture ... this is not ... well, what I will tell you is nothing to do with that.'

Twenty-five times he has performed this unenviable task. He can never guess what kind of reaction he might receive, and has learned he must never assume anything. His friend Halldór had thrown a horseshoe at him, and then rolled his anger and disbelief into a ball of defiance. Halldór committed suicide on the longest day of the year. It was one of the worst days of their lives in a string of worst days.

His dear friend Margrét had laughed in his face. He thought she was laughing at him – he understood the absurdity. She confessed that she had recently been worried that she had the cancer, and was naturally giddy for days thereafter to discover that she was not ill, until, finally, the reality of her new life sobered her.

Out of all of those in their group, it was Múli who spoke of enchantment, who insisted that this was the work of the trolls and elves that permeate their lore. He believed that a reward was finally his and he had entered another realm through a dream, a gift that stemmed from his devotion. It was for Stefán to convince him otherwise.

At present, the room grows darker as the fog rolls in, accompanied by the low whine of a wind. Stefán can delay no longer.

'The pool you came upon – the pool that is different from all the water sources where you took your lunch – its water has ... properties. We are unsure if it is water, or another form of liquid.' He pauses. 'The liquid has changed your body, your very existence.'

Elísabet and Jón sit silently, waiting to hear more.

'There must be some sort of scientific explanation for this, but we have not yet discovered it,' Stefán continues. 'We try. We work every single day towards understanding. 'So. How has your body changed? This is your first question. We call it "extended mortality" and it will seem to you, a miracle. I suppose it is, until the day we discover otherwise. You are not immortal, but now that you've ingested the liquid from the pool, the only way you will die is if you drink from it again.'

The couple stare blankly at him.

'If you return to the pool and drink even a handful, you will die instantly,' he repeats.

'It makes no sense,' Jón says.

A loud banging on the door startles them. Stefán hesitates, and then hurries through the passageway.

'He is mad,' Elísabet says.

And perhaps dangerous, Jón thinks.

'What will we do? Do you think we should leave straight away, in the storm? Is it too late now?' Elísabet whispers.

Stefán returns and notices the couple hold hands whilst they stare uncomfortably at the floor, their bodies rigid. It is no surprise to him. He is familiar with this reaction, and the denial and disbelief. Now they will have an overwhelming urge to run from this place; he doesn't blame them. Stefán summons an even calmer countenance.

'I will continue, though I know you have questions.' He pauses; the slower he goes, the better, otherwise he knows a quick barrage will further unnerve them. 'We have discovered through bitter experience, through trial and error, that too much of the liquid will kill you.' In his narrative Stefán omits the horror of the very early days, the burial mounds of those whose lives were lost from ignorance, greed and experimentation, and the stories of the Watcher who guards their secrets.

'You will not age, but you will not become any younger. You will be the most vibrant, healthy, strong and fit as you can be for your current ages. If an accident befalls you, you will recover; however, you will not live without physical pain. Deformities have occurred. One of our group's ...'

'Group?' Jón stands.

'Wait, Jón. Let him speak,' Elísabet says.

Jón sits again, and Stefán acknowledges Elísabet with a grateful nod.

'One of our group's hand was mangled in an accident. It has healed, but not perfectly. Normally, he would have lost the use of it. These are small things, considering. Believe me, the physical challenges are few. It is the mental and emotional toll for which you must prepare.'

'We have heard enough. Thank you for the coffee. We will prepare the horses.' Jón stands again and motions for Elísabet to join him.

'Please, wait! There is much more to tell you,' Stefán says. 'You really must not leave here before you're fully prepared. It would be dangerous.'

'Wait, Jón.' Elísabet turns to Stefán. 'There are no children on this farm. At least, none came out to greet us.'

'Yes, you are right.' Stefán is eager to engage her.

'And the people who live here, they are not your family?'

'No. We are a community, made of people like you and Jón, who purely by accident, stumbled upon the pool.'

They stand awkwardly at the door in the dark passageway, neither coming, nor going. The lava walls feel too close. There is not enough room to breathe.

'I urge you to stay the night ... this is no weather for travelling. I can try to answer all your questions.'

Jón exchanges a look with Elísabet. 'Very well,' he says reluctantly. 'Until the weather improves.'

Greatly relieved, Stefán tosses a brick of turf into the fire and blows. Then he pulls on an outer coat and steps out for a few minutes to round up food from a neighbour.

Jón paces. His thoughts lead him back to his first reaction, one of utter disbelief.

'Has your curiosity been satisfied, Elísabet?'

'No, Jón, it has not. I want to hear more. I don't know what it is, but something is wrong here.'

'Of course something is wrong. We've been unlucky to come across a farm of, I don't know ... I don't know what they are. Surely, you don't believe him?'

'No, of course not.' She pauses. 'I don't think I do.'

Stefán returns carrying a steaming pot, and the woman they met earlier, Margrét, follows him with more food. She places an assortment of bowls on the table, and then opens her arms to the couple in the customary, uninhibited way of greeting – as if things were still normal. She welcomes them both with hugs, and kisses Elísabet's cheeks.

Margrét serves chunks of salted mutton, swedes, a plate of hot lentils and pot bread. She passes a bowl in which a mound of chopped black potato and hard-boiled egg are covered with a brown sauce and sprinkled with pepper, sugar and vinegar.

'We're grateful.' Elísabet smiles at her. 'So much food!'

'It is very good. Thank you.' Jón, who thought he could not eat, is suddenly ravenous.

'There is herring and cheese when you are ready. Do you have enough coffee for after?' Margrét asks Stefán.

'Yes, thank you, Margrét,' he replies, and signals for her to leave them.

'How old are you, Stefán?' Jón asks.

Stefán smiles at this. Jón has waited longer than most to ask.

'Ninety-seven.'

Elísabet drops her spoon. 'It cannot be. You look . . . no, it is not possible.'

'I was fifty when I first drank.'

Elísabet calculates. He survived the Skaftá fires. She places her bowl on the table, struggling to keep her supper down. An acrid taste rises in her throat. Suddenly, she is fearful that everything he has told them is true.

CHAPTER TWELVE

1831

It is June. Soon they will again be under the spell of the salty tang of the sea. Elísabet rides comfortably enough. Jón is overly cautious and asks too often how she fares. She must stop frequently to relieve her bladder and her husband's infinite patience verges on irritating. She might like him to sigh, or make a humorous remark, but he sits in a watchful blaze of pride and is immovable in it. It is their last journey before the birth of their first child.

Neither Jón nor Elísabet could resist Stefán's offer to fish from the portion of his land that borders the sea. When his letter arrived, the first personal post they had ever received, they had been discussing a way to supplement their stores for the oncoming winter. Stefán will allow them to keep what fish they need and then trade or sell any extra.

Her body moves with her horse's gait and her thoughts stray to a seafaring foreigner, the man who so recklessly played with her life. How quickly he lost interest in her the day he first met her sister.

'Elísabet? Where are your thoughts?' Jón beams at her. 'We're almost there.'

She smiles at him, erasing the past that fretfully reappears.

When they arrive at Stefán's farm to rest for the night, Elísabet is surprised that the buildings seem larger and more numerous than she remembered. The farmland sprawls further than she recalled from that first strange visit.

As it is still daylight Jón gives the customary three knocks. The door opens and Stefán's broad and welcoming smile slowly fades to that of surprise and confusion on sight of Elísabet.

'I'm sorry.' Stefán recovers. 'Please, please, come happy.' He offers the normal greeting.

After Elísabet and Jón are made comfortable, Stefán wastes no time.

'I must speak frankly.'

Jón nods in agreement.

'I am astonished. You are the first of us to conceive under these circumstances. I am unsure what this means.'

'Surely it just means we are going to have a child,' Jón says, confused.

'No, you don't understand. Forgive me – congratulations to you both. But we don't know what your child will ... if the baby will have been affected by your condition.'

'Stefán.' Elísabet speaks carefully. 'These past few months we've thought about this, and we still have not grasped the full meaning of "our condition" as you call it. It is so hard to fathom. We do not feel different.'

'I understand, I do ... you haven't told anyone of what happened to you both, have you?'

'No. We gave you our word.'

'And neither of you has yet been taken with the long sleep I warned you of?'

'No, not yet. But we remember your instructions and if this strange sleep occurs, we will follow them, I assure you.'

'Good. Have either of you noticed any strangers or foreigners near your farm, or on your journey here?'

'Just yesterday, we gave way to a traveller who rode behind us for a while. He gave no greeting when he passed. Elísabet, you observed his riding?' Jón looks to her.

'Yes, he seemed uncomfortable on his horse. But then he went ahead of us. Why?'

How much to tell them now, Stefán wonders. Perhaps a small healthy dose of the truth.

'There are ... people ... A Danish group who are suspicious of us. But you must be hungry and tired. Perhaps it is better to speak of this in the morning.'

'I think Elísabet needs to rest before we eat, but I want to hear more about the Danish,' Jón says.

Stefán looks through the window hole to check the sun's position. 'While the daymark is still before mid-evening I must take my turn on watch. Would you care to join me?'

'My legs are stiff and aching for a walk. But I will stay with Elísabet,' Jón says.

'No, Jón, please go. I will rest. It's fine,' she reassures him.

A light mist falls as Stefán and Jón tread past a massive heap of sheep dung. Stefán points to a patch of low shrub.

'Just past the shrub the path will lead to a small stream, there you will find a grassy ledge. Just beyond the ledge the mountains will appear on the horizon. They are our octant marks. Each night, before mid-evening our men walk the perimeter. We search for our enemy.'

'Enemy?'

Just as Stefán begins to explain, a man covered in blood runs after them. He shouts to Stefán.

'There is trouble with the ram!'

'I must go back,' Stefán says.

'Do you need help?' Jón offers, as any farmer would.

'No, thank you. Please. Continue your walk. We will speak later.' Stefán turns to go, and then turns back. 'Not too far, yes?'

Jón nods in agreement, waves and sets off.

Bright patches of bog cotton, white and spotless, shimmer through the mist. Cows and sheep graze in small familial clusters. June's midnight sunset is still hours away when the copper-coloured head of Jón Eymundsson disappears through a meadow of brilliant yellow-green grass.

Elísabet wakes later in a drowsy cloud, perplexed until she gains her bearings. She stands holding her heavy belly, feeling famished and nursing a strong craving for something sweet. She moves slowly down the long tunnel-like hall into the common room where Margrét greets her.

'I hope you had a good rest. I am happy for you and your husband.' Margrét embraces and kisses her. 'What would you like to eat? I picked blueberries earlier today.'

'You are a magician, Margrét. They are exactly what I want. But surely you will save them for a special occasion.'

'This is a special occasion.' Margrét serves the blueberries with a large bowl of sweetened cream. She likes this woman with her strange and handsome beauty. Margrét is somehow put at ease in her presence.

'Do you know the time? Has Jón returned?'

'Not yet.' Margrét pauses. 'His appetite will bring him back.'

The women smile at how easy it is to guess a man's motivations.

'The evening looks promising, perhaps you'd like a bit of fresh air?'

'Yes, I'd welcome that. I'll go out and wait for Jón.'

She steps into the evening air just as Stefán rushes by the front of the hut, followed by several other men. These men would normally be using every bit of the daylight to attend the animals and prepare for next month's haymaking season. It is now that she realizes she must have slept longer than she thought. Jón has been gone too long.

'Jón is not with you?' she asks Stefán.

'I had to come back to see to a ram. I directed him to a walking path, but he hasn't returned yet. We're off to search for him now.'

'I will come, too.'

'There's no need. I think it would be best if you ...'

'No. I'll go with you.'

There is such finality in her voice that Stefán doesn't argue, and when they begin walking he's surprised that she is more than capable of keeping up. She strides in silence, eyes ahead, searching.

The mist has cleared leaving the tall grass damp. A wind blows south and carries wafts of sweet-smelling thyme that grows in clumps along the path. After walking a short while, the party reaches the spot from where in the distance the peaks of the cold blue mountains shoot up into the charcoal cocoons of clouds.

They call Jón's name. Stefán entertains thoughts of what might have happened: a broken bone from a misstep, or perhaps it was time for Jón's long sleep. He reproaches himself for allowing him to go alone.

It is a beautiful time of day. The sky is flushed rose. The grey-leaved shrubs glisten. But as she continues forward, Elísabet sees the shrubs are smashed, dented with impressions of a struggle. She walks on. A mist has fallen in front of her like a curtain. The soles of a pair of boots protrude from the mist: they seem to hover just above ground like footprints of spirits. She edges closer to the boots, faintly hearing Stefán's call for her to wait. She will not. Her heart rises to her throat. It looks like Jón's body, lying near a stream of glacial water. She cannot get to him quickly enough. She thinks, hopes, he is sleeping, but the fine weave of his vest, her weave, is torn, buttons lost. Her eyes travel up his body and stare unbeliev-ingly into his beautiful face turned ghastly. His eyes bulge and his swollen tongue protrudes from his mouth as if in a grotesque thrust. His hair has taken the moisture of the mist and matts thick and dark against his head. And now she sees that his arms lie stiff, pinned beneath him.

Elísabet crumples beside her husband.

'Search the area, I'll stay here,' Stefán says to the other men. 'Be cautious.'

The six men form into pairs and set off with grim faces.

Elísabet removes the long muslin handling that flows down from her waist and places it over her husband's face. Then she turns on Stefán in a fury.

'What is this? How could this have happened?'

'I do not know. I am sorry.' Stefán musters a calm he does not feel. 'Elísabet, this is very important. Where does Jón keep his phial?'

Stunned she asks, 'Is that what you think?'

'No, not by his own hand. We know he would not have taken the contents of the phial by choice. But we also know that it's the only way this ... this tragedy could have occurred.'

As she moves Jón's body to search for his phial they discover that his hands are tied behind his back. Elísabet looks at Stefán wildly, her face hot and her eyes brimming.

'Who would do this? Why? Why would they do this?'

She searches the pockets of her husband's jacket and then his trousers. She looks in his socks. Her hands move fast, patting him down, feeling every inch of him, his crotch, even his armpits, searching for the phial.

Gone.

Panicked, she reaches for her own phial, which hangs from a necklace hidden beneath her clothing; it feels warm against her skin; she had forgotten it was there. She clasps it now seeking further confirmation that it is secure while her mind verges on accepting the incredible.

The outlines of black-clad figures move towards her in a dark squall. Four men approach with their hands up to signal surrender. It is an old custom, one that is still used in this sparsely populated land. One of the men looks first at Elísabet and then speaks to Stefán. 'Nothing.'

'Who has done this?' she manages to ask. 'His phial is missing. He ... he just went for a walk.' She tries to be rational, but nothing makes sense.

Elísabet moans as Stefán helps her to her feet.

'Come. We'll take you back,' he says.

'No. I want to go home. You must help me take Jón home. Please, untie his hands.'

'You cannot travel right now and remain safe. Think of the child.'

'How dare you. I think of nothing but the child.' A flash of anger overwhelms her as she turns away from them, but the truth is that this miracle she carries weakens her resolve to bear it alone. Of course she must stay with them. She cannot manage the journey home on her own. Owing to this act of violence she assumes the mantle of their secret. Yes, she nods, she will accept their help. She would be a fool to forgo it.

A rustle from the dwarf shrubs nearby alerts them. The other two men in their group emerge and quickly take Stefán aside. His head bowed, he listens, nods and then looks up at them, his face stamped with surprise.

'We need to go back, Elísabet.'

She leans heavily on two of the men, suddenly exhausted after her exertion; she's moved by their shyness with her. Stefán and the other four men lift Jón's body and carry it like a coffin.

Doors open at the sound of the group's return. Men and women stop work to witness the arrival of Jón's body with open-faced bewilderment. Their wadmal clothing forms a black moving blanket as they approach his body. Confused glances pass between them and they look from Elísabet's ashen face to their leader.

'He is dead? How can that be?' a man asks Stefán.

'Margrét, please take Elísabet to my house.'

Stefán then addresses the group. 'Please, complete anything that is pressing if you must, and then gather in the meeting house as soon as possible.'

Nothing is more pressing than the discovery of the body of Jón Eymundsson. The group immediately files into a hut reserved for communal meetings. They take their seats on two long benches placed around one equally long table.

'Our enemy looks like us,' Stefán begins. 'He dresses as we do. He speaks as we do. But he is Danish. I can confirm that Copenhagen's Falk family pursue our secrets. For those of you who don't know the extent of their power and resources, the Falks' wealth is made from the slave trade and sugar.'

A murmur floats through the hut.

'How do you know this?' asks Múli.

Stefán hesitates and the six men who tracked the Danish men earlier throw glances at each other.

'Because there were three men following Jón this afternoon. One of them fell and broke his leg. His companions left him with stab wounds in the bushes, most likely thinking he would die before we found him – evidence of their ruthlessness. But he was not yet dead – and he talked. And now the birds feed upon his body.'

'What did he say?' they all want to know.

'The elder Falk, he has always believed in the existence of the pool and he means to find it – and us. And ...' Stefán pauses. 'He knows my ancestors. He has heard a rumour that I am still alive and do not age. It is why I moved here.'

'So you have brought this danger to us,' a woman says.

Fists pound the table in disagreement, silencing her.

'I do not accept that. Any one of us can bring danger unwittingly. The point is that today the Falks' hired men know for certain that the amount we carry in our phials leads to death.'

This new truth sits heavily on them.

'If the child survives the birth, it will be the first amongst us,' another woman, Pála, says. 'And therefore, will be another danger to us all.'

'Dangerous, but also very important to us,' Stefán reminds them. 'We must contemplate how to keep Elísabet safe until the birth – and afterwards. Tomorrow morning, after sunrise, we meet again.'

At his house, Stefán pauses a moment before he knocks on the wall of his second sleeping room. Elísabet rests, propped up by eiderdown cushions, her eyes closed, her thick lashes damp with tears. Margrét works quietly as she collects the remnants of a meal of dried fish, butter, and a bowl of whey. She nods to Stefán before she leaves and tells him that Elísabet is awake.

'You must be very tired. I'll be brief,' Stefán says.

Her brow wrinkles at hearing his voice: it reminds her of the horrific events of the day. She cannot forget her husband's face in its grotesque death mask.

'Elísabet. You and your child will always be cared for and protected.'

'For how long, Stefán?'

'Forever.'

Elísabet looks him straight in the eye and calls upon her strength to say what has been so hard, so maddeningly difficult to admit.

'The meaning of "forever" has changed.'

CHAPTER THIRTEEN

Before sunrise the roof holes of the huts emit swirls of smoke. Elísabet wakes to the sloshing of hot water in a wide basin. Margrét negotiates the doorway, a cloth draped over her shoulder and soap in her pocket. Elísabet's clothing has been brushed, her shoes cleaned.

The warm water soothes her and she takes her time, gently moving the cloth over her belly, which seems heavier than yesterday. Her back aches and she wonders at the fact that she is hungry. She dresses, grateful for the patience Margrét has shown in removing the tendrils of grass and the dirt smudges from her skirt.

Now Margrét prepares a bowl of fish and cheese in the small, raised kitchen while Elísabet paces near her.

'There you are,' Margrét says to Stefán when he appears, the morning mist beading his jacket. 'You look as if you too need a hearty breakfast.'

'I've eaten, Margrét. Thank you.'

'You haven't slept.' Elísabet notices his weary, grey eyes.

He pulls a chair to the fire and waits for Margrét to leave the hut.

'I feel that I am responsible for the death of your husband.'

She slowly picks at her bowl of food. 'How so?'

'You and Jón were the first people who did not join us. Both of you convinced me that you could live alone. You were a new breed of survivalists, I thought. Yet, you are the youngest among us and I made the terrible error of ... I should have been more persuasive.

And now, with your pregnancy . . . if you had been living here with us we could have . . .'

'No. You cannot tell a man who is soon to become a father what is best for his child. Jón would never have listened to anyone else. We never expected a child – he was fiercely proud.'

Stefán cannot suppress a deep sigh.

'What is it?' Elísabet asks.

'I ask that you listen to me – someone you hardly know – and heed my advice. You are right. I have not slept for thinking of any other way to keep your child safe. What we have, who we are now, is as dangerous as it is miraculous. But, Elísabet, I . . .' Stefán stops. 'Goddamn, I cannot do this.'

'What? What is it that you cannot say?'

'We must take great care to protect your baby, to hide the child . . .'

'Yes, of course. I'm not an imbecile, I'm aware . . .'

'No. You do not understand. Your baby will not be safe in this country.'

'What are you saying?'

'Your sister, in England . . . Koldís?'

Elísabet stiffens. 'How do you know of her?'

'When I realized my mistake . . . when I was unsuccessful with my plea for you to join us, I made an effort to protect you both. It involved asking questions about your families.'

Elísabet stands abruptly, her chair falls over with a loud crash.

'Jón's father and mine will come to collect my husband's body.' Her tone is harsh, her words clipped. 'If you will please allow me to borrow a horse, I promise they will return it. Thank you for your kindness.'

'Elísabet . . . wait. Please trust me when I say that I have no other motive than to keep you and your child safe. I can think of only one way, one choice that gives you and your baby a chance of escaping the fate of your husband.'

'Why? Why are you and your community safe and I am not? Why

is it that my husband, who is – who was – an intelligent and practical man, is dead and not one of you?'

'For many reasons! We have been evolving, changing our habits for years now. You have no idea yet what it is truly like to live as we do.' He lowers his voice. 'I am sorry, that sounded harsh.'

Elísabet knows he's right. Jón insisted they remain isolated from this farmstead and its people. He never really believed that what had happened to them was actually real. A new wave of fear washes over her. Feeling unsteady, she sits again just as the clang of the bell that signals meetings peels out a call.

Margrét comes again and informs Stefán that everyone is assembled.

'I'll leave you for now, Elísabet. If you need anything, Margrét will be here for you. Call upon her.'

The community of men and women are seated in the meeting hut. Under their feet, hidden beneath the table where they are now gathered, the entrance to the tunnel is narrow. One must crawl head first, forcing a delay in pursuit to anyone who attempts to follow them. The tunnel leads deeper into the ground, then widens, and it is there, stored in specially handcrafted casks, where their most precious contents lie. The Icelanders sit atop the stores of the iridescent liquid.

The woman named Pála pours the coffee, taking great care not to fill the cups to the rims. A superstitious act, but there has been trouble and now is no time to court bad luck.

'Now,' Stefán begins, 'the child.'

Outside the meeting hut the weather takes a sharp cold turn. A gust of wind cuts through the unheated room and mocks their fortitude to think clearly and creatively. Margrét arrives with a bundle of sheepskins and they huddle under them warming their hands with steaming coffee cups.

Four hours pass. The chores of the day wait as the discussion continues until noon. This soul searching is not a simple one; after all, they have no claim to the child. However, they have scissored through the muck to devise a clear direction, and a plan, though incredibly complex, emerges. A proposal is agreed.

Afterwards Stefán pauses before entering his house, his forehead rests on the door as he takes a moment to prepare for his awful task. He finds Elísabet sitting in his common room. For a moment he is disoriented to see her knitting, her head bowed, exactly at the angle his wife used to find comfortable, and sitting a little sideways in the chair to face the best light. He winces, it seems like yesterday.

'I hope you do not mind my boldness. It calms me . . . the needles were lying there as if . . .' She looks up at him and sees that he has changed in some way. 'I am sorry.' She folds her hands over the needles.

'No, it . . . my wife always struggled with the needles; unlike you, your fingers fly.'

'Is she, did she . . . die? Apologies . . . of course she has.' Embarrassed, Elísabet turns back to knitting.

'It happened before we knew . . . before any of us changed . . . and began to form our group. I lost her and the children before I could begin to make even some small sense of all this . . . she never knew. This is why I come to you now.'

'You have a proposition for me,' she interrupts. 'You, all of you, want me to live within your community. I guessed as much.'

Stefán sits beside her.

'That is part of it, yes . . .' He pauses. 'First. Would you agree that the single most important task is to secure the safety of your baby?'

'Of course. Please. Speak plainly. I am not a child.'

'No, of course not. I didn't mean . . . I am asking you to do the most difficult thing you will ever do.' He pauses. This is a damnable job. 'Give your baby to Koldís to raise, until it is safe to bring the child back.'

'Never.'

'Please hear me out. We, all of us without exception, put it to you that when your child is born, the same group that murdered your husband will no doubt come for your child. Perhaps not right away, but one day they will come. There will not be a single safe haven in this country. We believe, temporarily, the best place for your baby is with your sister in England. We have the means for the voyage, and the child will want for nothing. It will give us time to plan for the future.'

Elísabet knows that what is important in this moment is to keep her composure; it is imperative to conceal the rage that immediately overwhelms her thoughts, and which threatens to overtake her entire being and become madness. She must make certain that not Stefán, nor any of them, later accuse her of that madness, though what she feels at his suggestion is wholly untethered.

'Please. Listen carefully,' Stefán pleads.

She strokes her belly and the baby that moves inside her and turns away from him.

'We are a small country that sometimes seems vast. It is true that when the winter comes we are isolated on our farm, and we all know what it is to feel separated from the other farmsteads by ice and snow. There is a false sense of security in that. If our enemy discovers where your child is they will do anything to get to it. Your child would be nothing more than some living thing upon which to experiment. My God, Elísabet! I hate to think of what they might to do to the child. They have already spied on your husband, tracked him down and killed him – solely for experimentation. And due to their murderous act they have learned of one of the properties of the water – the most dangerous one.'

'My husband is not yet a day dead and you ask this of me? No. *I* will protect my child. I will go away ... to the north.'

'Do you need any more evidence that you cannot cut yourself off from us entirely? Jón's death is proof of that. And if both you and your child were to live here, it would no doubt bring danger to us all. Our plan, our suggestion to you is that you stay with us. We will care for you and protect you. And Koldís . . .'

'Do not . . .'

Stefán sighs. Their acquaintance is a new one, but he has learned the story of her past and he is loath to broach it now.

'It was a bad business,' he says.

Elísabet's hands tighten around the knitting needles.

For a few minutes they are silent until Elísabet responds in a soft, thick voice.

'I was much happier and more fulfilled in my life with Jón than I ever could have been in England with the man that became my sister's husband. They were both cruel to me. Sister or no. Lover or no. Jón was a patient man. He healed me.'

She stands and walks to the small hole in the wall, richly-covered with a pane of glass from which she views the jagged dark blue peaks of the glacier set against the sparkling, green grass.

'Koldís . . .' Stefán attempts the subject again.

'She is no longer known by that name. She is called Clovis now. And she takes the name of her husband, as they do there. Fowler. Clovis Fowler.'

'Ah. That is in our favour,' he says. 'They will search for Koldís Ingólfsdóttir.'

'What do you mean?' she turns to him. 'Do you expect they would go all that distance to find my child?'

'Yes, of course. Eventually.'

Elísabet is stunned, grasped by a new awareness that ripples through her and leaves her weak.

'Leave me to think on this,' she whispers.

Stefán brightens at this first hopeful sign that she may change her mind. 'Of course. I'll go now. Please let Margrét attend you. She is fond of you.'

He lingers at the door and turns to her again.

'It is with great regret that we ask this of you. There is nothing we want more than to have you and your baby live here with us. I promise that we will devise a way to watch the situation carefully. It will be difficult to manage, Elísabet, but we *will* manage it.'

'Am I to lose everything I love?'

Her lovely eyes seem to bore straight into him and he is taken unaware by the lump of emotion that lodges in this throat. He knows what it is to lose everything.

'You will know your child one day,' he promises.

Her face holds the kind of sorrow he has witnessed too often in his long life. Sometimes the others knock on his door in the dark hours when the nightmares come. It is not unusual to find one of them out walking before daylight in an effort to shake off their demons. They come to him begging for some kind of understanding of what they have endured. The anguish of losing his own wife and children has not provided him with any answers regarding the deep well of grief from which they are all forced to drink. So he listens to them, unable to offer much advice; as the years march on there are times he feels he may die from the exhaustion of it – if only he could.

When he looks to Elísabet for a small acknowledgment that she will co-operate, something changes in her. Her eyes grow wide with hope; her face transforms, and a wild, frantic woman looks back at him.

'I could go as well! I would endure anything. Yes. I will.' She is already planning the voyage. 'Why did I not think of it? We could leave soon after the birth.' Her whole being expands with hope.

'We did discuss that possibility as a solution, but can't you see? They will expect you to take that course. What they will never believe is that that you would part from your baby.'

'What kind of mother would?'

'A mother who wants to save her child from some unspeakable horror.'

The next morning when Margrét brings Elísabet's breakfast bowl to the room, she lingers, hesitant, but clearly wanting to speak.

'What is it Margrét?'

'There is something the others have not been told. Something only Stefán knows. He chose not to alarm the others at the time, and I agreed with him. But you should know. I understand the decision facing you. I speak to you as a woman, but also as someone who has seen the unspeakable ... evil ... of the Falks.' Margrét's voice cracks a little as she loses composure.

'Margrét, here sit beside me.'

'No, please, do not be kind to me, I will not be able to speak.'

She reaches in her pocket for her handkerchief and mops her damp face.

'My husband and I. We were blessed with a child very late in life. It was before ... before we changed. Such a loving little girl, she made me ache with joy. She was with us the day we drank from the pool. I was going to give her a sip from my travelling cup, but the Watcher appeared. He frightened me so that I dropped the cup. He was kind. He told us to bring her back when she was older. Then he directed us to Stefán. But on the path, when we were almost a day's ride from the pool ...' Margrét stops.

'You do not have go on. It's all right, Margrét.'

'No! It is not all right!' She lowers her voice. 'The Falks. They rode it seemed out of the sky, suddenly four of them surrounded us. They said nothing. They asked no questions. And before we could get our bearings they took her.'

Elísabet gasps. Instinctively her hand clutches her belly.

'The Falks were just guessing, we had seen them before, but they had no way of knowing if she had changed, or anything at all. My husband found her discarded body in the following spring's thaw. He refused to let me see her. What they did to her body, the experiments, haunted him. My husband drank the contents of his phial a year later. Your child will not be safe here, Elísabet.'

Elísabet bows her head, her tears stream down and fall into her lap; tears shed for Margrét and for herself.

'How old was your daughter?'

'She was in her sixth year.'

LONDON
1831

CHAPTER FOURTEEN

'Fuck. Fuck me into the light. I'm up to my knees in shit.'

Finn Fowler adjusts his lantern as he leads his crew on a race against the tide in a tunnel as black as midnight. He lowers the neckerchief that protects his nose and mouth from the noxious air.

'Hold 'em up, hold 'em up. Don't drop that fuckin' cargo, you beasts.'

Sugar, tobacco, lace and chocolate, all they can carry of the stuff, is transported in a caravan of men who stretch the fabric of their dirty canvas trousers and troop under the streets. It becomes a simple run once they dupe their easy target – the lighterman who abandoned his goods for a draught of purl. Then, unpredictably, the current changes, along with the warning sound of the oncoming sewage, with its rats the size of cats, and everything dead comes rushing their way. At thirty-three years of age Finn can still outrun any of the river police through the streets and across the boats and ships, but down in the catacombs of underground avenues where people live forever divorced from light, where secrets are kept, and thievery muddies their boots, he cannot outrun the sludge.

'The fuckin' grate is two feet from us – prepare yourselves, you thieving girls.'

The six behind him slow down, and when Finn gives the signal of his raised hand in the shadows, they come to a dead stop.

Finn shuts the slide on the bullseye lantern that protrudes from the buckle on his belt. Not a ray escapes and they are plunged into a hellish black. His ear is tuned to overhead footfall, but no restless walkers, no drunken brawlers darken the grate. He opens the slide to emit a glow that shines out full strength, chasing the dark away. The men carry on. Their torsos lean forward with the weight of their treasures but their feet cling and sink into the sticky excrement of man and animal, until at last, their legs pull free and they are released. Disgruntled, they trudge forward once more, burdened by their heavy sacks. Three more grates hinder their progress before they approach the concealed exit.

Their watcher kneels by the exit listening for signs of his investment to rise from lower London. And here they are! Gasping for fresh air and so covered in filth that he almost loses his digesting pork chops there on the spot. He will never grow accustomed to it, and this is the reason Finn allows him to be the lookout. He relieves them of the first load until a chain forms and within minutes the cart is loaded, covered, and on its way to the apothecary's cellar, where there is access to another tunnel passage.

Owen Mockett is upstairs in his bed, exhausted from the evening's romp with his wife. This is his pact with Finn: Mockett gives access to the river, receives his share of the plunder, and if anything should go wrong he remains the simple apothecary who knows nothing.

The men scatter, having shed their grimy clothes for some poor washerwoman to deal with in the morning. Finn stops at a pump to rinse his hands with what remains of the day's water, then quickly runs his shoes through the last trickling drops. His eyes dart, looking out for strange followers who may be spies. His gang is intentionally few in number, hardly a gang at all. He courts no competition with the larger gangs who would rather slice each other's throats than negotiate territory. Nevertheless, he'd be a fool not to be wary.

He struggles with an urge to visit Madam Liesel's; the German runs the best bawdy house this side of the river. He is instantly aroused with the memory of Anna from Bavaria and that special thing she does to his member that tempts him back tonight. But he feels filthy and smells worse and Madam Liesel would never allow him near her house in this state.

The eastern edge of London never really slumbers. Candlelight suffuses a random spread of front rooms down the streets. He hopes his wife's little puppet is heating the water for his bath. It's been three years now since Clovis plucked Willa from the orphan asylum. Christ, what a quivering mass of nerves the girl was.

The heat of the bakehouse interrupts his thoughts and his stomach grumbles as he walks through its steamy door. He reaches into his jacket for a small pack of tobacco for Carson and a measure of lace for the baker's wife.

'All right there, Carson?'

With outstretched blistered arms the baker presents his offering with a lukewarm greeting. In the early hours of the morning the basket full of warm bread is company to two large meat pies and one of Carson's special cakes made with the sugar Finn traded with him last week.

Across the street the shadow of a man in a dark-brown suit is drawn on the cobblestones from the dull glow of a single street lamp. The outline of his tired, black topper elongates as he turns away when Finn leaves the bakehouse. The dark-brown suit moves on. The baker spits after Finn's departure.

The thrill of Finn's rich booty and the heady satisfaction of a smooth run are wearing off, leaving him tired and hungry. The shutters of his front windows are closed but he can just make out a strip of light in the joins. He gives the signal of four raps in quick succession followed by a pause and one single knock.

The hour is three in the morning but no one is asleep in the Fowler household. On the evenings when Finn makes a run they call his time away 'the dark hours'. Never knowing if he'll be snatched by the paws of the newly formed Metropolitan Police – how bloody inconvenient of them – or meet his end at the hands of violence, those who depend on his risky occupation anxiously await his safe return.

Willa opens the door and stands well back. Her master reeks this morning. She has saved enough water for a good wash and he follows her straight to the kitchen where under her watchful eye the water simmers in a big pot over the fire.

Clovis appears and stands quietly in the frame of the door. She motions for Willa to leave them. As a precaution she still wears her day dress during the dark hours when Finn is away in the event there's call for a swift departure. Her hair is unpinned and falls down in thick waves to settle on a fabric of midnight-blue.

'All is well?'

'If Jonesy is back, then yes.' He pours a pitcher of water over his head savouring its journey down his body to the stone floor.

'He has returned. Everything is safe with Mockett.'

'What is that?' He points at the paper she holds in her hand.

'I want to speak to you about this. A letter from Denmark.'

'What? A fucking fortune then!'

'No, Finn. Delivered by a boy, not a letter carrier. We did not pay for delivery.'

'Denmark? Not Iceland?'

'I do not know why it's marked Copenhagen.'

'Well. Go on then.'

'It seems we are going to be parents.'

'Not bloody likely.'

Finn wipes his fingers across the plate and sucks the crumbs from them. He considers himself to be somewhat of a pie aficionado. Carson had dipped into his good flour stores for this meaty pie; the secret lies in the lightness of the crust. He tastes the difference in the high quality shortening. Papery flakes fall as golden flecks on Finn's shirt.

Clovis conceals her disgust at his carelessness. There's a bit of lettuce on the floor and a ring of red wine on the tablecloth, as though he marks his territory, or must leave evidence.

'Finn, I prefer that you not eat in the bedroom.'

'You prefer? Another word you've picked up at those lectures of yours? I'll eat where I like.'

'I thought it would please you. I try to improve my English.'

Clovis waits for a response, but he eats and drinks and grows weary – weary of her. His wife's beauty no longer interests him. There is no gown, no simple or complicated design that is capable of dimming her voluptuous body, yet he no longer has the addiction he once did for her. In this, most men would think him quite mad, or a sodomite, but a man, especially a man like Finn, does not like to be used, and the feeling in his tackle goes limp whenever he thinks of her trickery. So he dines in silence.

Clovis is nothing if not patient. Her chair near the window is comfortable enough and from her position she waits for the right moment to strike. She counts the number of times he fills his goblet. It will be soon.

Outside their bedroom window commerce is slowly beginning its daily march. The dustman's 'Dust-ho!' followed by a sharp ring of his bell, brings Willa pattering down the stairs. Yesterday's ashes swept from the fireplaces are ready for collection.

Clovis adjusts the shutter to allow a sliver of light to stream in while Finn continues to eat. She looks down at the milk pail being lowered from the milkmaid's string where, having run back down to the basement kitchen, Willa unhooks it with her calloused fingers.

Clovis continues her vigil at the window. The smacking of his lips, she thinks, and the way he sucks his fingers – hateful.

When they first met, Finn told her he was a horologist. He had set sail from London in late March of 1828. On board, Dr Von Torben, an eminent geologist, three draughtsmen, two writers, several seamen and fishermen, an Icelandic interpreter, and an astronomer made forty men.

They reached Iceland three weeks later and the terrible and beautiful ruggedness that stretched out before them led them to believe that no humans could possibly inhabit the island. So gigantic was that first view of desolate nakedness that they forgot to be afraid. If the shore had not been covered with boats they might have despaired that the scenery held nothing for them but that nakedness.

Finn arrived on the island with his clocks: ships' clocks, striking clocks, pendulum clocks, and a few pocket watches. The interpreter had insisted that this country's people had no use for and no means of investing in a clock, and now he was proven correct. Icelanders mark the time in a completely different way according to their long hours of sunlight in the summer and their short dark days of winter. So Finn, ever resourceful, became the astronomer's indispensable assistant.

That summer Clovis had returned to her father's farm from the north where she'd spent two gruelling months assisting her aunt during the birth of her fifth child. She despised every moment of the clinging children, her needy aunt, the constant drudgery of the work, and the cold. God curse the cold! She thought she'd never be warm again. Near the dead lands of the southern coast they always speak of the beauty of the north, but she found nothing redeeming, nothing worthwhile and the journey was never-ending and unbearable.

She returned home to find two foreign men camped near their hut; they had traded with her father while she was away. What kind of man traded good boots and tools for the opportunity to look at the skies from a poor farmer's scratch of land?

The one called Finn amused her with his vulgar tale that from the first time he saw her riding along the path by the meadow, with the white-capped mountains painted against her flying red hair, he became so stiff he thought he would have to relieve himself there and then. As she rode nearer and he saw that she was real and not an exquisite dream, the intimacy he had shared with her sister vanished like the steam of a hot boiling spring. And that was how he admitted what he had done while Clovis was away with her hands in baby shit and ignorant of his presence.

That was when he was drunk with just the thought of her.

But today, Clovis's breasts rise without desire, and her lips part not from wanting, but because she is pulsing with an entirely new lease on life. Here it is in her hands in the form of an extraordinary letter. If Finn would only look at her, he would recognize ambition racing through her.

'So go on then. Read it.'

The street below continues to wake as Clovis allows more light to filter in.

To my sister and her husband,

You will be surprised to hear from me. I am surprised that I write – I do so because I must. There is much I cannot tell you and you will have many questions. They will be answered at another time.

My husband is dead. He has met with a terrible accident. I am to have his child four months from now. My child cannot remain in Iceland. I will be honest with you, my last choice, but my only choice, is to have the baby raised by you and your husband as your own. A fuller explanation will come at a later date – and it will not be from my hand. You will not hear from me again.

Considering events of the past, I find it difficult to ask you to do this. I know you are moved only by incentives. A handsome amount will be offered annually to ensure your loyalty and comfort, but most especially for the safety, comfort and education of my child.

Make no mistake – a supporter will be appointed to monitor my baby's progress, so think carefully before you accept. You will be monitored.

If you agree, we must move swiftly to prepare for the baby's arrival and subsequent journey. There are a number of things you will need to do, not least of these is to begin the facade of your pregnancy. This you must do. No questions must be raised.

As you know, the yearly postal boat arrives in Iceland from Denmark in late October. So more expedient means of communicating must be employed. A messenger will call on you in two days to collect your reply.

Again, think carefully on this. Once the child is with you there is no undoing this agreement.
Elísabet

'Damn you, damn Elísabet, damn me and damn God,' Finn roars.

Clovis sits down beside him and rests her hand on the meat of his upper thigh.

'Aren't you just a little intrigued by this, Finn?'

'No, fuck no.'

'The money. Think of the money. It must be a large sum.'

'There's something not right about this. Elísabet's not the kind to give up her baby. Especially after . . . And good Christ, you a mother? I hate to think.'

She is not stung. There are already three children under this roof, she says to herself. Her thoughts keep turning, turning. There must be some scandal, or some deeply foreign secret that has created this chain of events. A smile begins to form because she knows she is right. She can feel it.

'We will be rich, Finn.'

'Your sister is not rich, and now that she's lost her husband she has nothing. She is trying to unload that child on us, Clovis.' He raises his voice again. 'Our pockets are not going to be lined with gold, you stupid, stupid woman.'

Clovis stands perfectly still with her eyes tamed on Finn. And when she is certain that his full attention is turned upon her, after he has licked away the remainder of the pie, she speaks.

'I think we both know that I am not stupid. See me here, Finn Fowler. I live in the greatest city in the world, in my own house with two servants. One day you will remember this moment when I say this child will make us rich. You will never call me stupid again. Things are going to change in this house. Hear me well: I would rather kill you than allow you to endanger what is to come.'

She has gone cold. A woman does not like to be used.

CHAPTER FIFTEEN

The exchange with Finn has left her feeling restless. She waits until he sleeps before she prepares the parlour. When everything is in place she summons Willa.

'I am ready for you.'

'Yes, mistress.'

Willa sits and immediately thrusts her hand into her pocket to clasp her tokens of comfort.

Clovis studies the porcelain head that sits on a pedestal, its mysteries mapped out in shiny lines and sections. Her finger traces the black marking of the line from the centre of the forehead, all the way to the top of the head where she stops at the benevolence organ. She calculates and memorizes the trajectory, mentally tracing it on the head of her servant who sits nervously in the chair.

Willa fingers a miniature heart-shaped pin cushion in her right hand. The soft, blue velvet calms her. What will Mistress make her do this time? She wonders as she traces the threads of the embroidered horseshoe in the centre of the cushion that she stitched in so expert a fashion.

'Close your eyes.' Clovis instructs.

Willa obeys, and after a moment's pause Clovis passes her hands over the girl's head.

The fire needs stoking, but neither of them will attend it now. There is a pause in the bustle of commerce outside in the street. Clovis chooses the quiet of this moment to apply firm pressure to the end of Willa's little finger, progressing slowly to the root of her nail. This she does patiently, methodically with each of the girl's fingers.

The amulet falls from Willa's other hand, her head lolls. Clovis stifles a gasp. She has commanded a hypnotic state in a few efficient movements. But now she must recall exactly what she witnessed on the stage and also the instructions in the pamphlet.

'Willa.' Clovis uses an unhesitating and positive tone. 'Remain asleep. Lift your head, keep your eyes closed.'

The girl slowly raises her head. She appears comfortable, calm and restful.

Clovis begins the next procedure. It is her first effort to test her ability to affect the organs of the brain. Calling upon her excellent memory she imagines her idol in her mind's eye. She sees the great mesmerist before her and the way in which he magnetized the entire lecture hall. She glances once more at the porcelain head gleaming in the darkening room that grows colder by the minute.

Clovis locates the spot easily enough and wills herself to feel supreme confidence as she places her finger on the organ of benevolence on Willa's head. After a short time, the girl's face undergoes a remarkable change. Her sleepy expression transforms to one of such intense pity that Clovis takes a step back.

Willa still sleeps, and apparently with no awareness of the continued pressure of Clovis's finger, she reaches into her pockets and produces an array of amulets and charms, bits of thread and ribbons, until her pockets are empty. She then holds these pitiful offerings in her palms, as if to give them all away.

Willa stands and takes a few steps forward. Her palms face up as she moves slowly to and fro, as if searching for someone to receive her treasures. Clovis quickly adjusts her position to accommodate the roaming girl and takes the bits from her, while her other finger remains on the girl's head. Willa is aware that her hands are empty and relaxes again.

The drawing room, normally cosy from the heat of a substantial fire is now chilled, which makes the girl's next movements even more remarkable. She begins to undress. Clovis stands transfixed as first one item of clothing then another falls to the floor, until the thin skeleton of Willa Robinson stands completely naked.

Clovis does nothing to protect the poor girl's modesty. Her heart is close to bursting, pounding with excitement. This unbridled joy cares not for the shame and embarrassment should someone happen upon this scene. Willa is a tool, her subject, and nothing more. Clovis Fowler swells with a new-found power.

Now shivering, Willa gathers all of her clothing into a neat, folded bundle and offers the square to Clovis. Benevolence. Charity. Humanity. Clovis removes her finger from the spot, and with that simple act, Willa sits in the chair again.

'Dress yourself,' Clovis orders.

Willa stands again and in a dream-like state she slowly dresses as Clovis provides her clothes item by item. Clovis now looks for a false moment, or for a break in the trance. But Willa shows no sign of faltering, even when she begins the intricate task of lacing her stays. Her hands work fastidiously, while her gaze seems absorbed entirely on a different plane.

'Sit,' Clovis commands, when the girl is fully clothed.

Clovis reaches into her pocket and produces a handkerchief. It billows out with a few shakes, and with it she fans Willa's face and head. There is no immediate reaction. She commands herself to remain calm, passes her hands over Willa's head three times, and continues to fan for another minute or so. Willa begins to stir. Quickly, Clovis retrieves the pincushion and places it in Willa's hand. She fills her servant's pockets with the trinkets.

The girl wakes at Clovis's instruction.

'Willa?' Clovis asks in her kindest voice. 'How do you feel?'

Willa glances at her mistress and then surveys the room as if she sees it for the first time.

''Tis so cold, mistress, I should tend the fire.'

Willa makes an effort to stand, but Clovis places her hands on her shoulder and presses her down.

Willa shrinks from her, disoriented that her mistress would touch her.

'I have a question first.'

'Yes, mistress.'

'What do you remember of our session today?'

Willa's large, green eyes narrow as she tries to remember her actions since she first stepped into the room.

'Well, mistress, I came into the room . . . and . . . well, I think you told me to sit in this chair . . . and . . . then, nothing. It is cold.'

'Is there anything else? You must be forthright, Willa.'

'Nothing at all, mistress. Well, there is one thing. I might be a bit more . . .' She searches for an inspired word.

'More what? '

'Calm.'

'Do you remember our conversation when we first met? That I could help you?'

'Why yes, mistress, I certainly do.' She is awed by the kept promise.

'You may fetch more coal now.'

CHAPTER SIXTEEN

It was three years ago when Clovis disembarked at Westminster Bridge, on the marshy corner of Lambeth that seems to serve as a receptacle for the misbegotten.

In scouring the newspapers for charities that sought employers for their charges, Clovis learned there of a pinch in funds at the House of Refuge for Orphan Girls. The Refuge takes great pride in their fervent work to save girls from a life of prostitution and immorality, and happily for Clovis, administrators have recently relaxed their rules. Jobs are less closely investigated and the girls are being processed and let back into the world more easily.

Clovis sails with confidence into this atmosphere of need and want. On this day she has chosen a fashionable woven-silk dress, the fabric of which was stolen from a vessel returned from China. Figures of hand-painted dove breasts and black flowers are scattered across the heavy, white satin. Heads turn at her elegant walk – one she has so painstakingly developed. Women who are near the front gate when she steps out of the sedan chair track her with envy, their eyes follow her down the path. Her black-and-white silhouette, crowned by brilliant red hair that falls perfectly from her large matching hat, brightens the dimly lit entry of the asylum.

The administrators have made it perfectly clear that it is preferable that those women employed at the Home of Refuge for Orphan Girls are widowed, and they must have unexceptionable characters of sobriety and honesty. From where she stands in the presence of

Matron Jennet, Clovis weighs the arrogance of one such woman. If ever two women possessed more scrutiny ... Matron Jennet's right eyebrow could not be more arched, and Mrs Fowler's human form shifts to that of a stalking tiger, immediately sensing a foe. A shaft of morning sun falls on the floor between the two as though marking a divide.

Mrs Fowler is invited to sit to discuss her needs. Mrs Fowler would rather stand. Then the light from the skylight shifts ever so slightly with the wave of passing clouds and falls on a dark corner where, like the breast of one of Clovis's printed doves on silk, Willa Robinson stirs.

Clovis brings her attention to the girl while Matron Jennet darts to the corner where the little bird sits crouched on a stool, busy with her needlework. Matron seems eager to hide the girl by stepping in front her, a ridiculous effort that only arouses Clovis's curiosity further.

'Why, Matron Jennet. What have we here? How quiet she is. What beautiful work, Miss ... ?' Clovis looks to Matron.

Defeated, Matron steps aside. 'Stand and introduce yourself,' she orders the girl, flustered.

The girl is as thin as a spindle, and her head is unusually large. Equally large are her almond-shaped green eyes with which, when she summons the courage, glance not quite into the beautiful lady's face but settle somewhere near her neck.

'Willa Robinson, madam.' She curtsies.

'Well, Miss Robinson, where did you learn such precise needlework?'

Willa looks for approval from Matron before speaking.

'Here, madam. Mrs Arnold, the seamstress, she teaches all us girls.'

'And what else have you learned?' Clovis gives her a most radiant smile.

'Knitting, making linens, curing, pickling.'

'And can you read, Miss Robinson?'

'All of our girls are taught reading and spelling and they each have the same branches of housekeeping skills as Miss Robinson,' Matron interjects.

Thank Christ, Clovis says to herself, I don't want that responsibility. For though she despised every moment of her reading lessons in that smoky, turf cottage, she would not be here today if she had not applied herself.

'May I escort you to the dining hall where the girls will soon gather for their dinner? You can meet all of our young women who have completed their training and who are ready and eager to secure a position.' Matron is in a rush to exit.

Clovis now sends Matron an equally winning and patient smile, but turns her attention more intensely on Willa. So it goes for the better part of an hour, in which Matron Jennet makes every effort to lead Clovis's gaze from Willa to the discussion of other young ladies. Yet, the more robustly Matron puts forth her suggestions, the firmer Clovis stands against them.

Luck plays its part in the day when Matron is called to attend the arrival of an administrator.

There is something awry here, of this Clovis is certain. The girl is of age and fully trained, yet Matron clearly asserts a proprietary stance.

'Please excuse me for a moment, Mrs Fowler. Come, Willa. Come with me.'

Willa jumps up like a trained pony.

'Matron Jennet, please, may Miss Robinson wait here with me?' Clovis flashes another winning smile. 'It will allow me a moment to tell her about my small household and what we might expect of her.'

'I am afraid that will not be possible.'

'Because, Matron Jennet, it will save me returning with Mr Fowler to address the administrators at a later date. I would so love to tell them how co-operative you have been . . .' She pauses. 'Rather than the opposite. If you understand my meaning.'

Matron's lips close tightly, her eyes blink like the wings of a trapped moth.

'Well. Yes. Yes, Mrs Fowler, I understand you perfectly.'

Matron throws a portentous glance at Willa before her stiff petti-coats swish away to suck the air from another room.

'Now, Willa Robinson. Do come nearer.'

Willa hesitates before inching forward. Other than a desk and three chairs the room is unadorned. The girl is so nervous that she places her hand on the desk to steady herself.

'It is my wish that very soon I shall employ you.' Clovis captures Willa's eyes and does not let them go.

'You know, Willa – I shall call you by your given name – and a very pretty name it is, too.'

Willa is quite entranced now. Clovis positions two chairs directly across from each other, sits in one and invites the girl to take the other. Then she leans in just enough to appear conspiratorial.

'It appears that you are a little frightened of something?'

Willa casts a worried glance at the door.

'How old are you, girl?'

'Fifteen, madam.'

'And have you ever been chosen for employment before?'

Willa pauses, glances towards the door again, and with a directness that she has not yet shown, she whispers. 'Many times.'

'Ah. I see. I will tell you a little secret. You mustn't tell anyone.'

'No, I won't, madam.'

'I know how to make people feel better. What do you think of that?'

'How do you mean, madam?'

There it was again, the fear jumped onto her. Willa's eyes grow wider until they look as if any moment they may pop out.

'Well, in the same way that you have spent these years learning to sew and read and cook, I have been studying, too . . . in the realm of science. I will tell you all about it when you come to live with me. But this must remain a secret, yes?'

Willa nods, obviously relieved and thankful for the nature of science.

'Now, I have confided my very important secret, do you have one to tell me?'

The girl's face reddens and she slips her hand into the pocket tied at her waist.

'What have you there?'

''Tis a hand, madam. I sewed it from scraps. It protects from the evil eye.'

'How intricate it is, too. Is that your secret then?'

Willa searches the lady's face; what she hopes to find she does not know. Salvation? Protection? Her eyes fill up.

'Is there another secret, Willa?' Clovis says, with a delicacy of which she never thought she was capable, false though it is.

'Mrs Fowler.' Matron Jennet appears again. Willa starts, but Clovis has no reaction at all to her sudden appearance. Matron, however, is slightly breathless, to Clovis's amusement.

'Please, Mrs Fowler, I must kindly insist that your experience with us today is a full one. If you'd be kind enough to follow me to the dining hall.'

'I will not. But thank you, Matron, my business here is completed for the present.'

'But . . . what do you mean?'

'Forgive my directness, but I have already made my decision. I shall return in seven days to collect Willa Robinson. Good day, Matron Jennet.' Another alluring smile and then, 'Willa, would you escort me to the gate, please? If Matron agrees, of course.'

Matron manages a slight bow of her head, thoroughly defeated. Her face drains of colour, as there can be no doubt that this creature has cast a spell on Willa. Matron stands impotent as Willa follows in the wake of the Fowler woman.

'Now, my little bird.' Clovis slips her hands through first one glove, then another and adjusts her hat in the tall mirror in the reception hall. 'Tell me, is Matron Jennet terribly fond of you?'

Willa's legs will not carry her further.

'Now, now. You mustn't be frightened, Willa. Is this your secret?'

Nothing from the girl. She continues her slope-shouldered walk.

When they are outside the Refuge's dim corridors and the influence of Matron Jennet, Clovis motions for Willa to follow her to the small front garden, near the gate and safely away from the windows. Willa's uniform of dark-brown petticoats, white apron and cap looks drab and spiritless in the company of this woman who towers over her, whose hair is even more brilliant against the rich, green leaves of the trees and their bowing branches.

'Have you ever been outside these gates before?'

'Not often, madam. Once, near Christmas, we carted our knitting to the market. It were a special occasion for us. That night, I suppose because of the holiday so near and everything, Matron, she was on the gin. "Tain't allowed, madam. Not here. Never.'

Now that Willa has found her tongue she forgets to breathe.

'I were dead asleep, long day and all, when Matron is rattling my shoulder. She were without candle even. It scared me so to see her standin' over me in the dark like that. She said I must come with her and to be quick and quiet about it. But Mary, who was in the next one over, she put up such a fit and fuss. I were awed by her bravery. My only friend ever in this world. So Matron, she turned around sharp-like and left. She were very cross. Mary were placed directly after that in the New Year. I dunno know where she is.'

Clovis approaches slowly and deliberately. 'Willa, has Matron ever touched you in a manner of . . . fondness? In a way that makes you feel uncomfortable?'

A guttural sound sticks in Willa's throat. She freezes in her steps and her face turns pale. Then her fingers ply against her thigh, each slender tip moves singularly up and down, up and down, as though she must perform this counting motion in order to save her life.

'Once. But she tries many times. I has to think quick.'

'Hmm. Yes, I thought as much. Your secret is safe with me. I will be as silent as the grave.'

'Please, please, madam. You will not say anything, will you? Matron is very powerful.' Her fingers continue to tap.

'Oh Willa, that is not power. Matron is filled with fear. We will not speak of this again. You will not have that worry with me, or anyone in my household. But you will work very hard.'

'I like to work.'

'We shall see. Now, I think I will walk back to the bridge. Yes, a walk to celebrate today's business. Good day to you, Willa Robinson. Until next week.'

'Goodbye, madam . . . Madam?'

'Yes, what is it?'

'You won't tell, will you?'

'I am the soul of discretion.'

'Oh. Does that mean you won't?'

'It does. Now run along, will you?'

'Yes, madam. Thank you, madam.'

Willa feels as if a spell of bad luck has been broken as she stands at the gate and watches the magnificent vision of the lady's gown fade into the remainder of the day's sunlight. She has been saved! Saved from the monstrous Matron Jennet.

Willa wakes early the next morning and uses the extra time to prepare for her departure next week. A petticoat needs mending, and though her boots are clean, she rubs and buffs and shines them until her arms are sore. She had squirrelled away a piece of gnarly gristle from her stew and rendered its fat with the flame of a tallow. She rubs it on her rough hands and feet, working it in and smoothing it as if it were as rich as a pot of Pears' balm.

After the morning lessons she scurries to collects her charms and tokens from the hiding places in the asylum. Behind the heavy curtain of the sleeping-hall's window she pockets the acorn that serves as protection against lightning. From under the corner of her mattress she retrieves the wishbone bound in striped silk for protection against danger. She has only a few minutes left to dash to the chapel where behind the shelving, last year's Soul Mass cakes have become as solid as little bricks and the mice have had a good gnaw at them. She leaves them.

'You are late to dinner, Miss Robinson.'

Willa's back is to the door of the chapel and she is almost certain that the trembling that overtakes her is visible.

'I was replacin' a prayer book, Matron.'

Willa had managed to avoid the woman all morning. For the first time in her life she has reason to feel hopeful, and was so consumed with her tasks that there were moments when she was free from the weighty thought of Matron Jennet. Emboldened by her impending departure and new place in the world she turns to face Matron, but upon seeing the creature's knitted brows at the top of her bulldog face, Willa's fickle strength leaves her and fear shoots her down. She feels like one of the ducks or pigeons that famously fall to the ground in the surrounding Lambeth marshes when the men are at the hunt.

'There will be a day in your future when you will think on your time here. It may not be in a fortnight, or in one year's time, but that day will come.'

Matron's poisoned breath is at her ear and her breasts push against Willa's arm.

'And on that day you will ask yourself in quiet despair, why wasn't I a little kinder to Matron? It really would not have been so bad. Not as terrifying as this stranger . . . this woman who hides something black-hearted behind her seductive smile. Mark my words.' She pauses. 'Now get out of my sight.'

Willa runs out of chapel to the bathhouse where she washes her hands several times and then paces with her hand deep into her pocket, rubbing another of her tokens, a human tooth. Oh no, she has forgotten its use as a charm. What is the meaning, the purpose of the tooth? She cannot think. There is no comfort.

She has missed her lunch now and Cook is cross and will not give her a crust. She is late to help the younger girls with their baking lessons, which stirs their rowdiness when left on their own. Cook's sharp tongue and the chaotic kitchen reduce Willa to a limp bag of nerves.

Later that evening when the flames are extinguished and the snores and whimpers of the girls form the melody of the night, doubt overcomes her and she worries that the lady who has offered her a life outside these walls will not come again. What if she changes her mind? With a hand still greasy with gristle she reaches under her mattress to retrieve her most powerful charm, a copper, crescent moon. She holds it to her lips and rocks until finally she falls asleep.

CHAPTER SEVENTEEN

Willa's first employer arrives on this dismal morning dressed in the colour of the gunmetal sky. The outline of her body between the two columns of the portico appears sharper than the week before, her jacket more severe, she looks more like a governess than the colourful and blooming flower of last week. Willa stands at the edge of the first-floor window peering down, with her head slightly cocked at this inauspicious beginning. She can hardly say for sure, because she doesn't consider herself to be a good judge of character, but surely Mrs Fowler is a little less radiant today – but perhaps more powerful for it, Willa goes on to think; really it's just her own silly supposition, her own weak effort to form an opinion after her upset with Matron, that Mrs Fowler, perhaps not aware of being observed, bears the aura of menace. And as the lady in grey lifts her petticoats to climb the step, she turns her head to the left and looks up into the window, where Willa flinches and draws back from sight.

No one comes to offer Willa a farewell. No one wishes her well. She wore the invisible mark of Matron's Girl, which left her friendless during her time in the Refuge. She stands before Matron this morning her skin still red from the scrubbing she gave it last night. Her nails shine blue from her efforts to extract the essence of wild violets. Her desire to be and smell clean when travelling with her new mistress had almost made her ill and robbed her of sleep.

Whatever final business Matron and her new mistress may have attended is now concluded. With a slight nod Mrs Fowler turns on her heels and marches out of the Home of Refuge for Orphaned Girls with Willa following closely behind, clinging to her box of modest goods.

A two-wheeled, one-horse cab waits for them at the gates. Willa is unsure how to actually get in it, having never in her life ridden in or on anything, and though it looks simple enough, she is certain it is not. Clovis instructs her to climb in the cab before her, but the girl misjudges the height of the step, struggles with the box and becomes entangled in her petticoats, and with a dive forward lands with her face on the floor.

Clovis has not yet smiled at her servant today, but now she laughs. When the warmth of that bright beam of light shines on Willa, just as it did last week, it is worth a great deal more than a sore nose. In fact, the radiance so occupies her thoughts on their journey that she doesn't notice that the hansom has stopped. She assumes they have arrived, but she cannot make out the river stairs from the little window, nor is the great river itself to be seen. She edges forward a bit more for a better view of a sprawling and imposing building. Its centre dome seems to stare back at her as though it were a large eye drinking in her soul.

'Do you know what lies within this building, Willa?'

The cadence of her mistress's words, spoken with the trace of a foreign accent, sounds like a song and they are the first she has spoken to Willa today.

'No, mistress.'

'Men and women who have fallen out of themselves. Some will be restored and others have fallen so far they will never be seen again.'

'The madhouse?'

'Indeed. Bethlem. Leave your box here and come with me.'

Frightened that there has been some trick played and she will be left here, Willa protests.

'But, mistress! I don't want to. What are you going to ...'

Clovis turns on the girl with such fury and force in her expression, that the girl's confidence is shattered.

'I will not stand for disobedience. Nor will you ever question me again. If you doubt you are capable of either of those, then I shall return you to Matron Jennet at once.'

'Oh no, mistress. Please. Forgive me. Please. I thought that . . .'

'We will take the air here.'

Clovis steps down, adjusts her petticoats and begins to promenade along the perimeter of the formidable home of the forgotten. The cab waits.

'Many arrive here and most will never leave alive. The criminally insane have their own ward but often they are so clever that they find ways to infiltrate the other wards . . . the women's ward. I have also heard that a young woman's hands may be tied in such a way that she cannot freely do her counting, or rub her amulets and charms.'

Clovis's voice has become trance-like. 'Worse yet, Willa. There are hundreds of women within those walls who are exactly like Matron Jennet. But even these women, well, they are lightweights compared to the doctors, who apply leeches to a woman's labia.'

Here Clovis pauses to gauge Willa's understanding.

'Your quim. Imagine it.'

Willa tries desperately not to do so.

On the street the slow plodding donkeys bray against the rush of the horses and carriages. Fresh excrement steams in piles they build indiscriminately. The first drops of rain fall on Willa's face. Clovis's large, brimmed hat, wrapped in a long swath of grey chiffon, dramatically envelops her face and protects it from the mist. She is just beginning to warm to her subject.

'But all is not gloomy. There is a ballroom. What do they look like I wonder, Willa? Do they dance in tattered and stained gowns? Might their shaved, scorched heads, oozing with wounds, catch the flickering light? And how, I consider, do people who are mad take to the drink when they are offered ale and punch. I dare say it is not for the weak. Hmm?'

Clovis draws her chiffon mask higher still.

'Well. We must get back to the river before the heavens open. My goodness, but you are shivering. One of these days soon Willa Robinson, you are going to rub a hole in that pocket of yours. Whatever is the matter with you?' she asks innocently.

Willa may be naive and unworldly, she may possess a head full of spectacularly simple thoughts, but she is not stupid. She knows a threat when she feels it.

Before Clovis steps up into the cab, she turns again to face the hospital.

'A dead house stands behind those walls. An apothecary hacks off the heads of the dead patients and places them in pickling pans until the flesh falls off. A gruesome end, yes?'

'Yes, mistress.' Willa enunciates the words but her mind is free now, counting – one, two, three, four, five, six . . . and on and on until she crushes the panic.

The cab driver, who would normally curse and spit during the interminable wait, stands quietly as if under the spell of the unnerving place. After the jerk of the first turn of the hansom's wheels, Clovis turns her entombed head and unties the chiffon, until it falls down in long strands around her neck. She calculates that this would be an opportune moment to release another smile. It is after all a new beginning, a new relationship. So she summons it, warm and inviting, full and open, until Willa's shoulders relax, and the girl's hands are finally still.

Then Clovis lays forth the map to Willa's new appointment.

'Should the two of us ever come to any . . . disagreement . . . that we cannot remedy, or if you ever display a single act of disloyalty, that broad building where London deposits its mad will be your new home and its inhabitants your new family.'

Willa casts a timorous parting glance. Her mistress's sweet breath fills the cab.

CHAPTER EIGHTEEN

The smoke is as thick as a hand; the stench in the stifling room is born of ale and sweat. Finn Fowler's insides churn with the pure exuberance of what is sure to be a win.

It has only been a few months since Willa's arrival and the peopling of the Fowler household is near completion.

Around the table in the house of Far East whores, unshaven men murmur at the scene in progress, set for a climax and perhaps a fight. The Chinese proprietor's son perches on a tall stool with a knife in his hand. He scrapes away at a piece of wood and while he seems to be concentrating on the shape taking form, he also listens to the men who are carving the shape of another's life – his.

'Nothing left,' Mr Ling says.

'You have one asset.' Finn raises a brow at the boy.

The two men lock eyes.

'I need an apprentice,' Finn says.

'Premium?' The Chinese man asks and looks away, as if he's no longer interested.

Finn glances again at his cards.

'Twenty pound.'

Someone coughs.

'Count it,' Another man says.

'There ain't twenty on there,' says the man next to Finn, entirely drunk.

'Whatever sits shiny and hard on the table, the premium is twenty pound,' Finn says.

'Terms?' Mr Ling asks.

The men at the table groan. Their tough-skinned fingers impatiently strum the table and they adjust their itchy crotches.

'Agree the twenty, finish the hand. If I win, we sort out the rest tonight and I go back to Three Colt Street with the boy. If my hand's a crapper, well then, you keep the boy – for now.'

They lock eyes once again. The expression on Mr Ling's face is blank. He agrees with a swift nod.

The boy's knife stops its work. He reveals nothing. His stomach, however, churns at the events being played out before him. His future will be decided by a game of Put. His father prefers Fan-Tan, or Pak-ah-puh, but the rogues insisted on their English card game tonight and he was impotent against them.

'Fer fuck's sake, show yer cards,' another brays.

This has never happened before. Mr Ling has never allowed the stakes to stack up so high that he could not meet them. But things have been bad for him lately. The parish is becoming more dangerous for those who operate below the law. He has no allies and there is no other Chinese man who resides within this parish. He could die quickly and quietly and no one would notice, and those who would, well, they would be grateful to his murderer. People owe him. People despise him. There are those who find this foreigner too foreign.

The boy is long ruined. Ling first noticed it after his mother crept out of the door late one night and never returned. He heard she'd hidden on a ship in the docks that sailed the next day for the East, but was discovered during the voyage and thrown overboard like a morsel, fed to the insatiable sea. What a good idea, Ling thought. He was tempted to drown the boy. He is meant to treasure a male child. But he does not, not this one who pines after his grandmother from some shitty little province full of Jurchens.

Jonesy's mother had been running her entire life, first from an arranged marriage in Shanghai, then from the floating life of the canal brothels, and finally from him and his father. She had learned to travel light. Several of her tunics were left discarded in a sad pile on the floor, except for the green one that on an enlightening morning fell loosely from the boy's naked shoulders. Ling dreamed of wrapping Jonesy in the green tunic and tossing him into the Thames. He consulted the oracle. When he threw the yarrow sticks for guidance the reading was unclear. He had no wish to anger the ancestors, so he let the boy live.

The more he thinks on it the more he hopes his cards are shit. He could then leave this rank, black cloud of a country and return to Shanghai. He'll be hired to work his passage back, but has only enough money for one life when he arrives and he'll be hanged if he'll throw his savings in the mix tonight. Now that the circumstances are right in front of him, he prays to his ancestors to lose.

Finn needs only one more point to win and he holds a '3'. He has no need to bluff, but he allows the tension to build anyway.

'Put.' Finn says at long last.

All heads turn to Ling. He does not follow his opponent's advice to throw, or 'put' his card in, rather, he forces Finn to lead with his card. His aim is for everyone to witness how squarely Finn will triumph. There must be no dispute.

Finn pauses again, which sends the other men into an aching moment of anticipation, then he flips his '3' down in front of Ling. Unless Ling also holds a '3' the boy is Finn's.

A whoop goes up all around the table, and then another moment of complete silence prevails until the slow steady scraping commences when the boy takes up his knife again. He received his new name by means of his father's casual glance at an English newspaper, *Mr Jonesy Rawlins, who finished his apprenticeship on Tuesday* ... While he lay across his mother's breast, blood gushing from the place of her recent delivery until she almost bled to death, or so the midwife said when she insisted on increasing her compensation, he was named Yun, 'born in the clouds'.

Father and son have not exchanged glances during this game of ownership. Mr Ling places his card down as Jonesy's shavings fall silently to the floor.

The King card shows his face. Ling has lost. The boy is lost. And then a great roar of voices and the pounding of fists on the table are too much for the small room as they celebrate the birth of Jonesy's apprenticeship.

Three Colt Street is deserted at this late hour. The screeching sounds of fighting crows break the silence as they lay waste to a mound of discarded entrails the lazy butcher has tossed in an alley near his blood-splattered shop. A breeze carries the stench. The master and the apprentice walk in different forms of sobriety; Finn's ale has worn off after the thrill of his victory, and Jonesy entertains a thoughtful terror of the unknown.

Finn wends his way along expertly in the fog that speedily rolls in from the river. He is a late-night creature, a man who is comfortable in and with the darkness. Jonesy notes this and how efficiently his master slips his key in the front door.

'Follow me. I'll get you sorted tomorrow. Tonight you'll make do with a sleep in the scullery. At least you'll be warm.'

Jonesy bows his head and begins to express his thanks when a figure advances and moves the air in the room like the shadow puppets of his childhood. She looks like midnight meeting the waning sun. Her gown is a blue so dark it seems it's been dipped in a bottle of ink. He has never seen hair the colour of a Shanghai sunset, or the beauty of that sunset in a woman. It leaves him speechless. He is not aroused; the feeling is purer, as though he has stepped into a poem, her beauty encased in a couplet.

Clovis takes the measure of Jonesy with a vulture-like eye that seems to penetrate his deepest fears. She circles him; her nostrils flare at the clinging aroma of herbs and other men's games. She steps back and surveys the delicate manner in which he allows the observations. His thick, dark lashes fall to his cheeks when he lowers his eyes. He cannot bear to be scrutinized so, but he endures it.

'I have seen you skulking around the river front. You like to watch the ships. Yes?'

'Yes, mistress.'

'Hmm. What shall we do with that long plait hanging down your back?'

'Whatever Mistress wishes.'

This makes her laugh.

His queue is thick at the top and gradually tapers out to a few thin strands below the back of his knees.

For a moment her gaze travels from Finn to Jonesy and then back again.

'I think you can train him,' she says to Finn. 'But he won't last long.'

She offers him no bedding, nor food or drink.

Finn cuts a piece of cheese and points to the bread and a slice of meat pie.

'You look like a fuckin' skeleton. If you're gonna work for me, you need more flesh.'

No one has ever considered his strength, or lack of it. No one has ever considered him at all.

The stinking cheese tastes foul, but Jonesy scoffs it with the bread. He's smart enough not to refuse the food. In the past, a simple statement such as 'I do not care for cheese' could bring a slap, or worse.

Finn has made a bowl of punch, and this Jonesy does like. His senses sharpen after the first few gulps. He will not speak until he is allowed, but he would like to say that he is very glad to be here and away from his father's house where the walls never rest, where someone is always in need of extra care, where the days never end, they just turn darker. He'd like to say aloud to someone that already he breathes a larger share of the air than he ever has done in his life, but his English isn't up to it yet. He will do whatever job Mr Fowler asks of him, whatever dirty and low thing his master has in mind, he'll do it. And he vows to show the mistress who looks like a goddess that she is mistaken, that in her presence he will only grow stronger.

Shown into a small room, where short stacks of goods neatly line the walls, a bed is hastily made on the floor with fresh linen and a pile of some sort of packing cloth on which to lay his head. Jonesy slowly lies on his side – he never sleeps on his back – and extinguishes the tallow, closing the light on the stolen goods that he will soon learn to move around Limehouse and beyond with the speed of a flying dragon.

At the top of the house Willa tosses and turns in her bed. Change unsettles her. She finally puts her bare feet on the floor and from under the bed she retrieves her box, swinging it out and up between her legs and onto her lap. From it she scoops up a handkerchief, heavy with her calming charms, and selects the most precious of all, the small, velvet bag that holds a lock of her mother's hair. She chews on the brown, matted hair until she is comforted and falls into a dreamless sleep.

The next morning while Willa completes her morning chores, her attic room is in the process of transformation. It sounds like hell is entering it. There is scraping and banging and cursing and all this because the new boy is moving in on her territory, a space that has become sacred to her. When she has the courage to climb the steps to the eaves of the house a wave of anger passes through her. A heavy damask curtain hangs from a wire suspended across the room. In an uncharacteristic flash of temper, she casts it aside with a strong jerk. Pushed up against the wall is another bed. The middle of it sinks with the weight of a wooden box similar to hers, though slightly larger. Drawn to the strange script engraved on the top of it, she hesitates, and before she is aware of what moves her to do so, she tries to open it. Locked.

'I help?'

He stands in the doorframe, an angular silhouette. Willa is so astonished at the sight of him that she forgets to be embarrassed by her investigation.

'I . . . I did not hear you.'

This morning he had wrapped his queue around the top of his head so that he appears to be wearing a hat made of hair. She gawks outright. The front of his head is shaved, presenting a dichotomous image that confuses her, though it is his clothes that intrigue her most: a loose blue collarless jacket falls just below his knees. Long wide-legged trousers trail down to a pair of black, cotton slippers with platform soles made of cotton cording, perhaps with leather as well, she cannot tell. He looks monkish, a porcelain version. Though she is slowly becoming accustomed to the world's people who float in and out of Limehouse, this is a rare one.

Jonesy approaches his bed and Willa jumps back, startling them both when they crash into each other.

'The door,' he says, when he recovers. 'I will tap?'

She adjusts her cap and straightens her apron. The door opens into her side of the room; a further loss of her cherished privacy.

'Well. Mr – I do not know your name.'

'Jonesy.'

She pauses. Such a ridiculous name.

'Well, Mr Jonesy.'

'Jonesy Ling.'

Even more ridiculous, she thinks.

Her moving fingers distract him. She smells of grease and fire. He has seen another like her; madness is next if she is not careful. He sits down beside his box and opens it with the key he retrieves from his deep trouser pocket.

'Well, Mr Jonesy Ling, I been here a short time, but I'm much adjusted to my own company, in my own room. I am from a place that were crowded, where I slept in a room with many girls. But this, what we have here is different.' She bites the tip of her tongue to curb her chattering but it does not help.

''Tis too bad for me then that the door opens into my side of the room. So, no. I dunno know how you plan to spend your evenings, but I retire early. Do not wake me by tappin' on the door. And if you have any decency about you at all, when you open the door, focus your entire self on this curtain. And then close it tight. And be quiet about it, if you please.'

He didn't understand much of what she said, but feels he needs to offer her something.

'Move? I sleep there?' He points to her bed.

She cannot move her things. She has her rituals, everything is in its place, and she has access to the window. She shakes her head and her fingers commence their tapping again. Her breathing is shallow.

She is so visibly disturbed that he assures her. 'No! No move, no move.'

Jonesy opens his wooden box and rattles around in it until he produces a bright green silk pouch. He unties the black string and empties its contents into his palm.

'Cicada.' How can he explain it to her?

'Oh what a beautiful piece, Jonesy Ling.' Her defences fall, she is suddenly transfixed.

Then she squints at him as if he has done something very bad.

'Where did you get such a thing?'

'I carve. White jade. Cicada.'

'You carve? It looks cool, like ice. And smooth as cream.'

'For you.'

'Oh no, Jonesy Ling.' She drops it on the bed. 'It were wrong. I do not take gifts.' She recalls many occasions upon which Matron tried to tempt her with gifts. A gift is never without conditions.

'Friends.' He offers again.

'No, I cannot.' She's hesitant, but moved, and weakening because she has never received a genuine gift.

'Please.'

Well, she thinks, it *is* very beautiful. And she cannot quash her desire to touch it.

'Got nothin' for you but I can knit and sew.'

'Nothing required.' He bows low.

'Well, all right then, thank you, Jonesy Ling.'

'Jonesy, please.' Before he gives it to her he strokes the outline of the wings that are carved to appear folded underneath the insect.

'Cicada. Chinese symbol for, um, very long life. Survives underground for long time, then comes up and flies. Flies to the sky. Um, forever . . . Symbol for . . . undying.' He struggles to find the word.

'Immortal?,' Willa says.

'Immortal,' Jonesy repeats.

CHAPTER NINETEEN

Francis Lawless diminishes each day from a withering illness that the doctors fail to identify; they consider he has lived a long life and as his death approaches there is really no need to label what overtakes him. Owen Mockett makes up the prescriptions for the laudanum to help ease his passing and cosset his dreams. It is the very least he can do for the Lawless family who have always been loyal customers.

George Fitzgerald's legal team puts Francis's affairs in order. There is more than a little sadness etched in the deep lines of his face. So intricately are the Lawless and Fitzgerald families entwined, with marriages, births and deaths.

Each time St Anne's bell tolls the sisters are certain it is their father's death knell. Claustrophobia settles in. There is no truly private place in the house. Their ailing father sleeps fitfully, and their well-intentioned cook, Bertie, their only live-in servant, has a natural ear to all conversation, even when she retires to an exhausted coma-like sleep.

An eagerness for a taste of the freedom that is a birthright of men has always gnawed at the sisters. How well their father knew it. As his dying countenance lies before her, Constance recalls that after the second tragedy of their lives bore down on them with the weight of iron, he gave them a choice. He would search for second husbands and she and Verity could live conventionally if they wished. Or, they could live their widowed lives unconventionally, as long as they applied themselves to something worthwhile. At the time, they were so heavy with grief they could not rise in the morning without dreading the day. He quickly realized they could make no such decision, so he made it for them. Francis whisked his daughters away from the scenes of their sorrows. He opened the doors of Europe to them in a Grand Tour wildly of his own making that followed no traditional itinerary. They returned to Limehouse forever changed.

During the restless years that followed, the sisters became primed to perform an act so daring that they would lay down their reputations for its cause.

Constance arrived home one day with a worn second-hand canvas haversack bulging with two suits of men's clothing. She revealed the accepted uniform of a casual worker: trousers, shirts, waistcoats, loose fitting long jackets, two flat cloth caps and two pairs of dull boots.

The trousers offered such an extraordinary feeling of vulnerability and at the same time release, that at first the sisters' gaits were awkward and exaggerated. At the completion of their transformation when they tucked their hair under the caps and wrapped neckerchiefs high to their chins, the mirror reflected that tall, thin men had come to roost. They sneaked from the house and stole into the night's crisp air. They walked as men, free to discover London's nocturnal underbelly.

On those nights when the wind suddenly howled, or when they were tired but still restless from their long walks, one of their father's warehouses served as their private salon. The sisters bribed their father's guards for two powerful hours of privacy in the dark fortress.

On these nights they became more of themselves when they shed a thin layer of the skin of their society. A society that of late seems to tighten and pinch like the corset that is a slave to the new waistline; its grip even more firm and prim in its quest for a curve.

It has been some months since they were last out. Gently they close the door that seals the deathbed air of their home and inhale the night as if it were their last breaths as well. They forgo their walk of discovery and stride quickly past the spars and rigging towering like menacing daggers thrust into the black sky.

Their father's employee, Lewis the guard, paces to and fro, peeling around the building's corners, stepping in time with the lapping water. He tips his hat to them. Verity slips a pouch of coins from her pocket and empties it into his leathery hand. Secrets are bought that might one day cause men to call them mad and scandalous, rather than two women who simply seek solace.

They grab the lanterns that rest on hooks by the door and take the stairs to the first floor. Carpets, rugs, and mats of all kinds are stored here, waiting to cover the floors of English parlours. They skirt past the corner where the skins of peacocks hang; their superior feathers still attached, fan out into the room.

The air is pungent with the smell of tobacco that shoots down from the attic. Their boots stick to the leaked sugar on the floor. Silently they search for a space that is free of goods. There are eight rooms on this floor and in the sixth they find an empty aisle amongst the pipes of port. The long barrels with tapered ends stretch down the length of the room. Constance unrolls a fine Turkish rug and secures it onto the cast iron window frame then nods to Verity to light the larger lanterns.

Constance sits with her back supported by one of the barrels and removes the contents of the haversack. She fills the bowl of a pipe with tobacco and uses the slender remains of a taper to light it.

Verity pours from a crude Bohemian glass flask into two beakers. Apricot brandy, sweet and hot, stings their throats. Soon they are a little drunk.

'I wish to talk about them tonight. I want to remember,' Constance says.

'I don't.'

'Why, Verity?'

'It is not enough to keep telling each other stories of their short lives. It is not bearable.' Verity's voice rises. 'The absent bodies ...

When we visit their empty graves and read aloud their names . . .' Her voice breaks.

'But you don't!' Constance shouts. 'You never say their names. You won't speak of them.'

'And you never cease! I hear you in your room late at night. You talk to them as if they were sat beside you. It really is unsettling, Constance. You treat them as if they are ghosts.'

'They *are* ghosts. And what of you? You retreat to your prayers to saints and clutch your beads and yet you still walk down to the water's edge. You would be dead if I had not found you.'

'That is not fair.' Verity stands. 'Do not dare speak of that one, single moment on an awful, awful night.'

They have drained their beakers and the flask, and the fug in the room makes Verity dizzy. Her burning eyes stream.

'Not fair? To even consider leaving me here on my own?' Constance accuses.

'I was not going to do it.'

Constance stands, too, and as they face each other their frames create exaggerated contours against the barrels in the light of the lanterns. Shadow play catches Constance inching towards her sister.

'William,' Constance says. 'My dear, lovely husband, William Fitzgerald.'

'Don't.' Verity walks away.

'Say it. Say his name, Verity.' She stalks her sister down the aisle. 'Say your husband's name.'

'Stop it.'

'Say it!'

Stunned by Constance's forcefulness, it tumbles out of her.

'Sterling. Sterling Fitzgerald.' Verity throws the words at her sister. 'My husband, Sterling.'

'Jack. My darling boy. My son, Jack Fitzgerald!' Constance holds her sister firmly by her shoulders, yet she too is trembling. 'Say it, Verity. Say your son's name.'

'Henry,' Verity whispers. 'Henry Fitzgerald, my lost son.'

The sisters, who had loved and married brothers, who had brought sons into the world, stagger after their roll call of the dead.

Leaning against a barrel, in the freedom of their trousers they slide to the floor, spent. It can take years for the purest bit of grief to crawl up out of its deep home.

'Look at us,' Constance says. 'What would they say if they could see us here in this corner dressed as lightermen, reeking, our limbs spread like drunks.'

She offers Verity a weak smile, but it is met with sombre thoughts.

'The lost bodies of our husbands and sons . . . it was like blotting out all traces of their existence.' Verity's frustration drops to a whisper. 'We needed their bodies, Constance.' She rests the back of her head against the cold, brick wall. 'Otherwise, there is only a haunting. Dead – yet not dead.'

'We will have our father's body – in burial,' Constance says.

'It is not enough for me.'

Still a little drunk and dry-mouthed from the tobacco, they have lost track of the time. Neither speaks while they vacate the building.

The guard sits up against one of the outdoor sheds fast asleep. Verity relishes these last few moments when she can walk the streets without wearing her dark spectacles. She gazes upon a different sort of darkness. Sharper, almost blunt images cavort before her. A cat slinks by in a brilliant stripe of orange. The lettering painted across the boats and barges is surprisingly shiny. The rift between the sisters is made small against the power of night.

'Constance, look there,' Verity whispers. 'Is that not Mrs Fowler from Three Colt Street?'

A woman in a long, dark cloak stands on a nearby boat, deserted but for the man who embraces her. The cloak's hood has fallen away leaving her red mane shooting like a flare into the black night.

'Indeed, it is. But that is not Mr Fowler who holds her close.'

Clovis jerks her head towards them as if she has heard the whispers.

Her attention fully upon them now, she is struck by the familiar. These two men she has seen before, here or there, but no, not in this form. She has made it her business to know the wealthy widows on sight; trousers and a cap do not fool her.

Clovis throws her hood over her head and the sound of her laughter clings to the sisters' backs as their footsteps recede.

Constance settles into her spot before the window on Fore Street, where she casts her gaze beyond the sail-less masts that look like crucifixes jutting up into the hovering mist. She shivers as the reliable London fog pushes in from the sea and travels above the water like a full sail, with only the single pane of glass between her and its wicked danger. She fears there is another danger to which Verity seems oblivious, and so she must grab it by the collar on her own.

When they go about their morning errands that lead them outdoors, and in the afternoon when the sisters take the air, Constance senses they are being watched. With that ever-present in her mind, she goes out alone today with the excuse of needing an item urgently from Mockett's Apothecary. But Constance does not go to the Commercial Road. She ambles through the neighbourhood's streets with no clear route. She makes herself seen on Three Colt Street and wends her way finally to St Anne's churchyard where she waits by a distinctive pyramid monument. The church clock chimes in the tower outlined against the sky, its angles and corners in perfect symmetry. Every fifteen minutes it rings and it is not five minutes past the current chiming before Clovis Fowler appears.

'Mrs Fitzgerald.' Clovis is slightly breathless. 'I have been looking forward to meeting you properly.'

'Mrs Fowler.' Constance's voice cuts the air.

'I was quite astonished to catch a glimpse of you and your sister a few nights ago.'

Constance is not drawn to reply.

'There may be several reasons why you choose to wear men's clothing. And really, it is of no concern to me. Although, I dare say others might attach a queer and abnormal reason,' Clovis says lightly. 'Equally, I trust that my presence that evening is no concern of yours. I would not like for a scene that was entirely innocent to be . . . misconstrued.' Clovis musters her most engaging smile.

'Mrs Fowler. If you follow me or my sister again, I will bring down the heavens upon your head.'

'My goodness. Are you threatening me, Mrs Fitzgerald?'

'Are you threatening *me*, Mrs Fowler?'

This has gone wrong. Clovis had intended to use their shared secrets to strike up a conversation – not to threaten or be threatened. Her desire is to cultivate an acquaintanceship with the wealthy widows. Her miscalculation be damned; she must salvage it.

'I apologize wholeheartedly.' Clovis lowers her eyes as if she is hurt. 'I have no intention of revealing your secret. I followed you only to seek a moment to speak to you without raising suspicion at your home, or mine.'

'Mrs Fowler, if you are as innocent as you say, why must you "not raise suspicion", as you put it?'

Clovis hesitates, annoyed that this has not gone her way.

'I will not trouble you further.'

Clovis makes a sweeping turn and saunters off, her skirts brushing against the tombstones. She holds her head high and curses under her breath.

Dettu niður dauður gömul kona.

Drop dead, old woman.

The midwife covers the expectant mother's eyes against the light of the Aurora to ease the pain of birth. Every fire in the settlement is lit to discourage supernatural interference. The midwife carries two delivery stones, wrapped in the hair of a virgin, to guarantee good health to mother and child.

His arrival is met with great joy and great sadness.

The law that requires the baby to be baptized in a church within seven days of birth is broken. This baby, born under a shroud of secrecy from the loins of the mother who has been changed, is taken to the Watcher before his journey across the sea.

CHAPTER TWENTY

1832

The tollhouse on the Commercial Road bulges today with the dock hauliers' heavy carts that form ruts in the setts on the street. The taverns heave with freemasons, press gangs and lonely sailors, all hungry for gossip and a game of backgammon. Yet within this Sailortown, on this edge of the river where men seem so dominant a fixture, a remarkable number of women are found in a variety of trades. Nuzzled securely in this coterie of middling sort of women, Nora Mockett pins her focus outside the apothecary with a keen eye trained on the shop's window.

Her husband has recently refilled the great, bulbous show globes with his mercurial solutions. Shaped like giant eggs, they hang from brass chains emitting their chemical glow. One displays the colour of a dark, glistening emerald, the other is filled with deep-red liquid, as rich in hue as a claret. There can be no better announcement, and few newcomers to the neighbourhood would doubt that Mockett's Apothecary is a modern and fully stocked establishment.

With finger to her chin, Mrs Mockett contemplates adding one or two potion bottles, or perhaps a collection of blue-and-white Faience novelties to tempt the ladies. She is stirred from her musings when she spots in the distance what is possibly the figure of Clovis Fowler and that of her servant, the odd young girl with the restless eyes – though her own eyes may be deceiving her. Nora strains and squints with a distance vision that is annoyingly blurred.

It is very simple. Nora Mockett does not trust Mrs Fowler. More than that, she loses her focus in the young woman's presence. She cannot think what to say, or what to do, and her hard-won confidence evaporates like the smoke of her husband's experiments. She fumbles with the door, rattles it, pounds on it until Owen Mockett comes running to help her.

'What is it?' He is just a bit impatient.

'The door sticks, tell the boy to repair it. We mustn't fall, Owen. We mustn't fall. And Clovis Fowler walks this way. There is something strange in her appearance.'

'All right, all right. Do calm yourself.'

Nora tidies the rows of opium pills she had helped prepare earlier this morning for the Saturday evening crowds who will lay down their money and receive the boxes without uttering a word. It really is a miracle cure for all the most common ailments. And oh heavens – the profit.

The shop's porcelain jars and glass bottles are completely free of dust, yet while Mrs Mockett waits for Mrs Fowler to arrive she runs a cloth down a line of vessels with nervous anticipation. Nora recalls her father's prejudices of ginger-haired people, especially women. His belief that the reds possess character faults was biblical. 'Poison,' he'd said.

When the door finally opens and Clovis Fowler enters the apothecary, Nora understands why Mrs Fowler's figure appeared foreign from a distance. She digs her nails into her fists. Faced once again with what she has been denied, she will remember this day and the precise hour when her path turns sour and wrong, when what begins as a small, hurtful jealousy grows into an appalling cancer. *Poison.*

'Good afternoon, Mrs Fowler.' Nora composes herself even as the words stick in her throat.

Upon witnessing the utter surprise on Nora Mockett's face, it is not difficult for Clovis to summon the contented smile of a luxuriating cat.

The condition that must be concealed as long as possible has been visited upon Mrs Fowler. Nora quickly calculates that Clovis must be at least six months gone, for no woman could be absolutely certain for the first five months. This she knows too well. How brazen of the Fowler woman to appear in public like this. Whatever can she be thinking? This is it you see, Nora thinks, this is where the foreigner in her comes to the fore. Uncouth.

'Good afternoon, Mrs Mockett.' Clovis makes no further effort at conversation, but instead waits to be served.

'How may I help you today?' Nora manages.

'Ah. Well. You may very well ask!' Another smile. 'I will require several items before The Little Stranger arrives.' She beams.

'Yes, of course.' Nora manages to spit out; mortified that Mrs Fowler would actually mention her condition in public. Perhaps Mrs Fowler will even pat her bump!

'I believe you've met Willa, my girl. She will collect whatever I need for the next few months and I'm sure you and Mr Mockett will accommodate her. Mr Fowler will see to the payments. After all, our husbands share business concerns.'

At that remark Nora flushes from head to toe and a deep anger begins to brew within her. Whatever business occurs in the damp dark of their cellar, how dare this woman speak of it in the company of their customers. How careless of her. The assistant and the patrons shoot questionable looks towards them now.

Mr Mockett intercedes at just the right moment.

'Ah, Mrs Fowler. How lovely to see you. Do not worry yourself with anything at all. How happy both Mrs Mockett and I are for you and Mr Fowler. We wish you great joy. Isn't that right, dear?'

'Oh, yes, yes of course,' Nora replies.

'May I offer you a chair, Mrs Fowler?' he asks.

Clovis turns her complete attention to Mr Mockett in the way that makes a man feel as if only he exists – even though his wife stands shoulder to shoulder with him.

'You are too kind. No, thank you. I won't stay long. You have met my girl, Mr Mockett? I was just informing Mrs Mockett that . . .'

A sharp breeze accosts the apothecary when the door creaks open again. Two women stand together Anubis-like in their mourning dress. The shop fills with the clanging of the Five Bells public house from Three Colt Street, as if to herald the sisters' entrance. Beginning at half past two in the afternoon, five times the bells toll to announce the afternoon's closing of the docks.

The fragrant odour of the botanicals and drying herbs of the apothecary fades against the overpowering incense that clings to the sisters' crepe clothing. They lift their skirts to climb the step into the shop revealing their grievous silk petticoats and plain black stockings. They are swathed in the black of the dead, a lustreless, sombre and depressing black. Their gloved hands grasp parasols of inky chiffon. Their faces cannot be distinguished behind their veiled hats, with the exception of the blue-tinted spectacles Verity wears that are intimidating and quite unnerving.

The fourth bell clangs.

No one moves or speaks; the ghostly sight strikes even Clovis mute. Willa retreats to a corner unsure what kind of protection she may need from these apparitions. Constance and Verity seem to have drawn all the air from the room. When they advance further into the shop towards the counter, row upon row of jet bead neck-laces shimmer around their necks, crunching whenever the sisters move. Mrs Mockett dashes over to them and relieves them of their parasols. The sisters appear very grand in a way they do not intend.

The tone of the fifth bell fades.

Owen Mockett comes to his senses and silently blesses his wife for insisting he change into a clean shirt after staining his first one at dinner. Surprised to see the sisters, he assumes they must be out of 'retirement' from the world and able to return to society in a limited way. He's been administering to them at their home regularly for over a year following the death of Mr Lawless. They have not been well. No, not at all. In fact, though there is no hint of it today, during their retirement he had never seen them quite so . . . vulnerable. And possibly, just slightly, unhinged.

'Good afternoon.' Constance's bell-sleeve droops down, like a bird with an exceedingly wide wingspread, as she raises her arm and points at the shelves of medicinal glass bottles.

'The last remedy was not as effective, Mr Mockett.' Her voice is hoarse, her delivery, deliberate. A wisp of her silvery-white hair floats with her breath, trapped as it is under her veil.

No, indeed it was not. Owen has been carefully monitoring Constance Fitzgerald who was without a doubt completely and wholly dependent. He hates to admit that he is not entirely without blame. It happened slowly over the past year, drop-by-drop. Each fortnight he had increased the strength of the formula. She requested, 'Stronger, more potent, please, Mr Mockett.' However, there is, for the first time since the drug gushed through the sluices of the country, some concern about opium and its effects. So Mockett politely refused her, a precaution he felt he must take for her sake, and because the eyes and ears of the Society of Apothecaries whose jurisdiction he is under are everywhere.

But Constance had sought another source. She was introduced to a rent-collector who was connected with a burying club. She had a bad reaction when she chewed a raw form of Turkish that blistered her mouth. An unforgiving case of pruritus claimed her so severely that she scratched holes in her body. Worse than all that, the opiate sleep upon which she relied, that always came like a soothing, red blanket, eluded her.

By the time she called upon Mr Mockett again for help, her fingers and mouth had acquired a blue tinge. She looked as if she had aged twenty years and her blistered gums were beginning to deteriorate. Mockett was alarmed at how quickly she had descended into what was sure to be a poisoned death.

Constance was anxious to conquer her dependency and he was

anxious to help her by devising a plan for a slow progression of withdrawal. Mr Mockett notices with relief that the tinge of blue at her fingertips is paler than it was the previous month, which is evidence that she is not waning and no longer as miserable a slave to the sleeping draught as she has been.

'Good afternoon, Mrs Fitzgerald and good day to you, Mrs Fitzgerald.' Mockett nods to the sisters.

Verity, whose attention has been drawn to the leech pots, turns to face him. Her nod is so slight that he thinks perhaps he has missed the acknowledgement. He feels as awkward in her presence here as he does in her own home simply because she refuses to speak unless absolutely necessary. He makes an effort to decipher her needs. Their father's death has hit them harder than he imagined.

'Would you like me to examine your eyes, Mrs Fitzgerald?'

No, she indicates by slowly moving her head.

'Then, would you like more ointment and another bottle of solution?'

Yes, she nods, that is what she requires.

Clovis has been watching and waiting for the opportunity to address the sisters. She glides over quietly, positioning herself between them. Captured by surprise they turn to her, and because they are both two important inches taller than Clovis, they look down on her with a united and protected force.

It is a thing to witness: Clovis Fowler caught slightly off her guard. She is not intimidated, yet their combined presence forces her to take a step back.

'My deepest condolences and regret for your loss.'

The sisters in one united movement turn further to glare at this creature. Verity's brow furrows as she thoroughly inspects the woman who has the impudence to address them and the further effrontery to refer to their 'loss'.

Verity detaches a steel pin with a dull, black head that secures her veil onto her hat. The gauze unwinds and falls into a soft ring around her neck. She removes her spectacles oblivious to the theatrics she creates and blatantly stares for a long moment at the swell in Clovis's skirts. Slowly she raises her naked eyes to the face of the Fowler woman who has held her nerve at the scrutiny until now. But when their eyes meet, Clovis falls short and looks away. Verity's pink lids, both upper and lower, appear as raw as a rare piece of meat. The inflammation and redness make the young beauty's eyes stream. But there is more – Clovis did not expect to see the hint of the madness of grief that stared back at her.

Verity retreats behind her spectacles once more. She throws the veil up and winds it round and round her hat and sticks the black-headed pin into place. Customers are beginning to spill into the shop now. Mr Mockett discreetly beckons the sisters to his corner table.

'Mrs Fitzgerald.' He addresses Constance. 'I have your bottle ready. The mixture is correct.' He gives her a stern voice and look to go with it.

Now he speaks to Verity. 'I have made these lozenges for you.' He opens a small box filled with flat coin-like tablets with the Mockett stamp embossed on each one.

'These are made with a mild concoction that is most effective in this form. They are light and easy to carry. To use one, crush it and mix it with a liquid – distilled water is best – and then apply it to your eyelids like a salve. You must only do this in the evening before retiring.' Because there are 4 drams of opium in this batch, he thinks, but doesn't say. The drug seems to have no effect on the younger sister. She scratches her eyes at night when she is unaware of this world and lost to another. He struggles and will be damned until he devises a potent formula.

'I wonder, Mrs Fitzgerald, why your eyes seem to be troubling you more than usual.'

Verity turns to Constance who offers an almost imperceptible nod.

'We are learning to swim, Mr Mockett.' She says.

A glass bottle crashes to the floor and explodes into crystal shards. Nora has dropped it spectacularly.

The assistant scrambles at once to sweep up and no one knows quite what to say, so uncomfortable are they all with the thought of the sisters submerged. Only Clovis looks slightly confused and much amused.

'Mr Mockett.' Constance nods. 'Mrs Mockett. Gloved and veiled once more, jet beads glistening and striking against each other, she makes for the door.

Verity adjusts her spectacles and follows, with the Mocketts fussing along behind them.

Clovis has positioned herself at the door and takes this opportunity to offer an unctuous farewell.

'Perhaps we will meet again soon. I wish you both a good day.'

Constance pauses at the door without turning to the woman who insists on making her presence felt.

'Take great care of your child, Mrs Fowler. The world can be a cruel place.'

Verity sniffs as if accosted by an unwelcome odour.

Willa steps out of the corner where she has made herself small. She is drawn to the window where she hopes to catch a last glance of the sisters. She feels remarkably calm and though it makes no sense to her, she feels the moment of peace was due to them. How inexplicably sad she is to see them go.

One by one Mockett's customers conclude their business and a lull falls on the apothecary, yet Clovis lingers.

'The Fitzgerald sisters. A strange pair, wouldn't you say?' she probes.

'Those women. They have lost too much.' Nora replies.

'How do you mean?'

'I was but twelve years old ...' Owen begins.

'Mr Mockett, this really isn't the time ...' Nora says.

'What does it matter? It's no secret. It was well reported in the London papers. Please do sit yourself down, Mrs Fowler.'

'Thank you, Mr Mockett. I am beginning to feel a bit fatigued and heavy and would like to rest before I leave. Please do continue.' Warm smile.

Perhaps she'd like to tell us how many months gone she is, or what her belly looks like unclothed! Nora thinks, feeling a headache approaching from grinding her teeth.

'It was thirty years ago. I was twelve years old,' he begins again. 'The first freeze of the winter brought us all out of our homes on the Sunday. The day before, the news was that the Serpentine was frozen. So from all corners of London, the young and the old, we all made our way to Hyde Park; the wealthy to parade their winter finery and the poor to get warm by the big fires. I went to skate . . .'

Nora produces a tray bearing tea, which brings an approving glance from her husband.

'My father and I joined hundreds, perhaps even thousands of others. I don't think we have experienced a big freeze since you've arrived in our city, Mrs Fowler. They are not as frequent or severe as those in your country, I dare say. For us, it was exciting until suddenly in the middle of the afternoon at the height of the numbers there was an awful roar. And the shout of 'men down, men down' had us all rushing to the shore for safety. From there, my father and I strained to witness the terrible sight of two men and two young boys flailing in the water where a large section of the ice had given way. The boys went under immediately. It looked as if the men, their fathers we assumed, were under the ice, too, but their heads popped back up for air – they were diving to find the boys.'

'Bystanders went to fetch ropes and the Royal Humane Society men raced across the lake in their flat-bottomed tub. The two fathers went under a second time, but emerged again shaking the ice and water from their hair and gasping, and now seized in panic. That is when we recognized the men – the Fitzgeralds. They dived under for a third time, but this time did not come up again.'

Nora dabs her eyes with her handkerchief. Her soft sighs accompany her husband's story.

'The Society men finally reached the location but more of the ice began to give way. It just wasn't safe enough, even with ropes tied around their waists. The sisters Fitzgerald had been in the Cheesecake House. It was their custom to retreat for a short while to the cake house after watching their husbands and their little lads skate. When my father spotted them walking over the footbridge he knew they did not yet know. He grabbed me and we pulled off our skates and ran towards the sisters with our shoes unlaced. You see, my father knew the Fitzgeralds quite well – we enjoyed their custom, and he once employed the men for legal advice.'

'Was there no further attempt to find them?' Clovis asks.

'That night there was a hard frost, and by morning the ice was as firm as brass. They searched the following spring. But there are mud deposits on the bottom . . . The sisters' husbands and their sons had disappeared.'

Another whip of wind gusts through the door again and a young sea captain enters followed by one of the mutes from the undertaker's down the road. Clovis and the Mocketts are returned to the present by the captain's complaint of a throbbing head and the mute's purchase of a second box of opium pills.

'Goodness! I thought the Fowler woman would stay the night!' Nora says, as they put out the last lamps. 'I have a bad taste in my mouth, Owen.'

'Well, spit it out, Nora.'

'Did you notice her reaction? How could a woman listen to such a tragic story and not be moved? I was afraid you were going to tell her about their mother, too!'

'No.' Owen says as he secures the locks. 'You are right as usual, Nora. It is unnatural for a woman to remain untouched by such a tragedy. If I am honest, I grow more and more uncomfortable with the Fowlers and this tunnel business. The risks are too great.'

'I am relieved to hear you say it, Owen. We mustn't fall.'

'As thieves go, Finn Fowler is not the worst of them … but his wife … I agree with you. I have a bad feeling about her, too.'

Nora sighs, long and deep – as a woman does when she feels the fear of the unknown dissipate; that inexplicable *knowing* that something dangerous has been avoided.

She wraps her arms around her husband's neck and kisses him, and in that kiss invites him to their bed.

'We mustn't fall, Owen.'

CHAPTER TWENTY-ONE

'Opin, vinsamlegast! Opin!'

'What the fucking hell!' Finn springs from the bed in the dead of night.

A persistent knocking accompanies the pelting rain. Clovis slips into her dressing gown and lights a taper from the embers in the fireplace. Finn is too rattled and impatient to have any concern about modesty or decorum and streaks down the stairs in his nightshirt.

'It must be midnight or later,' Clovis hisses. 'Who can this be?'

Then they hear the language they have not heard for years.

'Opin, vinsamlegast! Opin!'

The man is tall, middle-aged and handsome. The woman, older, carries a swaddled baby on her back. Weighed down by the dragging rain, the woman's mouth drops open a bit when she sees Clovis. Taken by a moment of jolting recognition, Margrét had not expected the sisters to appear so similar.

Undaunted, Stefán steps in uninvited, quickly, in the manner of a man on urgent business.

'My apologies for the late hour,' Stefán says in his language.

'Do you speak English?' Finn asks.

'If you prefer. Margrét is still learning.' Stefán's English is good.

The commotion has brought Willa and Jonesy down from the attic. Neither is sure what they should do, except relieve the strangers of their sodden outer jackets.

'Welcome. Forgive me. We are taken by surprise.' Clovis motions for the strangers to follow her.

'Our late hour is necessary for the safety of the child,' Stefán says.

Without further comment Clovis leads them into the front room. The visitors note right away that with the exception of their midnight arrival, Clovis is prepared. For there, dominating the corner opposite the armonica, suspended high off the floor from its base, a rocking cradle awaits an occupant.

Margrét carefully unties the baby's carrying cloth. She struggles in an awkward moment and looks to Clovis for help. But Clovis remains rooted and instead motions to Willa who is wrapped in her own blanket. The girl is relieved to have something useful to do.

'Tea.' Jonesy bows before he retreats to the kitchen.

'No. Coffee for our visitors. Hot and strong,' Clovis orders.

Once the baby is free from its bindings, Clovis takes the sleeping bundle from Willa and places it in the cradle. The dismal months looking after her aunt's newborn come to the fore now as she gently lowers the baby. She turns back to her audience beaming, as if she'd accomplished a great act.

An awkward silence settles on the guests and their hosts. In it, Stefán and Margrét take stock of the baby's future. In what kind of household will this child be raised? What might he report to Elísabet that will ease her mind? And who, exactly, has Koldís Ingólfsdóttir become?

Margrét has never been surrounded by so great a quantity of wood. And there are so many things made from wood in this country. Her eyes rove to a writing table, an occasional table, a screen, a round table, chairs and the sofa upon which she now uncomfortably sits. How heavy it all makes a place. There are, well, *things* every-where. Objects crowd the mantelpiece. There are cloths on tables, brackets tipping with china. Collectors of dust.

Stefán and Margrét offer Jonesy a grateful nod for the steaming coffee.

Upon yesterday's arrival, the claustrophobic, filthy London streets and the number of people in them quickly overwhelmed Margrét. There seem to be more people in one street than in all of Iceland. And now, in the weary midnight hour, this woman who has not even asked the name of her sister's child, is clearly concerned only with herself, and would try to steal their attention over that of the baby's. Margrét cannot hold silent.

'Would you like to know the name of the child?' she asks in Icelandic. 'Would you like to know its sex?'

Clovis hesitates and casts a glance at the judgemental faces that stare at her. Damnation. She must repair this.

'You read my thoughts exactly! I have been itching to know.'

'His name is Rafe,' Margrét says quite sternly, mixing the languages.

'It is Rafe Fowler now.' Clovis meets the woman's glare.

It is for Stefán to quash the potential storm brewing between the two women. Clovis's husband looks amused, which does not make their departure any easier. Their journey, the planning, and the resources used to deliver the child safely have clearly not been considered by these two Fowlers. Stefán stands and retrieves an envelope from his jacket and places it on top of the round table. Immune to Clovis's beauty and her trap of a smile, and not at all interested in her husband's thoughts, he delivers final instructions with a bare disregard of convention.

'You will keep the boy safe and healthy. His education is primary. If he develops any unusual aspects or habits, or displays any physical abnormalities you must contact our emissary immediately. A man named Benedikt will be looking after you. But you must only communicate with him as he directs.'

'What a lot of mystery there.' Finn finally speaks.

Stefán ignores him.

'If anyone else takes an interest in the boy – strangers asking questions, that sort of thing, stay out of their company and report it. Be detailed. You are being paid for such information.' He nods towards the envelope that contains a great deal of money.

'If you are involved in any illegal business, it must stop.' He registers Finn's glare. 'Well, you do not think that I believe this house, its furnishings, the two servants, and the gown your wife wears is a result of the sale of a few clocks, do you? Your decoration is paired with an income that does not match it by any other means. A vital part of our agreement is that you raise no questions, court no trouble.'

'Sir, I can assure you that . . .' Clovis starts.

'I think we have some right to know why this child needs such special protection and why Elísabet cannot raise it herself,' Finn says.

'No, you do not have a right. If there comes a time when you need to know, you will be informed.' Stefán hesitates. 'Honestly, we do not yet know all the answers ourselves. Your servants, they must honour our demands for secrecy.'

'Sir, I give you my word. You have no worry there.' Finn feels he must be heard and acknowledged.

Stefán nods, but will not make eye contact with this man, who has behaved so dishonourably in the past.

Clovis studies Stefán more closely. It is futile to probe him any longer about the baby, but perhaps she can learn more about him.

'My goodness. We do not even know your name, sir.'

Again, Stefán catches the tone, the insincerity.

'Come Margrét, it is time. We must go.'

His abruptness does not phase Clovis. While Margrét approaches the cradle for one last glance at the boy, Clovis edges closer to Stefán.

'Does my sister send any message for me?'

'None.'

She nods, a smug half-smile spreads across her face.

'Do you have any message for her?' he asks.

'None.'

'Well, there is this.' Margrét says as she opens a bag made of dyed and untreated seal skin. Sewn with overlapping seams to keep it watertight for their journey, its contents are precious. Margrét lays a number of folded knitted items on the table beside the envelope. She then carefully removes a delicate piece of linen and lace that is clearly a christening gown.

'Your sister's hands. The lacework, the embroidery – all the white work is hers. Her wish is that he be christened.' She reverts to Icelandic as she speaks.

Then Margrét takes one last item from the bag.

'Rafe is to be fed *dúsa* from this spoon. Meat, fish and butter.'

'Ah. Their marriage spoon.' Clovis, toneless, barely glances at it.

'Rafe is accustomed to dúsa from this spoon. He will soon grow out of the clothes and the boots, the mittens and caps. But he will always have the spoon. Your sister might find some comfort that he has it and requests that you keep it safe.'

Stefán places a hand on Margrét's shoulder. 'We must go now.'

Margrét nods and then fastens the silver buttons of her outer jacket. Her hands begin to shake when she picks up her cap, the style of which looks odd even in this mongrel neighbourhood, with its tassel dangling down to her shoulders. The anger she feels is thinly obscured when she gives it a strong jerk. The sadness, the hurt and the wicked unfairness of it all leave her overwhelmed and with an urge to grab the boy and run. But instead, she thinks of the enormous strength Elísabet has shown in the face of these most damnable events and reaches down into her own reserve and pulls herself up. She clears her throat.

'He'll want feeding in an hour.'

Stefán stops at the door.

'For as long as Benedikt reports that the boy is well – and make no mistake, he will know – then you will be paid regularly. But if any harm befalls him, there will be no more compensation and other arrangements will be made.'

The clouds have wrung themselves dry and steam rises from the pavement. The river fog eats the shadows of the two Icelanders.

Finn stands by the table holding the envelope, which he now opens.

'Bloody hell.'

'Let me see.'

This couple seldom share an agreeable moment these days. No sooner had the banns been read did the passion that previously directed all their actions begin to wane, and their interests split and separate like a ruined curd. They woke up one morning in their London marriage bed, exhausted from all their efforts of running from the scandal they had so famously created in Iceland. The domestication of their union did neither of them very good at all. They are best together when they are bad.

'I told you, Finn. And this is just the beginning.'

Her eyes dance over the notes and sovereigns. In this they find common ground.

Finn tucks the envelope of money under his arm. Before he makes his way to bed, Finn takes a good long look at the baby. A stirring, a memory, and he thinks how queer and mysterious it is that a child of Elísabet, a part of her, would find its way to him.

'Mistress?' A bleary-eyed Willa yearning for sleep pops her head in. 'Is there anything else?'

'The remains of the cold joint. I'd like that and the butter. Bring them in here in a bowl. And fetch another bowl.'

Willa is sure she can hear her muscles whimpering over the sound of the second stroke of the clock. She must be up at five because she has not yet laid the morning's fire in the kitchen.

Jonesy is still awake and hovers by the kitchen worktable.

'You might as well help. Standing around like that for no reason. You might lay the fire for the morning. If you know how,' Willa says to him, cross and spent.

She monitors the strange, young man as he works the fireplace. He is precise, she will give him that.

They hear the baby's cries along with Mistress's call to hurry it up. Quickly, Willa lays a tray with a bowl of sliced meat, the butter dish and an empty bowl.

'Hurry, will you? He irritates me. Christ! Didn't I make myself clear?'

'Yes, mistress. Sorry, mistress.'

Clovis slathers a coating of butter on a slice of meat and begins chewing. There are many things about her country that she does not miss, one of which is the sour butter that was a staple of their diet. The rancid stuff never agreed with her. Upon her first taste of the sweet butter of the Irish she was a convert.

'Willa, where are you going? Come back here. You must watch. I certainly will not do this each time he needs feeding. Jonesy, you, too.'

Clovis suddenly points her knife at her two servants, using it to punctuate her words. 'If either of you ever disclose our secret arrangement with Iceland I'll kill you. Both of you.'

Then she chews, exaggerating the mastication until finally she spits it out into the empty bowl. She places more food in her mouth and begins again. When she has thoroughly ground a spoon full of the moistened beef and butter, she dips the baby's spoon so that a small amount rests on the tip.

'Bring him over, Willa.'

Willa's hand has been in her pocket, rubbing the back of the jade cicada. She is so distressed from her mistress's threat and what she fears is about to take place, her fingers are sore. She does as her mistress asks.

Clovis holds him like she might a loaf of bread, loosely, with one hand under his head. She places the tip of the spoon to his pouty mouth. His cheeks move as he sucks, first slowly, then ferociously.

In an appearance of unexpected kindness, Clovis orders Willa and Jonesy to bed.

'We can't have you dead on your feet tomorrow. Off with you both.'

'Thank you, mistress. I'm sure I'm very grateful.'

'I stay, if you wish,' Jonesy says.

Clovis looks up at him and considers. 'Yes. You can sleep downstairs tonight near the baby. Feed him more of this when he wakes. But leave me with him for a few moments. Here. Put him back in the cradle.'

Jonesy seems adept at handling a baby, or he is doing a fine job of pretending. He is so eager to please his mistress that he bows deeply before going off to gather the makings of a pallet for the floor.

Finally, alone with the child, Clovis begins to undress him. Off come the knitted dress and the cap, which she will discard in the morning along with the others that the bristly Margrét brought. She refuses to have any further reminders of her sister in the house. The baby is quite enough. And she has just noticed after removing the cap that his hair has a pale reddish hue. She throws her head back and laughs. He squirms as her laughter fades and now she stares at him coldly.

At the beginning of their union, each month she waited, hoping for a sign that she would carry Finn's child. She caught the look of relief on his face when no such thing occurred, though he tried to disguise it month after month, year after year. She suspected something within her had withered, and so too did her hope. Now, just in case, she takes the reins in the matter to prevent a thing so clearly unwanted.

In the small cupboard on the stair's landing she has stored a newborn's layette, the result of Willa's seamstress skills. She removes a white cotton undershirt, long dress and nightcap, and with these, puts her stamp on him and erases her sister's.

As she towers over him he screws up his face and forms little fists in preparation for a fit.

'No,' she warns.

His legs begin pedalling while he stares up at her.

'No,' she says again more firmly.

He blinks and searches for another view.

'I've been instructed to teach you both English and Icelandic. Let your first lesson commence. My bitter old father once sang this lullaby to me.'

> *Sofur thu svid thitt*
> *Svartur i augum*
> *Far i fulan pytt*
> *Fullan af draugum*

She then sings in English.

> *Sleep, you black-eyed pig.*
> *Fall into a deep pit of ghosts.*

CHAPTER TWENTY-TWO

'Outrageous! What could the woman possibly be thinking?' Verity asks.

'Something mischievous no doubt. That one's a spider.'

'Yes, constantly weaving.'

At eight o'clock the setting sun hangs on behind a wall of cloud; impotent against an approaching storm. A wind is building tonight, and though it is late summer the fire in their parlour on Fore Street is blazing.

Bertie stands with her arms folded awaiting their decision. Late for her appointment with her evening bottle of beer, impatience pinches her face.

'What do I tell her? How about, "come again at a decent hour"? Or, "wait 'till yer invited, hussy"? Imagine. Bringing her whole clan to this doorstep, like vagabonds.' Bertie punctuates with sourness.

'She does not come alone at this hour?' asks Verity.

'She is escorted by a nervous young woman and a Chinaman.'

'Indeed?'

'And she carries a baby. Indecent.'

The steel nib of Verity's quill halts its scratching. Constance rises.

'I'll send them away.' Bertie turns to leave.

'No,' Constance says. 'Show her into the drawing room. See that the other two are fed something. I don't know, are there any buns left? And marmalade?'

'They'll be servants, not guests!'

'Bertie, do as Constance wishes, please,' Verity says.

Clovis Fowler is led into the entry hall. Her gaze flows high and low, taking in an array of decorative items: busts sit crowded together on a table, heavy ferns whip against her skirts, a long oval mirror that looks as if it comes from an ancient place reflects her handsome figure.

'Come along,' Bertie says.

Clovis starts at the sharp-voiced servant, but recovers and raises her chin an inch.

Through a sliver of light behind a half-open door Clovis catches a glimpse of the fire. But Bertie directs her to the door opposite, to a less personal room, more formal and intended for guests. There is no fire laid in its hearth tonight; in fact, it is completely dark. As she awaits the sisters, Clovis senses the room has the smell of money, a great deal of it.

The door opens and yet again Clovis is startled by their appearance. The banyan-attired women enter clutching candelabras. They look so entirely different from the afternoon at Mockett's when their theatre of gloom piqued her curiosity. Their man robes fall just above their ankles in the new, more form-fitting style. Clovis strives to remain passive, but she cannot quite conceal her interest and absorbs the details without modesty. A sting of jealousy overcomes her at the sight of Constance almost floating in a white, quilted robe sprayed with brilliant blue and red flowers and green creeping vines. Her white hair is loose and rests on her shoulders. She has a fire in her eyes and her skin is strongly coloured with life, and these attributes, this ethereal image somehow grounds her very much into the reality of this world.

Behind Constance, the light of Verity's candelabrum clashes with her gold damask banyan. Clovis gazes at the line of her robe, trailing down to Verity's matching slippers, which make her appear as if she is walking on golden light. The two long plaits that hang down her back are the colour of the silvered prickets she clasps with her ink-stained fingers. Verity's pink-rimmed eyes rest on the baby.

Clovis Fowler has never before felt so dull, her beauty eclipsed by women who must be three times her age.

Constance glances past Clovis to the squirming child, whose tiny hands grasp the edges of a crocheted blanket. She places her candelabrum on the table by the window and indicates that Clovis should sit on the settee.

'It is late to be calling so unexpectedly. Yet, here you are.' Constance is short on decorum this evening.

'My great apologies to you both.' Clovis bows her head for a moment. 'I have come this way on an urgent business matter at another address near this street concerning and requiring all in my household.' A lie told efficiently. 'I have had a pressing question to ask you for some time and could not pass on this opportunity while I was so near. I am, again, sorry for the inconvenience.'

Verity slowly slippers her way behind the settee, while Constance stands in front, sandwiching Clovis between them. The sisters are perfectly silent. The hour is too late for polite conversation, and Constance notes that Clovis does not seem at all nervous or awkward with the absence of chatter, as most would. The red-haired woman has a bold and powerful eye that remains steady. The baby sleeps with a laboured breath.

'Please come to it, then.' Verity breaks the silence.

'I have here a son!'

The sisters glance at each other.

'Well, yes,' Constance says. 'Congratulations to you.'

'He is the reason I have intruded. Mr Fowler and I would, *humbly*, ask that you, Mrs Fitzgerald, and you, Mrs Fitzgerald, would do us, and our child, the honour of becoming his godparents.'

A mirror stretches over the mantelpiece across the room. From where she sits Clovis witnesses the reflection of Verity Fitzgerald stiffen like a plank.

Constance folds her arms as if to contain a web of complex feelings before they expand and overtake her, one of which is distrust. She puts her fist to her lips and clears her throat before she responds.

'Why?'

'We have no family here, Mrs Fitzgerald. You are known for your good deeds, and you have experienced loss, which transforms a person, does it not . . . to the sort of person who cherishes life.'

'Be very careful, Mrs Fowler,' Constance warns.

Verity catches Constance's eye and then lifts her chin slightly to indicate, let me handle this.

'Mrs Fowler.' Verity slowly makes her way around the sofa to stand before the woman who seems to have an unending supply of gall.

'What do you consider to be the role of the godparent?'

'After their participation in the baptism, to be present and active in the matters of the well-being of the child.' Clovis has rehearsed.

'Because . . .' Verity interjects before Clovis can continue. 'My sister and I, well, we are Catholic. We have been Catholic all our lives. Catholic when it was dangerous and illegal, and Catholic when it was thought vile to be so, and Catholic still, in the face of prejudice. In that light, we would consider such a relationship with your son to be a spiritual kinship.'

'Yes . . .'

'And,' Verity quickly continues. 'My sister and I, we are not your friends, we are hardly acquaintances. So, Mrs Fowler, that could only mean that we are the richest women you do not know, whom you would like to know. And you would use your son to make it so. Would that not be uncomfortable for you?'

Cloves raises her eyebrows and shakes her head no.

An oval-backed armchair sits forlornly in the corner by the shelving. Constance drags it close to the settee in front of Clovis. Still the woman does not blink! Constance sits with her back shooting straight up like a proud tree and speaks so softly that Clovis must lean forward.

'Do not think us foolish, Mrs Fowler. Do not think you know our sorrow. Do not think you can play upon it.'

Clovis does not flinch. Then there is a change. A tear forms and drops. Her face transforms with embarrassment. A vulnerable smile in way of an apology is offered. Then she folds the blanket back until the baby's soft tufts of ginger hair appear. She keeps her gaze on the child as she speaks.

'I do not think that at all, Mrs Fitzgerald. I assure you. I am sorry if I have given you that impression. It is only the child I think of. Mr Fowler and I know of none better than yourselves. I lost my mother when I was very young and know what it is to need the guidance and comfort of a female. I would wish for my son to have such influence ...' She raises her head. 'Your influence, should anything terrible befall me. This world is so unpredictable and ... well, there is no one else.' Clovis believes this. For if there *were* danger enough in the air, the kind for which Elísabet would give up her son, then Clovis is truly alone.

The sisters, despite the tinge of threat in their manner, are thawing. They detect a genuine note in the woman's plea and exchange a glance when they hear it. Neither have dared study the boy. They cannot allow themselves to look too closely.

'What about the Mocketts?' Verity asks. 'They are younger, more suited.'

'And they have always wished for a child,' Constance adds.

'Have they? I did not know.' Clovis lies effortlessly and offers no more conversation on that topic as she now turns the baby to face Constance and Verity, positioning him on her lap.

Tiny patches of eyebrows furrow as he stares first at Constance and then turns his focus to Verity. Something not unlike a smile forms on his face, and a noise that the sisters will later swear was a giggle erupts, along with a feisty punch into the air.

Clovis summons a demure flutter of her eyes to both sisters. Inside, she is reeling with joy. How well the boy has performed, and so innocently, completely unaware of the enchantment he casts. These two old women are besotted. The answer is not yet secure, but she is certain they are seduced.

'I have overstayed my welcome. I will take no more of your time. Mr Fowler and I can only hope that you will consider our invitation. I thank you for your attention and your hospitality at my interruption.'

Clovis then makes a show of overcoming the dilemma of rising from the sofa with the baby in her hands. Constance reaches out for him. It is a natural reflex and Verity's hands open too, welcoming the child like a treasure, a delicate golden treasure.

'Oh thank you. If you don't mind holding him for a moment while I ...'

'What do you call him?' Constance asks.

'Rafe.'

'Rafe,' Constance and Verity repeat together.

They are falling ... falling ... falling ...

'You will have our decision in a few days, Mrs Fowler.'

After Clovis departs, the sisters return to their private parlour.

'I think there is nothing more comforting than a good fire. Do you agree, sister?' Verity asks.

'Hmm, yes.'

'We're going to do it aren't we?'

'Yes. Yes, we are, sister.'

They sit quietly for some time, each with the single thought of this extraordinary invitation and all that it implies, turning it over and over, examining it for its consequences. For an hour or more they lose track of time and every now and then glance at each other with an intimacy that requires no words. They share the same thoughts, the thoughts of a child in their lives again after a long emptiness.

The stubborn wind does not find its calm and creates a song, a swirling melody. Bertie comes bursting through the parlour door, her face the hue of a bright plum from her beer and she shakes her head in wonderment.

'Blessed Mother of Christ. What is this night like then?'

CHAPTER TWENTY-THREE

Her small stomach swelling by the minute with buns and marmalade, Willa stumbles over the question of Jonesy's absence from the Fitzgerald kitchen. After they depart Fore Street, Clovis and Willa locate Jonesy on the bank of the river.

'What is that boy doing?' Clovis asks.

'He said he needed the air, mistress.'

'The air – by the river? Idiot.'

Clovis is in a particularly amiable mood, otherwise Willa would not like to think of what her mistress might do to Jonesy.

He does not see them at first, and is therefore unaware that he is being observed in this particular way, out of his element. He stands amongst the flotsam and jetsam that the tide has washed up. The wind and the currents have delivered dead dogs, bits of coal, bottles and human bones. A battered boat is beached and another is raised on logs for repair. Beside Jonesy, a flaxen-haired sailor stands so closely that a sheet of paper would struggle to fit between them. Jonesy shyly raises his eyes to the young man's face.

Willa thinks Jonesy looks somehow more present and attentive than usual. He is ugly, she has always thought so, but here in the light of a waning day, beside the sailor who seems to be torn from a piece of the sun, he looks hideous. With his golden hair and skin, the sailor is an image of everything bright; piercing, shiny eyes and teeth so white that when he smiles at Jonesy she can see them sparkling from where she stands. Now she is caught up in the design of the sailor's uniform not having noticed it on the streets before now. Not in this way. It is a new cut. How revealing it is. The sailor seems entirely comfortable, if not quite the cockerel in his short jacket. The shape of his buttocks is defined, the muscles perfectly formed as he stands in the dusk. All these wondrous aspects are usually hidden from view under a man's long coat. The sailor turns now. The flap of his horizontal crotch is tightly buttoned against him, exposing a distinct bulge. A blush rises to Willa's face and something in her stirs.

Jonesy notices Willa now, and Mistress, too. His expression changes. Willa expects a friendly wave, but he wears that ill look again. He turns away and says something to the sailor, who laughs, but Jonesy does not. He quickly runs towards his mistress, his long, layered tunics billowing, his sandals flapping against the uneven shore. The sailor laughs again. Jonesy must have said something amusing, which is not like him at all, or perhaps the sailor is laughing at Jonesy's bad English? she thinks.

This is not at all what Clovis mulls over. She nurtures her own thoughts and they are quite different. Well, this evening has taken a turn. Her head tilts slightly as Jonesy runs even faster towards them. He has not far to run, but he breathes heavily and bows low and asks for forgiveness for not remaining in the Fitzgerald's kitchen with Willa.

'Look at me,' Clovis commands.

When he rises from his deep bow, his head remains lowered.

'I will not tell you again.'

He raises his head and looks into her scrutinizing eyes.

What he beholds is so subtle, but so powerful that he feels his thudding pulse and blood coursing through him. He cannot control the lantern rattling in his hand. Clovis has a dangerous look about her that conveys to him what she has deduced. Her lips form the slightest of knowing smiles.

Her gaze remains locked on Jonesy as she says to Willa, 'Here, take it. It smells.' She hands over the baby as if it is diseased. 'Home now,' she orders. 'The wind becomes angry.'

In their short walk back to Three Colt Street the changeover from day industry to evening is everywhere apparent. Here on the fringe of the city they pass the ropery where much of the work is done outdoors. During the day the scene is rich with hearty men hand-dressing and spinning, twisting and walking backwards and forwards over the ground until they cover miles in the same stretch of land – their ropewalk. Wrapped around the men's waists like skirts, the fibre bundles are pulled and drawn around a twisting wheel. Tonight the rope-makers scurry against the force of the thrashing wind to secure the long strands of yarn into the sheds. The sharp stink of tar carries into the streets. Willa covers the baby's face as they hurry past.

A black-clothed, slender figure of a man skirts the edges of the ropewalk. A beaver low topper, also black, protects his head and he tilts its worn rim forward keeping his eyes trained on the three who round the corner to Three Colt Street. Every detail of his grooming suggests his place in society. His suit of clothing is worn but not yet shiny or frayed. A clean shirt sits stiffly under his waistcoat. His moustache is neat and tidy. He has achieved his wish to appear as 'any man', and therefore has the ability to fade from view in the crowded streets and dark alleys of Sailortown. He follows Clovis and her wards, barely a shadow behind them. When the fog thickens and almost extinguishes the light of the man's lantern, the baby's cries guide him. The shadow man, Benedikt, picks up his pace. The cries are louder and hint at distress. He edges too close, for the young man with the long plait stops, turns and raises the lantern higher, seeking to discover who follows. The man falls back and flattens his body against the brick wall of a jutting house. When they reach their doorstep, Benedikt strides past them, taking the curve of the street and disappears from view.

The baby has not stopped crying since they left the Fitzgeralds.

He still cries when they open the door on Three Colt Street. Clovis speaks above the racket.

'See to him right away, Willa. And Jonesy, bring up hot water, I ... Why are you sitting there like that?' she says to her husband.

'Why have you been gone so long?' Finn sits on the step at the bottom of the staircase.

'Well, what are you waiting for?' she says crossly to her servants, and waits until they are out of earshot.

'I told you. I called on the sisters Fitzgerald this evening ... to ask them to be the boy's godparents. What is it? What is wrong?'

Finn sits too still. Always a fidgety sort of man there is something strange about his restraint.

'Mockett has closed his tunnel to us.'

'What?'

'He says it is too dangerous. There are rumours. The river police say they are coming for the water rats who rob and steal from the shipping on the river, and they will have us one day for dinner.'

'Does Mockett mean to forfeit his handsome income then?'

'He does indeed.'

'Damn him. But, it is timely, Finn.'

'See to that baby,' he says. 'I do not want to fucking hear that all night.'

'I am seeing to it.'

'There is something else. Did you mention this Fitzgerald godparent malarkey to Mockett's wife?'

Clovis considers her answer.

'I might have. In passing. What has it to do with anything?'

He does not raise his voice. He shows no sign of agitation. He responds in a tone of cold disregard.

'Nora Mockett has her husband's ear. I am certain she persuaded him to act sooner on closing off the tunnel. He gives us no time to set up elsewhere. We are out on our arses. Your wish to hurt her has hurt us all. It was not necessary. You are fucking insatiable – that's what you are.'

The baby strains its lungs now, aggravating the couple at the foot of the stairs. Willa appears, rocking him gently, with fear firmly settled on her face.

'Mistress, I changed him, and I tried to feed him, but he won't take it. Something is wrong. His head is mighty warm.'

'Think on your feet, damn you! Put a cool cloth on his forehead and take that blanket off him.'

'But I'm not sure ...'

'Just do it. Can you not see I am occupied?' she shouts over the wailing child.

'Yes, mistress.' Willa hurries away.

Clovis turns again to Finn, 'So, I am to blame for the tunnel closing because Nora Mockett cannot bear a child? I am to blame because I did not choose them to be godparents? You are foolish. There would have been another reason, another excuse. We cannot break our agreement with Iceland. If we are caught it will ruin everything.'

Now it is Jonesy who interrupts, also bearing a look of alarm.

'Baby not well. Very hot. Umm, waterings, pers, persp, perspires.'

Clovis turns on him, fuming. Jonesy's tunic is damp against his chest where he has been holding the baby.

'For Christ's sake! Bring him to me.'

Jonesy returns with Willa who is drenched as well. She holds the baby out to Clovis. Rafe drips to form a pool of moisture on the floor. He sweats from every pore and his face is now as red as his hair. He looks around wildly, not knowing from what he suffers, only that he does. His tiny stomach and ribs heave up and down as he tries to catch air through the sobs.

Clovis takes him from Willa.

'Hush. Hush. What is it, you little worry ...' Hardly affectionate, but she shows the first signs of concern.

His hair sticks to his head in small, damp clumps. He soaks Clovis in a fast fury.

'We must go to Mockett,' Clovis says.

'It's after ten. He's shut,' Finn reminds her.

'What do I care of that? We are going. Here, take him while I make ready.' She hands the baby over to Finn.

'Willa, I need a fresh blanket. Jonesy, a lantern. Now!' she orders.

'Bloody hell! He's like a water pump. My shirt is sopping already. Good Christ! Hurry, Clovis.'

Nora and Owen Mockett separate their sweaty bodies at the sound of ceaseless pounding on the door downstairs. He pulls on his britches, thoroughly annoyed at the interruption of a streak of good sex his wife has so willingly and hungrily bestowed. He has no clue if Nora's sudden voraciousness has anything to do with the closure of the tunnel, and he does not care two coins. She is completely naked, too. None of this lifting of the gown, either. Damnation! Who disturbs them? He opens the shutter a slice and silently spews further curses.

'Who is it, love?' says Nora.

'The Fowlers, the both of them. I must go down.' He does not tell her the baby is in Mrs Fowler's arms, though she will know soon enough.

Not wishing to spoil the mood of their bed, Nora remains silent. She turns on her side and watches him pull on his shirt, but when he leaves their bedroom, her jaw tightens and she lies back waiting to learn why that venomous woman would keep her husband from their bed at such an hour.

Nora learns instantly when the door rattles open that it is the baby who needs attention. She will not go down. No. She will not. No matter what. Why should she help? But the child, he is innocent. Oh bother! She sighs. She grabs her wrapping gown that drapes the chair and opens the door a crack to better hear the news.

'He has a fever.' Mockett takes the baby from Mrs Fowler.

'I know that!' Clovis snaps. 'What is to be done about it?'

The short walk to the Commercial Road had given Clovis time enough to clear her head. She must keep this baby alive, especially now that the tunnel is closed to them. Finn will need time to re-organize. Iceland must continue to pay. Thoughts of lost income race through her head. She imagines the coins falling away from her.

'I have never witnessed such profuse perspiring. It cannot be tooth fever . . . the heat is too severe. When did it begin?' Soaked through with the baby's sweat, Mockett rolls up his sleeves and gently places him on the countertop.

'When?' Clovis demands from Jonesy.

Uncomfortably the centre of attention, Jonesy cannot think straight.

'After we leave the, sorry no name . . . the Mrs Sisters . . . when walking home.'

'So, it came on suddenly then, is that right?' Mockett asks.

'Yes.' Jonesy bows.

'What time of day was that?'

'Well over two hours ago,' Clovis says.

'Will he be all right?' asks Finn, genuinely worried for the boy and not the coin.

'Too soon to tell you more.' Mockett pours liquid into a one-ounce bottle.

'Could it be deadly?' Clovis asks.

'Honestly, yes. But you mustn't worry yet. This is a fever tincture.' He holds an amber-coloured bottle to the candlelight. 'I need to dilute it quite a bit for the child.'

Clovis refrains from ordering him to be quick about it.

Upstairs it is Nora who notices first. She has been struggling; one foot in her shoe, one foot out. Her heart is with the baby, though her mind is sore with hurt and anger. She has been foolish and knows it. Why she ever thought the Fowler woman would select them to be godparents . . . Why she ever let herself imagine that there still might be a child in her life, though not her own . . . Foolish, foolish. Owen has forgotten the compresses of willow tree bark and meadow-sweet that are complementary to the tincture. She should be preparing them now, slender strips of cloth for the baby's forehead. She is wistful.

If the hand of fate could be seen as a living thing in this moment, its grasp is so firm it would choke Nora Mockett. It is now when her pride wrestles her like a demon – it is in this very second that she decides to offer her help – and in the next second that follows when she changes her mind, that her future is determined. Suddenly the house is absent of the cries of the baby's misery.

Downstairs they had become immune to the screams and accus-tomed to speaking over it, and it is some minutes before they fall quiet and notice the child sleeps.

The silence is then pierced by Mockett's voice.

'Good God, man!' He tugs at Finn's sleeve.

'Is he dead?' Finn asks.

'No, he lives. And he lives without the fever. Look, his face is a good colour. Feel his forehead and arms . . . they are cool. He is dry as the desert sand. What ailed him has completely disappeared.'

'Thank fuck for that. What did you do?' Finn is visibly relieved and grateful.

'He has done nothing,' Clovis scoffs. 'The boy is simply no longer ill.'

'Enough. You forget yourself, woman.' Finn cuts her with a sharp warning.

She has broken their agreement. She is forbidden to cross him in public.

'Take this tincture with you should it come again in the night. Watch him closely tonight at regular intervals. Hopefully, this is the end of it.'

Finn takes the bottle as Clovis makes no move towards it.

'Thank you. I am sorry we have disturbed you.' Clovis makes a small effort.

'And Mrs Mockett. Apologies to her,' says Finn.

'Quite all right, and my apologies that this tunnel business has come about so quickly. Be careful, there are rumours flying. They seek to hold someone up to the public, tar them, all of it. It will be bad.'

'Warning received with thanks. I'll have the readies for you tomorrow for your trouble.'

'No, not at all. Consider it an act of friendship.'

'No.' Clovis says sharply. Then more kindly, 'No, thank you. We will see to the account. I insist.'

It is midnight when the Fowlers and Jonesy step out into the street. It is the hour when the nightmen begin their work. They do not come to the cesspools frequently enough in this area. The shit is heavy and malodorous. The Fowlers cover their faces, damning their timing.

Doors of the infamous houses remain open. Publicans line their pockets. Rum blokes stagger. It is raining gin. The violin of the mariner's night still plays at this hour, serenading the sailors whose opium lozenges have overtaken them and dumped them at their wit's edge.

The Fowlers turn off the Commercial Road to a more docile scene. Benedikt breezes quickly past them. They do not notice.

'Why do you insist that we settle with Mockett?' Finn asks.

God, I am weary of this. Weary of explaining my actions, my thoughts, my decisions, thinks Clovis, her patience spent.

'I do not wish to be in Mockett's debt. And certainly not his wife's.'

'If it had been mine, I would have closed the tunnel, too. It's time to find a new route.'

'How kind of you. When did you become so forgiving?'

'When did you turn so fucking hard?' he puts to her.

'Turn? I have never turned.'

When they are home Jonesy stands in the doorway as the man in the black suit and beaver topper crosses over to the other side of the street. His thoughts rest with something other than Benedikt, who now moves on into the night. He loosens his plait and frees his long, silky hair, but it does not help, it does not keep the knot in his stomach from twisting, rousting up a truth. He is recovered from months of blindness and it brings a feeling of the deepest dread. His beautiful mistress . . . he was wrong about her.

Finally, the Fowler home rests. Clovis and Finn dream of filling their coffers with Icelandic money. Willa sleeps soundly with her whole being weary from this frightful night, and Jonesy entertains dreams of the sailor while the cloud of his mistress's spite hovers over him. Owen Mockett sleeps in a splendid stupor, drunken by more of his wife's juices.

The baby Rafe sleeps innocently, unaware of the remarkable transformation his dripping sweat has wrought on those who held him.

CHAPTER TWENTY-FOUR

'Christ! There is enough to do without this annoyance.' Clovis tosses the letter on the table.

> *Clovis Fowler,*
>
> *We are disappointed that there has been no return message from you. We were clear in our previous letter that a report is required regarding the health of your son. Every detail is expected. We know of his fever; now you must inform us of exactly the circumstances before, during, and after his recovery.*
>
> *Any information we ask of you is vital to your safety as well as his.*
>
> *You have no doubt noticed that your monthly allowance has not yet been arranged. Leave your correspondence at the new location in three days' time or you will not receive this month's instalment.*

The new collection place – she cannot think where the new collection place is because it is so often changed. All the day's demands and still more to do. Composing a tedious – and irrelevant – letter about a baby's feverous sweat is a ridiculous distraction.

The priest is visiting today. Excruciating. When he is gone she must perfect the christening luncheon plans. The sisters Fitzgerald have agreed to attend as the honoured godparents and Clovis means to win them over entirely.

Then there is the long evening ahead. Finn and Jonesy are underfoot, clearing more space in the cellar for receiving the riches of another night's haul. Curse the Mocketts. Simmering in her thoughts in particular is Nora Mockett, who of late takes up too much of her time, who must one day pay for the trouble she has caused. The thought that she will find a way to bring about the woman's reckoning quickens her blood.

Clovis sniffs and turns around the room.

'Damnation! What is that horrible odour?' she screams, her patience at an end. 'Willa!'

'Mistress?' Willa runs in from the kitchen.

'It smells like the water of Iceland in here.'

'That would be my Lucifers.'

'Your WHAT?'

Willa proudly presents the sulphur friction matches.

'Much quicker than the flint and the tinderbox, mistress.'

'Get rid of them.'

'But mistress, they are free, a gift from Mrs Mockett.'

'Mrs Mockett! Throw them away.'

Willa pauses, worries her fingers and then bravely adds, 'They give me time to do more work, mistress.'

Clovis casts her a sideways glance.

'Then do something about that smell. Now out of my sight.'

Later, after food and drink have been taken, the house falls silent with sleep. The baby complies this evening and does not stir for hours. Finn's private knocker-upper taps on their bedroom window at midnight. He has his orders – not until the street is empty does he raise his pole to tap the lightest, quickest taps.

The boards creak as Willa's feet swing from the bed and touch the floor. She is the first downstairs to boil water, followed by Jonesy who replenishes the fires. Both go about their preparations for the work that will keep the roof over their heads, the food at table, and such luxuries as lie scattered about.

When Finn and Jonesy leave through the rear door of the house to rendezvous with the other men, Clovis sits by the parlour window surrounded by a stack of journals and manuals. While her husband goes about plundering tangible goods, she turns to perfecting the art and science of mental theft. Tonight she chooses from a selection of mesmeric manuals, one of which devotes a great deal of focus on the process of 'demesmerizing'. She mimics reverse hand passes, mirroring the drawings in the journal. Practising with her handkerchief, she waves it slowly in front of an imaginary subject and then quickens her movements to short, staccato passes. She is pleased with her accuracy in this display of manipulation and force.

On these nights when Willa awaits the safe return of Master and Jonesy, she tackles her sewing basket. When the mending is light she does crewelwork on cushions for Mistress's bed. It is her favourite thing to do. Her hands are so engaged that her fingers have no need for stones or shells. The design itself is her charm, the wool her token.

She has changed her opinion about Jonesy. He surprised her with a rabbit's foot. Its soothing soft fur delighted her. His attention brought a surprising blush to her cheeks. She had taken down the heavy curtain in their room to add to the laundry, and replaced it temporarily with a thin piece of muslin. That night, when he came upstairs to bed, she secretly stole glances at him.

He is thin, but with her needlewoman's eye she determines that he is well formed. His skin is smooth and his long hair shines against the candlelight. She has misjudged his face. He closes his eyes while he re-plaits his hair; she notes his thick, lustrous lashes. The sharp angles of his face are so unlike the swollen Limehouse faces, the sailors whose eyes are puffed with drink, and whose noses are jagged and broken.

She wonders at the stirring she felt at the sight of the flaxen-haired sailor and how it seems to have transferred. For she feels it now, between her legs, and it is moistening her quim. She wants to touch herself while her gaze is fixed on him, but she dares not. He is so close that she can see his ribs rise with each breath and she matches it with hers. He looks up at her. She is caught! He smiles. Burning with embarrassment she turns over on her side, her back to him.

Now, as the hour reaches long past midnight she contemplates that night, a thought the size of her needle's point stabs her. When he smiled at her, his demeanour seemed to be missing a component that she did not even know she desired. He was being polite. That is all.

There is a rattle of the rear door and the grunting voices of the men of the house. A shock of damp air whistles into the kitchen fire.

'We've lost two men tonight, lay your work down and help us.'

Master is in a foul mood.

Still Willa sits.

'Move it!'

'But sir, I am not to touch the goods. I mean to say, I am not involved . . .'

'Not involved?' Clovis stands at the kitchen door. 'You little hypocrite. You are involved with your food, are you not? You are involved with a warm fire, and just last month you were involved with a new pair of boots, if I recall. Get right off your high horse. Get to work.'

An assembly line is formed. Hands and backs move goods from the rear of the house to the cellar. With more force than necessary, Clovis shoves the sacks at Willa, when a loud knock and then a great banging assaults the front door. The four are frozen with goods in hand.

'Fuck,' Finn says under his breath. 'Fuck, fuck, fuck.'

They had been working so intently that not one of them was aware of the light of the lanterns gathering in the street. Finn raises his hand signalling them to be still, to wait. He tidies his shirt and waistcoat, wipes his hands on his britches, and smooths his hair.

There could be a neighbour in distress at their door, or a warning of fire.

Finn steps carefully towards the parlour window and narrows his eye to look through the shutter's crack. The men are in private clothes. He cannot tell how many there are. One continually pounds with a flat hand upon his door. It's obvious they have come for him.

The night watch should have warned him, but tonight the decrepit old man who is easily bribed has accepted a second compensation, and now keeps happily drunk and warm as he sits with the publican on the bend of Three Colt Street.

The pounding stops, the men outside are suddenly still. They have seen the shadow of movement by the shutter; though slight, it is enough. The men wait for the phantom to make his move.

With one foot slowly creeping in front of the other Finn steps on the weakest floor plank, which sends out a reverberating groan. He will never know if the Thames police did actually hear his misstep from the doorway, but they most definitely hear him try to recover when he knocks up against the blasted armonica in the dark. With one concerted effort the constables push through the door like a tempest felling a ship.

'Peelers!' Finn shouts out.

The warning call is too late. Willa and Jonesy are trapped in the cellar surrounded by the piles of goods that tower to the ceiling. They make a futile attempt to squeeze in behind a wooden cask. The constables know exactly where the door to the cellar is located, and in all the chaos and the shouting this strikes Finn as both odd and important.

'You, sir, have fallen foul of the law for the last time. And you take down all these here with you who have been on the game.' This from the burly man in charge.

Jonesy and Willa are discovered and dragged out of the cellar. It is at this moment that they and Finn first become aware of the fact that Clovis Fowler is nowhere to be seen.

CHAPTER TWENTY-FIVE

Clovis flees to Fore Street in a night that has turned damp and threatening. In a gust of wind the baby's white blanket leaves a tail that skims along behind her. She pauses for a brief moment when she hears footfall on the slick pavement. From the corner of her eye she recognizes the figure that follows her every step these days. Unlike her, he does not breath heavily. Well, follow me if you wish, even if it may be to hell, she thinks, and fleetingly wonders at Benedikt's commitment.

She is on the move again. Though it appears that she speaks to the fog in front of her, her words are meant for the man at her heels.

'I go to the sisters Fitzgerald.'

No response.

'I must tell them about you. It will be unavoidable if you want to be informed of the boy's progress.'

Still nothing.

'We will need a great deal of money or else we will hang. Tell Iceland I will not be deported. I will take my own life first.'

Clovis picks up her pace again, as does Benedikt.

When she reaches Fore Street she pauses once more.

'He will be safe here.'

She then turns to face him but he has already melded into the indefatigable fog.

It is three o'clock in the morning, a sombre hour to be alone on any London street. Clovis has no torch or protection now that Bendikt has disappeared again. She expects to wake the entire street when she beats on the Fitzgerald sisters' door but is taken aback when it opens immediately.

In spite of Clovis's mission, her astonishment tumbles out. 'I find you awake?'

The house is alive with brilliant light suffusing the hallway, where both sisters stand bathed in a pale, yellow glow. They are all sleeves, large gigot sleeves of matching black gowns with broad, white collars. Clovis wonders if a ritual is performed in this house tonight. A violin's melancholic tune continues, despite her interruption. The sisters' faces are warm from cognac, their breathing heavy from dancing to the violin's song.

'We do not follow rules of day and night. And you?' Constance asks.

Clovis summons her nerve, a different sort than she has relied upon in the past. For a woman about to be charged, she displays a remarkable presence of mind.

'A great emergency has occurred. May I be admitted?'

Constance opens the door wider for her to enter.

'There has been a grave error . . . A terrible misunderstanding . . . A mistake has been made.' Clovis clenches her jaw for stumbling, for sounding needy.

With a furrowed brow Constance looks to the baby, then to Clovis. 'What is it that brings you out at this hour? What would encourage you to endanger your child in this way?'

Clovis ignores the admonishment. 'I have little time to tell you. My entire household is arrested. I have absconded with the boy for his safety. I plead with you ladies, who are to be his godparents, that you look after him until I return. And return I will, rest assured of that. These charges . . . they are unfounded.'

Verity has hold of Constance's arm in such a tight squeeze that Constance winces and gently removes it.

The three women stand like statues, each filling up with past regrets and wild thoughts of the future. Verity makes a low choking noise and turns her head away.

A child. A boy.

'Well.' Constance finds her voice. 'It is a great responsibility.'

'I do not have the luxury of time. You must take him this very moment, or I will find another solution.'

'Yes,' Constance says. 'We will have him.'

Verity nods in agreement.

'I ask that you visit Mr Mockett. Please,' Clovis adds. 'Ask him to watch over our home.'

'As you wish,' Constance agrees.

'There is something else. There is a man. He . . .' Clovis has not had time to think this through, nor time to concoct an explanation for Benedikt's presence. 'He acts for us as a . . . protector. The baby's protector. He will come and go, he will communicate with you by way of written correspondence. He may bring you word of our proceedings. You can trust him. You *must* trust him.'

'How extremely odd,' Constance says.

Clovis places the baby in Constance's arms.

'There is a final matter. I have no time for delicacy.' Soon to be arrested, Clovis is still capable of picking her moment. 'We will most likely need your help with financial burdens that may be ahead. I would not impose if . . .'

Constance lifts her gaze from the baby and meets her squarely. 'You are very bold in your troubles, Mrs Fowler. But we will help where we see fit.'

'Thank you, Mrs Fitzgerald. We will repay you, of course.'

'Of course.'

'The boy, Mrs Fowler. Are there any instructions for the boy?' Verity asks.

'The boy? Oh. Yes.' Clovis shakes her head, as if she has just remembered Rafe exists. 'He is ready for pap and milk. His feeding has been in the Icelandic way until now. There has been no time to collect his clothes.'

'We will see to it all tomorrow.'

'I must go.'

Clovis turns. She runs into the night and does not look back.

'Extraordinary,' Verity says. 'She does not love this child.'

'No, sister, she does not. She loves only herself.'

'Why would he need a protector?' Verity asks.

'Curious, indeed.' Constance sways gently with the child in her arms. 'Carry the lamp into the kitchen, sister. We'll feed him when he wakes.'

The evidence of Bertie's absence from this bizarre turn of events stands upright on the kitchen table. Three empty bottles of ale it is tonight. She will be snoring in her room, her jaw slack, and her mind oblivious of the surprise to which she will wake.

Verity cuts through the bread and warms a splash of milk. Soon a slice torn of its crust turns soggy. The sisters gaze at the baby's tiny sucking mouth, his cheeks doing their work to take nourishment. His eyes are fixed on these new adoring faces that look at him so intently.

'Arthur. I am sorry! Do sit for a glass.' Verity beckons to the violinist, who has been standing forgotten and ignored in the doorway.

Verity pours cognac and indicates for him to sit.

The wind has left them and blows, perhaps out to sea, maybe to the west; wherever it flies a hush is left in its wake. The boy is satisfied and struggles against sleep. He kicks a bit and his wee fingers splay. The musician drains his glass then places his chin upon his violin and picks up his bow.

It is but a hint of a melody, soft and slow, yet the sisters recognize the old tune. They look at each other with their shared pasts between them, with 'who would have thought it' written across their faces. Constance begins to sing hesitantly, unsure if she is still capable of it. The old man plays on and when he begins a new verse her voice reaches the baby in a whisper.

> *I'd rock my own sweet childie to rest*
> *In a cradle of gold on a bough of the willow.*
> *To the shosheen ho of the wind of the west*
> *And the shularoo of the soft sea billow.*
> *Sleep, baby dear,*
> *Sleep without fear.*

CHAPTER TWENTY-SIX

There is nothing more entertaining for the people of London than to see a man hanged.

At the junction of Holborn and Newgate Street townspeople gag and cover their noses when they pass under the windows of a particular building five storeys high. Male prisoners piss out of the windows onto the heads of unsuspecting free people. Along with gambling, fucking and drinking, it is one of the inmates' favourite pastimes.

Rotting. Filthy. Stinking. Verminous. Everything that is dark and putrid festers within Newgate Prison. The Tower, the royal palaces, none are as awe-inspiring. There is no place more famous. All eyes are on Newgate.

The men who snatch these notorious criminals, made wicked by their crimes, have their own stories to tell. Two will hone their tale, shaping it to please a rapt audience: the night they captured the ravishing woman, who is as cold as the country from whence she came.

They were waiting for Clovis when she returned home. She knew they would be there, and rather than run until her life was in even more danger, she stole into the back garden and, with her hands, dug into the ground to unearth one of the purses of coins buried there. She dug fast and deep, like an animal burrowing, until she struck gold. The rest could be got at later; this would buy their immediate comfort.

It was almost four when she entered her home to find she could have dug the rest of the night had she wished. The remaining constables who had been assigned to this evening's raid had helped themselves to Finn's sherry. They were half drunk when she flew inside, panting, with her face flushed and hands caked in dirt. One of the constables caught up in her whirl made a grab for her and groped her breasts, then his scaly hand moved down her skirts searching for a prize. She knocked him over in one fell swoop. The crack of his cranium on the table's edge sent a shock through her.

He lay like a dead man. The other constable was instantly sobered. He curled his lip and pointed a stub of a finger at her.

'Oh yer done for it now. Murderess.'

'I defended myself. It was an accident.'

'Really, now. Let's see how the jury sees it then.'

'If you tell the jury the truth they will see it as it was.'

'If. Now that's a word, ain't it?'

Clovis took his measure, thinking. What kind of bribe will tempt him most? Sex? Money? Both? She found herself warming to the challenge.

Then, from the floor came a groan. He stirred, as alive as his head was sore.

'Assault. It's still a capital, now, ain't it.'

The constable stood, took aim and spat on the floor.

Clovis and Finn had discussed their plan of action should this day ever dawn. They rehearsed their defence, depending on the circumstances. Not in any act of chivalry or sense of duty, but rather, from a thin and shrivelled sense of family, and a desire to secure their loyalty, they agreed to protect Willa and Jonesy.

Finn had wanted to entrust the baby to Benedikt, should the need arise. But Clovis was immovable, a veritable fortress on her stance that the boy would, in the end, save them all and must be cared for by a more known situation.

If she knew nothing else on this godforsaken earth, she was certain there was something about the boy that was worth the enormous sum required to secure their safety. When the door of freedom closed behind her, she knew that even if condemned to death, she would not hang. She showed no fear because she had none.

By the time the sun sets this day, a sun that never shone in the cells, the Fowler purse is half empty. Everything they do, everything they need, is at a cost. They pay dearly for a room without lice crackling on footfall, a room in which they might sleep on a plank and not wake on a cold slab of floor, their eyes level with a pile of their own shit. On the first day, they had avoided being stripped, beaten and abused.

The next morning Finn learns from other prisoners' tattle that he and Clovis are attracting the sort of attention that catches like wildfire. When informed that trials are moving quickly he is gripped by a wave of terror and also relief, for they cannot afford to live here in this place that is more expensive a home than almost anywhere in London. They bleed money.

Willa cannot stop pacing. Clovis aims to calm her with assurances, but she will not be persuaded. The girl is certain she will either die in this hell, or hang beside her mistress.

'Everything happened so quickly. One moment I am sewing, the next, I am dying,' she sobs.

Clovis slaps her face.

'How ungrateful you are. Would you rather be downstairs in the cellar where you will be raped and torn at like a piece of meat? Or perhaps you would prefer to be separated from us in the Common women's hold, with a hundred half-crazed rotting females?'

The slap and sharp words have their desired effect. Willa places her hand on her red-marked cheek.

'No, please, mistress.'

'You are not going to die. None of us are going to die.'

'It is just that I have had such a small life, mistress.'

'Shut up.'

Clovis does not know their future. She cannot predict exactly how they will one day return home, but she knows they will. She depends on Iceland to secure it.

'Have strength, Willa. Look to me for safety.'

Jonesy is not so easily convinced. On the third night of their incarceration he moves quietly from his straw bed to kneel beside Willa, who clutches a torn blanket. He whispers for her to join him in the corner of the room and places a finger to his lips, motioning for her silence. He takes off one of his sandals. There, in the sole, his fingers prise open a hidden compartment. He removes two packets of powder. He points at her and then at himself. Leaning in closely, his cold lips in her ear, he whispers, 'Poison.'

Willa squeezes her eyes shut and nods – she understands. In a world where their position renders them powerless, Jonesy keeps a claim to their deaths in the worn, pavement-beaten sandal that she had once so easily mocked. They will not hang and they will not be deported.

The next day the Fowlers are called to the visitors' room. From the moment he steps onto the damp gravel in front of the gaol and enters into the gloom of a little room adjacent to the governor's house, Owen Mockett feels enveloped in a cowl of misery and very nearly turns back, his task incomplete. Only Nora's voice chanting her plea 'not to fall' steadies his nerve, and he waits with his scented handkerchief, holding it close, almost a mask across his face.

Mockett expects the Fowlers to look worse than they do when the officer leads them in. And how polite the officer is! How heavily Fowler must be lining the officers' pockets for their easement. Mockett comes with food and drink. A measure of brandy is served. A change of clothing, a full purse of coins, soap, tallows and two blankets – he could carry no more.

Arrangements are made. In exchange for his evidence as to the goodness of the Fowlers' characters, Mockett will not be implicated. The tunnel-opening in his cellar remains a secret and his involvement will go unpunished. The weight of this news relieves him. Fowler is a nobler man than he had ever hoped. He readily agrees to watch over their home and keep it safe. Clovis stands at the small window, her red locks framed against the iron bars. Mockett cannot understand her remarkably calm manner. It is as if she just patiently bides her time, certain of her release.

Straw is laid down on Old Bailey Street today; a thick layer deadens the noise of passing carriages indicating it is a trial day.

The baker Carson sings like a skylark.

'Twas the cruel and demanding fist of Finn Fowler that had forced him to receive stolen goods in exchange for his best pies, bread and cakes.

It is recorded in the newspapers. Carson tells the jury of how Fowler terrorized the neighbourhood with threats of violence if they did not trade with him. With a red and blistering face his gestures grow broader, until he finishes with a triumphant glare at the accused.

When the constable who witnessed the alleged assault upon Mrs Fowler is called for the defence he does not appear. The court is told he is feeling too poorly to raise his head from his bed.

Their trials last less than nine minutes and the verdicts and sentences are announced.

JONESY LING – indicted for stealing. **GUILTY. Aged nineteen years. Transported for twelve years.**
WILLA ROBINSON – indicted for stealing. **GUILTY. Aged nineteen years. Transported for twelve years.**
FINN FOWLER – indicted for stealing. **GUILTY. Aged thirty-three years. DEATH.**
CLOVIS FOWLER – indicted for assault, stealing. **GUILTY. Aged twenty-nine years. DEATH.**

Finn Fowler holds no hope, no belief in the possibility of a pardon. He cannot grasp the dream of a reprieve or a lighter sentence. He sits on a rotten bench, shackled in the men's Condemned Hold, sick with something entirely unfamiliar. Sprouting in his gut, remorse takes hold of him like a weed. He is resigned to death, but did not expect regret.

The Ordinary is quick to notice when a man turns.

'You must repent, prisoner. You may tell me your confession. It is my duty as your chaplain to hear it.'

Foul of breath, stick-thin and scowling, the Ordinary would like to record Finn's confession, for the accused did not give it at his trial. But the formerly unrepentant Finn is aware of those who will turn a profit from his death and turns away from the Ordinary without a word.

On Sunday, the small prison chapel at the top of the gaol is filled to capacity. The Ordinary makes opening remarks of his Condemned Sermon and moves on to punishment, sorrow, childless parents, broken hearts and death tomorrow morning.

Allowed to sit beside his wife on the pew for the condemned, Finn detects a sliver of amusement in her face.

'I have received a message from Benedikt.' Clovis keeps her gaze forward. 'He works towards a reprieve.'

'For you, perhaps.'

'No, for us both.'

'It will not happen.'

'It will.'

'How are you?'

She turns to look at him.

'What?'

'I . . . I am sorry.'

'For what?'

Clovis regards him through narrowed eyes. 'If you are truly sorry, then answer this honestly.' She pauses, overcome by a wave of unexpected emotion. 'Does your heart still beat for her?'

'What?' He looks at her astonished. 'No. And I did not think you gave two fucks one way or the other.'

Clovis holds his gaze for a second longer before looking away silently.

The Ordinary drones on from the pulpit, bellowing out a reading from Scripture, supplemented with a constant chant calling for the prisoners to repent and confess.

'Do not give the Ordinary your confession. I have paid him well. He will allow you a longer speech on the gallows if we need more time.' Clovis now instructs Finn.

'Yours will be a crueller death if you do not forget this hope for a pardon. Prepare yourself.'

'No. I will not. You underestimate me, Finn. You always have.'

'We will not meet again, Clovis Fowler. You are still the most beautiful woman.'

'Oh, but we will meet again. I do not know when, there are difficult years ahead, but I will see you again, Finn Fowler.'

They turn from each other and face the Ordinary for his final words of the service.

'May the Lord have mercy upon your souls.'

CHAPTER TWENTY-SEVEN

In four separate corners of Newgate the members of the Fowler household are for the first time separately housed.

Jonesy sits on his portion of the floor with a straight back, his crossed legs form a lap upon which lays his sandal, and this he opens, removing the packet. He closes his eyes and conjures the image of the flaxen-headed sailor, who did not come to his trial. Jonesy wonders if the favour he performed for the under-sheriff in exchange for the delivery of a letter was for nothing. He feels hopelessly stained by all he had learned in his father's house of whores.

The powdery poison tastes bitter and feels like dust in his dry mouth. He has had no food or drink today; the emptier his stomach, the quicker and more violent the reaction. All over soon.

The female holding cell for transports is overcrowded tonight. They swarm around Willa seeking stories of Mistress Fowler. She begins to rock and her fingers count on both hands. The candles sputter to darkness one by one until she can no longer make out the women but for their figures walking past her like ghosts. Her hands search along her hem until they fall upon the packet.

She thinks of her former home and Matron's haunting words arrive now. What was a little groping compared to a life? Could she have born the violations more readily than the pit of despair and submission she was sure to suffer from her gaolers in New South Wales? The women speak of it for hours on end inside these walls.

Willa holds the packet as if it is precious gold. She must not spill a grain. Her fingers find her mouth in the dark and she opens wide.

Clovis stands in her cell alone and waiting, anticipating the arrival of a notice. The hard melody of metal announces the gaoler's path to the female Condemned Hold. He grows fatter with midnight messages. She hears the heavy footsteps near the ward's passage, and yes, they stop at her cell. He turns the key in the gate.

Now in the last hours, a certain constable has made a remarkable recovery and has gone to great lengths to swear an oath that on the evening of the arrest, Clovis Fowler did indeed strike out in self-defence. A reprieve. What is to be done with her will be made known in the morning.

'You have friends in high places.' The gaoler shakes his head as he removes her shackles.

After the gaoler secures the gate and makes his way back to his warm bed, Clovis reaches for the wall for support. Once steady, she lies on the plank and searches for the ceiling that remains hidden in the unlit cell. Her ankles and wrists ache. Her resolve to hold her nerve had wavered for a few moments. It returns now, ever stronger. Events unfold as she had predicted.

One more hurdle. She closes her eyes and while she rests, the crows that perch on the portable gallows below her barred window flutter past Debtors' Door.

The gaol's restless prisoners are not yet finished with this night. There is trouble in another cell. Willa cannot stop heaving. The vomiting began almost immediately after she ingested the poison. A fire rages in her belly and it wants out. She cannot be sure that she is not spitting flames. Jonesy had not warned her of this.

The other women call out for help. A few are concerned for the girl, but most are frightened of contagion. None of them have seen such fierce retching.

In the men's hold they are not so kind. Jonesy is pushed and kicked into a corner as he spews vomit on inmates. The prisoners are easily riled the night before a hanging, and their disturbed sleep foments unrest and violence.

A bell hangs in the cellar over the High Hall stairs. A single ringing calls the turnkey; for an alarm it is rung twice. The gaoler is gruff and in bad humour with this second intrusion of the night. He will demand more for his coffers.

'Can you walk?' he barks. Then he orders one of the prisoners to lift Jonesy to his feet.

'You dare not puke on me. I'll kill you.'

The cellmate drags Jonesy behind the gaoler, through the gates and over to the Common side, where Clovis is still held in the condemned ward.

He throws Jonesy into the cell with Clovis.

'Here,' he says. 'If he's going to cat all night, let it be in your cell.'

Five minutes later he is back with the same prisoner who now half carries Willa.

'You need to pay the swabbers to clean up their mess. There's two cells full of their sick. I will not have a fuckin' epidemic on my hands.'

If he expects Clovis to flinch, he will be disappointed.

'Sir. I would like wine. The watered down variety that is so famous here.'

'Why you . . .' Then he laughs. 'It will cost you.'

'Need you even say it?'

He points at her before he leaves. 'I will miss you, woman. By God, I will.'

In less than half an hour Jonesy and Willa appear completely recovered.

'So. You live.' Clovis splashes watery wine into crude metal cups. Black smoke rises from the candles that accompanied the wine.

'What? What is it?' she asks them. 'These flames cast shadows on your faces that tell me you are not pleased.'

Jonesy opens his mouth to speak but cannot find the words.

Clovis looks from him to Willa.

'Stop it,' Clovis commands her. 'Stop it right there. Do not drop one tear. What is going on here? I warn you. I am in no mood for anything other than the truth – and be quick about it.'

'We should be dead,' Jonesy says.

Willa nods, while Clovis is impatient.

'We should all be hanging by our necks tomorrow,' Clovis says. 'And if not for me you would be. Speak plainly for Christ's sake.'

'What Jonesy means is . . . we took a powder. A poisonous powder. We do not want to be transported, mistress. We would rather die,' Willa says.

'This poison . . . very strong.' Jonesy adds.

'Obviously not strong enough, you fools.'

'No, mistress,' Jonesy says. 'This powder . . . it is right one. We take twice amount, to be sure of quick death. Something not right.'

'Do you have more of it?' Clovis asks.

'No, mistress. Willa and me, we take all of it.'

'Well then. If you have taken the right powder and you have had enough of it, you would be dead.'

'Yes, mistress,' he says.

'I am disappointed that you do not trust me. You will not be transported. I am weary of repeating it. Wait and see. We will all be at Limehouse by this time tomorrow.'

Jonesy is not persuaded. He waits until he hears their slow and steady sleeping breaths and then he takes off his sandal. His fingers dig deeper inside the hidden compartment of the sole, past where the packet was, to almost the edge. Hidden there is a sliver of a blade. It is the tip of a knife, short, thin, but sharp.

'Goodbye,' he whispers.

He runs the point of the knife across his wrist. Drops of blood fall on his tunic. He recalls the old whore past her use who showed him this way to cut. Then he thinks of his mother. She wears a pink silk robe with cherry blossoms in bloom across her body. He wants to sleep now. The warm trickle slows its course. No! This is not right. His head is heavy when he moves it to look down at his wrist. The blood stops. No more blood.

Jonesy crawls across the filthy floor to the window. He feels the cold bars against his bloodied wrist. His lips move soundlessly as he summons the spirit of his grandmother to fly to him and help him understand why he cannot die.

Met with silence, he cannot breathe for the fear.

CHAPTER TWENTY-EIGHT

Hundreds are gathered at four o'clock this Monday morning. The pavements are cleanest at this hour. The crowd is calm, the weather mild. Spectators mark their places as near to the gallows as possible. Two young men will also swing today, but the crowd is here for the Fowler man and his wife; they wait oblivious to her fortunate news. In ignorant bliss they mingle at the place where the scaffold will stand.

Finn is brought the breakfast of the condemned. Tea, coffee and a little bread and butter are his fare. The Ordinary stays planted at his side, still trying his best to coax a confession between prayers. Finn has had none of the breakfast, and refuses the Ordinary.

Now the scaffold is wheeled from the Sessions House to Debtors' Door where it juts out a bit, like a crowning babe not quite ready to make its long-awaited appearance. Three cheers go up when the crowd catches sight of it.

At six o'clock the mass grows denser and people who have rented spaces begin to appear in shop windows and on the roofs of the surrounding streets.

The crowd swells ever greater, and grows more festive. Jokes are wending through the clusters of friends, and laughter follows. All is deliciously merry, as if an opera is expected.

The baker, Carson, arrives. Shouts of, 'Witness coming through!' afford him and his wife a better view, closer to the scaffold. Other tradesmen are here with their wives. The Mocketts are not among them. Their desire is to be unnoticed today, weighted as they are with relief that they were not implicated in the crimes.

It is seven o'clock – three hours have passed. Numbers grow greater with each minute until thousands fill every space. Now the Sheriffs' carriages arrive; their procession arranges itself with great show and they wave to their peers.

St Sepulchre's clock strikes the half hour. Five more minutes pass and the crowd settles down, eager, but quiet. They wonder what the condemned are doing in their last half hour on this earth.

The bell tolls the quarter hour.

The scaffold stands before the throng, the black chain hanging down from the beam, ready for the day's work. It is eight minutes to the hour of execution. The crowd is feverish. The morning has passed so swiftly and yet now it creeps along to hanging time. The wall of people extends as far as the eye can see when the bell begins its toll of eight. The spectators settle into a quiet awe as they await the procession.

No one comes.

Necks strain, then a murmur is let loose. The message spreads through the masses like a breeze carrying smoke: the murdering boy has hung himself in his cell. They will be denied his young face.

Some in the crowd fold their arms and nod their heads.

'Always a possibility.'

'Did not think he had the fortitude, frankly.'

Still no one comes from the door.

'Wait, wait. There is more news.' The tattle spreads.

'The sodomite. He has been murdered in his cell.'

The crowd sends out an approving roar. The last minutes before execution are always pregnant with a turn of fortunes. Reprieves, suicides, even murders – they are part and parcel of their expectations.

The attention turns back to the scaffold. Just then a shockingly white head of hair appears out of the black door. The mane is long, and tied back with a trailing black ribbon that lies against the man's black suit-jacket.

'A new hangman.' Ripples run through the spectators.

They were expecting a short, stout frame with beefy arms. This long reed of a man that stands before them is somehow more sinister-looking in his slimness. The sharp lines of his body move like an ebony blade.

A man follows the executioner with his arms tied in front of him. He too wears a black suit, a new one, with a bright, white shirt. Supported by a turnkey, he mounts the scaffold. There is an awful silence. Finn Fowler is not the swashbuckler the crowd expects. Even if he tried, he cannot stand the hero. His supporter makes an effort to prop him up before the Newgate drop, but Finn trembles so, his strength has left him. There is call for a chair. The white-haired executioner lifts a skeletal arm.

'Halt! No chair. Stand on your feet, Finn Fowler.' His razor-like voice cuts through the air.

The Ordinary helps hold this felon who is entirely stripped of courage. Finn has refused the attentions of the Ordinary until now. If he could speak, he would give the man his story and then he would beg for his life. He would tell him that his only education as a child was the art of thievery, foisted on him by his parents. A beating, or a loaf of bread, these were his options when he was but four years of age. He stole the first loaf from the elder Carson, the baker, whose son witnessed Finn's first act of thievery and stands glowering before him now.

Finn shakes his head to empty it of the memory until his hair falls loose.

'How handsome you are, Finn Fowler!' A nosegay lands at his feet.

'Farewell, Finn!'

The crowd waits for her to appear. This Fowler woman, by God, they have imagined her over and over again and are now impatient to gaze upon her in the flesh. They anticipate her flowing, red hair, and her beauty, which is rumoured to be outrageous and envied, even by those in the Palace. There is a flush of pleasure in the excitement while they wait for their fantasies to be played out. Some admit to being sexually aroused.

She does not appear.

Caterwauls and whistles begin to voice the unrest in the audience. The feeling of being cheated is rising and spreading throughout. Those in charge are aware of the danger of an unruly mob and serve the announcement of Clovis Fowler's reprieve in haste. Not one cheer goes up in her favour. Hissing and spitting rains down in nasty wet globs. The burden now rests on Finn and they have no faith that his will be a spectacular death. The draw was always the married couple. There are only eight hanging days a year at Newgate, and in this one they are short-changed.

The executioner removes a thin, white cotton cloth from his pocket. Finn stares at it dazed. Here is his last opportunity to speak and he will be given ample time as a pitiful offering to appease the crowd.

The executioner turns Finn's body to afford the onlookers a better view. Finn recalls Clovis whispering in his ear, instructing him to make his speech a long one; he remembers this vividly, as though she were next to him at this moment. He opens his mouth, but nothing comes. Warm urine runs down his leg.

He looks to the crowd, for what, he does not know, but his eyes find Carson the baker. Finn's expression turns quizzical. He is confused with the image of Carson the young boy – even while he looks into the face of the older version before him. Carson returns his gaze with a cold and lifted brow.

'He does not die game!' Carson shouts to reach those farthest away.

Laughter peels from those close to the scaffold.

'Will you not speak?' The Ordinary pleads.

Then Finn remembers what he is searching for. At the last hour he lost all hope for a reprieve, but he renews his hopes for it now.

Clovis promised him it would come, but first he must draw out a speech to buy more time. He cannot.

In one swift motion the covering is placed over his head. The crowd yells its approval. His bowels loosen. The head-covering does little to erase this day; he can still see through the lightweight cotton.

'Hats off!' Thousands of hats swish off to allow a clearer view.

From the front of the gallows the hush of the crowd concertinas to those farthest back.

Finn catches the scent of the rope and his mind flees to Limehouse, where he breathed the work of the ropemakers. When the rope goes around his neck a scream escapes him. The women jump back, as if his unexpected voice pushes them away.

The executioner pulls the bolt and the drop falls. Finn will not go so easily. Astonishingly, he draws himself up, and his feet find purchase on the side of the drop. The executioner pushes him off. Finn lodges his feet on the side again. The crowd emits a collective, 'Ah!'

A third time he saves himself.

When he is pushed again, the rope breaks.

A yell bursts out from the viewers and echoes back through the swell of people. They laugh a strange, uncomfortable laugh. This man, this Finn Fowler, he fights to live and they are with him, by God.

Another rope is placed around his neck. The hangman is gruff this time, showing no mercy. The Ordinary shouts a prayer, only to be met with disapproving and mocking hisses. The knot in the rope slips around to the back of Finn's neck. It will be a slow death.

The executioner turns him this way and that to disorient him. Finn's feet cannot find the edge this time and he drops. He kicks at the Ordinary and the hangman. The head-covering falls off. His lips and nostrils ooze a frothy, bloody mucous. His face balloons. His eyes bulge and his lips and ears begin to swell. Signs of distress settle on the faces in the crowd. As if to mirror their turmoil, dark clouds dirty the sky.

Finn is clearly still sensible and knows he is hanging. His feet search for the platform. The executioner pushes him again. The people roar. Finn visibly soils his britches.

Just as is a pillow pressed on the face, hanging is suffocation. The longer Finn hangs, the more uncomfortable the crowd becomes and they direct their jeering to the hangman now.

Finn is completely unaware that his penis has become erect and an involuntary ejaculation further dampens his britches. There are a few who gesture, but none find it amusing. The people are turning.

At nine o'clock no movement is detected. A group of women have come forward. They have paid a large sum to test the miracles of the gallows. One woman bares her breasts. The hand of a hanged man is believed to cure tumours. She mounts the scaffold. She has no fear, no hesitation, as she takes Finn's hand in hers. Just as she raises it to her breast, his head rolls and his eyes open and meet hers. The woman faints clean away.

His struggle to take air is too much for the onlookers and they begin to cry out.

'Cut him down! Cut him down!'

The hangman who until now has been a model of control yells, 'God almighty!' and steps back from the gallows.

The Ordinary clasps his prayer book to his chest and recites a prayer, his eyes tightly shut.

Finn's distorted features have played upon the people until they are wholly changed and awed by his agony. Their eyes flash back their tears. A different sort of passion overtakes them and leaves them soured.

Then the words Finn thought he would never hear are repeated over and over again.

'Reprieve!' The word creates a soothing blanket over the crowd. 'Reprieve!'

The executioner is given a blade to cut him down.

When the rope is loosened the pain is so great that Finn wishes he were indeed dead. His ears ring with the explosive sound of people cheering. He scarcely knows where or who he is.

He should not be alive. Finn knows it, the hangman and the Ordinary are sure of it, and the onlookers will speak of nothing else for months.

Clovis Fowler leans against the wall of the cell in which she had bought the three of them a view of her husband's execution. Willa and Jonesy have locked hands throughout the horrible, unfolding scene. Through the double row of bars, Clovis looks down upon the gaping faces of the crowd, people who still cannot believe what they have witnessed. As time passed and the reprieve did not come Finn did indeed appear as dead as a man could be. She had felt her own jaw clench, a knot of panic sticking in her throat, as he'd dangled like a blackened piece of fruit. Near the end of the hour when his lifeless body began to move again, Willa and Jonesy let out screams louder than any of the free people below. The blood drained from their faces, replaced by the haunted sheen of death masks.

'It cannot be,' Jonesy says to Willa.

It would seem I have three miracles on my hands, is Clovis's first thought. But she does not believe in miracles. Surely Jonesy made a mistake and did not actually ingest poison, but some other substance. And as for Finn, cruel as it may be, hangings have been reported to last an hour or more. The difference here is that eventually the result is always the same – whether it be minutes or an hour, death is met at the end of the rope. Remarkably, there was no death today. A queer and freakish idea forms; its nature is persistent.

Clovis turns her attention from the extraordinary scene below and grasps Jonesy's chin, turning his face to meet hers.

'How do you know it was poison? It might have been a bad batch, or a mistake.'

'I take it from jar myself.' And then with a steely countenance he has not shown before, 'I know poison. I buy myself from trusted trader of my father.'

Then he thrusts his wrist at Clovis.

'I will not bleed out. Twice I have tried.'

She examines the cuts and searches his face, he tells the truth.

Willa turns ashen and begins to rock.

Clovis looks out of the window again. People still linger around the gallows, looking and pointing as if Finn were still there. At the corner of the platform nearest her window, Benedikt appears seemingly out of thin air, for she did not notice him before now. He wears a pair of dark, green-lensed spectacles today, which, in addition to his hat, almost entirely conceal his face. He gazes up as if he can see her behind the bars. When he turns to leave, Clovis notes something familiar in his stride. She dismisses it. Benedikt snakes through the ocean of people until he becomes a black speck and disappears.

Finn Fowler is taken to a small room near the boiling pot of human parts. A doctor who witnessed his ordeal volunteers his services. His genuine desire to make Finn more comfortable sits alongside his innate curiosity. How could this man possibly still be alive?

The doctor removes Finn's soiled clothing and washes him. He examines the man's ragged-looking throat, inside and out.

'It will be some time before you will be able to speak again.'

In defiance, Finn struggles. He rises up and motions to the door.

'What? What do you want?' the doctor asks.

'Ordinary,' he rasps.

Minutes later, the Ordinary sweeps into the cell, his chest puffed with importance now that the hanged man who lives asks for him.

'Make way, make way!' He pushes the turnkeys and wardsmen who have gathered round for a glimpse.

'I am here, Finn Fowler. I am here.'

Finn rests his head on a ragged blanket, as if comforted by the

Ordinary's presence. Yet there is some mischief in his expression. Come close, he motions to the man who clenches his prayer-book.

The Ordinary leans in. Closer, Finn indicates. Awkwardly, the Ordinary turns his ear until he feels the warmth of Finn's rancid breath.

'There . . .' Finn coughs. 'There is nothing . . . after death. No heaven.' He pauses to swallow and wipe his slobbering mouth. 'No hell.' His voice scratches. 'There is nothing.'

Shaken, the Ordinary springs back as if Finn Fowler had laid his hand upon his heart and strangled it.

CHAPTER TWENTY-NINE

The river flows like dirty moss. The wind chops the Thames and forces the lighters to bang into each other, making an awful racket. There is no mercy on this river. The sound of the waves pushing against the wharves and wooden stilts diminishes the barking cries of the seagulls. Work is abandoned momentarily for hot cups of tea and, for many river men, something stronger at the nearest tavern. The criers are out walking the slick pavement with fresh cockles, silver mackerels and whelks.

Constance stands at the bowed parlour window peering down into the rising tide. The past swells up to a painful pinpoint in her heart, when, for a moment, she imagines her mother's body floating by. The water rises so close, so high, that she could reach out to invade its threatening currents, grab her mother's skirts and pull her out of the river's clutch. This time, Averil Lawless would be saved.

Verity sits on the sofa behind her sister with their elderly father-in-law and his youngest son who will soon take the reins of Fitzgerald & Fitzgerald.

All around the room stand boxes and packages, bundles and stacks.

'Constance, are you listening?' she calls to her sister.

'What? Yes.'

'I was just saying to Percy and George that there is still no other talk from Limehouse to the Tower but that of the Fowlers,' Verity says.

'Astonishing.' The old man shakes his head.

'From gallows to transportation, it is not that unusual,' Percy Fitzgerald suggests.

'It is when you are pronounced dead,' Verity counters.

'Well, yes, that aspect of the tale is curious indeed,' Percy says.

'When the Fowlers return ... ' Constance begins.

'The Fowlers will not return. Van Diemen's Land is no New South Wales. The latter is near to being a desirable place to settle now. The convicts are happy to stay.' George is firm. 'Twelve years each, I believe is their sentence? No, you will not see them again.'

'I wish we could be certain of it. I would rest easier.'

'I too, Verity,' Constance agrees.

'Excuse me, Father. We mustn't assume anything at this point. They have not yet left England,' Percy says. 'And I would not like to see my sisters-in-law's hopes dashed. If they do return ...' his voice grows gentler to cushion the truth, 'Mrs Fowler will still be the babe's mother. And Mr Fowler his father.'

'Quite right you are. But if I were to wager, I would say they are not made of the stuff to survive.' George insists.

'Sister.' Verity peers at her around the teetering piles. 'All right?'

Now that the day has arrived, Constance is not certain that she is all right.

'I hope we have made the right decision,' she says.

Bertie comes bounding in with the baby in her arms. She is stopped short by the silence in the room.

'Thank you, Bertie. We'll have luncheon when you can manage it.' Constance takes the boy.

'I'm far ahead of you. 'Tis ready now.' Bertie makes a lively manoeuvre, skirting the baskets filled with linen and clothing. 'It won't be much longer now. Soon as you've had your lunch, it will be time. Now I'll just make another sweep through the rooms again.'

'Well, at least Bertie has no second thoughts,' Constance says.

'I am certain it's best for the boy. Think of the fresh air, the village life. What a lucky lad!' Percy says.

'It is a very beautiful house,' Verity adds.

'Of course it is. Stunning. And you will still have a home by the water. A kinder body of water, I dare say,' George adds.

'It seems on the other end of the earth.' Constance hands Rafe to Verity.

There is cheese and cold meat. Pickles, bread and cakes fill the plates in their laps and the afternoon sun glints through the sherry glasses.

The workmen arrive, are fed, and begin loading the carts.

When it is time to depart Constance looks back into the empty rooms, surprised by the feeling welling up in her. The last time they left this place they lifted the hems of their wedding gowns and stepped up into the carriage that waited at the door. They didn't go far, only a few streets away. Fore Street will survive the thrashing the Thames gives it each day. It will go on without them.

'Come, sister,' Verity calls out to her.

Bertie carries Rafe, and pauses at the door of the carriage. She turns back to the house, lifting his tiny arm in a farewell wave.

Constance looks ahead at the boy and what is left of her family as she closes the door to the house on Fore Street.

Everywhere the eye roams in Regent's Canal Dock, cargo is shifted. Salt, ice, timber, rice and coal – tons and tons of coal – are transported on the Regent's Canal.

Here in this dock, hundreds of narrowboats wait in the lay-by. These long, wooden boats lack the majesty of the tall-masted ships that carry wild-eyed men off to sea. The narrowboat retreats from currents and tides and shifting shoal, and turns instead to the still, inland water.

It is mid-afternoon when the sisters' carriage arrives at the edge of the crowded, noisy dock.

'We are in luck with the weather today.' Verity steps down from the carriage and adjusts her dark green spectacles.

The coachman hands Bertie the last of the small bags and a large hamper.

Swaddled in a soft, red blanket, Rafe struggles to be released from Constance's firm hold.

'He's restless today. Seems to know he is in unfamiliar territory,' she says.

George Fitzgerald pokes his head out of the carriage door and pleads with the sisters to be sensible.

'Why must you take one of these ... well, I can scarcely call it a boat? Percy is perfectly capable of protecting your goods on his own. You will not be comfortable and the journey will take hours longer. You must take a carriage. The water, Constance, such a long time on the water. And the boy.'

'George, do not worry about us. We will be safe. We are not as feeble as you may think.'

Perhaps this change in the sisters' lives unsettles George Fitzgerald, or perhaps he is feeling sentimental in his old age, for his eyes turn glassy and he places his aged and quivering hands upon the their faces.

'Of course you are not. My sons always took pride in how utterly fearless you both are. Ah! There is Percy.' He dabs his nose with his handkerchief.

'Farewell, George. You must promise to visit us when we are settled,' Constance says.

'Father, Camden Town is not on the continent. Actually, Constance and Verity will be nearer to us now. Off you go. I will meet with you tomorrow.' He sees to his father's comfort before he nods to the coachman and the carriage claims the roads to Holborn.

Normally, the captain's boat would be loaded with tons of cargo, but today, makeshift seating is arranged near the bow and along the hull.

Captain Emil Unger is in charge of this commission. When Verity and Constance offer their handshakes he looks at them as if they have just slapped his face. Unsettled, he wipes his hands on his trousers, but doesn't quite know what to do with them.

The captain cannot understand why these women would have any desire to passenger a hauling boat on the canal. He doesn't normally carry passengers, and certainly not the likes of these wealthy women, who are past the middle of their lives. It will be a tight fit, and they are sure to get in the way.

'Good afternoon, sir . . . We place ourselves in your capable hands.' Constance's hand remains outstretched.

Surprised that he is addressed in such a friendly way, he relaxes and shakes her hand. What sort of woman offers a handshake? He glances from the child to the sisters and back again, and another question forms on his face.

'He is our ward,' Verity explains. 'His parents have met with difficulty. This is Rafe, our godson. Say hello to Captain Emil, Rafe.'

The baby gurgles and blinks. He stares at the Captain's weathered face and then throws his head back, opens his mouth wide and erupts with the most enormous peel of laughter. His tiny belly shakes, his laugh grows, as if he has just discovered the thing itself.

Completely won over, the captain's face softens further when Rafe reaches out to clasp the boatman's plump, rough finger.

'There now, hearty lad, catch your breath,' he says.

'I have the toll money here,' Constance says to the captain. 'And half the agreed wages.'

'That's fine then, madam. We'll be off soon. We normally start out much earlier than this, but we shouldn't have too much traffic later. Hard to know.'

Percy steps from the second boat over to the third and after more vigorous greeting and handshaking, the bargees demonstrate how securely the furniture is tied and protected under the sheeting.

The boats are well stocked with food and the water cans are full.

'All aboard!' Captain Emil calls.

The bargees pole off and enter the queue at the entrance to the yawning jaw of the Regent's Canal.

It is only now after all the checking and double-checking, after all the securing and preparing, that an elaborate bonnet first appears, peeking out from the panelled door of the cabin of the lead boat. In a moment, the bonnet's owner steps out of the cabin. Weathered, crinkled hands tuck her bibless apron under her thick leather belt; her arms, beneath leg-of-mutton sleeves, are as muscular as any man's. In her fortieth year, she looks ten years older. She keeps her eyes down in a wasted effort to conceal how incredibly shy she is at this particular moment.

When she dares to look up, her eyes fall on the baby. In her smile there is a black square where one of her front teeth should be.

'Ah! Look at the little one. He's a right beautiful boy. What a fine babe, a fine babe. I'll just be putting on a boil for coffee.' Finally, she raises her eyes. 'Coffee? I spice my own.'

'Yes, thank you Mrs Unger.'

'Angela. Feel free to call me Angela.'

'Angela then. I am Constance and this is my sister, Verity. This is Rafe.'

'Now that's a strange name, ain't it? If you don't mind me sayin'.'

'Yes, but it suits him, I think.'

Angela steps back into her nestled domain with the strings of her bonnet streaming down her back, heavy boots clomping the linoleum. Each time she moves, a swish of her striped, cotton skirts fall upon all the surfaces in the space she dwarfs. The outside of the cabin, and the sides and doors, are decorated with colourful motifs of castles and roses. Brass hoops are on the chimney and the portholes shine from tender polishing.

'Look ahead!' Captain Emil calls out to the other boatmen.

Emil and Angela's three sons give the horses a tug and they begin to tow along the path of one of the premier freight arteries of the country. The horses lean steadily into their collars, until the stretchy cotton towline is taut. With a minute or two's effort of sustained heavy pulling, the first load is on the way. The captain's narrowboat leads the other two, and as it rises up, meeting the first of twelve locks, the aroma of Angela's special spiced coffee greets the passengers.

The sisters stand like figureheads, their lavender and blue cloaks rippling against a faint breeze. All they see and hear embraces their senses. It is during the unexpected excitement of seeing a great balloon blowing across the strawberry fields of Hackney that Constance first notices two men on the towpath, both dressed in unusual black jackets, their silver buttons gleaming in the mid-afternoon sun. They pull their caps down, place their hands in their pockets and walk along close to the edge. Her palms go sweaty and she is astonished to feel fear grab her throat.

'Verity, look. Are those two men following us?'

'Captain Emil, do you know those men?' Verity asks.

'No, never seen them before.' One hand on the rudder, he waves to them.

When his greeting is not returned, the captain calls out.

'Hallo! You must have permission to walk the towpath.'

Still there is no acknowledgement from the two strangers, except a further tug on their caps.

'The Inspector will grab them soon, I'd imagine. We'll keep an eye on 'em.'

Onward they drift, as the eastern landscape of London diminishes with each clip of the horses' studded shoes. Coffee is welcome just at this moment. Soothing, warm and thick, it coats their throats and lifts their spirits.

Angela's dark head appears through the cabin hatch, and from down below the mouth-watering aroma of frying onions travels the length of the boat. She whistles a long, low sound that signals their early teatime. The men are famished; their last meal was taken at past ten this morning and it is now five o'clock. Before the gaunt wharves of east London disappear and the highway of water takes them further north into the City Road Basin, they eat.

Bertie has been itching to enter Angela's domain and takes this opportunity to haul her hamper to the galley door. At the heart of it all stands Angela at the black-leaded range, the centre of their home.

'To share.' Bertie opens the hamper.

Angela glances down at the densely-packed food.

'The wages. They include your meals,' she says. 'You are our guests.'

Angela removes the top of the bargee pail: a large cauldron filled with two earthenware pots that rests on the flat top of the range. Simmering in a rich broth in one of the pots is a substantial knuckle of ham, the other is filled with vegetables. Tucked in beside the pots are three linen-wrapped parcels of suet pudding, one filled with beef and ale, another with lamb and kidney, and the last is a sweet pudding of cinnamon and raisin. Angela has removed the lid of the well-stoked coalhole on top of the corner of the range and placed a spider pan over the fire; the potatoes and onions it contains continue to sizzle in animal fat.

'I'm afraid I have poor offerings to share compared to this feast,' Bertie says.

Angela turns her face away to hide her blush. She is at once proud and embarrassed.

Constance sits near the bow without a plate of food. Another sighting of the two men who followed them earlier has diminished her appetite.

'You are quiet, sister,' Verity steadies herself. 'Have you not eaten? Bertie is beside herself. She is rattling on about the best suet pudding ever to reach her lips. I must say that Angela has ... Constance, what is it?'

Constance looks straight ahead at the low-hanging trees. She remains perfectly still.

'There. Under the weeping willow. One of the men.'

Verity tries to move further starboard.

'No. Stop.' Constance grabs her sister's skirts and pulls her back. 'Do not let them see you searching for them. The other man . . . No, Verity, do not remove your spectacles. The other is a few feet north, near the timber yard.'

Both men weave in and out of stacks of planks until their short, square-shaped, black jackets fade from view.

'I will alert Captain Emil. If they are thieves, may they melt off the earth like snow off the ditch. What else could they possibly want?' She turns towards the cabin. 'And I'll return with a plate of food. You must eat, Constance.'

Rafe has been fed and lies beside Constance in the hamper, which is now empty of food and cushioned with bedding and linens. She reaches over to straighten the blanket that he has kicked off and which lies in a messy pile at his feet. His hair is turning just a tinge darker, less fiery than when he first came into their care. She smoothes it with a gentle hand.

Then a thought intrudes and she feels as if her stomach drops deeper into her body. Surely not! Why? What would two men want with a baby? She tries to shake the idea from her mind when the captain appears by her side.

'Here, madam.' He places one of Angela's china plates in her hands.

She looks up at him; the fear of the unthinkable written on her face.

'Madam.' He cannot call her by her given name as she asked. 'Whatever those men want, they'll only find at the end of my fist. All of us, and my Angela, too, we fight if we have to.'

She does not tell him her strange and dreadful notion. He will think her mad.

'Soon we stop to change the horses. Then we enter the long tunnel. You must eat now. It ain't for the faint-hearted.'

'Yes. Yes, of course. Thank you.'

She picks up her fork and pokes at the food before taking a bite of the shredded ham. Her eye is trained on the towpath. The pudding is meaty and moist, the carrots sweet. She feels a murderous boil in her blood. She will do whatever necessary to protect the child. The fried potatoes are glorious.

CHAPTER THIRTY

'Curses and more curses.' Captain Emil spits into the canal with a low-voiced growl.

There is a delay at City Road Basin. The Islington tunnel has no towpath and the steamboat that would pull them through the dark abyss needs a new boiler. Misery.

It is the busiest time of the day. Between five and six o'clock wagons pour into the basin laden with goods. The wharves are crammed with boats, in which the name of Pickfords dominates. The captain locates three moorings; it is a tight fit but the narrowboats manoeuvre and tie up.

Preoccupied with finding extra men to help leg them through the tunnel, he assigns tasks to his crew. Supplies must be purchased, the boys are sent to the stables to change horses, and arrangements must be made to reload freight on their return. Before he steps onto the bank, Captain Emil speaks to Angela in the patois of the boatpeople. Constance hears a few words but they make no sense to her. 'Foreign,' he says, and something about the cabin box. Angela seems to reassure him with a firm nod of her head. He gives her arm an affectionate squeeze before he enters the fray on the bank of the canal.

Dusk descends upon the basin. Grey smoke rises from the boats' chimneys and drifts towards the flour wharves, then disappears into the Scandinavian timber yard. Angela lights the lamps inside the cabin. One of the boys sees to the lighting at the bow and stern of each boat. The lanterns are richly painted; the blushing, pink roses and purple pansies create the effect of a glowing, evening garden.

Constance paces the wooden planks and looks out across the basin as it comes alive with lamplight. One by one the canal-side workers illuminate the expanse of the basin. She can just glimpse Bertie and Percy as they wander off in search of tobacco and beer.

Verity emerges from the cabin having added extra layers of warmth to Rafe's clothing. He is drawn to the reflection of the lanterns' light in the water and leans out from Verity's grasp, his arms stretching to touch the image of floating, waving light.

'Shall we go to your Aunt Constance?' she asks him. He looks all around him when he hears Constance's name.

As Verity comes towards her, Constance is struck with a very clear vision. As if she has been in a long, deep sleep and a slap of cold air has rattled and shaken her, she wakes fully aware: the men, all the men, are absent from our boats. She surveys their location again. How vulnerable they seem to be. The night has come now and it falls down upon her in a bad way. Her eyes dart around at the empty barges and boats, whose masters are doing business on land. She raises her hand to Verity to stop where she stands. She would very much like to tell her to take Rafe back inside the cabin. But she is too late, for there are the two men who have been following them. They appear like swift phantoms and are on board in an instant. The men's faces are covered with black kerchiefs.

One of them, the taller of the two, positions himself behind Verity. He grabs her and spins her around, then reaches for the boy. The other man blocks Constance, creating a barrier between the sisters.

Verity tries to fight off her attacker as best she can while still clinging to Rafe. She lets out a scream that does not sound human.

Constance scratches at the eyes of the man who holds her back. He hits her in the face with his fist. She drops.

The man struggling with Verity suddenly relinquishes her as he feels cold hard steel against the back of his neck.

'There ain't no delay when I pull this trigger. So move away, or

I have a large heavy bullet for you. One for your friend, too.' Angela has stripped off the robe of shyness.

Astonishingly, despite the gun at his head, the man acts as if he has not heard or understood Angela, and lurches forward again to try and tear the baby from Verity's arms. Angela brings the handle of her pistol down hard. She intends to hit his temple, but he turns and she misses; the pistol smacks his shoulder. He grunts.

There is a third man. They hear his running steps before they see him in the faded light. He leaps onto the narrowboat and lands beside Verity. He too wears a kerchief around his face, and the night is too dark to see him clearly. The third man surprises the attacker when he knocks his hat off, grabs a handful of his hair, and pulls him away from the child. Angela keeps her pistol trained on Verity's attacker.

A loud splash in the water distracts them. The man who assaulted Constance has jumped into the canal and is swimming away from the boat's bow. The other attacker takes advantage of the diversion and leaps from the stern onto the next boat. The third man does not waste a moment. His black coat sweeps through the night air as he pursues the man who now jumps from boat to boat.

Brandishing her pistol, Angela strides to the bow.

'Get the babe down to the cabin,' she says to Constance.

She takes aim and fires into the water.

Verity does not flinch at the sound of gunfire, but stands fixed, glued in fear.

'Take him to the cabin,' Constance tells her. 'Verity!'

Verity stares dumbly. Her shoulders tremble and she seems oblivious to Rafe's terrified cries.

Constance's eye throbs and her vision begins to blur. Her good eye tracks the third man and the attacker as they flee in an acrobatic chase across empty barges. The attacker reaches the bank and runs to a timber yard. The mountainous stacks of long planks soon swallow both men.

Constance approaches Verity with great care. She has known her sister in this trance-like state of shock before. Gently, she places her hands on Verity's shoulders.

'Verity. It's Constance, darling. Everything is fine. Look at me, Verity. See here? You have Rafe safely in your arms. I am here. We are all safe.'

Verity turns her gaze to Constance.

'There is blood coming from your eye, sister.'

Constance reaches up to her swollen eye.

'So there is. Come now, we shall go down into the cabin and sit by the range.'

Angela reloads and fires a second time into the water, but the man is an excellent swimmer and is beyond the bullet's reach.

Men with great, white cloths tucked under their chins, who seconds ago were enjoying their picnic suppers on the small parcels of green near the bank, scramble for safe cover, unsure of what has caused the melee.

Several men give chase on the towpath towards the City Road Lock. Impeded by their weapons and lanterns, the attacker outruns them. Though he is drenched, his nimble legs carry him further and further to safety in the pitch-black evening.

With a storm on his face Captain Emil comes barrelling towards his boats. Then there is Percy, breathlessly sprinting from barge to barge. Last comes Bertie, who finds it difficult to negotiate the slope of a hill and drops her basket, lifts her skirts and eases her way back to the mooring.

In the cabin, huddled near the range on bunk seats, Constance holds Rafe and rocks him until his whimpering begins to subside. The warmth from the stove is welcoming. Ashen-faced, Verity sits beside them with her head bowed and her hands clasped. She chants a prayer in Latin. Over and over her voice quakes with the same phrase that no one else understands, not even Constance.

On deck, Angela's arm hangs down by her side, the pistol heavy in her hand. Captain Emil parts the crowd gathered near his boats. He is yet to know what, exactly, has happened and stops short when he sees his wife standing on the boat. Angela looks at him with a strange expression on her face. He approaches her slowly, then when he is upon her, he reaches down and eases the pistol out of her hand. He begins to speak, but she places her hand over his mouth. No, not yet. But he is bursting with questions.

'Are you all right?'

'Yes.'

'The ladies?'

'I think not.'

'I know the bastards ran with empty hands. What were they after?'

'The baby.'

'What? I don' understand.'

'None of us do. Give 'em a minute. They need a drink . . . something strong.'

His crew is still on land helping to search the timber yard, although they have lost hope that the attackers are still near. The guilty will not be found tonight.

Bertie stifles a cry when she finally reaches the sisters and sees their faces, shadowed by lamplight. Constance's gruesome eye glows red with blood. Verity mumbles like a lunatic through her blue lips.

'Sweet Mary and Jesus and all the saints preserve us,' Bertie says.

'Ah, Bertie, there you are. Where is Percy?' Constance asks.

'He's off to find the authorities. He knows you three are safe. With great thanks to Angela here.'

The boat is heavy with people again. Angela motions for Bertie to join her on deck, and there speaks softly to her, receiving quick nods in return. 'Yes,' Bertie says, 'bring it quickly, too.' Angela fetches the whisky from the stern.

No one has noticed that the temperature has dropped except the three boys who care for the horses. They carry a collection of blankets they've gathered from the other boats.

'Here, Mrs Fitzgerald,' says the eldest. 'You shiver so.'

Constance looks up at the boy from where she sits with her head held back and resting on the cabin's scumbled panel. She holds her handkerchief over her eye.

'You are the son of the captain and Angela?' she asks.

He grins at her and nods. 'And them two runts up there be my brothers.'

Captain Emil stands at the door, gives his son an approving glance and then motions for him to move along. 'We will leave here soon. Make ready, Marland.'

Angela pours a round into teacups.

'Madam, a bit better?' he asks Constance.

'Yes, captain.' She takes the whisky in one gulp. 'I have never been struck before. I do not recommend it.'

'Angela will see to you. She has a talented hand at the medicinal, 'specially the leeches.'

'And what about you, madam? All right?'

Verity manages a weak nod.

'They were after the boy,' she says.

'I heard. Don't you worry. Won't happen again. You ladies and the little one are safe now. You'll not be out of my sight.'

'Thank you, Captain,' Constance says, though her voice belies her fears and she sounds very worried indeed.

'Right.' Angela enters the cabin. 'Your eye. 'Tis bad.'

Inside, behind the swagged, lace curtain Angela rummages around in a concealed cupboard.

'We realize this is your private space and we regret invading your home,' Constance says.

'You are welcome here,' Angela says matter-of-factly.

She gently removes the handkerchief from Constance's eye.

Verity gasps.

'Can you see out of that eye?' Angela asks, as she cleans the area with a fresh wad of muslin.

'Yes, I am relieved to say.'

'You're a brave lady.'

'Constance has always been brave,' Verity says.

Angela pauses, and then turns to Verity. 'You held on to the babe mighty fierce. You are both brave.'

All that is not said here now is breathed in sighs and held fast in their throats and hearts. How could they say, 'We could not lose another child, now could we ... For surely that would be the end of us.'

Angela has swiftly mixed a poultice.

'Madam, the treatment? Your permission?'

'Yes, of course.'

A few moments of silence are broken when Percy appears in the door.

'Good Lord! My dear Constance!' he says upon seeing her eye.

'She is quite all right, aren't you, Constance?' Verity says.

'I am indeed, by some miracle. What news, Percy?'

'We will be on our way again soon. I have just returned from the lock-keeper's cottage. He has dispatched a man to New Scotland Yard. The Peeler on the beat tonight is policing a violent brawl just north of the basin. He can be of no service to us here. It may be that we cannot report the assault until we reach Horsefall Basin.'

'We must not be followed to Camden Town, Percy. Whoever those brutes are they mustn't know the location of our new home! The very thought chokes me,' Verity says.

'They will not. With the kind help of Captain Emil and his connections we have a formidable escort on the towpath.'

'I'll just be takin' this up, then.' Angela carries two plates that serve as trays for the teacups.

Percy makes way for her and then continues. 'There is talk of a gang in the area.'

'They were not men in a gang. I am sure of it. And what would a gang want with a baby?' Constance says.

'Why are you so certain, sister?' Verity asks.

'Did you not smell it? Oh. Perhaps your attacker ...'

'Smell what?'

'The Danish tobacco. The man reeked of it. His coat, his hands, he smelled like a walking pipe from Copenhagen. It was the scent of our father.'

'But that does not prove anything. Many smoke Danish,' Percy says.

'It is a particular blend. Only available in Denmark. Those despicable men are foreigners.' Constance is firm.

'All aboard!' Captain Emil calls.

Finally, the boat moves forward in a night that is clear and cold. The canal shimmers under the yellow ochre of a nearly full moon. Yet the pall of the unfortunate event hangs over them, and what might have been a livelier evening ride along the water is much more subdued. The passengers and boatpeople are alert to the moving shadows of overhanging trees. The sound of rising and falling through the next lock is somehow more sinister. Each of them anticipates with dread passing through the arch and into the endless void of the Islington tunnel.

Everyone has a job to do as they wait their turn to enter.

Constance and Verity, alone in the cabin, add their whispers to the heavy hobnailed boots and the muffled grunts and voices.

'The third man, Verity.' Constance holds her sister's hand. 'I think it was the man Clovis Fowler spoke of – Benedikt. Did you see him?'

'Only his back. It is a revolving nightmare in my mind. Horrible images that I want to forget, not remember, Constance.'

'The tobacco. Father said it could only be had from Copenhagen. It cannot be purchased in London. And their clothing ... It is made from the same wool as the swaddling blanket that was wrapped around Rafe when Mrs Fowler brought him to us. Can you see that they must be foreign?'

'I do not know! Stop this! We've only just been attacked and you wish it all to be sorted.' There is a pause in the movement of those on board.

'I am sorry, Constance. I want off this boat and I want to be in our new home, away from these troubles and far from our former lives.'

The sisters fall silent for a moment as the boat moves closer to the darkness.

'Will you be all right, Verity?'

'I suppose.'

'No, I mean, will you be all right?' Constance turns her sister's face to meet hers so that there is no escaping her meaning.

'I will be ... for the boy.' She looks away.

'Come, sister. Let us go up and witness this tunnel business,' Constance says.

The two leggers are in position. They lie on their backs and place their hobnailed boots on the tunnel wall. Their legs hang over the boat, above the water, with a slight bend at their knees. A shout goes up from one of the leggers and then begins the first echoing sounds of heavy boots on the damp walls, like organized clapping. The right boot swings over the left, and they paw their way down the tunnel, one sweeping over the other.

Through the blackness the lantern splashes eerie shadows on the tunnel walls created by the dance-like movements of four legs.

'Marland, give us a song, lad.'

When young Marland sings the first clear note the tensions of their journey drop away. His exquisite voice joins the echoing tunnel and sends them to place without toil and worry.

> *Swift to its close ebbs out life's little day;*
> *Earth's joys grow dim; its glories pass away;*
> *Change and decay in all around I see;*
> *O Thou who changest not, abide with me.*

CHAPTER THIRTY-ONE

The leggers jump out where boats are moored at Mr Horsefall's basin, and slip away under the shadows of the wharf buildings. Percy asks that they halt their journey for a few minutes to await the Peeler who never arrives. Onward.

As the boats meander just beyond the workhouse buildings at St Pancras, the sisters notice the outline of a man with a torch who stands under a bulbous gas lamp centred above the entry gate. When he lowers his torch, its orange glow reveals his short black jacket and silver buttons.

'Look, it is the third man.' Verity points at him. 'He follows us, sister!'

'Shh! Do not alarm the others. You are right – it is Mr Benedikt. Look. He tips his hat. He wants us to know he is watching.'

'How extraordinary. Constance, what is it about the boy? I think I shall go mad with not knowing.'

'Whatever it is, he is an innocent and helpless, and we must protect him.'

The boatmen scurry about, preparing to enter the last three locks before their course veers onto the spur that leads to the Cumberland Basin. The country sky opens here, and beneath it unfolds a secluded, peaceful valley. The change in the air is remarkable.

The narrowboats settle into the curve of the canal with a short sprint upstream. The evidence of a new town on the edge of London spreads before them. Across the fields, through which the canal navigates, sparsely occupied streets are laid out; a church spire, a sprinkling of commerce, yet Camden Town still sleeps and will only slowly awaken in its development.

On the northern edge of the new Regent's Park, the canal cuts in two directions. Here the captain steers onto the canal spur that borders and separates two villages, Park East and Park West, and runs south to the spur's end at the new hay market in the Cumberland Basin.

Standing in a slight valley and set in private gardens railed off from the street, a few villas are scattered in Park East in a haphazard way; no two are alike and they are not in line with their neighbours.

'There's yer castle, madams,' Captain Emil tells them.

Tower Lodge looks as if it is on fire. Huge braziers flare with bright flames to light their way from the bank. Men with torches stand in the garden at the ready to help unload. Inside, the shutters are folded back to reveal sparkling, flame-lit chandeliers and candelabra shining through the glass. From the boats the sisters behold the welcome sight of the parlour fire beckoning cold hands and feet.

'I feel I'm eavesdropping on another's life,' Verity says.

A turret rises up four floors to dominate the north side of the house. Torches staggered across the first-floor balcony create jagged shadows that leap around the circular landing. The spectacle renders them silent. Even the great shires stand perfectly still, their feedbags motionless, as they adjust to the towering wall of light that radiates through the tenebrous countryside.

A figure stands inside the house at one of the imposing Gothic windows, and another waves from the Tower Room. Their petite frames turn away and disappear. The featured, tall chimney stacks lend the house a fortress personality, but the gables and classical design of the main body of the house softens the aspect. When the two young women seen in the windows throw open the garden door, the house seems to invite an attachment, as if it would like nothing more than a long romance.

'These will be the day maids.' Bertie chuckles. 'I told 'em they'd be working a long day today. I wanted them here to welcome you. I hope they've readied the house as I instructed.'

'Day maids. Two. Think of it, sister,' Verity says.

When Verity was nine years old she had asked her father if they were wealthy.

'Yes,' he'd said. 'Very.'

'And for how long will we be so?' Constance had asked.

'With your mother's help, because she is very clever and holds land and wealth of her own, you will always be secure.'

'Even if we live to be one hundred?'

His gaze had rested on his daughter's faces, which seemed to always hold quizzical looks and wrinkled brows.

'Yes, if you should be so fortunate.'

When the sisters first asked the advice of George Fitzgerald regarding their possible purchase of a ninety-nine-year lease on a house so large and removed from the life they had known, he advised them to follow their instincts because the money was certainly there, and though the well of their fortune was not bottomless, they could easily afford *many* of the homes in this secluded area in all of their assorted shapes and sizes.

After they are moored at the bottom of the garden, the unloading begins and everyone has a hand in it.

'Bertie. The champagne, please.' Constance says.

In the light of all the fires with the motley group of people standing by, their work nearly done, Constance raises the bottle of champagne and gives it a good whack against the wall.

'Lawless House,' she says.

'Lawless House,' repeats Verity.

When the last box and the last basket are safely delivered into Lawless House, the sisters step on board the captain's boat once again.

'We wish all of you well and happy in your new home,' Angela says.

'That we do. That we do,' echoes Captain Emil.

'Thank you and I shall settle up with you now.' Constance takes him aside.

'There is this. And there is this.' She places two pouches in his hands.

'But madam . . . I . . .'

'One is the wages, the other is something for the winter. I'll hear nothing about it. Now, do wave to us on your journeys, and when you have time, a mooring here is always welcome, Captain Emil.'

'Whenever we pass Lawless House we will have an eye out for the boy,' Angela says.

'Should you ever need anything Angela, come to us. We should like to help.'

The boatwoman's eyes glisten and she nods, but is unable to speak.

'We are sincere, Angela. This is not a farewell trifle we offer.'

Angela nods, her fierce pride momentarily suspended.

'Honoured to have met you, Mrs Fitzgerald.'

Verity walks along the towpath where the boys, still working, check the horses' shoes.

'Thank you for being so kind to a boat full of women who are old enough to be your grandmothers. I hope it was not too trying a day for you.' She offers each of them a small pouch. They stare slack-jawed at the coins, murmuring their thanks.

The water laps against the hulls of the boats as the men push off and the horses lean into the first big pull away from the bank. A final wave sends them off into the night, enriched by both healthier pockets and wealthier spirits.

A carriage for Percy, horses for the men, cabs for the maids, the business of travelling home for all those who helped is attended to until, finally, the exhausted women of Lawless House sit in a pile of disarray in the drawing room. They are aching to fall into the beds that await them, made splendidly fresh with new linen by the day maids. They yawn and stretch and feel as if they cannot bring themselves to rise to climb another floor to their bedrooms. Rafe is holding court in his new cradle. The boy is wide awake and chattering to innumerable invisible listeners. Bertie begins to place one tired, leaden leg in front of the other to go to him, but Constance stops her.

'Bertie, you look like death. Go to bed this instant.'

'I will not argue with you this time.'

'You are a treasure. Thank you for everything,' Verity says.

Bertie waves off the remarks and slowly makes her way to the second floor.

Verity lifts Rafe from his cradle and carries him to the windows. Now that he has someone's attention his babbling lecture continues.

'Look down upon the lovely garden, Rafe. This is your little plot of land. We will play on nice days and wave when the boats pass. We will watch storms in blowy weather and marvel at the snowfall.'

Below, his body concealed behind the garden wall of the neighbouring villa, Benedikt places his telescope back into his coat pocket. They are safely home. He rests his eyes for a moment and leans against the wall. On this cold night he wipes the sweat from his face with a handkerchief, replaces his hat, climbs the wall, and with a stealth that has become second nature to him now, he retreats along the towpath.

Verity turns from the window eager now to put Rafe to bed. He squirms and whimpers. She dips soaked bread into a small bowl of milk, but he turns away.

'Rafe? What is the matter poor boy? He is very restless, Constance,' she says.

'I see he is. Here, I'll have him for a while. Go to bed.'

But Constance cannot calm him either. Rafe's chatter has turned to fussing, his legs kick out and his arms fight the air.

'He is very warm, sister.' Constance places the back of her hand on his face.

'Oh good great God, Constance. He's pink all over.'

'And he's sweating now, it's pouring off him.'

'I'll fetch Bertie.'

'No, let her sleep, the poor dear looked dreadful.'

'I'll make cool cloths then. Yes? Yes, that's what I shall do.'

Constance removes the baby's outer blanket and gasps. His night-clothes are dripping.

'And bring a change of nightclothes, Verity.'

'I have no idea where they are. They could be in any one of these baskets.'

'A blanket then, anything, he's drenched.'

Verity rummages through the baskets and boxes, tossing cushions and clothing until she pauses, exasperated.

'We should have had the priest here to bless the house before the move. I begged you to allow it,' she snaps at Constance, who ignores her. 'I fail to understand why you preferred to wait until . . . This would not be happening if . . . He would not be ill if only the house had been blessed.'

Constance closes her eyes, one of which is throbbing, and sighs from weariness.

'Verity. Rafe is not ill because the house has not yet been blessed. Please. Find something to cover him.'

As Constance pats him down his sweat dampens her sleeves, until they cling to her arms. She lifts him to her cheek and his hands reach out for her face. When his arms flail and brush against her bruised eye she winces.

'Let me have him now,' Verity says. 'My God, you are soaked through, too. Constance!'

She places cool cloths all over Rafe's body, but he only screams louder. She quickly removes them and he calms a bit.

'He does not like them, Constance.'

'Then just hold him and I shall dig around in the baskets for his clean nightclothes.'

Moments later Verity too is drenched with Rafe's perspiration.

'This is not normal. He needs a man of medicine or … do we know where the nearest apothecary may be? The time. What time is it? Oh, sister, what should we do?'

'We shall keep him as comfortable as possible. There is nothing else we can do until morning.' Her voice wavers.

'I have never seen such a fever.'

They cannot locate his bedclothes and instead improvise with their shifts, which he promptly leaves sodden, and which irritate him. Not until he is left naked and free to squirm on a blanket on the floor does he begin to show signs of relief.

In the early hours of the morning Rafe lies perfectly still. Verity lumbers from the sofa.

'Constance, come here.'

Constance stands at the window where first light climbs across the garden, too terrified to turn her attention to the boy.

'Is he dead?' she asks.

Verity clamours to the floor and kneels beside him. She looks up at her sister and smiles.

'It is gone. The fever is gone.'

She lifts the naked baby and turns him to face Constance. He opens his arms to her and exercises his fingers.

Constance takes him, holds him to her bosom and again faces the window.

'Look Rafe, the sun is risen.'

The boy's sweat has turned them. The doting women will never be the same.

CHAPTER THIRTY-TWO

On any good map of London may be found the evil-looking starfish that appears as if it might actually slither across the paper. Spread like a poisonous flower of six petal-shaped wings, with each panopticon arranged around a single watchtower, the first sight of Millbank Penitentiary has been responsible for the spontaneous soiling of many a man's trousers.

The hour is upon them and the open cart bearing the Fowlers, Willa, and Jonesy, approaches 'the tench' in fits and starts. In the wake of the pandemonium at Newgate to transport the now notorious passengers, a mistake was made and the new Black Maria police van departed without them. Heads will roll, but in the meantime, the prisoners are escorted through the London streets with as much visibility as those who at one time were paraded to Tyburn.

They sit on boxes in the crude wagon, cuffed, but without an officer. At the same hour that the wagon nears Millbank, from the outer gates a queue of convicts marches by. Chained together in groups of ten, they shuffle down to the riverside where embarkation awaits them.

Rather than cast their eyes at the place of suffering that lies before them, the Fowlers crane their necks to soak up the last view of freedom behind them. It is low tide, and an old bargee has run his boats aground, making them the first to form a plank leading to the steam tug that will take the shackled queue of prisoners to the ship. Old Dan has an agreement that allows him this scheme. This morning, as the fog lifts in that religious way it is wont to do, his attention strays from the shackled men and falls upon the ginger-haired prisoner in the wagon who wholly distracts him. He waves at Clovis and puckers, gives the air a big kiss, grabs his crotch, and then laughs at her. Old Dan pollutes her last view of the river before the wagon jerks away.

The feeling of a dead zone persists. A stagnant moat surrounds the building, most likely meant to enforce its fortress-like position. An unfriendly blanket of low cloud covers the cobblestones, rumoured to protect the bones stacked underneath in one of the pits of the Great Plague. Things do manage to grow in the fevered, waterlogged earth, vegetables in the prison garden and such, but they are seeded adjacent to Millbank's own recently buried dead.

During her short stay in Newgate, Clovis gathered information on how to become a model prisoner, if events should turn this way. Her concern is not a question of survival, for that is a given now, her concern is rather, how to survive well. 'Don't cry over your hair,' she was told. 'Matrons sort out the weak from the strong when they shear women and men like sheep.' Good to know. 'Don't play mad – they is clever, those warders is. They is seen too many and knows those that is false.' Clovis will use that, too.

Then Clovis worked up her saliva and in a demonstrative gesture she swallowed her fear. And, when the fright of what was to become of her, of them, had been digested and put forever to rest, she faced the new possibility that had slipped into their lives. The delicious, quicksilver gift, that seems entirely impossible, but nevertheless stares her in the face. It is the thing that she will fiercely contemplate during her days and nights at Millbank – her immortality.

As the cart wobbles along, Jonesy studies Clovis, perhaps for the last time before they are all gobbled up by the giant starfish. He wonders why her eyes dance and glitter. He is confused that she is not at all panicked, unlike Willa, whose fingers have not stopped tapping against her cuffs. Or why, he asks, is his mistress not comatose with fear and bewilderment like her husband? And what is wrong with her that she, who is supposedly a talent for the magnetism, cannot see the ghost of his ancestors who sit beside him and float above his head? After all, he, Willa and Master Fowler, should all be dead. Perhaps he *is* actually dead, he thinks, and the messengers are taking him to the god of walls and moats for his preliminary hearing. This seems to be most likely, because in front of them a lifeless moat circles the unspeakably intimidating turrets. Jonesy is certain he is destined for the tenth court of hell for immediate rebirth.

Clovis, aware that Jonesy watches her, tries to stand but cannot keep her balance without the use of her hands and is thrown back. She recovers and summons his attention.

'Remember what I told you,' she says.

Last night, when they were still on the vile plot of Newgate land, she sat with each of them privately, two chairs, one facing the other. First, she made solid eye contact, which drew upon their exhaustion and made them drowsy so quickly that she was taken aback. She held their hands until they tingled and grew warm. The faces and figures of those around them dissolved until they vanished completely and the only face that was in their consciousness was hers.

'Bow your head a bit,' she instructed each of them.

When their chins rested calmly on their chests, she leaned into them, so close they could sense her beating heart and the light lift of her breasts as she breathed. She put her lips to their ears and, one by one, she whispered until the only thing in the world they desired was what she desired. She comforted them with the assurance that they would be together, that she would make it so. The years coming would seem like minutes flying by. They have all the time in the world. She whispered, until she too believed every word she said.

'Something has happened to us. It is a great secret that belongs only to the four of us. You must never tell anyone.'

And to her husband she said, 'If anyone asks why you still live, say that you do not know, it surely must be a miracle. When you come back to your senses from your ordeal, and when you are no longer disoriented, you must spend your time thinking of a way to earn a great deal of money. We will need it in the coming years. This time, Finn, within the law.'

She told them that they must be seen to turn to God. Their time at Millbank will include suffocating religious tutoring and they must bear it and play to it. After a few more instructions, specific to each of them, she awakened them and they remarked that somehow they felt better, and that their world was not ending as they previously thought, but only just now beginning.

Now they are arrived at the grand experiment atop the marshlands of Pimlico, where the weeds strangle the yellow-tinged building and its walls strangle hopes.

It is a prison of contradictions: clean, yet so rank with damp that filthy diseases race through the bodies of its convicts. The use of separate cells as punishment drives prisoners to seek company with the force of a magnet, often with violence; and the rule of strict silence is a mocking sort of entertainment, given that the ventilation system allows sound to travel so easily. Convicts will always find the ways and means to communicate.

The prisoners of Millbank are prohibited any news of the world outside. Visits with family members are carefully monitored. Despite this, the pentagons are full of sharp chatter when the news of the recent arrivals seeps into the prison's population.

The Fowlers and their servants are received into the prison and led through corridors into the governor's room where he sits at his large desk. They take their positions behind the rope, placed as it is across the room to serve as a barrier. The room is cast in almost complete darkness; a dim coating of light crawls through the double set of bars on the single window.

The governor whips out a large handkerchief and sprinkles it with a strong-smelling vinegar solution. The prisoners have the odour of Newgate upon them still. Normally they would have first been sent to the medical officer in the receiving ward to bathe, however, the governor senses the onset of one of his blinding headaches and must take to a darkened room before he passes out from nausea. This last task regarding these wretched thieves must be accomplished before he gives himself over to the laudanum.

The governor peers down at the neat pile of papers on his desk. The forefinger of one hand rests against his throbbing temple.

'Your sentence of transportation has been commuted. The length of your sentence is reduced from twelve years to nine.'

He is met with silence and the top of their heads, as the new inmates look down at their feet.

The governor remains glued to his papers, but he is well aware that this news that greets his famous prisoners has hit them in a powerful way. His eyes lift slightly to catch the trembling legs and skirts of . . . hmm . . . three of the four who foul his room. The skirts of another remain quiet. With his finger still pressed to his temple he raises his head an excruciating inch. For a blessed moment the pain lessens as the vision of Clovis Fowler appears. God help him, he feels the spur of an erection.

'Take them,' he says abruptly.

The prisoners are ushered to reception.

CHAPTER THIRTY-THREE

When a woman is very bad at Millbank, she is broken. She will not be reasoned with. When she begins to deteriorate it happens quickly and she often becomes outrageously violent. The matrons of Millbank are under instruction to identify those who would do war with them in the female pentagon. So well trained are they in confronting the female and her evil ways that they are unsettled when Clovis Fowler meets none of those expectations. When she was stripped naked Clovis bore her humiliation very well indeed. She projected just the right degree of shyness and a touch of humility but also, she subtly positioned her body in such a way as to enhance the curve of her back, and slowly turned a shapely thigh. By the end of her bath, and after they had spread the crack of her buttocks, she gained her first admirers amongst the hardened matrons.

When they cut her hair the moment of truth arrived. This was often the female inmates' breaking point; the harsh sawing sound of dull scissors followed by clumps of their femininity falling to the floor. Yet Clovis sits patiently, careful not to show defiance, nor anger, yet helplessness is absent in her. There is nothing of her behaviour to criticize.

She closes her eyes while her head is jerked right and left and thinks of the cloak of protection she has been given. With every passing moment she becomes more certain that like Finn, Willa and Jonesy, she too has been given the ability to live when others would surely die. When the last snip of the scissors leaves her hair short and uneven, she knows within the deepest part of her that the reason for this lies with the boy, Rafe. The exuberance given to his protection, and the care and intensity of it, concerns the dark magic he must surely possess. He is Icelandic, and therefore, it is feasible that its supernatural hand has touched him – she can think of no other reason.

The matron who gives Clovis her prison cap remarks later to the chief matron that she had never before witnessed the kind of strange, disturbing smile she received from prisoner 1089 after being shorn. 'It were of the other world, mistress.'

Another matron, while bent down gathering their filthy clothes, was unaware that Clovis noticed the moment her mourning necklace fell from under her jacket and dangled for a few seconds until she replaced it. Before the matron left to take the clothes to the laundry, Clovis stopped her.

'Excuse me, may I speak?'

'What is it?'

'I am sorry for your loss,' Clovis says, in a most meaningful and sympathetic manner.

'But how ... how did you know?'

Clovis shrugs and lowers her head in modesty. 'They say I have ... I am too embarrassed to say, matron.'

'The gift?' Matron's eyes bulge.

'I would never claim ... No, I would never even think it.'

The matron, quite in the dark as to the new prisoner's real character, and quite awed by her, vows to pardon all her offences should she commit any under her guard.

There is a clandestine agreement at Millbank Penitentiary in which all are complicit. There are many reasons to secrete the Fowlers away from the regular wards and onto B Ward, Pentagon No. 4. Not the least of these is the bothersome fact of their fame. It is, however, something entirely more bewitching that instigates their complete seclusion.

It begins their first night. In each cell a small, barred window set high in the wall looks out onto the pentagon yards. At dusk a warder arrives with a lamp to light the small gas jets in each cell. When the chimes in the clock tower of Westminster Palace fill the quiet, the lights of the Millbank cells adopt the semblance of the sacred in the inky night.

In their separate cells, each of the four new prisoners takes down the wooden plank that stands against the wall and secures it on the raised wooden platform extending across the length of the cell. Upon it they place a hard mattress that forms their bed, and then a coarse linen sheet. There are no pillows.

Whether the prisoner is at work or sleep, the warders and matrons have full view of them in their cells through a slit in the wall alongside the door. In Pentagon No. 2 Jonesy hears heavy boots approaching and catches a glimpse of the shiny key box that protrudes from the warder's hip. The warder pauses in front of his cell. He is a green one from the countryside, new to London, and this is his first encounter with a Chinaman. He lingers at the door to observe Jonesy sitting on the edge of his bed with his head in his hands. The warder has a perfect view of the shaved portion of the prisoner's head, just above his temples, which forms the traditional style of his people. Jonesy's braid was hacked off upon arrival with a swift snip of the prison's scissors, leaving a mass of silky, black clumps. The gossip from the reception room is that he bore his shame well. The young warder, blond and pale, is curious. Jonesy lifts his head and resists the urge to call out to him that he feels light-headed.

Upstairs, in a different ward, Finn collapses on top of his messy half-made bed, dizzy from the spinning room. When his warder looks through the slit he is of course curious, as anyone would be to see a Lazarus in person, but he jumps back. Struck by the vision of Finn's neck fully displayed, bruised in an array of colours, the warder cannot recall anything quite as ugly, and he has seen ugly in his career. He moves on without disturbing him. A reprimand for his untidy bed can be delayed until tomorrow.

In the women's pentagon, Clovis begins to feel unsteady as she smooths the rough blanket. Certain it stems from her first encounter with the evening gruel, she begins to undress. Willa, too, suffers from a wave of nausea in her cell as small beads of perspiration form a line across her upper lip.

From a room in the building at the centre of the six pentagons, situated like the hub of a wheel, the governor, along with any other staff allowed, is able to survey the entire prison. Each cell can be monitored at any time of day or night. One of the officers claims it is similar to peering into an absurd doll's house, looking down into the various rooms, one thousand and thirty of them, from a tall tower.

Four cells, four new prisoners, all of the same household, occupy different wards on their first night at Millbank. A chief officer will recall that on this night, he noticed nothing unusual before the lights were extinguished.

The next morning at six o'clock, the bell that is loud enough to wake all of Pimlico and Westminster sounds for the prisoners to rise. Finn, Jonesy, Clovis and Willa stay fast asleep.

'Oh no you don't!' shouts the warder. 'This is no way to begin your time with me.' He bends down to yell into Finn's ear. 'Get your arse up, 1090.'

Nothing. No response at all.

Another officer on the floor below, not the pale blond, but a brawny, older man, throws open the doors, grabs Jonesy's signal stick and pokes him with it.

'1091!' The warder yells like a siren. 'Up, up, I say!'

Jonesy remains as motionless as a corpse.

In the female pentagon, the iron gate of Clovis's cell stands wide open, as does the wooden door. The matrons of her ward stand in a gaggle around her bed.

'What should we do?' says one.

'Send for the doctor.' The chief matron, usually annoyed and quick to throw punishment, is clearly concerned. The prisoner is not dead, but does not respond to a pinch, a flick of cold water, or a slap in the face.

On the floor above, in Ward C, a young matron new to Millbank shakes Willa in a violent panic, worried that the girl has died during the night.

Two weeks pass. Millbank pulses with rumour. The inmates whisper that the Fowlers and their servants have been poisoned. The warders and matrons gossip from ward to ward, from pentagon to pentagon, until there are so many different versions of what befell the sleeping prisoners that the entire Millbank population is perched on a nervous, excited edge. The power of the stories breaks the monotony of their days and nights. Wagers are placed on whether they will awaken or die.

On the fifteenth day, Clovis opens her eyes to find herself in a large room. Her gaze fixes on blue, checked curtains and she wonders why her windows are covered with such a hideous pattern. She is so hungry that she could eat her own cooking, which is an affirmation of her voraciousness. She turns her head. Oh . . . This is not my home, not my bedroom. Finn looks dead in the next bed. She rises to her elbows. There is Willa further down, and on the fourth bed, Jonesy still sleeps.

The infirmary warder, who has the reputation for being a savage, jumps up from his chair and knocks it over, making an awful racket. He calls out with frightened, bulging eyes.

'Doctor! Doctor! She wakes. They are all waking.' He scurries around not knowing what to do, and then runs into the next room, 'I say! Doctor, come quick.'

The doctor approaches them warily and must make an effort to steady his hands when he examines them. He probes, glares into their nostrils and throats, and tests their reflexes. Finding them remarkably well, he stands back from their beds quite astounded.

'I feel giddy with hunger,' Clovis says.

'Yes, yes, please, doctor,' the others chime in.

They are fed a tremendous amount of bread and are given several cups of hot cocoa.

'Might we be allowed a cup of tea?' Clovis asks.

'No,' the warder says, hatefully. 'You've been dead to the world for two weeks. You've done no work, no cleaning, sleeping like innocent babes while the rest of the inmates here—'

'That's enough. Fetch them tea. And be quick about it,' the doctor orders him.

'What?' Finn asks, dumbfounded. 'Two weeks?'

'What is wrong with us?' Willa throws off her blanket and surveys her body, as if the answers might be written upon her limbs.

Jonesy, not fully awake, wonders if this then is the preliminary hearing of his death, and if so, where is Cheng Huang, the god who will hear his case. And who is this man probing his nostril with a cold instrument? He wonders, too, if he has any chance whatsoever of entering one of the Buddhist paradises. No, he thinks, probably not. He feels wayward strands of hair in his eyes and remembers – he has no queue and its absence is considered non-compliance. If he is not currently dead, the gods will execute him for treason for his missing queue. He hears the voices of the English. There are no English in paradise. He sits up and stares at the white men and women who surround him. Jonesy promptly falls back onto the bed.

A Millbank prisoner never knows how long their stay will be and are given no warning until they hear the words, 'collect your letters' – at which moment they will be sent on to a probationary prison to complete their sentence. But the Fowler group will not be sent on. Not to Brixton, not to a hulk, nor any other prison. These four are quarantined.

They are awake only a few hours before they are moved to one of the special wards near the infirmary in Pentagon No. 4. Clovis and Willa occupy three cells that have been fitted together to form a large, sleeping room, and a workroom, normally reserved for special cases. Finn and Jonesy are relegated the same arrangement down the corridor.

On that first night in the new cells, at a quarter to ten, when all lights are out, the flame from a large lamp glows through the slit in Clovis's door. The keys are thrust in the lock and suddenly the chief matron stands at the door.

'Cover yourselves. The governor comes with the doctor.'

Clovis throws her blanket over her shoulders and Willa reaches for her prison dress.

'Leave us.' The governor is brusque to the matron. 'Doctor Lemmings, proceed, please.'

The doctor clears his throat and hesitates.

'Out with it, sir.' The governor softens a notch.

'You, all of you, may be suffering from a sleeping sickness . . .' the doctor begins.

Clovis looks first at the doctor and then to the governor.

Willa taps her temples. Three taps, a pause, three more. Repeat.

'During the time you were asleep, we scoured your paperwork for whom we should notify in the event of your deaths. The same name appeared for each of you – an apothecary on the Commercial Road, Mr Owen Mockett,' the doctor continues. 'Odd, but nevertheless, it has proven to be a wise choice. He has presented me with a remedy of sorts, and a better understanding of what you can expect of your symptoms.'

'Do get on with it, Dr Lemmings,' the governor snaps.

'Yes, well . . .' The doctor removes two glass phials from his pocket. 'Mr Mockett tells me that you are now under strict instructions from a doctor, a Mr Benedikt. You must take two drops and only two drops upon waking from any prolonged sleep you may experience. He was most adamant about this. The phials are made specifically to administer one drop at a time.'

All of Clovis's senses and every fibre of her being are tuned to the doctor and the phials. At the mention of Mockett and Benedikt, she is on the edge of losing her composure. 'Doctor' Benedikt, indeed.

'Mr Benedikt informed Mr Mockett that this sleeping sickness will most likely occur again this year in roughly six months' time.'

Clovis's thoughts are spinning, trying to arrange themselves into coherent compartments.

'This is most unusual, and I am forced to allow for your special needs for one reason only, otherwise I would have you removed from here,' the governor says. 'This Mr Mockett cannot tell us if your condition is contagious.'

Willa rocks back and forth, back and forth. Clovis is not allowed to touch her. She is in no position to go against the governor, but she is weary of this man's seething anger.

'Sir, this is quite a shock. May I comfort her?' she asks smoothly.

The governor does not acknowledge her. He cannot look at her without becoming aroused. She does not press.

The doctor places two phials on the table and edges ever closer to the cell door – as if he is fearful.

'Two drops. Tomorrow we will discuss this further and I will collect the phials. They will be in my charge. And now we go to Fowler and the young Chinaman.' Dr Lemmings is anxious to leave.

Clovis notices he does not call them by their numbers. The sleeping sickness has frightened a spark of humanity from him.

The governor stands at the door with his back to Clovis. He looks ahead into the dark corridor where the doctor waits for him and turns his head ever so slightly, yet not enough that Clovis might see his face.

'I shall consider leniency and perhaps your regular clothing.' He pauses. 'You have ... awakened sympathies.'

She fully understands his meaning, and though her capacity for astonishment is currently low, she is surprised he shows himself so quickly. A dark horse, this man.

'Thank you, Governor, sir.' She ignores that she is wrapped in an ugly blanket, that her hair no longer falls to her shoulders and her nails need cleaning. 'I would be grateful, sir ...'

'The girl ... you may console her if you wish.'

'I do, sir, thank you a second time.'

His dark coat-tail disappears down the corridor.

One by one, the rules of Millbank are broken, all of them.

Clovis leads Willa over to the bed, which is noticeably sturdier in this cell and the mattress is stuffed with plenty of coir. She folds the blankets around Willa and kneels beside her. The flagstones are whiter but still as cold as a glacier, so she wraps the remaining blanket around her own knees and legs. She holds the phial to Willa's mouth. 'Take it.' Willa parts her lips. Two drops touch her tongue.

Clovis leans in closer to Willa's ear and begins the whispering cure. The words seem kind at first, spoken with warmth and in a soothing cadence. Willa fights to stay awake, terrified to ever give over to sleep again. Her mistress's voice persists, coaxing, calming. Just as Willa's head rolls to the side and her eyelids are too heavy to open, Clovis adjusts her tone. She demands obedience and loyalty and plants seeds of fear of the consequences should Willa ever wish to stray from her.

It is cold. She hears the governor and the doctor leave Finn's cell, but she remains on the floor, her knees cuddled up against her body. Her thoughts whirl. She's beginning to feel good again. There is a massive mountain of information to consider: Mockett, Benedikt, the sleep and what it means. She thinks of the governor and how she will make him her path to remaining sane in this god forsaken place. She considers how to use Finn, Willa and Jonesy – the people she is bound to in their long lives ahead. And the boy. It always comes back to the boy. A powerful idea brews.

CHAPTER THIRTY-FOUR

'Mr Moonlight' presents the knife to Jonesy. The pale, blond warder pauses for a fraction when their fingers meet on the handle. The moment is so quick, yet so electric that this time Jonesy is certain it is intentional. He feels sick with anticipation.

In the months that have worn on, each time Mr Moonlight passed his cell Jonesy's heart quickened. At first he was concerned that his master could in some way sense that his body became alert to Mr Moonlight's particularly light footfall. Or, did Master notice how quickly he surged to the gate when Mr Moonlight was on rounds, hoping to catch the smell of him.

Their work is carving, and the evidence of it spills out onto the floor in dusty piles. They shape the wooden handles for the prison's hairbrushes into monotonous squares. The privilege of working with a knife is great and they are constantly reminded how fortunate they are by the chief warden who frequently inspects their work. Jonesy is so accomplished and quick at it that he is promised more intricate work in the months to come.

Jonesy's days run together like a long dragon divorced from his auspicious powers, constantly searching to regain his strength, searching for the flaming pearl of spiritual energy and immortality. Jonesy learned of the dragons from the only honourable person in his family, his grandmother. She was a toothless old woman with a crooked back that prevented her from walking in a straight line. The smell of fish emanated from her pores as she regaled him with stories of the Eight Immortals.

She plaited his hair with her gnarled fingers while her peasant voice spun images of *Lan Caihe.*

'She, or he,' his grandmother said coyly. 'Some say a man; some say a woman. Eh.' She shrugged. 'Many say both. Lan Caihe don't care which one. His, or her, age is not known. Lan Caihe is wandering eccentric. She, or he, walks with one shoe on, one shoe off, in long blue gown. Lan carries basket of flowers of the divine. Life or death, they make no change for him, or her. Lan Caihe is least important of the Eight Immortals, but is most content.'

'To be peaceful within oneself, Yun, she called him by the name his no-good mother gave him, is the flaming pearl.' She poked him. 'Yes? You understand?'

He had been only four at the time and no, he did not understand the contradictions of Lan Caihe. He understood noodles and broth, fried chicken-feet and rice.

Jonesy stacks the brushes into the baskets to ready them for collection. *To be at peace within oneself.* Never was he at more odds with the world. Never more at war within himself than in this moment.

At six o'clock the gas flame has burned for two hours on this winter evening. The cell is chilly, and damp seeps through the whitewashed walls. Prisoners are becoming ill with diseases of the wet, but not him, not his mistress and master, and Willa is in perfect health, too. Though perhaps, he thinks, not in her mind.

Jonesy is lost in his musings, bending over the stacks of brushes and does not notice the pale warder standing at his cell door.

'1091.'

'Sir.' Jonesy bolts upright and turns to face Mr Moonlight.

'Fetch one of those baskets and come with me.'

Jonesy lifts the heaving basket filled with brushes and follows Mr Moonlight down the corridor.

Finn is occupied with sweeping and clearing away the day's mess. He pauses for a moment, places his hand to his throat and lightly massages the ring where the noose strangled him. He pushes the broom over to the door and peers down the dim hallway. The gas jets spit flames that swallow Jonesy's shadow.

Mr Moonlight strides slowly to a cell at the centre of the ward that has been converted to a storeroom to accommodate extra space for the infirmary's necessaries. He turns and motions for Jonesy to follow him into the cell.

'Place the basket here, 1091,' he says rather loudly, as if he wishes all to hear.

Jonesy does as he is told.

'Now to fetch another.'

The warder conducts a pattern of fetch, carry and deliver. He says or does nothing untoward, yet he never takes his eyes off Jonesy. This would be normal behaviour of any warder, Jonesy thinks, if not for the particular way the warder's gaze follows him. They do not speak or vary the ritual.

The warder also asks Finn to carry the baskets occasionally and so establishes such normality along the corridor that no one notices anything unusual when Mr Moonlight and Jonesy are occupied in the storeroom for a few minutes longer than usual.

It is the night before Christmas Eve. Jonesy follows the warder to the storeroom as he normally does and places the basket in the corner, to be collected in the morning. As he turns to go, Mr Moonlight grabs Jonesy's wrist, holding him back. He places his finger to his lips, signalling Jonesy to be silent. Then he closes the cell door leaving it unlocked.

Jonesy feels his knees weakening in a terrifying moment of uncertainty. The two are surrounded by rows of sheets, towels, pieces of soap and the finished wooden brushes that Jonesy has carved. The warder leans against a shelf of bath bricks, grabs Jonesy's wrist and pulls him closer. Jonesy is alarmed. What if he is contagious? If the sleeping sickness should pass on to the warder?

Mr Moonlight's finger is neither soft nor rough as it traces Jonesy's lips, which are parted and full of the warm breath of expectancy. His grandmother once told him that his mouth is shaped like a large plum, so ripe and swollen that it would one day fill a person with a great desire to bite it.

Jonesy wants to touch the man's face in return and reaches to stroke his pale skin, but Mr Moonlight's arm swiftly swats his hand away. 'No,' he says forcefully, with a silent frown. Just as quickly, he unbuttons his uniform trousers and guides Jonesy's hand down to his erection.

Mr Moonlight keeps his eyes trained on the door; the danger is both exciting and terrifying. They not only break the rules – they break the law.

He holds Jonesy's head with both of his hands and pushes him down to his knees. He sticks two fingers in Jonesy's mouth and when they're wet, he traces Jonesy's lips again with his own spit before he prises Jonesy's mouth open.

A different blond man, the sailor from Limehouse, taught Jonesy how to suck and play, and he is only getting started when the warder thrusts, thrusts once more, and is spent.

They are in the corridor again. Only a few minutes have passed.

The following week, with the baskets of handles sitting in the corner, and his mouth achingly open, he pleasures Mr Moonlight in silence. The week after is the same, and from then on, once a week, on randomly chosen days, Jonesy can expect to be at the service of a callous young man whose capacity for excitement is thankfully short.

Today, Jonesy sands the wooden brush handles to the rhythm of his master's regrets, which Finn constantly proclaims. While his master speaks on and on, Jonesy considers the differences between whoredom and freedom. He knows enough about the former through his father's pitiful rendition of a brothel. So in his limited experience he concludes that Mr Moonlight most definitely treats him like a whore; not once has the man offered anything in return. This, his grandmother would say, is dog treatment. Jonesy concludes, too, that he will surely lose more than his freedom if he is caught. Punishment sees him dead at the end of a rope.

Jonesy stops carving, his knife suspended mid-air. On my ancestors. I forgot. I cannot die, *he thinks.* He glances at the marks on his master's neck. London will forget one miracle, but not two. Another man dangling from a rope, a sod at that, an invert . . . There. I've said it. Even if only to myself. The weight of being found out is more frightening than death itself.

That night in the storeroom, once a retreat of intrigue where he had hoped that Mr Moonlight would touch his face and kiss his mouth, the shelves and crude necessities of prison life oppress him. Before he places the basket in the corner, Mr Moonlight's buttons are already unfastened and the bulge in his flannel throbs warm when Jonesy's hand is forced. He takes his hand away and shakes his head. The warder looks confused for a moment, then he angrily tries to force Jonesy down to his knees. When Jonesy plants his feet and resists, Mr Moonight strikes him. He uses the back of his hand, the way Jonesy's father used to do. The pain to the side of his face is not as frightening as the look of disgust in the warder's eyes.

It is time they leave, or their absence will be noticed.

'Jonesy. What the hell?' Finn's blood boils when he sees the imprint of the warder's hand on his face.

'Please. I beg you. Say nothing.'

Five more times Jonesy is subjected to Mr Moonlight's violent hand, until the day the warder disappears. It is said that he took a position at another prison, but the liars of Millbank do love to circulate rumours. He was quietly banned from prison work.

The governor is everywhere.

CHAPTER THIRTY-FIVE

'Your visitor has arrived. Follow me.'

Clovis moistens and bites her lips, the only act of vanity she allows the matron to witness. Her dress, her own blue dress is being brushed at present, which leaves her only the prison dress she first wore two years ago.

Millbank is a labyrinth of passages and corridors so complex that the warders and matrons loathe admitting they frequently take a wrong turn and are easily lost. The staircases are steep and unlit. When Clovis met Mockett in the small square visitors' house in one of the pentagons a year ago, she memorized the turns and counted the steps in the dizzying circular shafts of cells.

It was a harsh moment, facing him behind two sets of bars and wire mesh netting. A matron and an officer sat with them, which made for stilted, but enlightening conversation. She discovered that Nora Mockett is unchanged, and that Benedikt supplies Mockett's phials.

On that day, Clovis knew that whatever condition they have, curse or blessing, was born the night of the baby's fever. This thought presses upon her mind today as she is led into the visiting house.

There are two doors, one on each side of the room. Clovis enters on one side and waits for her visitor to walk through the opposite door. A principal warder takes his seat between the two iron gratings.

The room is bare and so completely unadorned that she is at the end of her patience when the heavy door creaks open. The warder and prisoner 1089 rise when Constance Fitzgerald enters the visiting house.

She is taller than Clovis remembers. Or it may be the hat – the grace of a beautiful hat has long been absent from her cloistered view. Its pale, blue silk looks almost obscene in this place, like furs and diamonds in a rookery. Clovis notes the fashion has changed; the waist is lower. All the comforts she forfeits come rushing at her now in a single rustle of the woman's exquisitely made dress. The sound of Mrs Fitzgerald's skirts as they settle in the visitor's chair drive her into a brief moment of madness. Clovis rises taller in her chair and raises her chin a touch higher.

Mrs Fowler, Constance surmises, appears amazingly well, considering. She had expected someone paler, more emaciated, to sit before her, but here she finds only a different version of Clovis Fowler, as if the woman were an actress now playing the role of a peasant. But now, she must focus on her task. She has been instructed to lie, to lie like a woman pleading for her life when she knows she is guilty and faces the gallows. Her lies must be cast in scents of truth to appease Mrs Fowler. She draws a deep breath from the less than fresh air.

'Good afternoon, Mrs Fowler.'

'Good of you to come, Mrs Fitzgerald. I had hoped that you would have my son with you. I have longed to see him.'

'I feel sure you will understand that this is no place for a young boy who has a touch of a cold.'

'Oh? I am sorry to hear it. Does he have a fever, Mrs Fitzgerald?'

There it is.

'No. No fever, just a slight cough.'

'Has he ever had a fever?'

There it is again.

'No, no, he has not. He enjoys very good health. We are near the fresh air of the Regent's Park now, as you know.'

'Yes, Mr Mockett informed me of your relocation. I was disappointed. I thought that I would have heard from you first.'

'And I thought I would have heard news of your freedom. The last we spoke, two years ago, you were in the midst of a misunderstanding, as you put it, not a conviction.'

Clovis hesitates, then she leans forward in her chair the way she does when she whispers to Willa and commands her to sleep. Lowering her voice and softening her gaze, she speaks slowly through the wirework.

'Tell me, Mrs Fitzgerald, does my son sleep well?'

'Very well, indeed.' Constance answers with an exact tone and in perfect tempo.

Clovis brings her chair a little closer with a glance at the warder.

'And you and your sister?' She lowers her voice a notch further. 'Do you both sleep well?'

'We sleep well, Mrs Fowler.'

'No irregularities then?'

'None.'

Her usual hypnotic voice having no effect, Clovis finds irritation rising in a flush on her neck. She tries a different approach, quietly forceful.

'Mrs Fitzgerald, I expect to see my son next year when you visit again.'

'Of course, Mrs Fowler, if he is willing.'

'A three-year-old does not know his own will.'

'Oh I disagree, Mrs Fowler. Rafe knows his own will even now.'

'He is my son, Mrs Fitzgerald.'

'Indeed. And my sister and I look after him very well. You've no need to worry. Is there anything else?'

Clovis glances at the warder. He nods. There are a few minutes remaining.

'Would you be kind enough to write to me of any changes in his sleeping patterns? Or if he should suddenly be ill with a fever?'

'As you wish. Would you like to be informed if he is ill with anything other than a fever?'

Clovis searches for the truth behind her visitor's question. Is this woman playing some sort of a game with her? Their eyes lock as she considers her reply. It is hard to discern if Mrs Fitzgerald has aged these past two years. Being so well cosseted all her life she looks fresher than most women her age. Mrs Fitzgerald's face is full and remarkably unlined, her hair shines and her eyes are clear and lively. It could be that her new home situated far from industry and the river brings her robust health. Today, Mrs Fitzgerald reveals nothing of miracles or strange occurrences. She's a hard one, she is. This visit is wasted and I am quickly falling into a foul mood, thinks Clovis, but she replies with cool politeness.

'Yes, of course. I would be grateful to receive your letters and visits, and any news of my son is always appreciated.'

Constance rises, nods to Clovis, and prepares to depart the ghastly place.

'Mrs Fitzgerald.'

Constance pauses.

'I hope you and your sister continue to sleep well.'

'And you, Mrs Fowler.'

Constance leaves through the door designated for visitors and breathes a huge sigh once it is closed and the prisoner is behind her. She is led through the inner gate by an assistant warder, then to the gravelled outer yard, and finally to her great relief, to the carriage that awaits her.

'I have never been happier to see you, Verity.'

'Was it awful? Were you convincing?'

'I do not know. I believe so. But, sister, she has been in that place of hell for two years and has not changed. Not at all.'

'Saints preserve us.'

As soon as Constance Fitzgerald is out of her sight Clovis kicks the iron bars.

'Calm down there, 1089,' the warder warns her.

She throws him a fuming glance. He leads her to the waiting matron who is in no mood herself for privileged prisoners and hurriedly escorts her back to her cell.

'There you are, mistress. How was your visit, then?' Willa looks up from her sewing.

Clovis waits until the fat matron has waddled away before she turns on Willa.

'Shut up. Do not say another word to me today.' She picks up her hairbrush and throws it at Willa. The handle cracks on the girl's skull and she cries out.

'Be quiet, or that onion-breath matron will have you for dinner.' Clovis retrieves the brush from the floor and places it back on the shelving, recovering calm. 'I should not have thrown it. It was wrong of me. It is this place.'

Willa chooses a long strand from a cord of threads that hangs around her neck. Squinting, she ties a knot, then changes the thread in her needle.

'Perhaps you could speak to the governor again, mistress? You are much calmer after you receive his good advice.'

'Why, Willa. You are a very clever, girl. The governor's wisdom is exactly what I need tonight.'

Clovis fits the red-tipped end of the wooden wand through the inspection hole, signalling that she would like to speak to the matron. It is not the heavy-footed woman who comes, but the older spinster matron who prefers night duty.

The governor comes right away.

'Ah. Prisoner 1089. What troubles you that you would take me from my visits on the other wards?'

'Sir. I apologize for my impudence. I . . . I seem to be on the edge of some great awakening, a stirring, if you will, sir, that I would like to discuss with you.'

Willa is quite in awe of her mistress, that as bold as she has known her to be, she would speak to the governor so freely.

'Indeed? Then you must come to me at once, 1089. Matron, bring this prisoner to my room in one half hour.'

It had begun over a year ago. Clovis chose her moment to approach him when he could not conceal that he suffered from a violent pain in his head. She made some pretence to see him privately when he attended their cell on one of his regular visits.

The curtain in the governor's room was drawn that day, a clear sign that he was ill. His writing desk was strewn with papers, the General Order Book was left open to a page, figures scrawled in the margins, and a cup and saucer thick with brown stains teetered on the edge of a pile of journals.

Clovis stood on a worn spot on a small, but expensive carpet. The governor did not bother with the rope of separation. His eyes followed the lines of her body from the tips of her prison boots to her neck until he reached her face.

He was distracted by the curves that refused to be hidden under her drab skirts and homely apron. Two urges coursed through him; a desire to point a revolver to the pain that pierced his head, and to relieve his untameable lust.

'Please sir, may I speak freely?'

'Yes.' He whispered.

'I know a technique that will help your distress . . . your headache.'

'Go on.'

'I will need cold water, a sponge, and a clean strip of cloth.'

He rang a bell which summoned a mouse of an assistant warder who regularly attends his needs. In quick measure, the items were placed on the writing desk. Clovis positioned a chair to face the governor. He watched her, wondering at her ease and her lack of intimidation.

She placed another chair by the writing desk and arranged the two to face each other.

'Would you please sit here?'

He rose, gave his jacket a tug, and then did as she asked. Clovis wet the sponge, wrung it, and gently placed it on the governor's forehead.

He closed his eyes. The damp coolness felt unimaginably refreshing. She removed the sponge and sat in the chair opposite him.

'Sir, may I have your permission to touch you to perform the New Science.'

He nodded.

Clovis placed her hands on his knees and drew them closer together. She spread her legs and placed his between hers so that he sat cradled by her thighs. He winced with pleasure. Then she leaned forward until he was enveloped in her warmth. She raised her hands above his head, her breasts so near him that she pulled back slightly. Just shy of touch, she made several passes over his head. She leaned back, paused, and then began again so that he felt a pattern of her energy. Her body plunged in towards him and then she receded, and the heat above his head came and went as over and over again she tirelessly gave him her attention.

Clovis monitored the changes in his face: his fluttering lids, a raised brow, his twitching mouth.

'Where is your pain now, sir?'

The pain had moved from his temples to the back of his head. He felt it transfer again to possess his shoulders until, after a few minutes more, it passed completely out of his body. He described these sensations in a voice absent of anger and the terse manner to which she was accustomed. He forgot himself entirely and spoke like a man.

She moved her chair back a few inches and stood, plucked his handkerchief from his pocket, and fanned his face to wake him.

The governor opened his eyes. His countenance had changed completely. Clovis fastened her gaze on his lips, which appeared much fuller. His face had relaxed and colour had returned to it. Dark lashes curled around his softened eyes that were previously slits of torment, and from the corner of one, a tear ran down.

'It often occurs; it is a release,' she offered in a whisper.

The pain was gone, yet he still struggled. Ever so slowly, he became sorely aware that Clovis perused him, following a trail from his mouth to his crotch. Her gaze moved up again to his mouth. She rose – he would remember her floating towards him – and before he could inhale again, her mouth met his and she kissed him in a way he had never before been kissed. She grasped his cock and he let out a groan.

Clovis replaced the chair giving him a moment to cover his wet trousers with his coat before he faced her. When men fall ill they have little power to conceal their desires.

'You will come again?' he asked. There was no demand, no insistence, no threat.

'Oh, yes. I shall come.'

Over the following months Clovis earned privileges for the four of them. They were so grateful that they did not question how. They relished and devoured even better food, more comfortable, warmer clothing, extra soap and candles, special books, and Clovis was given ointments to keep her skin soft, an entirely selfish privilege meted out by the governor.

Clovis considers these privileges a trifling, a pittance. She desires much more and tonight she begins her campaign.

It is during the supper hour that he summons her while the staff concentrates on monotonous tasks, and the prisoners fill their bellies with thick gruel, sweetened with treacle.

The governor has grown handsome. He does not know how changed he is, for when he peers into the looking-glass to trim his sideburns, it still captures the image of his sickness. He prepares for her as he would for a woman with a spotless reputation he would court. With a drop or two of unguent he coaxes a sheen into his hair. He recently purchased a new toothbrush and tooth powder, and keeps anise comfits in his pocket. He bites into one now.

The matron knocks and he buttons his coat to conceal his erection.

There the beauty stands, one hand clutching her Bible. He almost laughs but catches himself.

'Thank you, matron. Now, 1089, what is this about a revelation? Perhaps you should be speaking to the chaplain.'

The matron closes the door and clomps away to her supper.

Clovis puts her finger to her lips for silence and locks the door. The curtains are drawn. The governor sits in his leather chair. The scrolled arms are open-shaped, the seat deep.

Theirs have been rushed, frenetic couplings. She had allowed him his quick pleasure, but they are finished with that. Now she lingers, like smoke trapped in a room.

He has given her permission to let her hair grow again, provided she keeps her florid locks under her cap during the day. She removes it now. When her hair falls loose he catches the scent of rose water. Her ugly, prison dress buttons at the front, and he knows this is the reason she chose it tonight. His eyebrows lift when she deftly unbuttons it, unsure of what will happen next. He has never seen her naked. The petticoat, the stays, the chemise, in which she stands, are her own. As she peels off the layers, the linens and cottons form a cloth halo at her feet.

This creature in his room inches closer to him. Her breasts spill out of her stays and he thinks he may be close to death with the sight of her; surely his heart thumps out of his chest. Then she lifts her chemise and she is naked. She is more than perfect. He groans.

When he lurches forward, Clovis gently pushes him back into his chair and climbs on top of him. She guides his hands to her quim to stroke, and his head to her breasts to suck. She allows him in now and insists he moves slowly, and it is easy, she is wet, slippery. She clenches. When he is near to climax she reaches underneath him and massages his anus with her fingers. He gasps. But he does not miss a thrust. Just as she feels him tensing for the end, she slips a finger deep into his anus. His head falls back and he erupts with a shudder. She kisses his mouth to inhibit his cry.

Clovis, still wrapped around him, nestles her head near his and whispers. Her tongue rims his ear as she tells him what she wants and needs. He nods. God help him, she can have the keys to the whole, damned, stinking prison. Clovis Fowler can have anything she wants from him.

CHAPTER THIRTY-SIX

1837

In Camden Town the days hammer to the clamorous arms of industry that encroach upon Lawless House from all sides. The sisters need only to step out of the front door to feel the full force of the destruction lurking around the corner. Though the meadows and nursery gardens still border the canal's edge, Camden Town is the designated location of the terminus of the London and Birmingham Railway and the construction of its depot, which consumes the suburb.

The London Zoological Society overtakes more and more of their pretty little village. Several thousand people visit each day. A long parade of carriages waits ceremoniously to enter the gates, bringing astounding congestion on the Outer Circle.

In the haven of Lawless House the boy sits on the floor, a safe distance from the fireguard, where all around him lies Verity's collection of coloured glass spectacles. He is industrious and the proof is on his face. The pink tip of his tongue juts out of the corner of his mouth and his brows crease as he rubs the glass. The cloth, much larger than his hand, bunches up as he swishes to and fro 'cleaning' one pair after another. Later, when he is asleep, Verity and Constance will remove the smudges and straighten the wires he innocently twists and bends with his fierce little hands.

A long and lean five-year-old, Rafe's hair gleams in multiple shades of red; from fiery, striped with golden streaks, to the colour of dark orange burning coal. It falls with a faint wave just above his shoulders and he brushes it away from his face, annoyed that it interferes with his task. Verity offers him the stems of a pair of horn-rimmed spectacles.

'These need a good clean, Rafe.'

Absorbed now with arranging the spectacles to his liking, he scoots along the floor.

'Constance, what are you doing?' Verity asks.

Verity joins her sister, who stands in front of the elegant mirror hanging above the mantel. They are just tall enough to see the reflection of their faces, which stare back at them in perfect symmetry.

'I am sixty-eight years of age now, Verity. You are sixty-six. Is it possible that time has not touched our faces, not a single line, no fleshy jowl or drooping chin, these past five years?'

Verity tilts her head to the side.

'I cannot see a change, sister. But perhaps sharing the air with the trees and pastures has been kind to us?'

'I compare my face to Angela's. Their narrowboat passed by less than six months ago, and five years have noticeably aged her.'

'Angela!' Rafe repeats. Angela and the boats.'

'Yes, Rafe. That's right, clever boy.'

'And Marland and Captain Emil! They will promised a ride.'

'They *have* promised a ride. Not *will* promised.'

'They will have promised a ride!' Rafe announces.

'Theirs is a difficult life, Constance, always battling the elements. It is hardly a fair comparison.'

'It is not only that. Angela's back is rounding and she stoops a bit. Something is drained from her, and the captain as well. It is natural and I might not even notice, if it weren't for our situation.' She turns to her sister. 'Though I still do not believe it Verity, people are growing older around us.'

'It is the long sleep that unnerves me. When it occurs I fear one of us will not wake.'

'And yet we always do.'

Constance feels a tug on her skirts. Rafe stretches up his arms wishing to be held. She lifts him and swings him onto her hip.

'Let me see, let me see.' He reaches towards the mirror.

She lifts him higher and settles him on her waist so that he might see his reflection. He places his hand on her face while gazing into the mirror, using the reflection to guide his hands. He turns to Verity and traces the contours of her face as well. Then he looks into the mirror again as if he is trying to memorize their images.

'Auntie Connie and Auntie Very,' he says simply, studying their faces; he looks back and forth from the mirror to the breathing versions that hold him.

'Happy tears!' He catches Verity's tear and tastes it.

'Yes, Rafe, happy tears. Happy that you are with us.'

His face clouds with a frown. 'I want to be with you always,' he says to the mirror.

'You shall be, my darling,' Constance says.

'When will my mother take me away?' he asks.

'Not for a long while. You needn't worry about that right now. If that should happen, we will always be here, this will be your second home.'

'Do I look like my mother?'

'You have her colouring. She is very beautiful and you are very handsome,' Constance says.

'But do I look like her?'

'No, not really,' Verity admits.

'Verity!'

'Well. He does not and that is a simple fact. Only, as you say, the colouring. There is a faint resemblance.'

Constance studies him for a moment.

'Rafe, would you like to visit your mother?'

'No. I do not ever want to see her.'

'But she is your mother, Rafe. We have spoken of this before.'

'She must be very, very bad. I am punished for one day for throwing pebbles at the birds. She is punished for much longest.'

'Longer. Punished much longer.'

'Do not let her take me away, Auntie Very. Will you pray for me?'

'I pray for you every day, Rafe. Now, now, you are upsetting yourself. We do not know what the future brings, but there is no reason for you to worry.'

'I will not go.'

'Let's look at what you have made here, shall we?' Constance distracts him.

Verity's assorted spectacles are arranged on the floor in the shape of heart.

'Art,' Rafe says.

'It is beautiful.' Constance strokes his hair.

'Sacred heart for Auntie Very. I making a saint for you, Auntie Connie.'

He wriggles down from Constance's arms.

'Come.' He pulls their hands.

They follow him across the hallway to the library. He runs to a bookshelf where from the bottom row he edges out a thin volume. Squatting on the floor, stretching the velvet of his green skeleton suit, he opens the book and sheets of blue, loaf-sugar wrapping scatter at the sisters' feet. Rafe displays images of what appear to be a saint across the rug. Painted on the wrapping is a robed man with a long beard of deep crimson that tapers down to his waist. Above his elongated head fans a pale-pink aureole. It is crude, but the intention is clear.

'Rafe, did you paint these?'

'Yes, Auntie Connie. This one is for you.'

His eyes widen and sparkle as he thumbs through another volume. Slipped in its pages is the most recent, more refined version. The colours are more brilliant against the thick blue background, the eyes more lifelike.

'It is stunning, Rafe. I shall treasure it. How did you do it? What materials did you use?'

'Bertie gave me them. Beetroot juice and eggs, and flour, and the sparkly is salt. And the sugar paper. And the toothbrushes.'

'You painted these with a toothbrush?'

'Old ones. Am I naughty?'

'No, child! Not at all,' Verity says.

'And how did you make these colours?'

'Oh. Um, well, if you put a colour down on the paper and put the same one on top of it the next day it looks like this.' He points to the man's brilliant beard. 'This beard is three days. Tiny drops of water with the beetroot make pinks. A spicy powder makes a smelly yellow. Bertie gave me cloves to make it smell better. Eggs are stinky.'

'I did not know Bertie knew so much about painting.'

Rafe peals with laughter.

'That is jolly, Auntie Very. Bertie knows a whole much about kitchen things. Not about painting.'

Verity and Constance exchange glances.

'Rafe, would you enjoy having a paint set?' Constance asks.

'I would, Auntie Connie. What is it, please?'

Constance picks him up and swings him around.

'You are delicious. It is a box of colours that you may use to paint more pictures and we will buy you a proper paintbrush.'

'Now, it is time for our young artist's bedtime story. Up the stairs with you.'

In the evening, when the men have laid their equipment to rest and leave a bridge that is yet to lead anywhere suspended until the morning, when the Regent's Park Haymarket stalls are empty and covered, the soldiers are off to the taverns, and the gates to the zoological gardens are locked, the animals begin to stir. The monkeys cry and scream. The wild cats roar their discontent. The parrots screech in the unfamiliar cold. A chorus of squalls travels through the park and across the road until they reach the boy who sleeps in the Tower Room. While he dreams of being imprisoned, the sick monkeys wail in his ears until he forces himself to wake, screaming with the animals.

The sisters take turns of duty each night. In a bitter hour past midnight, it is Verity who tonight carries the lamp and a small cup of warm cocoa up the stairs. Rafe's wet red eyes, his hair damp against the pillow, and the look of despair on the face of the boy tear her heart into strips.

With a soft, dry muslin she gently swabs his face and feels his forehead for fever. His head is cool and he buries it in her chest.

'Auntie Very, I do not want to go to prison.' He gulps and moistens his words with sobs.

'Now, now my darling, you will never go to prison. We would never allow it. You are such a good boy ... Hush.' She kisses his face and rocks him.

When his eyes flutter into sleep, Verity picks up her old worry that the consensus is wrong. She rocks the boy thinking that perhaps Clovis Fowler will indeed survive the penitentiary. The possibility threatens her like the approach of a rabid dog. Prison has not weakened the Fowler woman as she had hoped it would, God forgive her. She crosses herself. Clovis Fowler does not wilt, nor does she grow ill. Her cold beauty is unscathed. Verity thinks that she must somehow prepare for it, yet she cannot, and it eats at her that she is not strong enough, not strong like Constance.

Down one flight, Constance throws on her crimson banyan and slippers. She cannot sleep and cannot read, so she uses the time to write.

Sir,

    I must say again, with all due respect, that I do not fully comprehend why we cannot meet and speak to each other in person. Frankly, the only reason I do not insist upon it is because I know that you are guarding

Rafe's safety by acting in such an extreme and anonymous fashion. For that reason, my sister and I continue to follow your instructions. You have garnered my respect and my admiration by demonstrating that your devotion has not faltered these five years. You are a mysterious fellow and we have come to rely upon you for many things, for as many reasons.

Our privacy is no longer cosseted, if it ever really was, living on the edge of the canal as we do. I am hearing noises again, and the feeling that someone watches us returns with a sense of unease and dread. I assure you, and I think you are aware, that we do our best to contribute to our mutual peace of mind by taking every precaution. Even so, just yesterday while in Park Street at the cheesemonger's, a man peered into the shop window and hovered outside until I departed, then proceeded to follow me. I changed my route several times, looking over my shoulder to find him close behind. There is no subtlety in that! Obviously, my sister and I nurse new worries.

Rafe continues to suffer from nightmares, but has had no fevers or illnesses of late. We have asked him several times if he would like to meet his mother, who requests his presence. I disagree with her vehemently, especially in light of his recurring dreams, and do not think he should meet her in prison. The matter is moot. We do not mention his father any more; Rafe has never questioned us about him and avoids the subject entirely. It is just as well, how do you tell a boy his father survived a hanging?

My sister and I will begin more rigorous lessons after the New Year. I hope that keeping him challenged will calm his fears and help to relieve him of his taunting dreams. He is a happy boy but for them, and, the dread of his mother appearing to take him away. We are the only mothers he has known.

One more item, before I close. I do not know if this is of interest to you, but I offer it just the same. He shows an early talent for art and is quite creative. We encourage him. It makes him happy and proud, in the best possible way.

Constance Fitzgerald

She makes seven folds in the writing sheet with more confidence than she feels, and firmly presses the creases when a loud thud from above jolts her. She hesitates, waiting to hear more. The sound seemed to emanate from Bertie's room, but the house is tranquil again. Bertie must have dropped something.

Upstairs now, Constance tiptoes down the corridor and gently knocks on Verity's bedroom door and edges it open an inch. Candles burn in every corner of her sister's room and a faint aroma of incense escapes. She is on her knees praying the rosary. The cloisonné beads glint in her hand.

'I'm sorry to disturb you. I'm stepping outside to Benedikt's box and did not want to alarm you. Did you hear that noise?'

Verity raises her hand for a brief moment to indicate she has heard. Her eyes remain trained on the images of the saints while her lips form chants. After the last silent word of her prayer she turns to Constance, her eyes filled with the lustre of her faith.

'I did. I think Bertie retired a bit pickled again. I'll check on her.'

When Constance opens the front door to the night, its sibilant air entreats her to remain for a moment. The universe never feels more alive than when others are sleeping. Frost clings to the patch of front garden and she thinks of how the earth either rests beneath her feet, or endeavours to push its weeds and buds up and out of it. She feels that same struggle within herself; a restlessness has pulsed through her for months. In the zoological gardens the animals' death throes juxtapose the canal's placid canal water and perfectly encapsulate her conflict.

The hooves of a horse and trap break the quiet. Trunks teeter dangerously beside the driver, who delivers for a neighbour returning from an apparently long journey. And when her mind pictures a journey, clarity happens, and Constance knows exactly what to do. They will go away for a while. Abroad. Not this year, nor next, for there is the new queen's coronation. Perhaps Percy will join them, too. Yes. That is it.

The tin cash box is hidden under a hessian bag, nestled between shrubberies. She unlocks it and places the letter in it. Also from underneath the bag she removes a petite, stuffed bird and positions it on top of the shrub to indicate a message. The paper, folded and tied with a ribbon appears small and unimportant in the empty box. The recipient would disagree.

The door creaks open behind her. Verity beckons.

'Oh Constance, come quickly. The night has taken Bertie. She is dead.'

CHAPTER THIRTY-SEVEN

In the misbegotten hours of Millbank nights, when a large population of criminals are too weary to make mischief, factions of inmates
come to life. None more so than those miserable creatures in the
darks.

Down the basement stairs of Pentagon No. 5 the smack of a
fungal odour clings to her clothes and seeps into her skin. Clovis
holds a flaming candle to air so thick with damp it is like walking
through mist. She bends down to avoid the low ceiling in an ante-
chamber that leads to the dark cells, one of which is empty. She
steps into an unspeakably cold space, so thick with darkness that
in spite of her light, her vision struggles to adjust. Creeping along
the wall like a blind person she finds the wooden plank and sets
her items upon it.

It is not completely unthinkable that a prisoner would roam the
dungeon of Millbank. For all its fortress-like qualities, it is entirely
possible to breach Millbank's codes, especially when the governor
is so devoted to her. Charles, as he insists she calls him when they
are alone, falls over himself to please her. He enjoys sexual positions
he never knew existed, and after five years he remains possessed.
They meet sparingly, which only fans the flame, for they must be
clever and vigilant. He is of the mind that, really, she asks very little
of him. She seeks no fortune or outrageous gifts, only access and a
certain degree of freedom within the prison, which he readily gives.

Tonight Clovis seeks the criminal skull. Dressed in a matron's uniform she places her candle tin on the flagstone and lifts the bar of the cell's massive outer iron-lined wooden door. Behind the grated gate a fingernail scratches at the wall of a room so dark that it is impossible to see its beginning or end. When Clovis holds the light up to the gate a female prisoner turns slowly to face her, and even with her steely resolve, Clovis's breath quickens. The woman has picked the whitewash from the walls and smeared it upon her face layer upon layer. Her hair is matted and sticks out from her head in short, dirty clumps. But it is her lips that make Clovis falter. They are cut and smeared with fresh blood. Dried blood gathers in thick globs at the corners of her mouth.

Clovis recovers and quickly thrusts her hand out, in her palm sits a large piece of soggy bread.

'It is fresh. I will break it up for you and give it to you through the grating.'

Over her brown prison dress the woman wears a coarse canvas, sack-like covering fastened with leather straps and screws. Her waist bears the burden of a chain that hangs to the floor and passes through a ring in the wall.

Clovis sets the light down and pulls off pieces of beef broth-soaked bread as if she is feeding a bird. She cannot see the thickness of dirt under the woman's scraggly nails as her hand greedily snatches the bread and stuffs her crimson mouth quicker and quicker, until it is all eaten.

'I will return with more bread and wine.'

The woman looks at her askance. *Wine?*

Clovis retrieves the wine and more of the broth bread from the empty cell. The woman inches closer to the grating.

'What is your name?' Clovis asks as she doles out the bread.

Her lip curls up in a snarl before she says, 'Antoinette.'

'Stop that scratching, Antoinette, or they will put you in the leather and you will lose the use of your hands.'

Silence.

Clovis opens a small glass pot. 'Lips to the iron.'

She soaks a sponge and puts it to the woman's lips.

'Yow!' Antoinette winces as the alcohol stings her lips, but sucks it with a greedy determination.

'Shhh!'

'What brings you to the darks, pretty matron? Not seen you in these parts before.'

'Why do you disfigure your face, Antoinette?'

'More wine.'

'No. Tell me first.'

Antoinette turns her back to Clovis and leans against the iron gate. Facing the far wall, which they cannot see, and the cold air from the grating that billows towards her, she begins to speak.

'I was a Mayfair beauty.' She pauses. 'I imagine your surprise. Could compete with you, I dare say. I am able to read and write; 'twas a great help with gaining custom of the richest whoremongers, one in particular. Apartments in Mayfair were being sought. But then I found myself perched on the sharp edge of scandal. He was a feisty, revolting one, of German descent, in the royal way, if you get my meaning.'

'I am bored now, Antoinette.'

The prisoner turns, jumps upon and clings to the grating like an animal. Clovis does not shrink an inch. Her candle's light creates a great stretching shadow on the wall that reflects Antoinette's wild, thistled head.

'Tell me why you act mad when you are not.'

'I want out of this dank, wet hell,' Antoinette hisses. 'I make them think I dress for an evening in Shepherd's Market. My lips are red; my face is powdered.'

She turns in a circle, her chain dragging, her arms thrust out to model her canvas-covered gown.

'I have made a bustle.'

Clovis sponges Antoinette's lips again.

'If you tell them that I am mad, matron, they will transfer me to the asylum and I will be out in months. I have means. I can make it worth your while.'

'I am not a matron. You are not going to the asylum. You will be conveyed to Van Diemen's Land where the men will wear you out, to your death. You will be fucked senseless and will no more remember your romping Mayfair nights than your real name, which is Henrietta.'

'Who are you?' Henrietta's voice goes cold and sharp like the sliver of glass she hides in her sleeve.

Clovis removes her cap releasing her brilliant hair. Henrietta takes a step back.

'Ah! Well, if it ain't Prisoner Fowler. The tattle about you flows through the tench—'

'I have no interest in rumours. Be silent. I can help you. But you must do as I say.'

'I would call you a liar, but here you are free to roam the darks disguised as a matron. You have somehow got your hands on wine, and even in light of a single flame, your skin shows nothing of the Millbank ghost, like the rest of us. Curious. So, what can you do for me?'

'How many years do you have?'

'Seven.'

'How many served?'

'Five, I entered only days before you.'

'You shall have better food. You will enjoy a return of visiting privileges. And there will be a pouch of coins waiting for you upon your ticket-of release. You will be free, avoiding deportation.'

Henrietta bursts into a high-pitched screech of laughter.

Clovis shakes the grating. 'Keep your voice down.'

'Why me and what do you want in return?'

'A great deal, Henrietta. I will demand a great deal. So think of your freedom and agree in your next breath, or I go.'

'Agree to what?'

'I will visit you each night while you remain in punishment. I have training in mesmerism, the New Science.'

'Oh my blind cupid. A quack.'

'I will leave you now, Henrietta. Enjoy your journey to Australia.'

Clovis turns to leave.

'No. Wait.'

There is only the sound of boots on flagstones.

'Wait. Please. Don't go.'

Clovis swings around, once again illuminating the dark cell.

'Sit down on the floor. Face the far wall, rest the back of your head against the grating.'

Henrietta arranges her chain and complies. Clovis slides her hands through the grating until they rest on Henrietta's filthy head. She closes her eyes to recall the Phrenological bust.

'Look ahead, Henrietta. Focus on the direction of the wall in front of you.'

The woman feels the warmth of Clovis's hand pass over her head and down her back. In less than five minutes, Henrietta's head rests heavily against the cold iron as she succumbs to somnolence.

Crouching down, and not without a whit of disgust at the woman's knotted locks, in which lice and mites have surely taken purchase, Clovis places her fingers on Henrietta's skull and begins to probe. Tracing the bumps and knots she settles first on the shape of the lower back of her head. There should be a projection of the bone where the organ that bestows an attachment to offspring is located, but it is almost non-existent. Underdeveloped. Indifference to those who are weak.

Henrietta's breathing is more laboured.

'I shall ask you several questions and you will answer truthfully.'

'Yes. I will.'

'Do you have children?'

'No.'

'Have you ever had a child?'

'Yes.'

'What happened to your child?'

'I left it somewhere.'

'Where? Where did you leave the child, Henrietta?'

'At the Barley Mow in Marylebone. In one of the booths, under the table.'

Her tone is almost chirpy, without an ounce of remorse.

Clovis's fingers crawl up Henrietta's head, tracing the contours of the top centre where her skull rises to a severe point.

Very deficient in Conscientiousness.

Her hands travel across, up and down and around the prostitute's head. *Combativeness, Destructiveness, Secretiveness, all overdeveloped and excessive.*

The potential for this woman to do harm is so great that Clovis is wary; if such a criminally-inclined woman falls so easily to her manipulation, perhaps Henrietta is acting. She will create a test to catch her out.

The night is waning and it is so cold in the damp dungeon that Clovis's breath visibly floats by the candlelight. She must hurry now. Breathing slowly and deeply, she anchors to her purpose.

'Stand up, Henrietta. Give your ear to the grating.'

The woman lifts her chain and stands with her profile to Clovis who positions herself flush to the grating and looks as if she is kissing the woman's ear. But there is no romance in her bidding. Her voice is low and forceful with all the instructions she now pours into Henrietta's consciousness. After her last whispered commands, she blows on the woman's neck to wake her. Henrietta comes around in a minute or two. Clovis steps back.

'Bloody hell. I have been in a fathomless sleep.'

'Do you remember anything?'

'Nothing.'

'I will leave you now. What was your work before you were banished to the darks?'

'Picking the nasty oakum.'

'You will be rid of the chain tomorrow. I will have you moved to the kitchen in a few days. A big room with light and better food will help. And you will not work alone. It makes the time go quicker. But I warn you. Best behaviour or you will be back withering in the darks.'

'You mustn't leave yet! I have something to tell you.'

'It is very late.' Clovis gathers the empty pot of wine, the candle, sponge and her cap.

'No, no, there is something I must tell you. I do not know why, but I must.'

'It will wait.' Clovis puts her off as part of the test.

'No, please. It cannot wait. It is urgent. I beg you.'

In the pitch black Clovis's satisfied smile goes unseen by the prisoner.

'Go ahead.'

'I am here for theft. But it is not my only crime. I planned and committed another. My baby. My second child.'

Henrietta pauses, thoroughly confused. She does not know why she has admitted this, her deepest, most dangerous secret. And words rise again, different words, terrible words stream out of her mouth like thick fumes.

'I set it up. I worked it so that another would be punished in my stead.' She continues just above a whisper, 'Hung by a rope as thick as my thigh.'

'Good night, Henrietta.' Clovis is deeply satisfied that her whispers proved successful.

'I ... I should not have said. No one knows. Not a soul. You mustn't tell anyone, Clovis Fowler.'

'One day I will come to you. You will do me a service. If on that day you are tempted to renege on our agreement, I promise you this: I will make you howl for your mother like a blind baby wolf.'

'What? What will you ask of me?'

A grave silence is her answer.

Henrietta lifts her chain and carries it to the wooden plank. The links feel heavier on this dank chill night. She has allowed this red witch to add to its weight in uncountable, invisible rings. She has stained her own future with her confession. She despairs not for her crime, but that a woman like Clovis Fowler should know of it.

CHAPTER THIRTY-EIGHT

1841

Soon the trees will be bare and bony. Summer is done, the harvest is in and London is brown and drab. Tobacco-coloured leaves crunch and crackle underfoot. Chimneys produce tunnels of thick, black smoke that choke the air. Winter is coming. The first day of November is mindful of death.

Lights for the departed suffuse Lawless House. Though maidens no longer go souling, soul cakes displayed on a silver platter await pitchers of cold milk to soothe and cool those in Purgatory. Rafe will go to bed tonight with a bag of broad beans and candies, a tradition honouring the link between past and present. The table in the formal dining room will be set for the dead to feast. The sisters began praying the novena for the departed on the 24th of October and it ends today on All Hallows. It is good to be home again. The fires of Lawless House do not dull the thrill of their time abroad.

The sisters meticulously planned an itinerary on the continent and were rewarded for their efforts when they witnessed the opening of a young mind.

'I see,' Rafe said, time and again, when he viewed the great works of art, the crumbling antiquities, and the Italian grandmothers who sat in the warm sun making magic with their olives and lemons, who then placed something gorgeous to eat in his hands.

Today the incense in Lawless House is as strong as the smoke that circled in the exquisite old churches of Europe and is sure to gently swirl up to the top floor of the house and awaken Rafe. Verity sets out a pitcher of water, a few soul cakes and the ossa dei morti, the traditional biscuits named the bones of the dead, made from the recipe a Palermo nun shared with them.

Constance recalls the lightning-bolt of jealousy that jumped from the pages when Clovis Fowler responded to her written request asking her permission to take Rafe to the continent. She relented for a hefty sum.

The day maids serve breakfast early this morning. Rafe dips a sweet roll in his cocoa.

'Do you think Bertie's body is incorrupt like the saints we visited in Italy?' He chews and contemplates.

'Do you have an opinion on it, Rafe?' Constance asks.

'She was very good, our Bertie. Whenever you or Auntie Very were long sleeping she made extra marmalade – she allowed me to eat it on buns until I burst – and sometimes she sang after she finished her beer. She was very brave, especially when the foreign men came.'

'The what? What foreign men?' Verity asks.

'A fortnight before she died. They came to the door and asked if Master Fowler lived here. She said, "Wait right there." Then she closed and locked the door and came into the library and told me to hide in the basement. She forgot that it is always locked. I hid in the pantry instead, behind the sacks. Then she fetched her rifle. Did you know Bertie had a rifle? Did you ever find it? She told me she shot one of them in the foot.'

'Rafe! Why did you ... why did she not tell us? Are you sure you remember correctly? You were only five years old when Bertie died.'

'Well, because she asked me not to! Yes, I remember exactly. Auntie Very was in the long sleep and you were at the penitentiary, Auntie Connie. Bertie said I must not worry you, that she had protected us all. They would never step foot on our doorstep again. Anyway, does that mean Bertie is a saint?'

'In a different meaning of the word, yes, Rafe, it does,' Constance says.

'I will not dress as a saint this year, aunties. I am too old for it and will wear my best suit. The Italian one.'

Despite their worry, the sisters share an amused glance.

'All right then, you had better change into your suit or we shall be late to Mass,' Verity reminds him.

He no longer wants to be a child. The boy has matured upon visiting the towns and cities of Europe. He is naturally curious and has a voracious appetite to learn, which made him an excellent travelling companion. He was drawn to every strange and beautiful morsel of culture the sisters had carefully curated.

Verity slips her hands into a pair of grey, kid driving gloves while Constance places a blue cashmere long shawl around her sister's shoulders.

'I'm taking the stanhope. Thomas has hitched the horse. Are you sure you will not join us?' Verity asks her.

'No, I shall help the girls with the feast preparations. That petite one, she is a terror with the china. Thomas should drive you to St Mary's.'

'No, you may need him here today. It's not far and I would quite like to drive myself. No virtue lost driving at my age. I do love a feast day, solemn as this one is. What a shock to hear about Bertie and the men. Do you think he exaggerates?'

'No, he is always truthful. We will speak to Percy as soon as possible. And I shall write to Benedikt and have a word with Thomas, too. Oh, there he is!' Constance beams.

'How handsome you look,' Verity says.

He looks like a painting standing on the landing. The sisters will remember it so. A finely tailored black coat cinches his waist, then flares out and flows down below his knees, revealing his first full-length trousers, starkly white.

There is something else. A rose gold chain flickers against the gold buttons. He squirrels around in his pockets. There are two more, one in each of his hands. And a smile to go with them that brims with self-satisfaction. He places the chain around Constance's neck. She bends down to accommodate him and he repeats his offering with Verity. It is then they notice the delicate rings: two golden hands joined together in the centre of the band.

'The day at the zoological gardens – and I will never go back there, never – when I was very bad and ran off and then found you again by searching for your blue and lavender cloaks, remember?'

Yes, they nod.

'You must always wear them and also these neck chains. Place your rings on them, look, just like mine. So that we will find each other if we are separated.'

'Why Rafe, what thoughts,' Verity says.

The sisters have no need to look at one another for they share the same trepidation in the pit of their stomachs. His intensity shakes them.

'Thank you, darling boy,' Constance says. 'It is a very good gift, a generous one, too. And such a clever idea.'

'Yes,' Verity says. 'How you must have saved! You are full of surprises. I hope you are not too grown up for a kiss from your aunties.'

With more seriousness than they would care to witness, he embraces them both, crooking his arms tightly around their necks.

'Now, you really will be late. More gifts when you return.' Constance chokes slightly on her words.

Constance passes a busy hour, and in spite of the butter-fingered maid, has almost completed the feast day arrangements. Their gifts to Rafe create a towering pile by his bed. The table by his window heaves with barmbrack. Downstairs, the pottage, his favourite dish, is ready for searing and the boxty pancake mixture awaits the sizzling griddle. She has changed into her new silk day dress, the colour of a heather field.

'I relish the thought of learning to pin my hair.' Constance offers a pin to the maid.

''Tis not done, madam.'

'Don't be foolish. My mother pinned her own hair until . . . until the day she died.'

'It is the only thing I do well. You don't sniff when I am finished,' the girl says, wounded.

'I do not sniff at all.'

'Yes, madam.' She smiles.

'And you do many things well . . .'

Someone has come down hard on the door knocker.

'Are you expecting visitors, madam?'

'None.'

The other maid raps on the bedroom door and pokes her head in.

'Madam?'

'Yes, come in.'

'A Mrs Fowler requests to see you.'

The glass pin holder crashes to the floor and splinters at Constance's feet.

She grabs the edges of the dressing table and holds on until her knuckles glare white. A perfect rage quells her panic. When she stands, the chair falls back and thumps against the floor.

'Madam?'

She cannot stop the tremors in her shoulders. The words repeat and repeat in her head until she has no other impulse than to expel them in a nasty stream of vomit. But she holds it back, even as it rises up in her.

I knew it. I knew it. I knew it.

All of those dear to her who said it would never happen, who were so certain that the Fowlers would die in prison, or would at least be gaoled until Rafe came of age, God help her, they were all wrong.

What shall I do with her? She paces the floor in an effort to command her shaking body to stillness.

Oh God no. Not yet, not yet.

'See her to the drawing room,' she says in a hoarse whisper. 'Ask her to be seated and then close the doors.'

'Yes, madam.'

Downstairs, Clovis Fowler examines every inch of the path from the foyer to the hallway that leads to the drawing room's double doors. She observes the maid is a well-fed, well-dressed young woman who nervously leads her through the corridor. Clovis makes no pretence in the presence of the maid and blatantly surveys the view and the furnishings, even the height of the ceilings. Several of the items she recalls from Fore Street; the same chandeliers, the mirror in which nine years ago the reflection of the Fitzgerald sisters dominated the room.

'Please be seated, Mrs Fowler.' The maid is intimidated by the woman's boldness.

'Thank you.'

But she does not sit. Instead she stands by the windows, her chin slightly lowered to gain a better view of the canal. As soon as the maid departs, Clovis returns to her review of the sisters' home. The house is impressive, as she expected. She notes the gas jets and the grand piano. Clovis recalls the day they first met and how the sisters brought to her mind the *huldufólk* of her country, strange, and condemned to live between heaven and hell.

The paintings that crowd the walls confuse her at first glance. She knows little of art, but surely the frames are worth much more than the amateurish paintings they protect. One is particularly rubescent; a canvas of halos in graded shades of yellow over which the outlines of red bearded men and veiled women seem to float amidst a rich red matrix, as if searching for the halo that belongs particularly to them. Clovis smirks. Something juvenile about them. Ah, she muses, must be the boy's work.

Footsteps. The door handles turn.

The years stand between them, but they do not make their mark on the women's faces, or in their movements or postures. There are, however, differences. Though her beauty has not diminished, Clovis has not yet stepped into the new decade. In the silence that follows it is clear how the world has moved forward without her. Her hair is wrong. It is too elaborate, too important in today's increasingly demure fashions. Her gown is out of date. The skirt is not full enough. Her bodice shoulder line is too high, her arms are too free, and her sleeves are ridiculously full, unlike Constance's narrow sleeves. Even her waistline is wrong compared to the woman who poses so assuredly in front of her, in a modern, more natural waistline.

Clovis does not expect to be so harshly affected by a bolt of cloth and a head of hair. She has had many years to think upon this moment and now that it has arrived she is angry that she cares too much about the outward signs that scream of her imprisonment. Forget about the goddamned frocks and locks, she tells herself. I mean to parry.

'I am here to collect my son.'

'He is with my sister in Hampstead. I do not know when they will return.'

'I will wait.'

Constance signals the maid to close the doors and takes a position by the fireplace. Elegant in her stance, she looks the picture of calm; the lavender sheen of her dress brilliantly offsets her silvery white hair. She clasps her hands in front of her to conceal the tremors.

'You have given us no notice. Perhaps, we might bring him to you after we have had time to prepare him and ...' She pauses. 'And pack his things.'

'I have only just arrived home last night. I am his mother, and I have a carriage waiting at great expense – you live far from Limehouse. I will take him when he returns.'

'My sister and I have cared for your son as we would our own.' She makes an effort to breathe. 'It will shock him to go so quickly.'

'Have you not already prepared him for this day, as we agreed?'

'I do not think a child can ever be fully prepared for this sort of monumental change. To be completely uprooted from everything he knows, surely it is best for him to make a gradual transition.'

'As his mother, I disagree. It is best that he is with his parents. We have been apart long enough.' Clovis advances. 'His best interests, you say. I do not know if it is in his best interests to spend one more moment in the presence of someone who has lied about his health.'

Constance remains steady. 'He is in perfect health.'

'Ah, but there was a time when in your care he was not. A time when he came down with a fever, a fever so hot and raw that he dripped pools of moisture.' She inches closer to Constance. 'His sweat covered you and your sister until you were as damp as he. And nothing you did or tried to do calmed that fever until it burned itself out, like a flame.' She snaps her fingers in Constance's face. 'And from that point on, you no longer aged.'

The unspeakable has been spoken. After a long, thick pause, Constance recovers.

'You came to us in the middle of the night, desperate for help. And we have given Rafe the best of care. When you meet him you will find a boy who has been loved and nurtured. What possible importance could you place on anything above that?'

Clovis smiles. 'All right, Mrs Fitzgerald. We will not speak of the mysterious Benedikt who plies you with phials, or the fact that your body is forced to sleep for fortnights at a time. Or the "miracle" that the boy has brought you.'

'No. You and I will never speak of such things. I would rather use this time to warn you and to entreat you to be vigilant.

'For what reason?' Clovis laughs.

'For the safety of your child!' Constance snaps. 'Have you already forgotten our last meeting at Millbank? There are men, possibly from your country, who have gone to extraordinary lengths to track his whereabouts.'

'I have it in hand.' Clovis says coldly. 'The boy is of no concern to you now.'

'Whatever do you mean?'

'You will have no further contact with him after this day.'

The doors are thrown open.

'There is a carriage outside . . .' Rafe begins.

Verity and Rafe are flushed with cold. Their expectant faces drop, their smiles vanish.

Constance rushes to him and kneels down, taking a firm hold of his shoulders.

'Darling boy.'

'Is she my mother, Auntie Connie?'

Clovis swans towards him.

'Yes, Rafe, I am your mother.'

He stares up at her for an uncomfortable moment, and all wait for his response.

'You look similar, but you do not look like me.'

Clovis stares back at him, undaunted by his remark. She takes him in with a swift glance and would of course never admit that the sisters have done a perfect job of moulding him into a little gentleman.

'I have come to take you home with me.'

'Today?' Verity gasps.

'Thank you, madam. But I do not wish to go,' he says.

'Please. We would like a few minutes alone with him,' Constance entreats her.

Clovis weighs this request. The boy begins to screw up his face and she cannot have that. Perhaps, she thinks, it is better to let them do this last, most difficult work rather than she.

'Why, of course. I completely understand. In the meantime, if your maid could call my girl inside to help.'

'Is your husband not with you, Mrs Fowler?' Verity asks.

'No, I am afraid he is attending to urgent business.'

'It must be very urgent indeed to be absent from this first encounter with his son.' Verity throws the remark over her shoulder as they usher Rafe up the stairs.

As soon as the door to the Tower Room is closed Rafe pushes his toy trunk to the door to block it.

'Please, aunties. Do not make me go with her.'

'Rafe.' Verity is shaking now. 'She is your mother.'

'I do not care! Please, Auntie Connie,' he pleads.

'Listen to me, Rafe. This is very important. I want you to repeat the agreement we made. Right now. You know the one. When you come of age . . .'

'No, no. I can't. I don't want to remember that. Please, aunties, please do not let her take me away.'

'Constance, why are you asking him do this? We should be telling him that he will visit us and we will visit him and there is so much to look forward . . .'

'Verity, please, trust me.' She draws a breath. 'Rafe, when you come of age . . . go ahead now, finish it.'

And now the tears come, and his nose runs, and his young voice, still high and clear, full of gulps and mucus, recites his instructions.

'When I am of age . . .'

'That's right, darling. Keep going.'

'When I am of age. I shall meet you in our special place on the 17th of December.'

'At what time, dear Rafe?'

'Three o'clock.'

'And should we not be there for reasons that we are unaware . . .' Constance prompts him.

'Then I will go each year until we meet again.'

'Yes, darling. Each year. If we are not there do not despair, come again the next year and the next.' Verity manages.

'Yes, aunties. Each year.'

'Never forget this, Rafe. No matter what happens. No matter how many years it takes.'

'But won't I see you before then?'

'I have always been honest with you, haven't I? I shall be so now. Your mother may very likely wish to have you to herself for a while . . . and . . .'

'No!' Verity says.

Constance throws a sharp glance at her sister.

'She has not seen you for such a long time, since you were a wee thing in her arms. And you have a father who will want to spend time with his fine, brave son. So, it may very well be that . . .' She cannot go on and looks to Verity for help.

'We will come to you as soon as we can. But we must respect your mother's wishes. We have our beautiful rings and our necklaces . . .' Verity adds.

'And will you always wear blue and lavender so that I may find you, aunties?'

In that moment, their hearts break. Another fracture to add to the scarring.

There is a soft knock on the door.

'Mrs Fowler is ready to leave, madam,' the petite maid, Rachael, says.

'Rachael.'

'Yes, madam?

'I would like you and Nancy to gather Rafe's things, as many things as you are able, pack them into the trunks. Be sure to include all of his painting boxes and utensils. Quickly, quickly. And for God's sake, tell Nancy not to break anything. Do not stand there with your mouth open. Go.' Constance turns back to Rafe.

'There are so many things we wish to tell you. You are so clever and good and your heart is strong and generous. Remember these things to be true. Continue with your painting and be vigilant about the way you experiment and play with your paints and materials. Be brave, Rafe. Most importantly, remember that we love you more than life itself.'

'And we will do everything in our power to see you again as soon as possible,' adds Verity.

'Even if she will not let you?

God above! How quick he is!

The sisters answer as one. 'Yes, my darling.'

The maids rush about, their faces red and upset.

Clovis waits in the foyer at the bottom of the stairs.

Rafe takes one step at a time, so slowly, as if any second he will turn back. When he reaches the last step Clovis offers her hand. He turns away and throws himself into Verity's skirts and clings to her legs.

'I cannot do it,' he says.

The sisters stand on the staircase, mute.

Clovis grabs Rafe's wrist with a firm hold and pulls him down. Not willing to risk his taking flight, she commands the maid to open the door.

Clovis drags Rafe out and through the front garden to the pathway where two people stand waiting outside the carriage. Constance and Verity follow, but stop short at the garden when they see that the Fowler servants are the picture of health, appearing as the exact same young people they were almost ten years ago. Distracted for a moment by this surprise, Rafe's crying shocks them back to their last sight of him.

Constance runs to the carriage and Rafe breaks free.

'Auntie Connie!'

Before he reaches her, Clovis snatches him back by the tail of his black coat.

'Remember, Rafe. Remember everything,' Constance calls out.

He nods to her and places his hand on his chest where under his white shirt he has hidden his chain.

The driver is anxious to depart and heads off with a crack of his whip. The horses lurch forward leaving their piles in the street.

Constance is unaware how long she stands in the cold before Rachael and Nancy come out with her cloak and gently place it on her shoulders. The lavender cashmere skims the sodden ground. Nancy and Rachael would not in usual circumstances dare touch their employer, but every rule has exceptions. The young women hold her firmly as they lead her back inside Lawless House. Constance roams from room to room where all the preparations for the feast day mock her. She cannot find her sister and has no voice to call out to her.

An awful sound emanates from the Tower Room. Constance finds Verity cowering on the floor, garbling some sort of indecipherable prayer in a voice that shrieks like a banshee. With no wish for the maids to see her sister so contorted, Constance begins the work of prising Verity away from the curve of the wall. It is a long, painstaking task for Verity does not want to be moved. Her arms flail and she stubbornly makes her legs heavy. Wisps of Constance's hair fly out from their pins and her full skirts are mangled in the effort as she drags her sister to Rafe's bed. Heaving her onto the mattress aggravates her sister's chanting and screeching. Constance can stand it no longer. She slaps her once into a desperate silence.

The day is done. They sit in the boy's room in darkness.

'I will offer her money,' Constance whispers, as the wind blows branches against the window. 'She has a weakness for it. We will buy three visits a week. No, perhaps one, one visit a week, to begin.'

Verity moans.

'We shall go to Limehouse tomorrow,' Constance continues. 'We will deliver more of his belongings. Clothes and things. What about that, sister?'

Verity does not respond. They sit in silence.

It is past the maids' time. They should be gone for the evening but Constance hears their footfall downstairs. With whatever they are occupied, their kindness knots her throat.

The night grows darker still, the Tower Room, frigid.
Verity stirs at last. Constance hears her open her dry mouth.
'She has not the slightest bit of tenderness towards him. No tenderness, Constance. He will have no love in Limehouse.'

CHAPTER THIRTY-NINE

On the busy Commercial Road, Nora Mockett dreams of the shops of Regent Street and their large plate-glass windows that can be illuminated by gaseliers all evening long. She imagines sliding the lights down to her chosen product, shining light directly on it. What joy.

The door of Mockett's shop opens and her lovely daydream disintegrates. With her metal nib poised mid-air, she cannot believe her eyes and actually blinks, in spite of herself. It is not possible . . .

Clovis Fowler stands before her – completely unchanged. How can it be? Dumbfounded, Nora simply stares at the radiant woman. She cannot tear her eyes away, even while she comprehends that Mrs Fowler is relishing every second of her stupefied gawking.

Clovis tilts her head an inch or two.

'Mrs Mockett?'

'Mrs Fowler,' Nora manages.

Nora is further astounded when from behind Clovis's enormous skirts the servant girl, she cannot remember her name, steps into view. She, too, is unchanged.

'I am here on business with Mr Mockett.'

'Indeed.' Nora gathers strength in spite of her light-headedness. 'And is he aware of your . . . return?'

'No, but I had hoped I would not need an appointment to see an old friend at his place of business.'

Nora might be mistaken, but she senses a proprietorial tone in

Mrs Fowler's voice and she is more than a bit uneasy about it. She must find her footing again.

'Mr Mockett is currently on a house call. I don't expect him until after the lunch hour.'

'Tell him I will return tomorrow, won't you?'

'Of course. I trust you found your home to your satisfaction?'

'Indeed. The attention to the boy's room is particularly noticeable.'

'And is your son home with you now?'

'He is. Perhaps I will let you meet him when I return.' She turns to leave and pauses. With her back to Nora, 'He is a handsome young thing.'

'The reason I enquired about your house ...'

'You were paid well to look after it,' Clovis clips. She loses patience with this woman.

'After you were taken away, your neighbours pelted the windows with rotten fruit and vegetables,' Nora continues. 'They smashed eggs against your front door. The knocker was torn off and auctioned to the highest bidder at the Black Horse. We bought another to replace it. Then we set a couple of boys on watch at the house until the revellers grew bored.'

'Who won the knocker?' Clovis asks.

'I do not know him.'

'You will be reimbursed. And then I wish to hear no more of your good deeds.'

'My word. Prison doesn't half strip you of your manners.'

The door slams.

Later that evening, while Owen works late to fill last-minute orders, Nora sits at her dressing table and pours three fingers of whisky. She opens her folded vanity mirror and sets it on the table. Positioning the three bevelled mirrors so that she may catch all angles of her face, she turns the lamp up a notch.

'Be brave,' she whispers.

The evidence stares back at her. The morning bloat takes a larger portion of the day to diminish, so that only now, late in the evening does it sink to wherever bloat goes. The beginning of a jowl disturbs her more than her crinkling smile. Puffed skin hangs above her eyelids. She positions one of the end mirrors to catch her profile. It is her first sight of a developing second chin. She closes her eyes. Until this day she had always considered that she was ageing well.

Her hands with their veins visibly pulsing under thin skin slide her dressing gown off her shoulders. They stroke the tiny crevices between her breasts. Nine years have done this to her. And nine years have not laid even a finger on Clovis Fowler, or her poor wispy slave.

Something stirs in the deepest part of her, from where all of her fears rise, from where all her sorrows are stored. She has not been – what? – strong enough, clever enough – to admit it. Even when he is overtaken with the terrifying long deep slumber and she waits for him to wake, she is so relieved when he does that she cannot bear to question the mystery. It is grotesque and too horrific to imagine.

Owen still has a full head of hair unlike most his age. Granted, it is bristly, but it is there, thick and plentiful, absent of the slightest grey. She glances at her mirror again. She has been experimenting with hair dye to hide her own grey strands that multiply daily. Whatever does this mean? Fear grabs her. He comes up the stairs now. She folds the mirror, turns the lamp down a notch and climbs into bed.

'Owen, do take your clothes off, I want you naked.'

'You only have to ask once.' He throbs at her suggestion.

When he is in bed, she throws the bedding off him and raises the lamp.

'I want to look at you.'

It is the only occasion in their marriage when Nora begins a night's lovemaking with dishonesty. She strokes him with one hand, the other holds a lamp while she conducts her survey. He is amused and flattered that her eyes appear to travel lustily down his body. It takes only a few minutes to discover what she needs to know. Now that she seeks it, it stares her in the face so blatantly, so obviously. He has not aged at all these last few years. She kisses his face, noting only two slim wrinkles resting near the corners of his eyes and nowhere else. He is fifty-four for God's sake!

There is an urgency in the way she takes him tonight. With her hands and her mouth, she does everything she can think of to him without allowing him that sweet release, and when he is almost in agony she finally places him in her. She changes positions to surprise him so that he holds on longer than he ever has before.

Nora Mockett abandons all her fear for one blessed moment until she is shuddering, and she screams out into the wicked, wicked night.

It took a year of diligence. A year of cajoling, planning, and explaining to Owen Mockett and the storm-faced boy how important it was to conduct tests. To warm the ten-year-old to the inevitable, Clovis mimicked family with Rafe. Once more she called upon her time in north Iceland, when her aunt's large family sat by the fire and pots hung from chains full of moss porridge and meat. When their vigorous storytelling set against the blasted, howling wind whittled away at the bleak sunless hours. Her interpretation of that setting reborn in east London was startlingly diminished when it became apparent that the only storytelling talent she possessed was that of lying. Surprisingly however, Finn, somewhat shyly at first, filled the boy's imagination with tales of his former seafaring life, and the summer of his astronomy-filled nights in Iceland. And once, upon the turn of the autumn into winter, the boy smiled at Finn's account of waking to the tongue of a sheep licking at his face.

In the meantime, Clovis filled Owen Mockett's thoughts with glory. Seduced by the possible results of replicating Rafe's magical essence, which included acknowledgement from royalty and making scientific history, he braced himself for the first day of experiments with those riches in mind.

So it was, that late at night while Nora Mockett slept upstairs, the first session began in the back room of the apothecary. It was the taking of skin that hurt most. Rafe shrank from the lancet. Mockett looked at Clovis and questioned her with his raised brow: Is this necessary? Her answer was given when she held the boy down.

CHAPTER FORTY

'I cannot find her anywhere. She is not at the market, nor on Park Street. The stanhope is here. The servants have not seen hide or hair of her. Where could she be?'

Constance paces in front of Percy, who has come directly from Holborn.

'She is always home before dark.' She realizes she repeats herself. 'She could have fallen into one of the train pits. Oh the damnable railways! They ruin us! Or, she has been accosted. Oh Percy, what if those awful foreign men have her? For God's sake. What shall we do?'

'Constance, calm yourself,' Percy entreats her. 'I will send for a constable immediately.'

'I have done it. God Almighty, Percy. Do you think me an idiot?'

'Of course not. Perhaps she is at St Mary's.'

'It was the first place I sent Thomas. It is that cruel woman who has twisted the knife. I offered her money and I could not believe it when she refused. She would not bend. We have been to Limehouse many times to see him. How humiliating it was, too. To stand on the street and be refused entry! She sent her husband out to tell us it was no good. We could not see Rafe, not even for a moment.'

'I am sorry. I am so sorry, dear Constance.'

'Weeks ago, I forget how many, he stood at the window crying. Crying, Percy! He revealed a world of unhappiness on his face in just those few moments. Then she pulled him away and it was our last glimpse of our poor boy.'

'You must keep trying. Persistence in all things, Constance.'

The drawing room is in disarray. Cushions are piled in one corner of the sofa; a few tumble to the floor. A tea tray with remnants of late night crumbs clutters the occasional table. The fireplace needs scrubbing.

'I have not let the maids in here since last week when we returned from Limehouse. It was a distressing journey home.'

'Do you think Verity is in Limehouse?'

'Well, Percy, I shall tell you now. The Fowlers are no longer in Limehouse.'

'What? Where are they?'

'We do not know. We have asked everyone in the neighbourhood. We have gone from door to door, from business to business, and they have disappeared like a night mist. The house sits empty. They owe no debts to anyone in Limehouse and they have not been turned out. They have stolen away with the boy.'

'I know a few men who will make enquiries. We will find them.'

'On that terrible day when our husbands and our sons ... when they died, I swore I would never let anyone I love slip from my grasp ever again. Look at me now, Percy. Rafe and Verity, both are gone.'

Verity had sneaked away from Lawless House earlier in the afternoon when Constance took her daily walk in Regent's Park. The clashing of china and the sounds of lunch being cleared away were her cue that now is the time to steal away without observation.

Her mourning dress, the same one she wore after her father's death, folds around her limbs so lightly. Compared to the current stiff and heavy petticoats it feels as if it is made of a few raven's feathers.

She strides up Park Street to the high street where the shopkeepers toss her a lean glance. The street never lacks a mourning ensemble and they pay scant attention to a veiled woman. Not so when she enters the Mother Black Cap on the high street. Heads turn and a path clears. Verity seeks the publican. She lifts her veil, and nudging her dark spectacles down her nose a bit, states that she is in need of a short stage, and asks at what time may she rely upon it.

'There ain't none reliable, madam, but one should stop soon.'

'As I thought,' she replies. 'Whisky.'

'Yes, madam. Right away, madam.'

She tastes the whisky and almost spits it out. Something is wrong with it. It burns her tongue and has lost its sweetness. She verges on purchasing another when she is told the short stage has arrived.

It has a gloomy sturdiness, older, smaller and less comfortable than a stagecoach. For two hours it rattles and rumbles, stops short, stops long and rolls. Four miles seem an eternity as the coachman commands it to unburden its chassis of passengers, and groan with new ones. The streets pass by but she has no interest in the vast swathes of the city unfolding in the approaching evening. At Fleet Street she grasps the leather strap and alights.

'Do I wait for you on my return trip?' the coachman asks.

'What?' Her attention is elsewhere. 'No, no thank you.'

Fleet Street abides its law of mayhem and frenzy with scuttling pedestrians and horse-drawn traffic at their peak. A solitary figure stands perfectly still in the lively and bustling entrance to Temple Bar; beckoned by the lavender girl with a few bunches, she empties her coin purse into the girl's basket.

'Cor! Thank you, mum.' She attempts a curtsy.

When Verity enters Temple Gardens the wind whips up, rustling the trees, shifting the gritty dirt. Stacks of law books dwarf the shadows of men in chambers. Young clerks scratch across the pages.

Verity has not visited the Mulberries since that day.

It was the empty house on Three Colt Street that shut her down. Hopeless and angry, she felt mechanically unable to keep going. She always knew the possibility existed, that Rafe would be taken from her and Constance, and now she is faced with the truth, that she never believed anything other than what she wished to believe.

Hunger did not ghost her when she tried starving herself to a slow death. Nor did weakness or pain from lack of nourishment. It is as it should be. Her failure brought her here, the place where sorrow first became her companion.

The black water is wild and forceful in its flow this evening. She waits for the river traffic to lighten at Temple Stairs, inching ever closer to the edge of the steps.

She marks the high tide and how the Thames spits angrily at her, spraying her face and sloshing her boots. Slowly, the water fades from her vision and is replaced with a spinning zoetrope of images. There is her son. She asks God's forgiveness, for she finds it difficult to recall the details of his face. Her husband is beside him, holding his hand. Then comes her exquisite mother who glows with life and reaches out to her.

The zoetrope disappears and the faces of those she loves shine up at her from the jet-coloured water. They are the faces of a family, her family, and all that ever mattered to her in the world.

With her veil and dark glasses still in place, Verity leans forward with her arms spread wide. She thinks of herself as an offering, like the tall, wooden cross the priest offers the river each year in the Blessing of the River ceremony. Her weight slowly transfers and she leaps.

Filth and sewage fill her nostrils. The roaring voice of the Thames muffles the cries of witnesses. The shock of the cold and the struggle to breathe does not frighten her. She welcomes the blackness as she sinks and the water pushes her north.

But what is this? The glow of the gas lamps flickers into her view. Her body floats to the surface as the currents throw her to the bank and deposit her shivering and as dirty as the Thames itself. Crawling back into the water, cursing the evil that would rob her of an instant death, she flings herself in again until she is carried along another mighty current. Again she goes under; deeply and forcefully it carries her down, down – and then again she floats up, up and is thrown back to the shore. *Impossible*, she thinks as she drags her limp body to its knees. Her veil and spectacles have been washed away and her long, silvery-white hair hangs wet down her back. Sediment clings to her drenched clothing.

Verity wipes muck from her face. What agony is this? She cannot still be alive.

Dazed and shivering, still kneeling, she turns to fix her view on something, anything recognizable. Pagoda-like piers. Winding stairs. A river busy with small steamers and their lamps glaring through an approaching fog. Human and boat traffic of the Thames. And she is still here. Utterly, shockingly, impossibly, still here. She crosses herself again and again.

She tests her legs; they lead her from the floating piers at the quay and up the winding stairs past a little wooden house with signs that direct passengers to 'Pay Here for Taking Boat'. She trudges past people who gawk at her. Onward she trails through the Hungerford market in which she descends the stairs to the fish market.

The mud on Verity's mourning gown attracts the fish scales and bones underfoot and, as if they are alive and entities unto themselves, they attach to her trailing skirts. When she reaches the narrow passageway lined with advertisements that lead her away from the market and the river, the nightlife of St Martin's Lane greets her and she shrinks from the cacophony it produces.

'I must walk ... I need to walk. Soho Square.' Her gravelly voice shocks her.

When Long Acre appears she turns off to navigate the small maze of streets in Soho. The longer she walks, the more she is mantled by shame and guilt. She expects her sister may never forgive her. But what is important now, this moment, is the fact of the miracle. She seeks Father O'Brien.

The privileged have long fled Soho. Prostitutes swan their way through their purlieus; music halls and small theatres have moved in. The buildings are crammed, and their open windows discharge the first smoke and song of the evening.

Verity toils on towards Soho Square, dragging her black skirts that glitter with mud spots of silver fish skin and scales. She recognizes the gardens as she draws closer. The poorest of the poor swing their children over the iron railings surrounding the garden so that they might relieve themselves before they are put to sleep with sips of gin in the nearby rookery.

Behind Carlisle House sits the two-storey Catholic chapel of St Patrick's. Francis Lawless had contributed heavily, moved as he was by the poor Irish trying to survive in desperate circumstances in the surrounding parish of St Giles.

Verity makes a fist and pounds on the door. Her eyes sting from the nasty river water. It takes more than one attempt before the door creaks open.

'Sister, I must see Father O'Brien,' Verity pleads.

The sister opens her mouth and shuts it straight away. She cannot fathom the creature she sees in the light of the gas lamp.

'I am a miracle, Sister, a miracle!'

'Yes, yes, aren't we all, aren't we all. I've over two hundred miracles that want feeding soup and bread this very moment. And Father O'Brien visits the rookery at the risk of his health.'

'But he must hear my confession, I must tell him about the miracle.'

The sister heaves a weary sigh. Another lost to the drink, she thinks.

'Go on now. We haven't room tonight. The father will be late returning and a good deal exhausted he'll be, too.'

'I am the daughter of Francis Lawless, who was one of the largest benefactors of this chapel.'

'Yes, dear, and I am related to Prince Albert.'

The door slams shut.

'Ah!'

She turns away, rendered speechless by the cold reception.

Overcome by the cruelties of the day, Verity sinks to the pavement in front of the iron fencing that borders the chapel.

Though her empty coin purse is lost in the Thames, she slips her hand in the side seams of her gown where between her under-petticoat and her petticoat her pocket is still tied to her waist. There is enough to procure a cab and suddenly she wants nothing more than to be at Lawless House with her sister. A hansom has just let down one of the square's residents. The driver leans down to hear the instructions, wary of her dreadful appearance, but when Verity offers him much more than his regular shilling a mile, he whistles in delight.

A fairly clean blanket is provided which she now pulls over her muddied and reeking gown. The cab jerks forward to begin its long journey to Camden Town.

'It is Verity! She is home! Come, Constance,' Percy shouts out from the front door of Lawless House.

Constance lifts her skirts and runs to the door. Percy leaps to the cab and opens the folding doors that cover Verity's legs.

'What a fright you gave us!' Constance steps out into the bitter evening air. And what a fright you look! Good Christ, Verity!'

'Constance, Percy. A miracle.' Verity calls out.

Once all are inside, Constance and Percy pace the drawing room, passing each other time after time while they wait for Verity to change her sodden clothes.

'Cognac, Constance?' Percy asks.

'No, I cannot drink it. Annoyingly, I have gone off it. I do not know why.'

'Finish your tea then, you need your strength, too.'

Finally, Verity is clean and dressed warmly under her white banyan. She nervously fingers her rosary beads.

'Where in the bloody hell have you been? Your sister and I have almost gone insane.' Percy is red-faced and unusually angry.

'Percy! I have never before heard you swear!' Constance is taken aback.

'This is a night for it, Constance.'

'Are we alone?' Verity asks.

'Yes, Thomas drives Rachael home now. He'll return the trap in the morning. What has happened to you Verity, we cannot wait a moment longer. And I am becoming very cross,' Constance says. 'Here, sit down by the fire.'

'You will be crosser, dear sister. And you, Percy.'

'Go on,' Percy says.

'God forgive me, I . . .' Verity sits and looks away from them and into the flames, ashamed.

Constance perches on an arm of the sofa squeezing a cushion, her knuckles white with tension. Percy pours another whisky and sits beside her. They wait.

'I have been to Temple Stairs.' Verity puts her fist to her lips and shakes her head. 'You see, I wished for nothing more than to be with those I love.'

Constance stares at her dumbly. Percy looks from one sister to another, also speechless.

'Do you mean that you tried to take your life?'

'I did not see it that way, sister.'

'What other way shall we see it, then?' Percy asks with a raised voice.

'I wanted to be with them, all of them.' A tired sigh deflates her.

'And what of us? What of me? Of Rafe? And Percy, and all the Fitzgeralds that are alive and well?' Constance demands.

'I am sorry. I was wrong and terribly selfish.'

In the silence that follows, Lawless House groans as if under the strain of Verity's confession. The fire pops and the windows rattle against a wind that accosts an early winter night. Verity turns her chair to face them more directly.

'There are unspeakable things that we must now face, sister,' Verity says.

'Perhaps I should leave you two to . . .' Percy begins.

'No, Percy. Please, stay. You must hear the rest. We need someone we can trust wholeheartedly,'

'Who came to your rescue? How?' Constance asks.

'God,' she answers.

'God?' Percy repeats, confused.

'God lifted me from that blackness.'

Verity stands and continues, 'I am in full possession of my senses. I will relate to you exactly what happened, the entire truth, and you may judge for yourselves.'

She tells them she should be dead, that no normal person could have survived the arms of the Thames twice. When she describes how long she was under water and how forcefully it overcame her, both of her listeners shrink with the horror of it and neither can repress their anguish.

'So you see, it was, it *is*, a miracle. God has brought me back from the dead.'

Another silence.

Then Constance stands and retrieves one of Rafe's halo paintings from where it hangs over the writing desk.

'No, Verity. God has nothing to do with this. It is the boy.'

'What?' Verity and Percy ask in unison.

'I never believed it until now. I am . . . I am terrified,' Constance whispers.

'Oh, sister. What are you thinking?' Verity asks.

'It is completely irrational, but it also makes sense in some bizarre way. Think of it. Why does Rafe need such stringent protection? Why is it that Clovis Fowler, her servant, and I assume, Mr Fowler and his apprentice have survived their ordeals? Especially Mr Fowler and his noose! And the long sleep, it is not a normal thing, Verity. It is to do with the boy. Think of the way in which

Clovis Fowler interrogated me about Rafe's fever. And Benedikt! There is a reason he devotes every hour to Rafe. Oh, heaven knows there are gaping holes and an immense number of unanswered questions, but . . .'

'Wait, wait. Hold right there, Constance,' Percy interrupts.

'Percy, we must confide in you now. We have not told you the entire story. You must promise us that you will never betray us.'

'Dear God, what have you done?'

'Nothing. Not a thing, except loved a child as if he were our own.'

They speak late into the night. They weigh the fantastical against the practical. Verity makes her view clear that even if the miracle is down to Rafe, it is the will of God and His power that makes Rafe special. Constance is not as certain.

Percy is so shaken that they send him home to his worrying wife and sleeping children. But he goes solid, and forever loyal and protective of the sisters, as the Fitzgerald family has always vowed to be.

'It is good that he knows. We will need him,' Verity says.

Constance draws a sharp breath. 'Did you think of me even once, Verity, before you threw yourself into the river? she asks.

'I was possessed of an overpowering desire, Constance. If I allowed myself even a moment's thought of you, I would not have been able to do it.'

Constance sighs. 'It will take me some time to forgive you.'

'I know.'

CHAPTER FORTY-ONE

1846

Spring comes late this year. In March the temperature in Hyde Park drops to below freezing. The trees' green-pointed buds are frozen beneath ice caplets. The haze over London is so dark and thick that travel is suddenly impossible. After the murk clears, heavy snow falls for two days, and after the snow comes a great frost. By the end of March, a bustling, wildly active scene is erected on the banks of the frozen Serpentine.

The lake area is noisy with barkers, music, sledges, children playing and drunks singing. Food is roasting and commerce is at its peak. Fires dot the area and offer warmth that many people cannot afford at home. Thousands of spectators marvel at the scene on the frozen Serpentine.

Chinese lanterns in red, blue, green and yellow throw splashes of vivid colour onto the ice. There are but a few short hours left of the daylight and this fact brings everyone onto the ice at once. The sisters had avoided the Serpentine entirely until Percy had persuaded them to join him, endeavouring to relieve them of their anxious fear of returning to the scene where the unthinkable had occurred.

Now that Percy is safely on his way home, the sisters are more relaxed in their wanderings. They stop for a piece of steaming gingerbread, not at all concerned that their gloves become sticky and soiled.

'It seems all of London is here today,' Constance says.

'Oh sister, look who comes. It is too late to avoid him.'

'Mrs Fitzgerald?'

Marland Unger's ears are red-tipped from the cold, yet he perspires from a long skating session. A little breathless, his broad smile turns strange when he takes the sisters in at close range.

'Marland, how well you look,' Constance says.

But Marland cannot coax his smile back, try as he might to pluck it from wherever it hides.

'The canals are frozen too are they not?' Verity asks.

He stares at them unable to look away. The power of speech fails him.

'I just remarked that it seems all of London is here today,' Constance perseveres, clutching her lavender cape more tightly.

Marland tips the corner of his flat cap.

'Good day to you both,' he mumbles, and skates away, casting back fearful glances.

'I did say, didn't I?' says Constance. 'His mother ages quickly, so it is even more pronounced that we do not.'

'I did not know it was that noticeable,' Verity says. 'I thought we had a few years left before we need worry about our appearances.'

Almost to the edge of the lake now, the sisters are moments from turning their back on the winter scene when a boy with flame-coloured hair catches Constance's eye. In a green-velvet coat that flips in the wind, he skates freely and without abandon, yet there is a wistful look upon his face that speaks volumes of how little he seems to be enjoying it.

Constance stops, paralyzed.

'What now?' Verity asks.

He looks younger than his fourteen years, not yet travelled through his adolescence.

Verity follows the trail to the object of her sister's view.

'Oh. Oh dear God,' she says.

Constance feels her heart stop and then it kicks another beat. There is the shimmer of the golden chain that hangs down his waistcoat. At the moment they recognize the ring swinging from the chain, the boy casts his gaze towards them.

He shouts out, calling the names that he used when he was young and could not pronounce their names.

'Auntie Connie! Auntie Very!'

How many people Constance pushes aside she does not know or care. The sisters shove and struggle to get closer to him, raising their voices to be heard over the raucous throng.

The Fowlers spot the sisters just as chaos erupts in the crowd.

'Oh, Constance, those men! They make their way to Rafe!'

The men are bearded and stocky and practised skaters. One carries a club of some kind that he uses to push people away, clearing a path to his target. Finn Fowler grabs the coat-tails of one of them, who swiftly bashes him until Finn falls on the ice. The other man sends Clovis flying with a massive shove.

Another flash of swishing, black cloth appears, cutting through the bystanders. Benedikt skates magnificently towards the two men just as they make an attempt to sweep Rafe away. He knocks them off their feet.

The crowd, which impedes the sisters' efforts to move in closer to Rafe, is stirred to protect the boy, but the weight of so many people on the same frame of ice is fatal. Beneath the pressure, the ice floor begins to bend and give. An awful cracking sound cuts the air. The sisters freeze in sheer terror and disbelief.

The men who were in pursuit of Rafe run away, lost amongst the stalls. Benedikt lets them go, his main concern is Rafe who is now sinking into the icy water. Benedikt dives in after him, both of them disappearing. Hundreds of people stand breathless, silent. A man unwraps his scarf and holds it above the break in the ice. But there is no hand to clasp it.

All are now certain of two deaths. The ice marshals try to break through the crowd but the density of the throng impedes their progress.

Constance whispers frantically into Verity's ear. 'I will not allow him to enter the frozen world of the dead. Not again. Never again.'

In the bitter cold of what is left of the day, Constance removes her shoes, then her cape, stole and hat. She slides in stockinged feet through the swarm of people. Not even Clovis can stop her now. Fearless, she approaches the edge of the ice break and steps down into the water. She vanishes.

Down, down Constance falls into the Serpentine. She begins to swim, her eyes open and searching. She swims until she spots Benedikt's black coat. He is still alive and still searching. He sees her, shakes his head 'no' and points in the other direction. Constance turns and swims away from him. Benedikt directs his search to another area.

Constance spots the red hair first. Rafe is floating along as if asleep. She captures him and cradles him in her arms. Her fingers clasp his wrist. Alive. She should not have doubted. Benedikt has turned back to witness the rescue. Her view of him is obscured by dirty slush, but Constance catches something in his eyes – some superhuman emotion is on the verge of erupting from this strange man, and then it is gone. There is something else about his eyes, something she recognizes in a hair's breadth and then it too is gone. She swims to find the opening, for she is unsure how far she has searched. Rafe's eyes open for a brief moment. He recognizes Constance and squeezes her hand. She did not think it possible to shed tears while immersed in icy water.

Swimming with one hand towards the dim light that illuminates the opening in the ice, her eyes feast upon every surface of him.

When they emerge from the water and after they have been pulled onto the safe ice, the crowd roars, 'Bravo!'

Then, when the moment passes, as if pulled by a magnet, they collectively step away – for how is this possible? How did these three people survive this ordeal? Impossible!

Clovis and a fully recovered Finn rush in and with brusque pushes against the remaining onlookers, they snatch the boy from

Constance's arms, swiftly removing him from the site of the commotion.

Willa and Jonesy cast a parting glance at the sisters. An acknowledgement of some sort is entangled within it, as if the four of them long to speak, but the young people are impotent under Clovis's furious orders. They reluctantly trail off after their master and mistress.

Still more confusion besets the scene as a covey of journalists descend on Constance. They surround her, panting like thirsty dogs with hanging tongues. They want their story of the silver headed heroine who mysteriously and outrageously survived the icy water of the Serpentine.

Verity wraps her stole around Constance and tries to stuff her hands into her hat.

'What are you doing? For God's sake Verity, run after them. Follow the Fowlers.'

'I will not leave you here like this, Constance.' Verity is incredulous.

'Go! Go! I am frozen and cannot move quickly enough. Go! Verity, please. I will live.'

'I will not abandon you.' Verity turns on the journalists. 'Leave us, you vultures.'

'Your names are Constance and Verity? Any surnames you'd care to help us with, ladies? Are you related? What happened under the ice? Who is the boy? You were under for over ten minutes – how do you explain it? Might you give us a word or two?'

'Come. Let us be away from here this instant,' Verity says.

Constance casts one more lingering glance into the crowd of dispersing people. For the second time they have lost him.

'I curse the Thames, the lake, I curse all bodies of water.' Constance tears through the house discarding her clothes, leaving them where they fall. She waves away the new maid who wishes to help her, and stands in her chemise at the top of the stairs. Her skin has a bluish tint and her veins add green to her alabaster skin.

Verity climbs midway up the stairs, stops short and gasps at the sight of her.

'Well. What?' Constance is furious. 'What do you think you looked like the night you decided to join our dead family?'

'That again,' Verity says.

'You should have gone after him.'

'I made a choice, Constance.'

'Yes, you did. The wrong one. Always, the wrong one.'

Verity shrinks from her sister's stinging truth.

'We have lost him *again*. We must begin searching *again*. I wasn't going to die today, Verity. All of this . . .' Her arm sweeps to emphasize her point. 'It has all changed. I was in no danger. I was just bloody freezing. It was stupid of you.'

'That is cruel, sister,' Verity says softly.

'No. I shall tell you what is cruel, shall I? The poor boy had marks and puncture wounds on his arms and his neck.'

'Wounds?' Verity stammers. 'Such as what – bruises, or swellings?'

'Such as cuts from lancets, and wound marks on his temples . . . like punctures! His hair . . .' Constance shrinks at the memory. 'His hair was floating up in the water, swishing every which way, and when I held him to me his head turned and I saw that a patch had been cut close to his scalp. They are taking pieces of him, Verity. And you let him go. He is with his monster mother now.'

'Oh, Constance. Oh, no. Why would she do such a thing? We must pray, we must go to Mass and ask God . . .'

'God? There is no God. What kind of God would allow this?'

Verity crosses herself. 'Constance. You are not well. I shall call for Percy.'

'Oh no. No, no, no. I am absolutely crystal-headed and fit as a race walker.'

'Surely, sister, you do not mean it.'

'Do not tell me what I mean. Please leave me now.'

'Shall I bring you tea, or cocoa, something warm, or brandy?'

'Go away, Verity.'

Exhausted, Constance changes into her dressing gown, grabs a blanket and waits to hear Verity retire. She eases down the steps with a lamp and into the drawing room to her writing desk. It takes the best part of two hours to gather her thoughts to compose a letter to Benedikt. When she's conquered the words, the nib flies as she relays her version of the day's events, her fears for Rafe, and a plea for Benedikt's assistance in locating him. She explains that when he was first taken they had no wish to keep him from his mother; they only asked to be a constant in his life. Now, she writes, she is certain the child is subjected to something devious.

And finally,

I am shaken with the anomaly of our situation. It will take some time to adjust. How ironic, for we have plenty of that stuff now. All the time. Time and nothing but time.

I better understand your purpose and the clandestine way in which you go about it. I wonder how many of us exist and of those, the count for good and compassion, and the count for evil . . .

Constance falls to sleep at last while contemplating the Serpentine. She took life back from it today. The boy would have lived, of that she is certain. But there was something about the actual taking of him that allows her to rest.

The next morning the newspaper hawkers begin their work, feeding the hungry public with the previous day's mysterious and miraculous events at the Serpentine. The amazing rescue garners unwanted attention to all involved.

Thomas, his arms full of tools, cannot quite meet their eyes at breakfast. His morning greeting is subdued and he goes quickly to work on the balcony repairs.

The privacy that residents on the street treasure and guard is sorely missing today at Lawless House. The maids cannot get on with their work for answering the door to callers who wish to steal a moment to congratulate Mrs Fitzgerald on her brave rescue of the boy. Constance turns them all away. She goes from room to room closing the shutters, drawing the curtains. Today, she intends to live the few precious hours of daylight in seclusion.

'Did you mean the things you said last night?' Verity asks her.

'Don't I ordinarily?'

'Yes, but these are extraordinary times.'

CHAPTER FORTY-TWO

'Owen was never secretive. Or nervous . . . He seems so very nervous.'

Nora Mockett has taken up talking aloud when she is alone. She finds it calming and is able to sort through her troubles and those things that niggle her.

'It is most certainly to do with the back room,' she says, as she repositions the Mockett's Mandrake Pills beside Mockett's Balm for the Skin. 'I do not know what it is he does back there in his inner sanctum, toiling away like a possessed sorcerer.' Her head bobs along as she resolves.

'And the Fowler boy, there is something not at all right about the Fowler boy.'

The screeching of the paperboy interrupts her monologue. He gives full range of his lungs with a gulp of the mucky air.

'Moooorning *Chronicle*! *Times*! *Times*! Former Limehouse Convict's Son Saved by the Sisters Fitzgerald!'

Nora throws open the door.

'That is a mouthful, you villain. Give me one of those!'

'Who's for today's news? News! News!' he crows.

'I say there, boy.'

'How many, mum? Ten?'

She shuts the door on the pitiable child after she pays him, tips him, and feeds him from her own breakfast with a large brick of bread and a half-round of cheese, which he promptly carries away to his mother. The employees have not yet arrived and it is still too early for Owen to come down. Nora sparkles in this, her golden hour. Perched on top of a high stool she sips her scalding coffee. From a chain around her neck she opens her mother-of-pearl-encased reading glass. Yet another sign of her weakening body.

'Now, let us see. Where are you?' She peruses the pages. 'There!'

Miracle at the Serpentine, it reads. The article recalls how three people, who by all rights should be dead, survived immersion into the Serpentine for longer than any would think possible. The trio rose from the icy water on an interminably cold March afternoon. The Fowler name is in print. A description of a tall, elderly lady with silvery-white hair is described as *the Heroine of the Day*.

'"One of the sisters Fitzgerald. Clovis and Finn Fowler . . . Their son . . ."' Nora's voice builds as she reads aloud. 'Owen!'

The queerest feeling rises in her. She is overcome by the sense that everything she once knew is no longer valid. With it, the oddest vulnerability crawls against her skin, something akin to what she always imagined madness to be and it portends a complete loss of control.

'Owen!'

'Nora? What is it?'

But Nora cannot answer. Her attention turns to the view of the street. She looks to the past, those years ago when the door was stubborn and stuck. The day Clovis Fowler and her pregnant belly taunted her until the sisters arrived and eclipsed the Fowler beauty. How Nora had savoured that moment. She recalls the atmosphere and how it was heavy with everyone, except her. That day mirrors her feelings now. Even the air can be pregnant, but she will never be, in any way. At last she turns to her husband's inquisitive face, knowing that she has been excluded in this as well. No matter how hard she works, or how hard she loves, it is not to be.

Nora rises from the stool. As certain as she is that her world has turned upside down, she is equally certain that her darling Owen is lost to her unless she takes action. She hands him the paper, picks up her bowl of coffee and retreats upstairs.

Owen reads the story of the miracle and drops the paper on the floor where he stands.

'Nora. Nora, dearest.'

He takes the stairs two at a time. She is found in their odd little parlour with its corner of windows that jut out onto the noisy Commercial Road. She studies her hands again; he often catches her at this. She turns them and strokes the faintly coloured spots. When she is aware of him, she places them in her lap. With a tilt of her head, she beckons him to sit with her.

'Tell me everything,' she says.

There have been difficult moments in their lives. The most bitter and lingering has always been that cruel absence in the cradle she insisted they purchase. Owen wonders if the circumstances were turned and she were to tell him the events that he now relays to her, if a cloud of disbelief might cross his mind. Would he be frightened of her, and for her?

He begins with the truth as he knows it and ends his story with hope. He tells her he seeks to replicate whatever strange and terrible essence the boy has running through his veins so that she too might join their number.

'That, dearest Nora is how I spend each spare moment of every day. My work is for you. The Fowlers are under the impression that I work for them, to bottle a miracle. I work to discover this boy's secret so that it may be shared with you.'

'You say it is in his fever.'

Owen expects laughter, disbelief, or an attempt at a note of levity, but not this dispassionate, flat response.

'It seems to be. You are the only one amongst us who never touched him while he was with fever.'

'I remember that night well. And the sisters Fitzgerald?'

'Yes. It would seem so.'

'And you have no sleeping sickness. It is a result of your condition?'
He nods.

'You know where the Fowlers make their home now. You have known all this time.'

Owen pauses. 'I cannot ...' He changes his mind. 'Yes.'

'You will tell me where I may find Clovis Fowler.' She is calm in her demand.

'They are in a temporary situation across the river in Bermondsey.'

'Bermondsey? Well. This news is almost as shocking as ... as the other. They have fallen.'

'They are far from destitute. They go where they are unknown, where people are occupied with survival.'

'And where will we go, Owen? When our customers and the people of the Commercial Road begin to notice how well you look compared to your wife – and compare their own ageing faces. I daresay they already gossip. Dear God in heaven.'

'It is the very reason I summon all my willpower to replicate this ... this ... thing.' He pauses. 'I am becoming a man of science and I will find a way to make all this right, Nora.'

She is not convinced.

The fourth week after Owen's confession, Nora remains ragged and in bad temper. She awakes boiling with so much anger that she could bite a brick and crumble it with the power of her jaw. Before Owen awakens she is warm with coffee and buttered buns, dressed, and out the door. The note she leaves explains her absence as an opportunity not to be missed in the West End.

Ten minutes from the Surrey side of London Bridge, Nora's fury has made her senseless. Forgoing a cab, she treads in unfamiliar territory. She feels no fear, even when accosted by the foulest smells she has ever encountered. Gagging not once, but thrice, she locates her vinaigrette in her reticule and inhales with a heaving bosom.

An innkeeper's directions have gone wrong and lead her to sights so macabre that she quite nearly turns back. Owen will strangle her if he learns of her strolling in this sparsely populated area, assaulted by the scent of blood amidst men in aprons and gaiters of raw hides. The tanners and their pits, the hide market, with its tens of thousands of soaking hides, is eerily quiet.

Ragged children share the weight of buckets of dog dung, for which the Bermondsey tanners pay up to ten pence a load. Nora stops a pair of them.

'You, there.'

She is aghast to see the children's faces and hands smeared with shit.

'Wha?'

'I seek Bermondsey Street.'

'Ha! Not fer noffin yer don't.'

She places tuppence on the ground in front of them. The urchins snatch them, laugh, and run away with the coin, leaving Nora none the wiser.

By some miracle she marches closer to Bermondsey Street, where the odour from the vinegar factory on Tanner Street moistens her eyes with its sting. Nora turns a corner and the street she seeks is suddenly underfoot. Her anger subsides for a heartbeat or two, replaced by, God forgive her, smugness. For the dismal street is so lacking in colour that it appears only in sepia tones. The houses crunch together, leaning in all directions, peeling plaster harshly covers their wooden frames.

Nora adds paint to the scene, turned out as she is for the West End in her purple ensemble. Her bonnet's ribbons fly behind her, trailing past the shoemakers and cobblers, and finally her marker, the Watch House on the corner from where the parish constables keep watch on the graveyard. On the opposite side of the street is the house, end of terrace, where the shopfront is closed up and shuttered, where the black door protects the Fowlers. Nora's ire returns.

There is no knocker, no invitation to call; she taps firmly with her fist. And again. On the third knock the door opens a crack and the servant girl's face appears.

'Mrs Mockett!' Willa cries.

Before Willa can react further Nora pushes against the door, nearly knocking the girl over.

Rafe appears in all of his awkwardness. The sight of him sends her into a spin of longing and regret, and she cannot stop from charging, holding his shoulders firm, she shakes him.

'Get it. Get it right now. Get the fever.'

He is wide-eyed and frightened and pulls away, but she is stronger.

'How often do you do it? Do it now. Let me feel your head.' Nora places one of her hands on his forehead, holding him fast with the other.

'Here, here! Stop that, Nora Mockett.' Finn appears and pulls Nora off Rafe.

Jonesy comes next and places his robed frame between Rafe and Nora.

'Take him away, Jonesy,' Finn orders.

'I am sorry to witness such a display. You are not at all well, Mrs Mockett.' The familiar voice, tinged with accent, causes Nora's eyes to close in a blind rage. 'Leave us,' Clovis says to Finn and Willa, before turning back to Nora. 'I have foreseen this day for years. You are predictable, Nora Mockett.'

'How often does the fever come?'

'It is of no business of yours . . . but I will tell you, not once since we have earned our tickets-of-leave.'

'It is very much my business. I am here today to tell you this. If I have not become a member of your miraculous party in six months' time, I will tell the world.'

Clovis laughs.

'Oh, Mrs Mockett.' She is genuinely amused. 'You will not place your husband in danger.'

'No, I will not, for he will be none of *your* business. You have no hold over him.'

Clovis changes her tack.

'None of us knows when or if Rafe will have the fever again. But if he should happen to be overtaken with it, I will send for you. You will have to be content with that offer, I know of no better solution.'

'Six months.'

'If you would like to limit the time, then do so. There is no predicting it.'

'Six months. Bring him to me. I shall not be "sent for".'

'Willa, see Mrs Mockett out.'

While Nora Mockett's plum skirts trail away from the Fowlers' house, Clovis continues to stare at the door, as if an imprint of the hysterical woman remained.

'Finn! Come here.'

'What now?' Her husband runs his fingers through his hair, a sign that the encounter has unnerved him.

'We are too long in Bermondsey Street, Finn.'

'Out of the area, then?'

'No, she would expect that. Wiser to stay near. There is a property on Magdalen Street.' She turns to him, 'See to it.'

Just before dark while those in the household are occupied with recovering from Nora's visit, there is one who cannot be at peace. Mrs Mockett has rattled him so that Rafe feels he might die if he does not get out of the house. At fourteen, he is not afraid of stealing away into a London night; he has evaded detection before and tonight he means to do it again.

Outside, the streets are changing over from the business of the day, to the business of the night. He strides to London Bridge in no time and crosses its busy path with the stampede. A thick wad of upset in his stomach produces gritty tears. He has searched for Auntie Connie and Auntie Very before, but when his mother callously informed him of their deaths after his rescue from the Serpentine, his quest changed. He seeks their place of burial. St Anne's graveyard pulls him towards Limehouse. Might they rest near their father?

An hour's continuous walking is uneventful but for a faint feeling of being followed. Each time he looks back, he blames his nerves when he detects only shadows. Full dark brings him to Shadwell High Street. There are whores everywhere, trawling the pavement, parading in short nightgowns, cheap silk and bare heads. His father has educated him regarding whores. Finn seems to know quite a lot about them.

Inside the Half Moon and Seven Stars where Rafe hopes to buy a pie, or a serving of soup, a clean-smelling woman catches his attention. Unlike the others, she is quietly dressed. She approaches him in a light grey mantle, a black silk coat, and ample crinoline. Her eye is drawn to his full pocket when he pays for his food. The publican winks at her.

'Young sir, forgive my boldness. Would you like to retire to a quiet and more orderly place to enjoy your meal?'

Rafe falls into her pretty smile and the glow of her yellow hair, and says yes, yes he would like that very much.

'Please call me Priss, as all my friends do.'

She takes him around the corner to an accommodation house where, for five shillings a turn, she entertains her punters in a clean room, with fresh linen and a large bed. She chats away while he eats and when he is finished she grabs his crotch. He pulls away from her so violently that he knocks over the pitcher of water in a basin that was meant for further cleanliness afterwards. His face is terror-stricken. He must not impregnate a woman. In achingly embarrassing discussions his mother has hammered into his consciousness that it is irrecoverably dangerous to do so. He has developed a further theory that his semen either in or out of a woman should not be touched, just as he must not be touched when in fever. This is the secrets he keeps. No one must know he still suffers from the fevers – especially his mother.

Priss's pretty smile transforms to a sneering, grotesque mask.

'I shall have my money, boy. You came up of your own free will. You are not so stupid to think I wanted your company, or you were to have mine for no coin! Mine is a night-time economy and I will have my due.'

Just then a buxom woman with high, white hair bursts through the door. Mrs Dripper, proprietress of the house of accommodation, is in a frenzy of anger.

'I have a hansom driver at the door insisting that the boy come down this instant. He is to take the cab home. What were you thinking, Priss? I shall raise your rate if you continue this bawdy nonsense.'

A man stands near the hansom. Rafe cannot see his face, but is sure he has seen him before. In the upset and confusion of the moment, and the dogged insistence of the driver to hurry Rafe into the cab, he takes no more notice of Benedikt. Even when the driver explains that he has his orders to deliver Rafe safely home, the boy does not seem to care to know the details.

The house on Bermondsey Street is brightly lit upon his return. His mother is engaged in a fuming disregard for his father who speaks to her in a low, reasonable voice. Rafe hears Finn defending Rafe's right to 'more freedom, and a life outside these walls'.

Clovis is so angry that when Rafe walks by her he thinks she may strike him.

'Do not touch me,' he warns, in a voice that contradicts his years.

In his room, he picks up a brush that lies in a row of drying brushes. He strokes his palm with it before dipping the tip in red. The canvas is primed and once more he conjures the sisters Fitzgerald into his room.

CHAPTER FORTY-THREE

Bandyleg Walk is dangerously situated amongst the never-ending narrow courts and winding streets of The Mint. Dilapidated houses, a few without roofs, are havens to fugitives from the law, debtors, and those who are driven from the slums by the men who build roads and railways. Henrietta from the penitentiary is found in The Mint off Borough High Street where she has embraced an opportunity to stitch together a life far from the alleys and corners of Mayfair.

The kitchen work to which Henrietta was assigned while in the tench, just as that frightening Fowler had promised, proved to be a boon. For she discovered that she was capable of rolling a crust and turned a fine hand to it. So pleased was Matron, that Henrietta was promoted to assistant cook for the Millbank staff and held the coveted position until she received her ticket-of-leave.

Here in Bandyleg Walk, on the ground floor of three crumbling storeys, a lodging house has prime place on the dingy corner where all the buildings are blackened from smoke. Henrietta made wise and frugal use of the purse of coins Clovis Fowler had tossed at her. She has set up and operates a soup-house. And by God, she cooked an outrageous amount of soup in the tench.

Steam rises in a smelly mist on the windows where basins and ladles are in full display for those who cannot read a bill of fare. For tuppence, a punter enjoys a prime basin of soup and a slice of bread. Add another penny and Henrietta throws in a potato. She is tough but fair; there are no handouts. She is known to employ two staff, always convicts returned to the world, but suffers no thieves or cheats on her staff. A burly lodger upstairs is her booter-outer. A sharp knife hides always within her reach.

Busy all day and half the night, the quantities she sells are large enough to afford a dream of a new venture. One day soon, away from this slum, she will have dining rooms. She is good at chops.

The supper rush is over and so efficiently run that Henrietta's frock is still fresh and unstained. She cannot say that she pines for her silk dresses and feathered and ribboned hats. Her plain, green wool suffices; though she could not resist sewing a neat row of small black velvet bows down the bodice.

Henrietta's back is to the door when it opens and the night air enters whilst the odour of twelve hours of simmering soup escapes.

'No more soup.' She does not bother to turn to her guest and continues scrubbing a rickety table.

'I am not here for soup.'

Henrietta pauses, and then wrings her rag. She scrubs again.

'What can I do for you, Clovis Fowler?'

Even people who are captains of their own ships form habits. Those who have the freedom to come and go as they please, rely on some ritual to mark their day. It is Nora Mockett's ritual to cross the Commercial Road when there is a lull in the traffic, well after the two-thirty bell tolls. Three weeks after her visit to Bermondsey Street she wraps a package for Mr Wright, the cabinetmaker across the road. He is a good customer, a loyal one who is in constant need of syrups, tonics and lozenges for his large family.

These last three weeks Nora has had to work a little harder to muster the smile she normally brings to his workshop. Lately she grows impatient with his neighbourhood gossip and is eager to return to her own place of business. Each day she awaits news from Bermondsey and would not like to miss a message.

When she has collected the payment and indulged Mr Wright for a short but polite time, the road is already moving again at a quick pace. Nora stands on the kerb waiting for the traffic to subside, with a chopped view of the Mockett shopfront. It really does outshine any others on the Commercial Road she thinks, and then turns her head to seek an empty slot so that she might make a dash. Suddenly she catches the odour of something like weak stew, with a prevailing scent of onion. She is hatless, and without her shawl, neither needed for her daily ritual, and so feels a warm breath on her neck.

Nora is on the verge of turning her head to see who crowds so close to her, when a firm hand is pressed onto her back. One shove and she goes down.

Nora hears a distinct crack near her temple. How cold the pavement feels against her cheek, she thinks. It is her last thought before a coach-and-four trample her. She lies dead, her eyes open, her neck broken, her body crushed.

A woman walks calmly away from the shambolic scene, pulling her cloak tightly around her green dress adorned with black velvet bows.

CHAPTER FORTY-FOUR

1852

Mockett feels he will lose his dinner when Clovis enters his shop. It seems the tip of a hot, searing blade slices at his innards. He has closed early, and now that she has arrived he hastily pulls down the canvas blinds with lightning jerks.

'Owen, you have lost your colour. Why do you secrete us here like this?'

Owen silently rages. *I could choke her over and over again. Though she cannot die, I would make her wish she could.*

He slams his fist on the counter.

'Do not speak!' he shouts at her.

Overwhelmed with a desire to grab her by her thick mane, hold her back and slit her throat, he forces his hand into his jacket pocket from where he produces a letter.

'Read it.' He thrusts it at her.

Clovis first takes a glance at the signature and then looks carefully at Owen.

'Read it,' he repeats.

Her face remains placid at first but as she reads on her expression changes to one of pity.

'I would laugh outright at these writings of a murderous woman if it did not soil the memory of the late Mrs Mockett. No, Nora and I were not the closest of friends, but my God, Owen. How could you think me capable of this?'

'I think you capable of anything,' he says, coldly.

'Henrietta Martin was guilty of infanticide. And she let another hang for the murder of her baby. *She* is the woman who killed your Nora. I tried to help her at Millbank because she wove a pitiful story of regret. Ask anyone and they will tell you it is true. But when she did not change her ways, and took advantage of my good will, I stopped wasting time on her and she turned on me. I will tell you this Owen, she is evil at her core. When I refused to help her again she threatened to one day ruin me, hence this, her false confession.'

Owen snatches the letter from her. Unshrinking, she approaches him gently.

'Owen, did Nora tell you that she came to visit us in Bermondsey? Did she tell you I promised that if Rafe ever came down with another fever that I would call for her immediately?'

'No. She never said.' Owen is uncertain of the truth of it.

'Do ask my entire household. They were all present, Owen, all witnesses to my promise to your wife. Ask any one of them.'

'Why didn't Nora tell me this herself?'

'Well . . .' Clovis looks away demurely.

'Well, what?' he snaps.

'She attacked Rafe.' Clovis appears to struggle. 'She demanded that he produce his fever, as if he could just turn it off and on. Again, ask Finn if you wish, he will not deny it. We wanted to spare your feelings and not cause trouble between you and your wife . . . knowing how difficult it must have been for her.'

All the fight drains from him. He can believe this to be true.

Clovis sees she has won and dares to touch his shoulder.

'It is time for you to do what you dearly love, Owen.'

His upper lip perspires with her so near him. He cannot help it.

'You cannot go on much longer here without raising questions.'

Damn her, she is right. As the years ticked over, his customers who once relied on him for relief of minor ailments began to seek a cure for deafness, gouty pains and other ailments of ageing. The comment, 'How well you look, Mr Mockett.' grows in number, and the women especially look at him askance while perusing his skin-enhancing formulas.

'We must go underground,' Clovis continues. 'That is our plight and one of the sacrifices we make. But you are the luckiest of us all. You can continue your studies in the sciences without the pressure of being in the shop each day. And once we set up your businesses anonymously, as we discussed, we'll secure finances for the coming years. I am at your disposal, Owen. I would never do anything to hinder our relationship.'

'Well, you can see how convincing the letter is. I could not fathom why she might make such a confession if it were not true. I wonder how she made the connection between Nora and you?'

'Oh, she was a cunning one. Always full of schemes. Your wife was well known. Nora was a respected member of this neighbourhood, and simple to locate. It would have been easy for her to make the connections. You visited us many times at Millbank and tongues wag and tales spin quickly. And Henrietta had nothing but time to think up her hateful deeds.'

'Then I suppose I owe you an apology.'

'No. Let us never speak of it again. Let us move forward as friends and partners.'

The day that Owen Mockett kills his name he stands alone in his shop on the Commercial Road surrounded by shelves and jars, filled with nothing but the scent of their former contents. The echoes of the neighbourhood footfall, the cries of sick babies and the jumble of voices that over the years filled this space, seep into his memory.

There will be no more Mockett pills, wafers, ointments, or anything bearing the Mockett name.

'Rest in peace, Mockett's Apothecary.' His voice echoes as he prepares to leave this life and form another.

The Parentations

I'll chain thee in the north for thy neglect,
Within the burning bowels of Mount Hecla;
I'll singe thy airy wings with sulphurous flames,
And choke thy tender nostrils with blue smoke;
At every hiccup of the belching mountain,
Thou shalt be lifted up to taste fresh air,
And then fall down again –

Prospero to Ariel, The Tempest

During Hekla's twelfth-century eruption people proclaimed the birds they watched fly into the mountain's fire were hovering souls. Until the nineteenth century, the belief that Hekla was the entrance to hell was firmly held. The legend persists that on Easter, witches gather to meet the devil on Hekla.

In 1913, having remained quiet for thirty-five years, Hekla's explosive eruptions spewed an average amount of lava, creating two large fissures.

The hidden pool's water rose brighter, and shimmered as green as polished malachite.

LONDON
1914

CHAPTER FORTY-FIVE

It happens so suddenly. Overnight London inhales, and when it exhales, its air hovers, thick with anticipation. Soldiers appear everywhere canvassing the streets in khaki. Thousands of Londoners who are strewn across the country and abroad to celebrate the August Bank Holiday weekend are pouring back into town. The atmosphere pulses with excitement and the sense that London life is on the precipice of changing forever.

When war is declared on the Tuesday there is fear of a rush to withdraw funds. The holiday is extended so that the banks may remain closed. But it is not money that is sought in Bermondsey. On Wednesday, Clovis Fowler stands at the counter in a Bermondsey grocer's shop with women who are throwing food. They swipe it off the shelves onto the floor and hurl it at the windows. The grocer has hiked the prices overnight and they are having none of it. Clovis throws her groceries down too, but not out of any protest. She would not even be here if she hadn't sent Willa and Jonesy to purchase buckets and sand. Her nerves are frayed and for once in her interminably long life she feels vulnerable. She elbows her way out and is safely away from the shop just as the police arrive. Down the street she marches in tempo with the monologue running in her head that refuses to quieten:

And just where are Finn and Rafe when Britain declares war on Germany? According to Finn's itinerary, in holy fucking godforsaken Berlin, that's where. The people in Iceland are furious with me. How was I to know that Rafe would sneak off? It is the first time. He's a grown man for God's sake. I cannot keep him tethered.

When she received Finn's telegram explaining Rafe had secretly booked passage, she first went limp with relief and then she snapped. She was so enraged that she shook Jonesy until his brains rattled; he swore he was unaware of the plan. Willa's eyes bulged with innocence.

Clovis is so engrossed in these thoughts that she forgets to avoid the recruiting office on Jamaica Road, where the queue of men runs down the long stretch and curls around the corner. She ignores the men whose eyes follow her proud figure as she crosses to the other side. Normally she relishes a man's raised eyebrow, but now their lust grows stale on her, like a dead mould. In the months that Rafe and Finn have been away she admits, if only to herself, that she misses them. And now with a war on there are so many concerns, so many possibilities that did not exist before. Mainly, what is to become of her men?

The owner of the photographic studio on Jamaica Road pulls the shade down just as Clovis arrives, but he beckons her to enter, eager for his payment. It was a whim, a moment of unabashed sentimentality when she defied Iceland's rule that forbids a visual record and insisted on a family photograph.

'Madam.' He twists his moustache and presents her with the photo.

Clovis stifles a gasp. Here they are, together, in the palm of her hand. How completely modern they look. She stands in the centre between Rafe and Finn, her narrow skirt of charmeuse satin falls just above her buckled pumps. Willa sits in a stiff pose, as straight-backed as the chair. How young she looks, still budding. And Jonesy, the exotic touch, perches on a low, tapestry footstool. Behind them, a muted pastoral scene. From this thick photographic card, Rafe's reserved gaze endures the scrutiny of the camera and Clovis is struck by his breathtaking resemblance to Elísabet.

*   *   *

The trade refers to him as the 'mysterious emperor of ancient things'. They are ignorant of his origins and the way in which he developed his eclectic taste, formed as it was in the sewers and tunnels under London. In the world of auction lots and bric-a-brac the only man who has knowledge of Finn's identity is not a man at all, but a female cross-dresser who knows how to keep a secret. Finn must trust someone, and she, Pauline, asks no questions.

Finn continued his apprenticeship, as he calls it, in a lowly manner. He attended scenes of misery; homes where people were cowed by their desperation for money, and where he then bundled their incongruous items to resell for a profit. Although there is no better pleasure than to buy cheap and sell dear, he could sustain no appetite for their misfortune.

For two decades he travelled to Britain's ports of entry at Hull and Yarmouth, where a healthy and seemingly endless bounty of imported furniture was his for the sniffing. When he began making a decent living, temptation straddled him like a hungry whore. The fakes and forgeries flowing in London's Wardour Street presented him with an opportunity to make a larger profit. Greed soared up in him and so clawed at his nerves that he gave a few spurious items to Jonesy and instructed him to mend and carve them into passable pieces of ancient furniture. How easy it was for Finn to proclaim his redemption while passing the hours in Millbank all those years ago. Now that temptation was before him, he almost fell flat on his face, for he ached for that shortcut to profit.

It was the lesbian Pauline who put him straight again before he tipped properly over the edge. The heft of her person and her extensive experience made her formidable on Wardour Street, where she sold Finn's merchandise. When he first met Pauline she was already too old to continue her buying journeys, and eventually when she was assured he possessed 'the eye' she anointed Finn with her knowledge of the golden route across the Continent, and more importantly, her contacts. She refused to sell his pieces of trumpery, though she praised Jonesy's fine and detailed work, and insisted that Finn take an oath to forswear thievery in all its forms, forever. He did so honestly, with an inner smirk at the word 'forever' and its particular meaning to him. Fifty years have seen the burial of Pauline and her brogues, and now a Mr Tiller fills new shoes.

Finn no longer crosses the Continent every other year, for it is gruelling, and as glamorous as a drunk at a christening. He rests his head on flat pillows in bad hotels and eats cheap food with the locals. The luxury itself is in being far away from London and the house on Magdalen Street. Travelling gives him perspective when he is tempted to forgo his drops and die a painful death, which he contemplates periodically. He plans his journeys around his long sleeps, departing a few weeks after he wakes. The profit proves so great that Clovis curbs her envy of his time away.

Low on stock this year, by June he relaxes in the Dover ferry's roomy saloon. He blinks at the vision striding towards him and then almost empties his bowels when he's sure of it.

'What in holy hell are you doing? You can't be here.'

'Calm down. I've left them a note. My sleep was a month ago, I wasn't followed, and there's no reason why I shouldn't come along.'

Rafe is unusually determined.

Finn almost lets it drop. He's near allowing the whole prolonged lie to unravel at last. What a bloody relief it would be to confess, 'I'm not your father. Go home.'

But it's too late for that, and too late to disembark.

The railway line between Paris and Marseilles travels smoothly. By the time they approach the southern port, Finn's anger subsides. There are small, awkward efforts of politeness: 'You take this bed, it's firmer.' 'No, you have it, I'm all right here.'

The wind of Marseilles is in Finn's favour and the whiff of it leads him to the enamelled pottery of the widow Perrin. The bargaining journey of 1914 begins.

In Stamboul they sample a few draws of cheroots and accept

lemonade from a new dealer. The air is different here, warm and fragrant with mint and sweet dust. Finn's challenge is to haunt the old places while making new contacts. He buys a beauty of a gilded pipe bowl. The smell of it makes him dizzy.

Like a shadow, Rafe follows Finn each day, through the souk and to each appointment, every coffee house. He's disquieted and doesn't seem to know what to do with himself. Finn assumed Rafe would take advantage of his freedom and explore, go a little wild, but he soon recognizes the mask of disorientation on his face.

'I know how you're feeling,' Finn offers. 'I felt the same way on my first trip abroad since . . . since we lost our freedom.'

Finn quickly picks up on Rafe's sigh.

'Our situation. It's not your fault, Rafe.'

'Of course it is.'

On the train to St Petersburg they sink into comfortable seats and sip strong, sweet tea. Their silences, made less awkward by their days together, are now filled with nods of acknowledgement of the sweeping Russian landscape.

The train rattles on for hours without offering a view of a single settlement, followed by frequent station stops, where hawkers wait on the platforms selling smoked fish the size of a large man's thigh. Having once sampled the chicken drowned in soured cream and cheese, Finn has since shunned the restaurant car. Today he buys fish and sausages from a kerchiefed woman on the platform who hunches with a bundle of birch twigs on her back. In their compartment Rafe mentions the pungent odour, but it is nothing compared to the fish paste the Mongolians have smuggled on board.

Their salty meal soon has Rafe searching for water and more tea. While he's away Finn picks up the sketchbook left lying on Rafe's seat.

'Bloody hell,' he says under his breath.

He flips through, not quite believing what he sees. Each dealer is perfectly captured; not only the likeness, but the very essence of the person. The Turk's possessive glare cast over his domain, and also his eagerness. The knitting grandmothers in the next compartment, their heads almost touching, assembled as they gossip. The Mongolian traders and their stash of alcohol, clothing and tobacco. All in remarkable detail, and so quickly drawn.

Finn turns another page. 'Ah,' he says. 'Well, well.'

He had always wondered what keeps Rafe going – who or what does he love. He knew it wasn't him – a surprising flush of shame – and sure as hell not Clovis. He thought perhaps Rafe nursed a lusty love for Willa. But Willa had changed and bathed him, dressed and fed him, the memory of which never faded. Whatever Rafe may have felt for her went unrequited.

Finn turns page after page of drawings of the sisters Fitzgerald. There's no mistaking their distinguished and elegant faces. The punch comes out of the blue, out of the rolling sky flying by his window. Gutted, he is. A baby first parted from his mother, then a little boy made miserable by being snatched away from the doting sisters. And Finn had done nothing. He'd done bugger all to turn a kinder hand to ease the boy's wretchedness. In fact, he admits, he has always been intimidated by him. Rafe had received more education by nine years of age than Finn had in his entire lifetime. And now, here in his hands is an extraordinary gift that he has failed to notice before; a hard-wrought, earthly talent to accompany that strange and otherworldly gift that Rafe has possessed since birth.

Regret constricts his throat as he reflects. I could have offered a soft word here and there instead of my cold indifference. It's no wonder he does not call me 'Father'. They've already lived a lifetime together. He feels like a grandfather who reminiscences with shame, for his memory is sharp and it cuts him.

It's appallingly late, and not nearly enough recompense, but a spark of an idea forms, something that calms him.

Finn returns the sketch book to the seat when the heavy compartment door rolls back. Rafe juggles glasses and a basket of sugary pastries, followed by a woman who expertly manages a tray of tea and water. I wonder that you're not full of hate. He offers Rafe a smile.

The train rattles on. Finn is pensive for the rest of the evening. He watches Rafe sleep; his broad chest gently rises and collapses. The light comes and goes whenever they pass through the remaining stations. When it falls on Rafe he turns in his sleep, and it's then that Finn recognizes the unmistakeably strong resemblance. How he missed it all these years is beyond him. Rafe's hands, folded above his waist, are Elísabet's hands. Her son dreams as the train rocks him to St. Petersburg.

They reach Berlin at the end of July and plan to scour the capital for two days before visiting Finn's most prudent dealer in Dresden. Jostled through the streets of Berlin by swarms of exuberant Germans, within an hour of their arrival they are consumed with panic. Young men sing patriotic songs in the cafés, and the popular Piccadilly Café is promptly renamed Kaffeehaus Vaterland; the city is rife with patriotic ardour. War with Britain is all but painted on their tongues.

'Thank Christ I shipped the goods I've bought so far. We're going home, Rafe.'

Zamovars, historical swords, silk and cashmere shawls and Venetian glass have been packed and shipped to England from St Petersburg. Finn wonders if he'll ever see his investment again. There will be no buying in Dresden, nor Madrid, nor Paris.

As they make their way back to the station to board the first available train to France, they are crushed in the onslaught. Finn grabs Rafe's wrist and directs his hand to Finn's shoulder.

'Don't let go,' Finn says.

Rafe swallows an unexpected knot of emotion. He offers a grateful nod to Finn, who for the first time in eighty years doesn't seem annoyed by his presence.

*   *   *

Never before was there such a sight. They stand in Victoria Station slack-jawed. It is impossible to take it all in. Great swirls of men, but also women – more women than they had ever seen in one place. Worry is written on their faces in a thousand different ways on only the third day since war has been declared.

'London is already changed,' Rafe whispers.

Sorely aware of their dark, three-piece suits amongst the great waves of khaki, their unease grows, as does the realization of their predicament. Rafe entertains images of being shot over and over again, of rising from the dust, the snow, the mud and the sea, like the great immortal monster he believes he is.

Finn's first thoughts are of equal alarm; one word, one scenario in their survival they have never before had to consider. Bombs.

They feel an urgency to be in their own home, another foreign notion neither had before experienced. A further surprise meets them outside the station. It seems travellers are forgoing motor taxis and one sporting the Union Jack on its bonnet coasts to the kerb in an instant to cart them home – never before so quickly. They sit on the edge of their seats to view the transformed city, in which there are flags everywhere – in shop windows, above entries, on hats, and in small versions pinned onto torsos. The pointing fingers of placards and recruitment posters flash by. Rafe elbows Finn and points back at the appeals for enlistments.

There is no visible pall of gloom over the house in Magdalen Street, yet they face their return with girded loins and dread. Rafe expects Clovis's wild anger, and an accusation of abandonment from Willa and Jonesy.

Clovis and Willa sit in the front room pouring over the newspapers when they hear the hum of the motor taxi idling in front of the house. Clovis nearly upsets the tea tray in a nervous jump from her seat. A flush of deep pink crawls up Willa's neck and face and she is unable to calm it. Jonesy bounds down the stairs.

When the door opens and the bags are set on the floor, Finn lifts his eyes to Clovis, anxious to face her wrath and be done with it.

'I'm sorry,' he says. 'There was no time to send a telegram. Germany was ...'

Clovis places her hand over her husband's mouth and there, in front of them all confesses, 'I thought I would never see you again, Finn Fowler.'

Later that night when they are fed, and when only a few swallows of wine make them woozy, Clovis climbs on top of Finn and drapes her naked body over him, like a snug, silk wrap. She takes him in her mouth until he shudders and takes him again and again during the night in a variety of ways and positions until he lays motionless, his legs spread, his manhood limp with exhaustion.

Finn awakens the following morning to the sound of boots on pavement that echo all the way from Tooley Street, the vibrations of which will be a constant for the next four years. Clovis stirs. Although he was surprised by her generosity last night, for weeks he'd noticed small indications that she was softening. Nothing monumental, but like a stiff shot of liquor, the slightest conversion took the edge off. No better time than the present to test her genuineness.

'I've been thinking,' he begins. 'Rafe needs a studio ... outside the house. Somewhere in the neighbourhood.'

'I agree. We might buy cheaply now with all the chaos. Iceland may help.'

Finn's back straightens. She makes no argument? There's no dismissal or bargaining?

'Good. I'll see to it.' He waits for her to change her mind; he expects it, as if their agreement were nothing but a hateful joke. Instead, she hums a tune he doesn't recognize.

'What's that?' He nods to the wooden figure of a man resting against the mirror over the fireplace in their bedroom.

'Jonesy. He's carving puppets. I'm encouraging him.'

Finn won't mention the phials today. One step at a time.

CHAPTER FORTY-SIX

1916

It began two years ago, on the third day after war was declared, when the sisters Fitzgerald, along with thousands of Londoners, traipsed to Victoria Station to view the spectacle. It was an event, and they must see it, for they were drawn to it just as forcibly as others were. None remained unmoved. It grabbed Constance first, a sense that she and Verity were no longer alone in their grief; that they stood with a whole nation of women who were forced to say farewell to those they love and may never see again. That this act was repeated in train stations all over the country sent a tremble through her limbs.

Now, two years later, on a rather cold, dull and wet June morning at Charing Cross Station, the worst but inevitable fears are realized as a constant flow of men return disabled, wounded, their faces ghostly and harrowed. People search in silence from shock and out of respect for the disfigured – a scene so tragically different from the cheers of excitement during the brave beginning. The news of a terrible battle at sea brings increasing numbers who besiege the stations.

Constance lets her gaze roam the whole of Charing Cross Station, and she acknowledges that another predominant colour joins the khaki uniforms – the black of mourning.

'Verity.' She turns to her sister.

'Why, Constance, you're as pale as death. What is it?'

'We must let him go.'

'I don't know what you mean.'

348

'Rafe. We mustn't search for him any more. It's time to rejoin the world as best we can. It's time to work.'

'What foreign thoughts. I don't know if I can do that.'

Constance grips her sister by her shoulders.

'Look around you, Verity. We've avoided this for two years. It's wrong and selfish.'

'What will we do?'

'I don't know yet. Come. Rafe is not here. Let's go home.'

Outside the station an additional crowd of people stand by the kerbs to watch the ambulances carry the wounded to Charing Cross Hospital. A long, white banner across the road flies a request: 'Quiet For The Wounded'.

A young, dark-skinned man walks briskly past the sisters with his head down, his cap sits low over his eyes. Verity stops short.

'How odd.' She removes her dark glasses.

'What is it?'

'That young man . . .' Verity gestures back towards the station entrance with the stem of her glasses. 'No, he's disappeared.'

'Was it Benedikt?'

'No . . . I had the strangest sense of . . . Never mind. I am shaken by this awful scene.'

That night, behind heavily-screened windows, Constance and Verity sit on the floor of the Tower Room packing Rafe's toys and books. All but the moon-faced man automaton and the mechanical bird will be donated to children who have lost their fathers. Yes, the toys may be old-fashioned, Constance surmises, but she hopes children in pain and fear will not mind. The sisters exchange few words, each lost in their memories of the boy. Finally, they come to his clothes; they stroke the little velveteen skeleton suits left behind after his hasty departure, and there lie his painting smocks and a pair of boots. How long ago.

'We'll keep and treasure his paintings, of course.' Constance says.

'Of course.'

'And we shall continue our visits to St Martin's every 17th of December, in his honour.'

'I agree.'

'Good.'

The next morning the sisters launch out before breakfast for a mind-clearing walk. They have become accustomed to the striking military landscape of The Regent's Park. They stroll on a muddied road past the Home Depot, a large wooden building where the post vans are being loaded with an astounding number of mail bags and Fortnum's hampers. Continuing on the edge of the military camp, they observe that the new recruits training on the drilling grounds are not as fresh-faced as the young men of two years ago, who were virginal in their knowledge of war. Fear and dread is in the air and the new recruits are both younger and older. The acrid odour of the anti-aircraft gun station and the experimental bombing ground persists this morning.

The sisters negotiate the route to the boating lake, where the juxtaposed calm water and lazily hanging tree branches is a welcome balm.

'Constance, look here.'

The sisters are joined lakeside by a queue of blind soldiers. Led by a seeing officer, they stand one behind the other, holding the shoulder of the blind man in front of them. Efficiently they board the rowing boats that await them, one for each soldier and their guiding companions.

Verity drops her umbrella where she stands and looks back, seeking the soldiers' place of origin. Without a word to Constance, she troops off on the path that leads to the gardens of a low handsome building adjoining the park, the hostel for newly blinded servicemen. Walking towards her is a man led by the hand of a young girl, whose head does not reach his waist. Verity later learns the girl is the gardener's daughter whose kindness is a fixture here. The soldier wears the same dark lenses as Verity, even their frames are similar.

'Do you need my other hand?' The young girl asks.

An idea strikes Verity like a thunderbolt. It comes so clearly that she wonders at the dullness of her intellect.

The sisters had dabbled in philanthropy, like birds testing seed. Their unsparing giving occupied the previous years in which their failure to find Rafe slowly withered their spirits. Percy had warned them, 'Do something. Find an additional purpose.' They studied charities and donated anonymously with Percy's guidance. Their hands were always in their purses, but they never really *did* anything.

'No, my darling girl,' Verity says to the child. 'I am here to give *my* hand.'

Jonesy knows what risks he takes in coming to Charing Cross Station. Although Britain is beginning to open its arms to the Chinese to fill the acute labour shortage, there are malevolent opposers to all foreigners. Already twice today the Specials have requested him to produce his medical exemption certificate, and he isn't entirely certain if it's technically their remit to do so.

He bears the harassment so that he may search the faces of returning servicemen. There's a word, a place, on everyone's lips that he doesn't understand. Jutland. Where is it? What is it? He longs to ask a stranger in the gathering throng. Since that word was first uttered the crowds have increased. He hears someone say, 'There is no reason to wait here. They're sewn up in hammocks and tossed over the side.' People speak in riddles, he thinks.

The boots pass him, so many soldiers' boots with dried, cracked mud still clinging to them. But Jonesy searches for a sailor, a young man named Stanley whose last letter was full of innuendo that only Jonesy could decipher. There were no thick, black strike-outs on the pages this time. A life together, Stanley promised between the lines.

He can only afford an hour before he must return to work in

Magdalen Street. Whittling for the war effort reminds him of his prison work: hairbrushes, shaving brushes, walking sticks. One workshop cannot fill all the orders for Punch and Judy puppets, and thus send the spill to Jonesy. These, at least, he actually enjoys making.

On his way into the station he caught the outline of two women wearing identical coats, one blue, the other lavender. They left an impression that washed over him, awakening his memory of two velvet capes of the same colours that once hung on pegs in the entry of a house on Fore Street. He and Willa visited with their mistress shortly after he began his apprenticeship; the night the long dead, golden sailor gazed at him playfully on the Thames shore. The fierce Irish woman in the kitchen fed them bread and marmalade, while Mistress met with the two women who lived there.

Jonesy refrains from looking closely at the women wrapped in blue and lavender at Charing Cross Station today. He avoids faces during these days of war, except when he attunes to returning sailors and searches for Stanley. His longing encompasses him in a bittersweet ache. Jonesy carries the ache home with him, no wiser on the subject of Jutland, or Stanley.

CHAPTER FORTY-SEVEN

1917

It occurs in broad daylight, a sunny bright day in June – the thing feared by everyone in the Fowler household. Iceland had warned them in a letter that Benedikt delivered to their box.

We cannot know what effect a high-explosive bomb might have on you. We suspect you will not survive a direct hit.

Now they too are caught up in the war's voracious maw.

Clovis had worked tirelessly these last three years to think of every scenario, every possibility to safeguard their existence. Mockett had produced medical exemptions for her men, not forged, but authentic certificates that Iceland had no way of producing.

She insisted that each of them contribute to the war effort should they ever be stopped and questioned. Willa has enough outwork to make a normal seamstress go blind. But each time she sits down with her foot on the peddle of the sewing machine she silently claims a victory. It took weeks to muster the courage to approach Finn.

'Sir, could you, would you, possibly consider a sewing machine for the household?'

'She won't like it.'

'Well, sir, of course she won't, but there are facts, sir.' She waits for an invitation.

'Go on.'

'It takes me fourteen hours to make you a dress shirt, sir. With the machine ...' she pauses for strength despite her milquetoast character, 'I can make a shirt in an hour and fifteen minutes.'

His attention is piqued.

'A dress, from ten hours to one hour, sir. I know a girl at the sewing factory. I've seen it.'

'Well, girl. You surprise me. Leave it to me.'

After registering false names and addresses, Rafe and Finn are assigned to guarding Tower Bridge at night. They blend in with other men in a melting pot of Londoners, who for one reason or another are not serving at the front.

Early on, when it became apparent that the war would not end quickly, Clovis felt triumphant when she collected enough phials to see them through the next few years. She frequently wrote to Benedikt who disappeared for weeks to return each time with another delivery. Now the supply has come to a halt. Her own engagement with the war effort is a restless wandering back and forth to Mocketts' laboratory in Limehouse. Women have no budget for frills these days, but the home medical kits that she suggested Mockett manufacture are a runaway success.

In the small hours of these dark nights, Willa whispers her hesitant hopes to Jonesy.

'It seems she's trying to protect us,' Willa says.

'Maybe.'

'We have a little more freedom,' she adds.

'To work,' Jonesy replies.

'Rafe has a studio now. That was unexpected.'

'She does what she has to do.'

'What do you mean?'

'There's an insect in China, the white wax insect. In August they build cocoons of pure, shining wax on the trees. By September the whole tree is covered with palaces of white, a quarter of an inch thick. Clovis is like the white insect. She secretes a wax cocoon around us.'

'But she has no feelings for us. So why does she do it? Why won't she just give us our phials and let us go.'

'I think she does not want to be alone. Her strength feeds off us.'

On a June morning, Londoners are caught unawares. The brazen flight of the Gothas mercilessly drop bombs at eleven thirty that morning and they do not leave Bermondsey unharmed. Only Clovis is at home and all day she paces. She cannot eat and every attempt to settle leaves her more agitated. In the late afternoon they begin to straggle in – all but Finn.

If he could, he'd get rip-roaring drunk. But alcohol scorches his gut now and he can tolerate only a sip or two – not nearly enough to escape for a few hours. Each night that he is on watch, Finn stares down into the tenebrous water of the Thames. Its power stirs his memory, which is too sharp and burdened by his lengthy life. Guarding the bridge in the wet and cold reminds him of his first journey north to the volcanic island that now, in a wildly queer way, sustains him.

One night whilst on watch, a small, innocent gesture knocked him back. Rafe offered Finn his extra pair of gloves. He handed them over with a smile, exactly as Elísabet had once offered him gloves, finely knitted by her own hands. He thought about what he had done to her. Since that night she will not leave his dreams – and he likes it, and eagerly waits to fall asleep to be with her again in Iceland. These thoughts of Elísabet fisted him, so wholly unexpected.

Then he had asked Clovis to release their phials. He'd calculated it was a good time to approach her; ever since his return from the Continent she'd been not her usual, horrible fucking self. The chaos of war seemed to intensify whatever change in her had emerged. But she refused him. Her manner was almost sorrowful, as if she honestly regretted that she couldn't release them.

Tonight he stuffs his hands in his trouser pockets. He's wandered far today, it's late. Walking towards Magdalen Street he looks skywards. Everyone in his path looks skywards. Bermondsey is on alert.

The fuss they make when he arrives home unnerves him and reinforces his mood.

'Albany Road was hit,' he says. 'The dairy. I was nowhere near it. You're all overreacting.'

In bed that night, when Clovis makes overtures that would send a believing man straight to heaven, Finn turns away.

'I'm tired.' He closes his eyes.

She strokes his face.

'I was worried about you, Finn.'

'There was no need, Elísabet.'

He feels her hand stiffen on his face.

They lie side by side in an eternal moment of silence in which Finn senses a chill rising from her skin.

He sighs. And then rolls out of bed.

'You lied to me at Millbank, in the chapel.' Each of her words are like tapered slivers of ice.

Sitting on the edge of the bed with his back to her he considers his response.

'I don't know, Clovis. I suppose I did. I didn't mean to.'

He steps naked and barefoot to the hallway and takes a sheet from the corner linen cupboard. Back in the bedroom that he will no longer claim, he steps into his combinations and then patiently fills the sheet with his clothing, his shoes and boots, everything. He ties it up, then tosses the large bundle over his shoulder and gently shuts the door behind him.

Finn spends a good hour setting up the opium bed in the conservatory where the view of the sky is worth the effort.

In the following days, when Willa hears Clovis's footsteps she braces herself for a torrent of criticism. Nothing pleases Mrs Fowler.

'Your attempt to economize is appalling,' Clovis shouts. 'You waste food like a silly child. I should send you to Iceland for a winter. You'd learn rationing there. The years have made you an ungrateful girl. I'm increasing your contribution amount to the household. And if you don't like it you can leave. There's a housing shortage in Bermondsey. I wonder how long you'd last out there on your own – without your drops.'

Their night sessions had become sporadic since the beginning of the war, but now Clovis drags Willa out of bed more frequently. And much to Willa's sleepy confusion, Clovis adds an odd kind of spiritualism to her repertoire. She claims to see the ghost of Willa's mother, and is so convincing that Willa jumps from the chair and runs from the room disturbed and anxious, leaving Clovis warmly satisfied.

Jonesy too feels as if the rug is pulled out from under him; there is no escaping her scorn.

'You've become careless,' Clovis accuses him. 'Stay away from the stations.'

'Have you been following me?' he asks, surprised.

She resists the urge to smack him across the room.

'Victoria Station in particular,' she shoots back, ignoring his question. 'You'll be mistaken for a prostitute. Have you forgotten – they arrest people like you, prostitute or not.'

He bites his lip until it bleeds. Jonesy wishes he could tell her that he haunts the stations just like thousands of other people who search for their loved ones among the returning wounded. Stanley. He only goes for Stanley. His presence at Victoria is not related to picking up men, even though the reputation of the station's surrounding streets is well known. But he can't tell her, he dares not say a word, for he sees her clenched fists and her dangerous eyes, and knows that today she would do violence to him given the slightest provocation.

Willa and Jonesy are aware that the wind that brings this frightful shift is sleeping in the conservatory now, separated from his marriage bed like curdled milk.

Then, quite unexpectedly, Clovis makes a swift departure from her daily habits. She instructs Willa to leave a breakfast tray outside her bedroom door instead of laying her usual place at the table. It is then curious to see Clovis descend the stairs in a two-piece black, tailored suit. The jacket borrows from the military in its design and the skirt is as full as a riding habit's. Her hair, drawn over a pompadour wire frame, accommodates her enormous black hat. As if she were in the deepest wartime mourning, she draws a thin veil over her face and proceeds out of the door without a word. There is no pattern to her days out except the number, which is four a week.

The house itself seems to sigh in relief when she goes.

There are so many dead young men. Is it any wonder that their families cannot quite believe that they would simply disappear across the sea to die on foreign soil? Might the mourner be forgiven for entertaining the idea that their cherished one makes some herculean effort to cross the torrid waters once more, unbound by death, to come home to lament and utter their final farewell? The number of women, and indeed men, who wish to contact the dead in the other world has never been greater.

Clovis operates from a first-floor flat, a room really, on the corner of Whittlesey Street just off Waterloo Road. It's a respectable distance from the prostitutes that beleaguer the area, and more importantly, hundreds of thousands of soldiers pass through Waterloo Station and King George's military hospital nearby. Where there are stations and hospitals, there are grieving people. She begins by stealing into St John's church where lonely people seek solace. In a single day, she procures her first two clients.

It is quite easy work. Clovis first senses and then sees an apparition of the departed in the room. She does not attempt to describe them. Things are murky in the world of the dead. Before long the distressed mother is describing her son, or husband, and Clovis has but to nod, *yes, that's exactly as I see it.* She never tries to guess names, or where the death occurred. Her clients are more interested in the message. And in this, Clovis excels, for she does not overact. Her soldier ghosts use words like 'if'.

If I did not say it, or never said it enough, I love you.

If when you think of me you feel sad, please know that I am at peace now. And so forth.

Clovis takes no pleasure or interest in any healing that may take place, she is not working to relieve anyone's tortured mind, or to soothe any pain but her own. The salve she seeks is money; soothing coins in her pocket, calming and powerful notes in her purse. She is in complete control, here in the shadow of the war's wounded. The years of her soft interlude are finished. Her edges are sharpened again. She has come back to herself. One day soon she will to return to Magdalen Street after her day's work to conquer her sister's wraith and blow its cobwebs from her house.

LONDON
1922

CHAPTER FORTY-EIGHT

Each time Verity teaches a man Braille, or when Constance sees the tension in a veteran's face soften after she has has read Tennyson aloud, they return to Lawless House slightly less empty, the salve of being needed having been applied. Their work with blind servicemen continued throughout the war's duration. Then Ireland's fight for independence brought more casualties who were blinded by mustard gas.

One boisterous morning when the sisters are enjoying a pot of tea with the ex-servicemen, a new blind veteran enters the lounge from the terrace of the hostel, guided by a volunteer. The men rise from their chairs and follow a strip of drugget that crosses the room and leads directly to the French door that opens onto the terrace. The men overwhelm the soldier with welcome so that at first the sisters do not gain a full view. But when the veterans finally peel away from the young man, Verity takes such a resounding gasp, that the men are quite alarmed.

'Please, what is it?' they ask in unison.

'It's just that . . .' Constance summons the words. 'My sister and I . . .'

'Sir.' Verity sweeps over to the new veteran. 'May I ask your name?'

'Henry Mason, madam.'

'Oh,' she says, her voice thick and sore. 'How do you do, Mr Mason.'

When he removes his service dress hat his auburn hair gives the sisters a start, but it is his dark glasses that spark a memory, a searing image of the boy playing with Verity's spectacles, placing them on his face, running through the garden, peering through them in wonder at the way Verity views the outdoors.

'We're very sorry,' Constance addresses the group. 'We thought we recognized you, Mr Mason.'

Like one who has a terrible addiction to the drink, who after years of abstinence accidentally picks up the wrong glass, their longing is unearthed by a mistake, and the sisters must now have more. Disturbed, because they have so swiftly and unexpectedly lost their footing and know they cannot fight it, they prepare to set out once more in search of Rafe.

But first, another shock. It isn't their neighbours, or their ever-changing housekeepers and gardeners, it is those who pass through their lives in other small ways who notice.

'Good morning.' The postwoman is surprised that one of the sisters answers the door.

'Good morning.' Constance reaches for the package.

'Dear me. I grow fatter, slower and greyer each year.' The post-woman's lingering gaze detects no change at all in the woman, who politely smiles at her pointed remark.

Hired at the beginning of the Great War, the postwoman retains her position, and during eight years of service she has come to believe that there is something queer about the residents of Lawless House.

Similarly, the elderly newsagent on Park Street often hesitates with a quizzical rheumy eye on Verity before he relinquishes the paper.

'After all this time, it is now, when Camden Town grows even more populated, that I feel we're in danger of losing our anonymity,' Verity says.

'Perhaps it's time to make more drastic efforts,' Constance suggests.

They are not often caught in a nostalgic web, but today their thoughts loom on the Limehouse of their past, where late on sultry nights they dressed as men.

'Will it be you? Or me?' Verity asks.

Constance studies her sister's face.

'Try a pair of your dark glasses.'

Verity chooses silver frames with dark green lenses and curls the wire around her ears.

'Definitely you,' Constance says.

'All right then, do it.'

Constance takes the scissors to her sister's hair and shears it like a hedge. With a little Brilliantine it rivals any man's cut in its accuracy. Verity steps into a pair of tweed trousers; the hairy wool grazes her naked skin. A man's shirt and waistcoat help fill out the suit's jacket. For an off the peg, it appears expertly tailored. The brogues are from Jermyn Street where a smirking snob of a man measured her feet. Admiring their sheen, she sits with her legs crossed, surpassing the *garçonne*, looking every bit the man.

'And now the derby.' Constance places the hat on her sister's cropped head. 'You will pass, but you must be confident. Practise your walk while I change.'

Constance stretches a wig over her pinned-up hair. The chestnut-brown bob takes ten years off her. A chemise-style dress with a dropped waist accentuates the angular lines of her body. A hat and gloves, a long lavender scarf that serves as a wrap, and ankle-strap, button shoes complete her ensemble. She looks unremarkable, and not herself.

On this Saturday they travel south on the electric railway, changing lines three times before they see the light of Wapping. The scent of the river encases them, reminding them that every structure, every path has tentacles that eventually reaches the Thames.

'You can relax, Verity. We are of no interest to this community. Look how it still clings to its identity.'

'It does, Constance. Men look happy to be out of uniform and back to work.'

'Those who returned,' Constance reminds her.

The docks have survived the horrors of the Zeppelins, but not without casualties. It is impossible to calculate how many young dock workers, sailors, merchants and wharfingers never returned to Sailortown. With their absence in mind, the sisters find the streets and dwellings teeming with people. Barefoot children spill out onto the pavement to collect manure and coal.

'Mr Atlee's in charge of Limehouse now. He has work to do here.' Constance murmurs.

Verity's confidence builds with each step on the cobbled streets. No one pays the slightest attention to the tall man with the dark glasses. Twenty minutes later they arrive at Three Colt Street. An artificial teeth-maker occupies the Fowler's former house. Displayed on velvet cloth in the front window, pink-gummed models varying in size seem to laugh at them in an entirely sinister way. Knots twist in their stomachs. A memory of Rafe's form standing in the first-floor window sears them.

'Come, Verity. Don't dwell here.'

They hurry past the artificial teeth, as if chased by their clomping bites, stopping a few feet down the street at a lively spit-and-sawdust pub. Seated at the Five Bells and Blade Bone they nurse their shandies with a ridiculous hope that someone will fling helpful gossip their way.

'That's my limit,' Constance says. 'I can't drink any more.' Her glass is still three quarters full.

Snatches of conversation hum in the background and then one voice hovers closer than the others.

'I am arrested by your appearances.'

A trace of accent clings to her delivery. The slight trill to her 'r' makes the sisters bolt up in their seats.

'Shhh. Do not say a word.' Clovis, with her back to their table, speaks over her shoulder. 'You place him in danger by coming east.'

Constance refuses to stay silent. 'Is he well?'

A chair scrapes the floor. Clovis slides into the empty banquette at the sisters' table. They are buttonholed by her muscular perfume and stupefied by this turn of events.

'Did you not hear me?'

The sisters heed this new vision of Clovis Fowler. Her hair is either cut and dyed or she wears a wig of dark brown finger-waves under her cloche hat. A box-shaped knitted dress clings to her torso and flares out into a pleated skirt. Her legs make their shapely appearance into the world. There is a moment's pause as the three women face up to their fresh transformations born in a new century.

'I know the reason you keep him from us. I saw the evidence years ago.' Suddenly clear-headed, Constance careers to the heart of their quest.

'You know nothing.'

'We have recently written again to Benedikt with our concerns.' Verity says.

'He has no power here.'

'That isn't true. More than once he has intervened ...'

'Yes.' Clovis snaps. 'Because you were careless. Twice they almost nabbed him.'

Verity feels as if she has been slapped. But Constance is livid. It looks as if she goes to pat Clovis's hand, and instead she grabs her wrist, pulling her arm under the table, digging her nails into her wrist until she draws blood.

'You will take us to him,' Constance says.

'I will not. The men from Copenhagen ... if they see us to-gether ...' She jerks her wrist from Constance's grasp. 'They haven't yet discovered where we live. If you and your sister haunt my home like a couple of old ghouls, you'll bring attention to us. If you really have his best interests at heart and not your own selfish wishes, then you will leave us alone.'

'We would never put him in harm's way.'

Clovis takes a handkerchief from her purse and dabs her wrist, then tosses the lace-trimmed linen on the table and stands.

'None of this matters.' Clovis looks down at them. 'He thinks you're both dead.'

'He . . . he what?' Verity stammers.

Clovis backs away from them expressionless, a witness to the effect of her blistering words.

The sisters long to lurch at her but they are thwarted by the lie, as if their limbs are screwed to their seats. Not until the door of the Five Bells and Blade Bone closes and the daylight disappears once again do they rouse, and then in a swift panic they bolt out after her.

Verity curses that she must wear her dark glasses and is no help to Constance who looks left and right until she catches sight of a swinging, pleated skirt. She spots Clovis turning onto the Commercial Road. Clovis moves like a dart to its target, and when she rounds the corner to Salmon Lane the sisters moan with what they face.

Saturday's commerce spills out into the great market street of the district. Clovis easily disappears into the densely packed throng. Assaulted by the stink of naphtha, the sisters quickly lose the woman's heady scent. They dodge the hanging, newly killed rabbits. Pushing past buyers and sellers they ask, 'Beautiful lady, dark green dress?' But an organ and coronet warm up to earn their Saturday shillings, drowning their enquiries. The sisters jostle past several fried-fish bars, forging on to the end of the market until they reek of frying oil.

'We've lost her,' Constance says.

They reach the bottom of Salmon Lane and stop to rest in front of the turtle warehouse. Its window boasts signage for 'the Real Turtle Soup' and inside, the calipash and calipee await transport to the city restaurants.

Verity uses her pocket handkerchief to remove a film of grime from her glasses.

'She's a liar. Even if she has told Rafe we are dead, he won't believe her. I know he won't,' she says.

'It doesn't matter. The important thing is that he's somewhere in London. We should not have doubted. We will not give up this time, Verity.'

A sea turtle thumps its shell against the window. It claims its freedom from the boiling pot for a while longer.

Clovis turns off Salmon Lane into Copenhagen Place. Wondering if it is somehow possible to crush the Fitzgeralds, to silence them forever, she takes a dusty path that leads to the back of a timber-framed building. The door opens before she knocks.

'I saw you through the window' Mockett says.

He bolts the door as she sweeps in.

'Your palace of science is a wreck,' Clovis says.

Mockett ignores her comment. His workspace is normally immaculate when he isn't creating a new product. She knows this.

She dips a finger into a concoction seeping through layers of muslin and sniffs.

'Mint and lavender?'

Mockett nods.

He deals the legal drug: cosmetics. It is almost robbery. Face creams keep him and the Fowlers comfortable.

'The mint is too strong.'

He nods again. She's probably right, she has a good nose.

Mockett's empire burgeons with a chain of chemist shops, but like the others, he cannot be acclaimed for his work. From his cavernous warehouse he doggedly protects his identity. There is no shortage of people with whom to do business; no one cares who he is as long as he produces and the profits soar. His medical, pharmaceutical, and science degrees, printed with pseudonyms, lie concealed in his desk drawer.

'I thought we were meeting at the Five Bells,' Rafe says to Clovis. 'We've just begun.'

'It's no longer safe to be seen there. The publican is suspicious.'

'Perhaps it's time to make yourself scarce in Limehouse.' Mockett suggests.

'What about you? You still live here.'

'I visit Wapping and Poplar. I never go to the Five Bells.'

Rafe sits in a dark corner, the laboratory section of Mockett's workspace. Mockett taps Rafe's vein. Another puncture, more blood. Tendrils of hair, nail-clippings, urine, a scraping of cuticles, and, did he remember to bring his semen, Mockett asks quietly. Clovis fastens her attention to the answer.

Rafe reaches into his trouser pocket. He's past humiliation, but not anger. His tutor teaches him to paint with fingers tipped with fire. Your power as an artist is in your anger, he said. Rafe will be sad to leave him, as he must when his tutor's sharp old eyes begin to notice.

'Spit please, Rafe.' Mockett holds a specimen jar to his lips.

Initially excited and challenged by Clovis's wild quest to replicate Rafe's fever sweat, row upon row of Rafe's samples are a grim reminder of Mockett's own arrogance. And now as he looks at the young man baring his arm, Mockett is awash with guilt for continuing useless experiments.

Rafe made his peace with Mockett one night when they were drunk as anything, both sick from a spit of ale. It was the night Mockett told Rafe what year he had stopped ageing. Painstaking record-keeping and monitoring of Rafe's secretions, skin and blood, did actually account for something and revealed that Rafe's body had not aged since 1867. They had guessed as much, but as science advances, it speaks clearer.

'I'm thirty-five?' Rafe had asked. 'Why thirty-five?'

'I have no fucking idea. It seems entirely random. Let's get drunk.'

On these occasions when Clovis is present, Rafe closes his eyes.

She tries to impress upon him the importance of what they do here, but he ignores her. Clovis and Mockett turn their discussion to cosmetic ventures.

The needle pricks again. Rafe recalls when once she had the audacity to mention love. The word was unnatural when she voiced it.

'One day you will fall in love,' she had said. 'You should have the option. You'll need a replica to keep her alive, if, as you claim, you have no more fevers.'

'That's rich,' he'd replied. 'You pretend to do this for me? If you really want to do something for me, you will give us what belongs to each of us. Give us back our phials.'

'I can't. It is for your safety, for everyone's safety, that I keep them.'

While Mockett gently clips his nails, Rafe thinks of the men from Copenhagen who search for him. Why him? he'd asked when he was young and still growing, still ageing. The fever, he was told, he is a carrier, the only carrier. And on that sobering day when he discovered a partial truth about himself, he decided to hide his fevers from Clovis. How many he had secretly suffered in his room in that first house in Bermondsey, he could not count. Now, when it arrives with its blistering heat, he retreats to his studio, locks the doors, and sweats it out alone.

From the moment she first appeared, tainting the doorway of Lawless House, he couldn't bear to be near Clovis Fowler. Those first years, she did not often touch him, but sometimes she placed her hand on his shoulder, or held him down until he understood what was required of him – the needles, and the lancet, and the scissors – and then he almost fainted from nausea. Her touch was worse than any bloodletting.

She often asks if he ever suffers from the fever to which he always replies that he does not, so convincingly that she only nods and then reminds him to let her know if that should change. He would never tell her the truth, because darkness rises in everything she does.

'Rafe. It's time to go. And we need to hurry, I think my long sleep is coming.'

Mockett and Rafe both supress the urge to acknowledge her remark. They have waited months for her next sleep to arrive. They have all waited.

CHAPTER FORTY-NINE

On a balmy evening two weeks later, both Finn and Clovis approach the end of their long sleep.

'That wasn't supposed to happen,' Jonesy says. 'Both of them at the same time. Now what are we going to do?'

'Before he fell asleep Finn insisted we continue as planned. That's what we'll do,' Rafe tells him.

'But he'll be in danger,' Willa adds.

Owen Mockett arrives to make their group complete.

'Have you locked her in?' Mockett asks.

'Yes, and she was completely unaware,' Rafe says.

The day after she fell asleep, Jonesy and Rafe moved Clovis from her bedroom into the anteroom, the small room sandwiched between the annex and the kitchen. They locked the door to the annex, and then locked the door to the kitchen. The room is bare but for a few boxes of books; there is nowhere in the space where the phials may be hidden. Willa searched Clovis for her chatelaine and a phial but nothing was concealed in her dressing gown.

'This would be an excellent moment for a whisky,' Mockett says.

'If anyone needs a drink, that'll be me.' Finn joins them.

'Finn!' Rafe says. 'Maybe we should call this off until her next sleep, when you don't need the drops, too.'

'No. I want to do it,' he addresses them all. 'I'm at peace with this.'

Mockett opens his physician's bag and begins to lay out a stethoscope, a blood-pressure cuff, a leather headband with a mirror, and a tongue depressor.

'Good Christ, Owen,' Finn says.

Mockett throws his hands up. 'I don't know what to expect.'

A quick rapping on the kitchen door restrains them.

'Finn? Open the door, Finn.'

'We want the phials, Clovis.'

'Open the door.'

'Not until you tell us where the phials are.'

She doesn't respond. Clovis hears breathing on the other side of the door, and the creaks in the floor as they adjust their weight. Now food is being prepared; they speak in low tones. Is that Mockett? Yes. He's there as well. She's ravenous. Bacon sizzles, there is toasting bread, a kettle is on. The intensity of hunger after the long sleep gnaws at her. How purposeful they are.

'Finn, I want to speak to you alone.' She raps on the door again. He nods to the others to give them privacy.

'They can't hear you. What is it?'

'I can't give them the phials. It's too dangerous.'

'How so?'

'Think about it. Willa, out there in the world not bothering to disguise herself. One day someone will become too curious. And Jonesy. God, Jonesy. He will choose the wrong man, the wrong place, and they will lock him up and then what will happen? Don't you see the danger?'

'I see that you're frightened everyone will leave you. Give them to us, Clovis.'

'No.'

The pains begin an hour later. Finn doubles over as if he's been punched. Clovis tries to stifle a moan but it escapes. A harrowing, haunting sound that shocks them.

Mockett wants to check his heart, but Finn waves him away.

'Water,' he whispers.

Willa, who fetches it, shakes at the sight of Finn in such agony and spills the water all over herself.

A scream pierces through the anteroom door and lands on all of them. Willa weakens.

'Isn't there another way?' She paces, her fingers counting and tapping.

'No,' Finn says. Then he puts his hand to his mouth. His tongue has thickened. His fingers curl up so that he cannot use them. They watch, stunned, as his hand turns to something claw-like covering his mouth.

Rafe goes to the door. 'Clovis, tell us where the phials are. You don't have much time left.'

Silence.

'Is she dead?' Jonesy asks.

'Rafe, unlock the door. She's your mother for God's sake,' Mockett implores him.

Again Finn says no. His eyes roll back in his head.

'This must stop now. His pulse, and his heart, they're poor.' Mockett shakes his head.

A weak sound persists against the door. They cannot see that Clovis lies against it in the foetal position. Her foot taps for attention. Urine seeps from the bottom edge of the door.

'Open it,' Finn rasps.

Mockett quickly opens the door to the anteroom. Clovis points to the opposite door that leads into the annex. He helps her to stand and she whispers the location. Steadying her body against the wall she watches Mockett search the tool shelf for the large tin of polishing wax.

'In here?' he asks.

She nods.

He opens the tin and takes out a small package wrapped in newspaper and opens it.

'One? Just one phial?' he asks with an incredulous gasp. 'Where are the others?'

She manages a smug smile before she doubles over again in pain.

LONDON
1956

CHAPTER FIFTY

The room is dripping in tat. A frayed lampshade sends a sickly, yellow glow into a grey corner that rivals the afternoon's clouds. Puckering across the single bed a dingy, blue blanket fails to disguise the lumpy mattress. A weathered, Lusty chair, meant for a garden and cocktails, sits beside a small, unused Victorian fireplace in this rented room in Pimlico. It's noisy, a bit smelly, and a hidden paradise. Kay Starr sings from a beaten up portable gramophone. Two men stand entwined in a small moon-shaped space in the centre of the room. To dance naked is unbearably exciting. Jonesy lets David take the lead.

'I love your long brown cock. It's the longest I ever seen.'

'And I love your short fat red one.' Jonesy laughs.

David smacks Jonesy's buttocks hard. 'Are you laughin' at mine?'

'That hurt. No. I said I love it, didn't I? I love you.'

Jonesy missteps, longing to hear if maybe today David will requite his love.

After David's hungry mouth and his short, square body are satisfied, he chooses another record, snaps it across his bare thigh, and throws the pieces onto the floor.

'I hate Doris fuckin' Day. That's all Tammy ever listens to. Fuckin' Doris Day.'

Jonesy ignores the mention of David's fiancée.

'I'll go out and get those cakes you like.' Jonesy wipes himself with a towel and pulls his trousers on.

'Get three of them lemon ones for me. I'm hungry. Bring us a tea.'

'Whatever you want.'

Jonesy makes no eye contact with any of the other men he passes in the dim corridor or on the stairs. This is a careful house; a room to let by the day doesn't necessarily mean it's a safe haven for two men to have sex. They don't wish to give the discreet landlady any reason to reconsider her business with them.

Uneasy in Pimlico, Jonesy walks swiftly past the rubble of building work. Each time he comes here, and it takes him forever because the Tube hasn't reached these parts, he discovers a little more of the area that borders his former miserable nine years of incarceration. He would have liked to witness the destruction of that gruesome fortress and shudders with wonder at how the four of them were released with their sanity intact. He knows how they survived physically, those two little magical drops, but he was so often sick with despair. The kind of despair he feels today, sore from the reminder that his rough lover upstairs will be married soon. Jonesy conceals his hurt in David's presence. Lust is a healing companion.

'Two, no, three lemon cakes and a custard slice, please.'

He always says please, hopeful of supressing a racist remark.

'Them's the lot,' she says. 'We can't keep 'em on the racks.'

'And two teas with milk and sugar, please.'

'For both?'

'Yes, please.'

Jonesy waits patiently; she's slow with the teas. Thank the goddesses there's plenty of sugar and butter again. Thirteen years they suffered without enough of those comforts.

That first night at the bathhouse, when David stood close to him with his towel wrapped well below his taut waist, the mechanic's greeting was, 'I'm not queer.'

God, hadn't he heard that before.

'Do you know how ridiculous that sounds in a room full of us?'

Jonesy had walked away with every intention of avoiding heartache.

But here he is, two years later, buying cake, saturated in his desire for a barely literate man who insists he is going to 'stop all of this' as soon as he's married.

Jonesy is not honest, either. He won't tell David about his family, such as it is, and he certainly won't reveal the dangerous secret that weighs on him.

'You're lookin' real smart today, young man,' the bakery girl says.

A reflex sends his hand to fiddle with his black roll-neck. He forgets that his body disguises his true age; blood always rushes to his face when he remembers.

'Thank you.'

'Look at your face! I didn't know your kind could blush.'

What an idiot, he thinks. She's a bottle blonde, always with a bit of gnawed pencil behind her ear, a huge gap between her front teeth – and she smells like over-baked sugar. He doesn't want a fuss.

On his way out with his hands full, she runs around to open the door for him and thrusts her body forward a bit, brushing against him.

'Nice coat. Where'd ya get it?'

Willa had pulled it out of one of her clothing chests. An authentic gem with engraved anchor buttons that make him nostalgic for his long-dead sailor. It's also thanks to Willa that his grey trousers are just on the right side of tight. She could make alterations to a rag and the result would be unique and beautiful.

'Friend gave it to me.'

'That's a friend you'll want to keep.'

'Yeah. See ya.'

'See ya.'

His brown jodhpur boots slide past the girl and he's on the street again. A light wind blows his chin-length hair into his eyes and he tucks it back behind his ears, balancing the cakes and teas in his hands. Just as he reaches the lodging house a man stops him to ask directions. Jonesy tries to help but doesn't really know how to guide him. The exchange is short and pleasant. The shears on the window upstairs twitch a couple of times.

Back in the room, he places the cake and tea on the slim fireplace mantel and when he turns around David punches him in the stomach. The breath is knocked right out of him.

'Flirting again?'

Another punch, this one to the ribs.

'Directions . . .' Jonesy tries to explain.

'You're disgusting.'

'So are you.' Jonesy is in a hell of a lot of pain, but he's not afraid. It's not like he's going to die.

A fist lands on his face.

'You're going to make Tammy miserable,' he whispers.

David grabs the soiled towel and twists it around Jonesy's neck.

'I'm not like you. I'm not queer. Say it. Say, "David you're not queer".'

He lets Jonesy breathe.

'David, you are an invert, a queer, a poof, a sodomite . . .'

David grabs the Lusty chair and smacks it across Jonesy's head. He goes down.

His rage spent, David sits on the bed and weeps.

Jonesy lies at his lover's feet, his head rests in a small puddle of blood and he takes a few minutes to come to his knees. As he does so, there is a pounding on the door.

'Raid! Move out!' The landlady warns them.

'What the bloody hell. It ain't a Friday night up the West End, it's bloody daylight in Pimlico,' a man hisses out in the corridor.

David doesn't hesitate. He hustles into his trousers, grabs his shirt and shoes, and after checking the corridor, he takes the rear set of steps that serve as a safeguard, the house popular for this reason. His lover of two years is not worth even a parting glance where he lies broken on the floor.

A few moments later a plain-clothes constable finds the door gaping.

'Hey, hey, hey, wait a minute there.'

Jonesy writhes on the floor trying to get up. Slowly, he raises his head and tilts it to face the voice.

The constable drops his guard.

'Holy fucking hell.'

Jonesy clenches the bed. Using the mattress, he labours first to one knee, then the other. His head has stopped bleeding. His jumper has soaked up much of the pool from the floor.

'Your face.'

Jonesy's hand goes to his jaw. Broken? He can barely make out the man in front of him. His age, he has no idea. His voice is kinder than that of his escaped lover, but he never trusts the police. The punches he can handle, but not the particular torture of the police. Not again.

Another constable pokes his head in.

'Anything doing in here?'

This one, no, he's not kind. Jonesy recognizes a hard-edged tone, holds his breath unconsciously and winces at what might be a broken rib. A hand tremor starts and in moments he's a full shaking mess.

'No, fine here. Check upstairs?'

'Right.'

Jonesy suppresses a cry of relief.

'Look. You're fully dressed. There's no one else here. Whoever made a dog's dinner of your face has scarpered. I'm not going to arrest you. I'll call an ambulance.'

'No. Please, no hospital.'

'You look bad.'

'Please.'

'Is there someone I can call? Where do you live?'

Jonesy's tries to remember if he has enough money to take a taxi home and then is sure he doesn't, it's too far.

'Do you have a phone?'

They do, but he won't enlighten the police.

'Phone box.'

'Do you know the number?'

'BER 2334,' he slurs.

'Bermondsey. What's your name?'

'Edward. Edward Moon.'

'Who do I ask for?'

'Edward Moon.' Their emergency code.

'You're not making any sense.'

'Please, just ask ... Edward Moon.'

His split lip bleeds again.

'Jesus. Okay, okay.'

Jonesy rests his head back; the vision of the constable fades and all he wants now is sleep.

'Hey, hey, Mr Moon.'

'Who is Mr. Moon?'

'You said you were. I'm going downstairs now to phone. You have to stay awake.'

'I'm not going to die.'

'Seriously, don't go to sleep.'

Jonesy fully expects the constable to return and blacken his other eye, or break one of his bones, some mark of violence to show that he does his job well.

He waits in the fading light, still on the floor, leaning against the bed. It isn't as dangerous as it used to be. They can't hang him. He has no reputation to ruin. But they can arrest him, lock him up, and then they will have their fun with him. He never again wants to be in a locked cell at the mercy of a policeman in denial of his own love for cock.

The constable is back. Jonesy can smell something on his clothing, a mix of tobacco and musk. The next moment he is being lifted with some difficulty onto the bed. He struggles to open his eye; the other is swollen shut. But when his good eye meets the constable's gaze his breath quickens, causing pain at his ribs. He's one of us. I can tell just by looking a man in his eyes. He has a thimble of hope that he will be left in peace to be collected, that the constable wasn't lying and will not arrest him.

'Why do you do this job?' Jonesy asks.

The constable switches on the lamp with the frayed shade. The commotion in the corridors and stairs has calmed.

'I have to go. You should at least go to the doctor.' He turns to leave.

'Constable. Thank you.'

'Stay out of trouble.'

An hour later, when every part of him is throbbing and the pain sends him near delirium, he can't tell whether Finn and Rafe are standing at the foot of the bed, or whether he is dreaming it.

'Who did this to you?' Rafe asks.

'Later,' Finn says. 'Let's get him home.'

They negotiate the stairs where, at the landing, the landlady asks for compensation. 'For my trouble.' Finn throws notes on the reception table and they carry Jonesy to the Hillman and ease him in with as little torture as possible, laying him across the rear seat.

Jonesy passes in and out of consciousness according to the health of the roads and the glare from the streetlights that land directly on his face. After they roll over the tram tracks of Vauxhall Bridge a new anxiety sets in.

'Is she very angry?' he asks.

Rafe looks at Finn who keeps his eyes on the road.

'Finn?' Jonesy persists.

'She's quiet. Relax.'

'That's not reassuring,' he says, before he passes out.

CHAPTER FIFTY-ONE

Clovis sits at the glass armonica, her tight, pencil skirt hugging her hips. When she hears the car pull up, her feet search for the high heels she'd kicked off by a table leg. She closes the top of the armonica and waits.

Finn and Rafe bring Jonesy into the house with his arms draped around their necks. Pausing at the door of the lounge, they wait for Clovis to acknowledge him. As she walks towards them, Jonesy lifts his pounding head an inch. Clovis closes the door, shutting him out, shutting them all out.

Willa stands at the kitchen door with her hand over her mouth, silencing a cry when Jonesy raises his head again.

'Take him up. I'll be there shortly,' she whispers.

Rafe tries to make Jonesy as comfortable as a beaten man can be, then sits beside the bed. After a few moments of silence, Jonesy reaches for Rafe's hand. His fingers lightly touch the bruise on the back of it.

'You've been to Mockett's again. Blood?' Jonesy asks, his speech as swollen as his face.

Rafe nods.

'Give me your other hand.'

He does.

'You painted today. Good. Red. Gold. Yellow. The same?'

'Don't try to talk. Yes, the same.'

Rafe adjusts Jonesy's pillow.

'Here's Willa. She's going to see to you.'

Willa cleans Jonesy's face with a gentle hand.

'You both think I'm foolish.'

'No. Not at all,' they say.

'But you are a hell of a magnet for the bad ones,' Rafe says. 'That has to change.'

'He's only been trying to change that for the last one hundred and twenty-five years,' Willa says.

Rafe and Willa share a soft trickle of irony-laced laughter, but their attempt to lighten the atmosphere leaves Jonesy quiet.

'Rest now,' she orders.

She turns the radiator up a notch before they close the door.

David invades his thoughts and keeps sleep away. Jonesy's body will heal from the welts, but the sickness that nests in his gut from such a cruel abandonment . . . He's not certain of a recovery.

Perched side by side on shelving, his puppets stare at him and tonight seem grotesque. Astonishingly to him, they're collectables, coveted by the rich. As their creator, Jonesy remains anonymous, which makes them even more desirable and valuable.

His most prized creation and the puppet he will never sell is Marshal Yin, the God of Time, with its three heads of flaming red hair. It sits next to The Cruel Female, dressed in black robes and with a menacing painted brow that arches over one eye. He has carved angry creases into her forehead. She's a bestseller.

The door cracks and he is pulled out of his fevered musing by the leathery scent of her brutal perfume. Her presence vexes him. He shifts. Clovis sits, crosses her legs, and as always he is struck by her beauty, as stunning and youthful as it was the first day he was tossed into her life.

'I'd give anything for morphine right now,' he whispers.

'You know you can't have any drugs. They make us sick.'

'I know.' He pauses. 'I'd just like a little relief. Just for a while.'

'I think the kind of relief you want is not from physical pain.'

He turns quiet.

'Because it's always going to be this way. Isn't it, Jonesy? Always placing us in danger. Bringing law enforcement, the vice squad, ever nearer to our door.'

She lets that sink in.

'What you are – I don't have any problem with it. I don't care who you fuck. But the law does – and that won't change. Ever.'

He turns his head away from her and stares at the wall.

'Your love for Rafe and Willa . . . and Finn. Is it so frail that you are careless enough to take risks in broad daylight?'

Her voice remains as soft as the fur on the street cat she reminds him of, the black one with white feet. He waits for her to show her claws.

'I don't know, maybe you like the thrill of risk-taking.'

'No.'

'Well, Jonesy, your words tell me one thing and your actions another. Every time you walk out of the door, you leave behind people who worry until you come home safely. We despair that you'll leave a trail for the police. Little crumbs from your love nests to our home. You are the only one amongst us who consistently throws caution to the wind.'

'I am careful. I'm not like many who . . . I'm looking to settle down.'

'Listen to yourself.' She points her words like tiny arrows. 'No one wants to settle down with you. It hasn't happened yet, has it? And you've prowled the streets for how many years?'

He's offended by 'prowled'.

'And what would you do if your prince did come along? Watch him grow older each year? Tell him that you are Dorian Gray come to life?'

He hasn't noticed that her hand has been loosely clenched in a fist.

'Dorian Gray? Is he one of us?'

'Christ. No. I only wish he were real, then he could be your companion.'

There's a knock on the door.

'What is it?' Clovis is sharp.

'Is Jonesy hungry? I have broth.'

'No, he's not. He's going to rest,' she answers.

She waits to hear the footsteps fade.

'How many more times will Finn be called to a police station? What will happen to you in prison? It won't be like Millbank, with all the privileges I worked so hard for there. Do you remember when you were arrested in '23? When you almost fell into the long sleep before we got you out? They will not be so gullible now.'

Clovis opens her palm. She holds a phial full of the green liquid. She stands, moves the chair closer to his bed, and places the phial on the seat within his reach.

He winces when he turns his head to face the phial and its damnable fluorescent sheen. Though his vision of her is hampered, there is no mistaking what sails between them.

'Good night, Jonesy.'

She throws a parting glance at the phial.

Clovis was wrong about one thing. Someone did want to settle down with him once. One of the thousands who live in secrecy with success: Stanley. So ordinary and forgettable, but he was the most adoring and kindest man to ever cross Jonesy's path. They had saved their pennies to rent a flat, a permanent love nest to use upon his return, even though Stanley knew he would die when he was called up and almost chopped off his leg to avoid it. He was found washed up on a Danish beach. Jonesy eventually learned the where and when of Jutland.

'I am not completely tragic, Clovis. My kind is not all doomed.' He speaks only to her fragrant vestige.

Jonesy rolls the phial on the seat of the wooden chair with his carving, calloused fingers.

He loves them all. Even his wicked mistress, he still loves her – and hates her. But he cannot change who he is. So he will never be able to keep his family safe. Everything else she said is true. The law won't change. Neither will the potency of the hate and the violence.

The room is still full of Clovis, her essence, her last glance so pointed with meaning as she turned and left him alone to make a decision.

Jonesy clasps the phial. Thinking of his grandmother now, he lifts the top. The dragon chases the flaming pearl of wisdom and truth – one of the Eight Treasures. 'To be peaceful within oneself, Yun, is the flaming pearl.'

Jonesy drinks the liquid. His hair fans on his pillow like a raven's wing and he waits for peace. His body convulses for several seconds. He is gone.

CHAPTER FIFTY-TWO

Willa stands in Jonesy's empty room, where his odour lingers, or is it just the memory of his scent. She is unsure. There, the vacant spot where his funny sandals should be. And there, scratch marks from his wooden box, when he scraped it across the floorboards' patina.

She imagines him sitting here shortly after they moved to Bermondsey, when he whispered a confidence. At the time she thought how burdened he must be, carrying his weighty secret. His eyebrows had arched with relief when he searched her large eyes and found them smiling with acceptance. She was embarrassed that she hadn't figured it out sooner. His painfully polite refusals of her timid touches were finally explained. She too felt relief when she stopped blaming herself for not being desirable enough for his libido.

A soft knock on the door and Rafe opens it a crack.

'Willa?'

He wants to go to her, to hold her, but her boundaries with him are clear. Sometimes she makes him feel so lonely.

'I'm okay.'

'Sure?'

'Sure.'

'I'm going now.'

She nods.

Now, alone in the house, her grief scares her. She closes Jonesy's door softly, as if his spirit sleeps there still.

In her room, strings of lucky acorns dangle from a nail head that juts out from an exposed beam. She rips them off the nail and crushes them with her heel; the stubborn, hardest ones enrage her.

She lifts the lid of a small, wooden box packed with miniature dented tin hands – to ward off the evil eye – and spills them onto the floor. Her heel comes down and she stomps until they are broken, the fingers splayed and distorted. Glass beads she once wrapped around Rafe's neck for protection, she smashes to smithereens.

'You do not do your job,' she accuses them.

Her arm sweeps over the windowsill knocking the rabbits' feet, the tiny horseshoe amulets and the shells and pebbles to the floor. The magic bones of toads and frogs she crushes with her fists. On she goes until she destroys every token, every charm she has ever owned. All but the jade cicada, litter her room.

The bolts of fabric standing in the corner anger her. The clothes and fabric rationing has been lifted, but the beautiful lace, the heavily floral and bright cloth that blazon her room do nothing to lift her.

In the days following, she continues to pat the doorknob in her newly bare room, her fingertips tap the empty windowsill and she counts ceaselessly. But these routines and patterns begin to agitate her. When her hands are this itchy she wants harder work. Clean. I need to clean.

Downstairs in Finn's annex, Willa attacks the dust covering the eccentric collection of furniture with one of her old cotton chemises. Her mind wanders to the other night, when they brought Jonesy home so battered and bruised. How long had he had the phial? Wouldn't he have told her? How was he able to leave his bed to retrieve it? She supposes he could have kept it hidden under his mattress. She puts her back into dusting the slats of a roll-top desk.

Clovis. Perspiring from the work and her suspicion, she pauses. No, she thinks, Clovis would never . . . And yet, here is one amongst them, an immortal who is dead.

She leans against a table upon which rests two volumes. Odd ones these. *A Dictionary of the English Language* by Samuel Johnson, 1775. She randomly opens one of the hefty volumes.

Mortal. 1. Subject to death; doomed sometime to die.

'Unbelievable,' she says.

Willa closes her eyes, opens the book to another page and points her finger.

Parentation. Something done or said in honour of the dead.

Her scream, high and hysterical lands on Finn when he steps into the annex.

'Willa?'

She turns to him, wild-eyed, with the dictionary in her hands, still open to *Parentation.*

'He wasn't supposed to die. Please Finn, we have to do something for Jonesy . . . to honour him.'

They are silent on the journey east to Wapping, a quartet in black. Willa is scorched with Jonesy's absence, felt more acutely confined as she is in their single-car cortege in the east London traffic.

Finn parks near the Town of Ramsgate pub. Along the side of the old building they walk the tight, ancient passage to the precarious, dilapidated Wapping Old Stairs.

The seagulls scavenge on the foreshore at low tide. Remnants of previous centuries lie scattered at their feet. The river meanders here, and where once the sugar ships were welcomed at Stepney Marsh, the river bends around a community that survived the Blitz, where wages have risen and almost everyone who works at the docks and factories can afford a television and a car. Not even Clovis can look across the Thames and fail to be astounded by the power of time.

Jonesy's sandals have left ghost prints on the Old Stairs where he once waited to greet his straw-headed sailor at the end of a voyage. Rafe holds a Chinese urn filled with his ashes. He lifts the lid and scatters a portion of Jonesy into the lapping water. Willa adds an armful of bright pink peonies. Finn almost drops the urn when he sees a small piece of bone protruding from the top of the remaining ashes. Tossing a portion, bone fragments and all, he then offers it to Clovis.

Reluctant, and with an awkward distaste, Clovis empties the last portion. But Jonesy will not go so easily. The breath of the Thames works against her, lifting Jonesy's dust and billowing it back into his mistress's face and hair. It enters her mouth. She spits and rages, while straggling peonies trap her feet. Black-headed gulls swoop down beside Clovis to fight over a fish carcass, their conversation quarrelsome and loud. She is trapped by dead things.

'I need a drink,' she shouts, retreating to the stairs.

'Just a minute,' Finn says to her.

'It stinks here and I'm cold,' she says, but she stops and turns back.

'We'll catch up with you.' Finn motions for Rafe and Willa to go on ahead.

'I'm sure you told us that you knew exactly how many phials we had. I remember how specific you were,' Finn says.

Clovis shrugs. 'I must have missed one. He obviously hid one from me.'

'That day, when you collected them from us, you were satisfied that every delivery was accounted for.'

'As I said, I must have miscalculated. Let's go.'

Unspoken suspicions trill in the dank air. The tide washes in fast. With each great, slosh of brown water, the mud grows thicker. Clovis is quick to climb the slimy stairs.

No. She is not so careless, Finn thinks. His feet broker small agreements with the stones of the foreshore as the remains take flight on the Thames, the parentations of Jonesy Ling concluded.

CHAPTER FIFTY-THREE

'Sometimes, I feel my bones jangling when I walk the streets of London. I catch an image of myself and all I see is a skeleton and wonder if everyone else sees the same,' Constance says to her sister.

'You're tired. Let's go home.' Verity takes her arm.

The sisters lumber along amid the evidence of decay, in their bleak return from St Martin's Gardens. Another year of disappointment leaves a bitter aftertaste.

'I really didn't expect to see him today,' Constance says, unconvincingly. 'Perhaps he believes his lying mother and thinks we're dead.'

'Never mind, sister. You'll feel differently next year.'

'Will I? I don't know.'

The desolate landscape of Camden Town mirrors their dragging skeletons. Earlier in the year the last horse-drawn cargo travelled on the canal, bringing an end to a way of life forever. Small factories, foundries, and all the supporting trades fall obsolete. Families packed up and moved out of the area to find work elsewhere.

Constance and Verity traipse down the high street where the facades of the dirty, blackened, old buildings still suffer the wounds of bomb damage, where shops are boarded up and vagrants display cupping palms. Everyone, everything is weary of time.

When they make the final turning into their street, the bridge that once crossed the canal at Gloucester Road appears as a strange folly. Under its arches where the boats once navigated towards the Cumberland Basin the soil and rubbish are piled up so high that it rises almost as tall as the bridge. Below its arches, the garden of Lawless House overgrows like a deep wooded dell.

Lawless House is in disrepair. Its famous and long deceased architect was more celebrated for his designs than for the quality of the build. It is the reason that James Fitzgerald sits in his car awaiting the return of his great aunts. He cannot remember how many greats are attached to their names. When he made the obvious decision to join the eponymous law firm, for the law runs through his blood thick and fast, his dying father Theo anointed him with the great family secret, just as Theo's father Percy had anointed him. That he must keep such an outrageous secret from his wife and children is not really very difficult, for his family are practical people, even the little ones, and they would certainly never believe him. He wouldn't care to worry them over his sanity.

James keeps the sisters as safe and secure as it is within his power to do; as safe as each generation of Fitzgeralds are wont to do. His aunts insist on paying him an exorbitant amount of money for his services, and he lives at peace with it now. Besides, he has five children to feed, clothe and educate. Ah! Here they come now. Good Lord, how Verity can possibly see in those dark glasses on a sunless December afternoon is beyond him.

Then he notes their slow ambles and their demeanours. They are flattened once again. Year after year he is witness to the crushing disappointment they endure.

Gathering his briefs and papers into his case, James greets the sisters and offers his condolences. He realizes this is damned bad timing on his part.

'James. You should have let yourself in,' Verity tells him.

Constance wrestles with her keys and shakes the gate in a small fit of temper.

'You know I'm not comfortable doing that,' says James.

After they're settled in the drawing room, he broaches the subject in the only way he knows. He's a straightforward man, without flourish.

'Your house is literally crumbling around you.'

'Well, great. Just bloody great,' Constance mutters.

'You really have no choice, I'm sorry to say. It will be an upheaval and you will have to move out temporarily but it is dangerous for you to continue to live here.'

'This is always a taxing day for us.' Verity glances at her sister.

'I know, and I'm sorry to have only added to it. Aside from your disappointment today ... Are you all right, Constance? You seem, I don't know ...' He changes tack. 'Please, don't let this house business unsettle you. I'll oversee everything. You'll have no worries over the expense. All of your finances are extremely healthy.'

'Good, good.' Constance takes an old, clay pipe out of the drawer, throws a pack of tobacco down on her writing desk and proceeds to fill it. Verity goes to speak in protest but clamps her mouth shut.

'Constance. I don't mean to belabour it, but are you quite sure you're all right?' James asks.

She coughs a bit and thumps her chest.

'God, I miss tobacco.'

'I think this change will do you the world of good,' James says. 'I'll leave you now to ponder. We'll speak next week about timings and I'll make enquires about a house to let in close vicinity.'

Approaching them, hefty and endearingly affectionate, James embraces both sisters and squeezes their hands.

'I am terribly, terribly sorry for your disappointment today.'

'Thank you, James,' Constance says.

Verity turns to her sister after James leaves. 'You're so pensive, Constance. I'll heat up the pottage.' Her voice trails off into the kitchen.

'None for me.' Constance stands by the windows.

She looks out onto the neglected garden. James is right. They should do something about it, who knows what or who has claimed it. The thing is enormous and its gnarled trees and creeping vines look as if they might crawl towards the house and strangle them. The house speaks to her; both day and night it cries for attention and mourns the absence of laughter and life. She is weary of its demands, just as she is weakened by constant disappointment.

Verity brings her a bowl of the special pottage.

'I can't eat it.'

Even the bowl, the same one from which Rafe once ate, upsets her today. She lets it sit untouched.

'I think it may be time, sister.'

'Time for what?' Verity places the needle on a record. 'Time for what?' she asks again.

'We don't even know what he looks like. Turn that thing off, please. We've been searching for so long. We comb the streets of London for red-haired men, young and old. I don't look at a man without a glance at his neck. He may have lost his chain. Perhaps he dyes his hair, just as we sometimes do. We watch the news, read the papers . . . what are the odds? What are the odds, Verity? I suddenly feel very foolish and every bit my age.'

'We are never in sync with this, are we?' Verity replies. 'I'm not thinking of dying right now. It's this house; it's making you morose. We must do as James says. Secure it, freshen it up, get the gardeners in. You'll feel renewed.'

'No, it's not the house. I need a sign, something, anything to give me a little hope. The smallest hope would satisfy me. We've failed at every attempt to follow Benedikt. He's never going to lead us to the Fowlers. Let's face it – we're lousy detectives. London has beaten us; the immensity of it has swallowed us whole. We've been chasing a ghost. A lovely ghost of a boy.'

'Constance, we mustn't give up.'

'I'm not giving up, it's not a matter of giving up . . . I'm tired. Oh. Oh, it's coming. Damn. Lemons, please sister. The sleep is coming.'

'Thank God for that. I'm glad. You'll feel better when you wake.'

Later in the evening, while her sister is lost in the wilds of a dreamless sleep, Verity begins a fast. Only water will pass her lips for twenty-four hours. The next morning, she sets off for Mass, which she attends everyday while on her mission for a miracle. She clasps her rosary and prays the joyful, luminous, sorrowful and glorious mysteries. Each night for two weeks she falls to her knees, entreating the saints for a sign.

By the end of the two weeks, she chants holy words in every breath she exhales. She prays for patience while she waits for Constance to wake and then, mindful that Constance always craves it after her sleep, Verity bolts out into the streets to purchase ingredients for a fish pie. She is dashing around single-mindedly, thinking of several stops she must make, when she passes the picture framer's shop. Her attention is captured by a glint of yellow. She stops. Then she sees it in full. Her hand flies up, covering her gaping mouth. A wave of heat races to her face. She crosses herself and enters the shop wherein she gesticulates wildly, conducts a brief conversation and then turns back towards home as fast as she possibly can.

Her breathless run is futile. Two hours she must wait. She paces, thinks of phoning James, decides against it, and makes a tray of cheese and bread, for there will be no fish pie today. She prays, lights candles, brews tea, and finally takes the tray of food upstairs and sits by Constance's bed and waits, nibbling on bread crusts.

Finally, Constance stirs.

'Goodness, Verity. What are you doing?'

'Sister, you must dress at once. Here are your drops. Stuff this bread and cheese down and then we must go. I have prayed and prayed and now my prayers have been answered. Hurry, sister, hurry.'

They are soon amongst the busy afternoon foot traffic of Park Street. Verity throws words at Constance so fast that she can scarcely understand. The greengrocer's queue impedes them before they turn onto the high street. Verity talks a streak.

'And he will not sell it. But of course you will make him change his mind. We must work out the provenance.'

'You haven't yet told me what it is! Slow down so that—'

Constance, still unsteady from having just come back to the world, seizes Verity's arm, and a distorted cry escapes her lips.

A painting rests in the corner of the framer's front window. The rough, thick-red background strikes her with a masculine force, bold and dramatic. Then the halos: delicate, flowing with spirit and searching, moving through the piece, radiant in yellow, clench her heart.

'It's his. Isn't it, sister?' Verity asks.

'Yes, yes. Of course it is. It bloody well is his.'

'Isn't it the most beautiful thing you have ever beheld?' Verity asks.

'Perfect, absolutely perfect.'

'You must speak with the owner. Don't weep!' She pushes Constance forward. 'It was a gift from his daughter, he says it's not for sale. Go on, you try.'

They learned it was purchased from the South London Gallery. Oddly, there is no signature, and when the framer's daughter questioned the gallery's director she was surprised to learn that the artist wished to remain anonymous. And no, the framer would never sell it; though she didn't pay a fortune for it, it was the first gift his daughter had ever given him.

Later that night the sisters plot with a new focus on museums, galleries, and bohemian enclaves. It's not that they had failed to haunt the creative spaces of London; rather, they failed to seek the obvious. They will hurl a new, studious eye to his nine years of paintings, which embellish every room of Lawless House.

The sisters are still awake when the moon disappears and gives way to dawn.

'I will never let you down again,' Constance says.

'Nor I you, sister.'

The creatures that crawl through their garden slink back into the overgrowth and hide from the weak, winter sun. The blackbirds warble warnings that things are shifting at Lawless House.

LONDON
1978

CHAPTER FIFTY-FOUR

The breath of stall workers rises in the five o'clock dark of a Saturday morning at Camden Lock. They orchestrate their pitches and the covers won't come down until midnight. The hour reminds Willa of her life before the advent of electricity, when she rose before dawn to light the fires and draw water. She luxuriates in electricity, it is her favourite invention.

Standing apart from her stall, she worries over the grubby hands that handle her garments, for she's not allowed to interfere. The workers have no clue that the fine treasures they handle are hers. An underground man through and through, Finn keeps Willa out of the public eye.

Since Jonesy's death Willa suffers dark spells that come in ferocious waves. Two years ago Rafe and Finn devised a plan to get her out of the house, to give her some relief from Clovis. They encouraged her to go through the trunks of clothing she had collected over the years and select enough for a stall at an emerging north London market.

'Every other table is full of junk, Willa. They're selling rags compared to your collection,' Finn told her. 'Trust me on this.'

Finn was right. Willa had begun by selecting a box full of decades-old clothing. She had then rummaged around until she found the frock she wanted to sell more than any other, Clovis's white, satin dress with the pretty black doves, the same one that had lit up the dreary orphaned girls' asylum on that fateful day. Still pristine, the costumiers for film and television who scour the market fought over that dress. Two hundred pounds it brought – an outrageous amount. Willa perked up.

Scattered amongst the originals, Willa includes her one-offs. A Georgian petticoat, to which she added patches of Victorian lace, a bustier made of denim and old silk trimmed with buttons made of carved bone. Odd combinations, wholly unique and hand-sewn in the hours when she cannot sleep. Everyone wants to know the face behind these creations.

That she receives no recognition, no acclaim, no acknowledgement of her talent worried Finn. So he gave her the same 'anonymous lecture' he gave Rafe when his current tutor itched to publicly thrust Rafe into the art scene. But Willa put him at ease right away. 'Finn,' she said, 'I've been anonymous since 1832. I'm not likely to catch the fame bug now.'

When the market opens, people queue to view her stall. By noon, the goats are roasting, and a steady flow of cash changes hands at Willa's stall. Everyone is in a jolly mood today, except Willa, who is concerned with other matters. Something she overheard on the bus yesterday; two words that won't leave her. *Stockholm Syndrome.* A woman in the seat in front of her said to her friend, 'It's a psychological phenomenon.' The woman went on about 'captives' and 'captors', about how the captive sometimes has positive feelings towards their captor. A famous American heiress was mentioned.

When Willa feels particularly low, words become confusing and she shuts herself in her room and reads *A Dictionary of the English Language* by Samuel Johnson, which oddly pacifies her. But last night she didn't find the disturbing words she'd heard in the old dictionary, so today she slips away from the market to the high street towards Mornington Crescent and the library.

Willa settles into a chair with her lap full of psychology books. The case histories she reads make her light-headed when she recognizes herself in them. She feels so nauseous that for a moment she fears she may be getting the long sleep, though it is not her time. A realization sends her staggering to the lavatory where she throws up her anxieties. She splashes cold water on her face, then wipes her mouth and drinks from the tap with her head in the sink.

Clarity comes. She knew. Clovis knew that I was particularly susceptible. And I let her take me. She plucked me from that place like a ripe piece of fruit. I willingly became her captive. I am like one of Jonesy's puppets.

The revelation that long ago she had been targeted for her weaknesses fills her throat until she fears another bilious attack. In the cracked sliver of a mirror above the sink she forces a glimpse.

'How stupid, how weak you've been, Willa Robinson. You've allowed her to rape your mind over and over again.'

Time, something about time makes her body want to rock. Time has passed so swiftly, decades gone in a blink. She's wasted so much of it already, she'll never get it back, and there is not enough time, never enough. Even though ... there is.

She suddenly remembers the market, and groans. She must get back.

The five-minute walk seems like fifteen. A film star strolls through the crowd unrecognized, in large sunglasses and a floppy hat. Hundreds descend on the club Dingwalls, for jazz at lunchtime. The market is relaxed and friendly at peak trading time and the only real worries are theft and rats. A large black one runs by Rafe's feet now, as he stands near her stall, anxiously looking for her.

'Where've you been? I bought you a sandwich.'

'We never talk about our freedom any more,' she says. 'Why don't we talk about it?'

Rafe frowns, glancing down at the sandwich in his hand and then back up at her. 'You want to talk about this now?'

'Yes. Right now.'

'Complacency? Shamefully. Because sometimes the act of getting on is all we can do. What's up with you?'

'I can't believe Jonesy's been dead for twenty-four years.'

'Willa. Hey. What's wrong?'

She is too humiliated to tell him the truth. Too ashamed to tell him, as they stand amongst hundreds of people, that she isn't strong enough to refuse the haunting notes Clovis plays to lure her. Too embarrassed to admit that she is addicted to the deep, calm place she inhabits when she gives over to the hypnotism. No matter how desperately alone she feels, or how much she would like to change, she cannot.

'Just missing Jonesy,' she says.

'Come on, let's go for a walk. Your stall's raking it in today. They want what you've got.'

Pink and chartreuse light from the budding trees wavers in the gloaming of the spring evening. Rafe leads the way to the dead canal spur. They stop across the street from Lawless House. The corner pub and the zoo invade their memories. Willa looks at the new gate of Lawless House, from where Clovis had dragged the nine-year-old to the carriage. Rafe recalls that if not for Willa's kind face that day, and her attempts to soothe his distress, he might have run away into the Limehouse night.

'Do you know who lives there now?' she asks.

'No. I don't come often. The shutters are always closed. The street is fiercely private. I came by one night hoping the lights would be on and the windows bare, but . . . I should stop coming here. I wish I knew where they're buried.'

'Are you still painting them?'

'Yeah.'

'Don't you ever want to paint anything else?'

'No. My new tutor . . . he's a portrait artist and he's been painting the same people for years.'

'I didn't mean anything was wrong with it.'

'I know.'

The parrots, screeching from inside the zoo, fill the silence between them.

'I have something I want to tell you, Willa. You seem so down, and I think it may help. But you can't let it slip. Clovis can't know.'

'Then maybe you shouldn't tell me. I try not to tell her anything ... She gets stronger you know. She studies all the time. She's reading psychology now. And she practises some kind of hypnotherapy. None of it ever worked on you or Finn – it makes me feel stupid.'

'You're not stupid. You should study, too. Learn how to beat her.'

'It would take years to catch up with her.'

'We have years.'

A small bit of laughter finds its way out of her.

'Are you still ... seeing people?' he asks.

'Do you mean, am I still having one-night stands with men I don't know?'

'Well, yes, if you put it that way. Are you being careful?'

'Of course.'

'Seriously, Willa. You forget that you still look seventeen ...'

'I'm careful.'

'Listen. If you ever meet someone, someone that you, well, like a partner – I can help.'

'Right. I'm really not in the mood.'

'I'm serious. I still get fevers.'

Willa searches his face. He *is* serious.

'I've been collecting my sweat.'

'You what? Collecting it? What do you do with it?'

'I collect it in sample jars. Mockett's tricks. I store it. Room temperature, refrigerated and frozen.'

'Oh my God. Does anyone else know?'

'No, of course not. Ironically, Clovis gave me the idea. She told me that all the testing and experiments to replicate my sweat are for my benefit – so that I can have a partner. She's insane. I can't believe she's my mother.'

She's not. If he's ever allowed to know the truth, Willa hopes he'll forgive her for not telling him. She's bursting to explain how Clovis threatened her, and how heavy this burden has been. She lets out a long sigh.

'I thought it might cheer you up, not make you sad,' he says.

'I'm thinking about Jonesy. And how the law has finally changed, and now, with your help, he could have had a partner. That's all he ever really wanted. But what about you?'

'Well, since you refused me I haven't been tempted.'

'Don't do that. I was your nanny for Christ's sake. Let's get back. The parrots are driving me mad.'

They walk to the corner and circumvent the growing crowd outside the pub.

'What if I were to choose the wrong man?' she asks. 'What if after a decade, or five, he turns nasty or can't handle the condition. Then what would I do?'

They look at each other.

'Overdose,' they say together.

'Just joking.'

'Yeah, me too.'

They turn the corner onto Park Street and then cross the street. They speak of the fireworks that will light up the market tonight, and the dragon attached to a canal boat that spits out fire and illuminates the canal's dark water. How Jonesy would have loved it.

On the other side of Park Street, the sisters Fitzgerald alight from a taxi, a few steps from the Indian restaurant, where they stop for a takeaway. An afternoon searching the galleries for Rafe's paintings has left them famished. They are busy paying the driver when the coat-tails of their lost boy whip around the corner.

ICELAND
1978

CHAPTER FIFTY-FIVE

Soon the whales will swim into the harbour. People plan picnics and children anticipate playing in the streets until midnight. The late spring brings tourists to a hoary, thawing Reykjavík, who use the slow-paced capital town as a stopover point to reach the real gem – the landscape.

Elísabet stretches awake and reaches for Stefán but finds only creases in the sheets. A rich, coffee aroma rises from Margrét's ground-floor apartment in the house. Elísabet takes two drops from her phial, grateful that the long sleep descends on her as predictably as the seasons; a gracious boon that makes her complicated life easier. But where is her partner?

Esja, the cold bulk of a mountain, stares at her from the kitchen window. There's a note from Stefán, which she reads while heating up the porridge he left for her. Her mind is crowded already with what she must do before she leaves today. Her body aches for a long jog. Taking her coffee into the bedroom she sets to packing her suitcase. Stefán's bag is ready, but he drives north today to view a farm for sale, and she flies south.

Elísabet picks up the photos Stefán left on the desk of four more Falk cousins. She memorizes their faces and feels herself tensing, winding up again, knowing these men have been identified as their enemies. She and Stefán still have the farm on the south-east coast near the pool, and this house in Reykjavík. To better boost security, their group have made homes in almost every area of the country now.

There's still time for a run. She chooses the big, circular route around the older part of town that connects two seaside paths. It feels incredible to be moving again in the sparkling air. Her wool cap is almost too warm. A half mile into her jog, she decides to turn off the main path to the Fossvogskirkjugarður Cemetery. Running through the wild, less cultivated graveyard is like being in a wood – where trees and untamed plants shoot up between the graves. She jogs on the various paths at a slower pace, but fast enough to keep the oxygen rushing to her muscles.

The cemetery is practically deserted, so she is alerted when the plod of another jogger begins to gain on her. He passes and nods, then reverses and runs backward, trying to get a look at her face. And she, his. She can't be certain that it isn't familiar. He slows up and looks back at her again. She loosens her long scarf; it will serve as a weapon if necessary. Then he comes towards her.

'Excuse me,' he says, with a wide grin.

Elísabet breezes past him.

'Wait!' he calls out, running after her.

She's certain she can outrun him, but she's going in the wrong direction and she needs to turn back. She can't miss her flight.

As she runs she flips through her mental files. Is he connected to the Falks? Is he one of the four in the photos? This is her main concern. Or is he another kind of criminal ...

She suddenly swerves and turns back, running wide of him.

'I just want to ask you a question,' he calls after her.

She sprints out of the cemetery.

By the time she arrives home, she's missed Stefán. She regrets her timing; it will be a long time before they meet again. After a shower and more food, Margrét knocks.

'Are you ready?'

'Yes, but there may be trouble.'

On the way to the airport Elísabet describes the man in the cemetery but Margrét hasn't noticed anyone suspicious near their house.

'It may be a coincidence.'

'Perhaps. I think you should tell Stefán though, and tell him I'll phone him soon.'

Margrét nods as she slows and stops.

'I will. Take great care of yourself.' Margrét squeezes Elísabet's hand.

'And you. Don't worry about me, Margrét.'

Just as Elísabet nears the military checkpoint inside the airport, she spots the jogger from the cemetery. Toting a briefcase and a small canvas bag, he surveys the busy departure lounge. She slowly turns her back to him and eases up on her approach to the checkpoint, avoiding detection.

As she suspected, he's boarding her flight. Elísabet considers changing her plans, but swings her way back to the check-in desk and upgrades to first class.

She lingers until the final call then places her woollen cap on, pulls it low and begins boarding. First class is almost empty and the seat adjacent to hers remains unoccupied. Her gamble is successful – he's in standard class.

She takes a sleeping mask out of her bag and asks the flight attendant not to waken her. After she's rearranged her cap and mask, her face is almost invisible. The long flight gives her time to plan her arrival. He's not the first to follow her.

LONDON
1997

CHAPTER FIFTY-SIX

On the evening of the autumn equinox Owen Mockett faces a despicable task. When Rafe and Finn arrive, he leads them directly through the lab and into his flat.

'Aren't you going to take samples?' Rafe asks him.

'Not tonight.'

'Christ, Owen. You look nervous. What is it?' Finn asks.

'You'd better sit down.'

Two sleek, leather sofas face each other in Owen's living room. Chrome curves and quiet taupe tones soften and relax the room, but for one, flaming burst of red. Rafe's painting, a gift to Owen, dominates the wall behind the sofa. Pin spotlights illuminate Rafe's interpretation of his own blood samples, and how his blood appears under the power of Owen's microscope. Rafe laboured for years painting over it, layering it, at times scraping it with his fingernails. Sometimes he applied paint using an eyedropper, drop by drop, the way his blood filled the sample phials. Anger and passion explode from the canvas.

'You know how much I hate taking your samples, Rafe . . .' Owen begins.

'I know, but we've all agreed to pacify her,' he says.

'Okay, well . . .' Owen looks warily at Finn.

'Spill it,' Finn says.

'I've been working with a sequencing facility on Rafe's DNA. I was hoping to make a big show of my commitment to this damnable magic formula that Clovis relentlessly pursues. The whole process is completely anonymous. I've used the facility several times to test their integrity and I trust them.

'And?' Finn tries not to display his alarm.

'I tested yours as well, Finn.'

'You what?'

'I was trying to prove something, something unrelated to the . . . My intentions were completely innocent. I wanted to prove to Clovis that there is no science that explains Rafe's condition . . . our condition. I thought if I could show DNA results . . . Anyway . . . oh, God.' He sighs.

'You should have asked our permission.' Finn is pacing now, wondering how to salvage this mess.

'Owen, you're making me uncomfortable,' Rafe says.

'All right.' Owen pauses. 'Finn, the results prove that you're not Rafe's biological father.'

'What? What did you just say? Are you sure?' Rafe asks.

'Certain.'

'Finn?' Rafe waits for an explanation.

'Bloody hell.' What else can he say. Of course he's not Rafe's father!

'Then who is my father?'

'I . . . I don't know,' Finn admits a half-truth. He doesn't even know the man's name.

'Did they give you a report, or a statement, or what, Owen?' Rafe asks.

'I downloaded it onto this laptop that I use for storing sensitive data. I'll print a copy for you and then delete it. It's secure,' Owen assures him as he opens it, finds the file, and hands the laptop to Finn.

'Scroll down to the bottom, past the number charts.'

'There. There it is.' Rafe reads aloud. 'The alleged father is excluded as the biological father of the tested child. Finn?'

'I don't know what to say.'

'There's something else,' Owen says.

From his desk drawer he produces an aged piece of paper, a prepaid penny-letter sheet.

'Read it. Both of you, read it,' Owen growls, like something wounded.

It's addressed to *Mr O. Mockett, Mockett Chemists, Commercial Road, Limehouse.* The year is stamped 1852; the month has faded completely. The hand is legible, but the creases make for slower reading.

'Owen, what is this?' Finn asks.

'Please, just read it.'

Dear Sir,

Regarding your late wife. I am in possession of the enclosed headline clipped from the Illustrated London News.

Fatal Accident on the Commercial Road

Wife of East London Chemist Trampled by Horses

Mrs Nora Mockett, wife of Mr Owen Mockett

Sir, I am a wicked, wicked woman. I am also a dying woman, and as such, I write to you my confession.

I had the misfortune to meet Clovis Fowler while incarcerated at Millbank. She sought me out, I suppose for my circumstances and my desperation, which at the time were worse than most. She discovered my darkest and most shameful secrets. In exchange for her silence and for enough badly needed coin to help me from returning to a former life, I was required to perform one task for her after I obtained my ticket-of-leave. I did not know what the task would entail, and at the time I am not certain she knew either.

I pushed your wife to her death on the order of Clovis Fowler. I cannot forgive myself, and could never hope to earn your forgiveness at this late date. I did not come forward sooner for my child's sake. I eventually married and was inexplicably blessed with a daughter late in life. They were taken from me – cholera – and as my life has consisted predominantly of misfortune, I expected that woe. The time I had with my husband and daughter was a little bit of undeserved heaven, but I have not had a moment of pure happiness since that afternoon, when out of fear, and desperate again with self-preservation, I performed that evil act.

I am truly sorry. I deserve your anger and disgust. The guilt has eaten me daily. I feel no relief as I write this. I only wish to warn you and should have done so before now. But as I said, I am a wicked woman and have waited until death stands at my bedside. I write to tell you that Clovis Fowler is far more evil than me. The devil himself has laid his hand on her. Do not allow yourself to become lost in her amber eyes for you never shall return.

With deepest regrets.
I am sincerely yours,
Henrietta Martin

Finn drops the letter sheet onto the desk.

'What the bloody hell, Owen? Why didn't you show this to me when you received it?'

'I didn't believe it.'

'Henrietta Martin. I know that name,' Finn recalls. 'There was gossip at the prison. Something about Clovis obtaining leniency for the woman and influencing her release from the dark cells. Ridiculous, I thought at the time. Millbank was nothing if not a den of gossip. I asked Clovis about the woman during one of our visits while we were still inside. She laughed – we both did – she said she didn't even know who I was talking about. Never heard of her.'

'Wait,' says Owen. 'Clovis said she'd never heard of Henrietta Martin?'

'Yes, I remember it clearly.'

'That she'd never even met her?' Owen presses.

'That's what she said ... that she'd never met anyone by that name.'

'Then she lied. She told me quite a different tale. She said she had met Miss Martin and was kind to her, but then Miss Martin took advantage of her and threatened to ruin her. I had no reason not to believe Clovis. Is it possible Finn? You were there.'

'Almost anything was possible at Millbank.' Finn is uneasy. 'But as I said, the place was crawling with outlandish stories.'

'What made you dig up that letter now?' Rafe asks.

'Something's always bothered me about it. The amber eyes. Miss Martin mentions Clovis's amber eyes. It's not a detail she is likely to have invented, it's too risky. The DNA test made me think of it again.'

'Nora visited you at your home in Bermondsey Street, didn't she?' Owen asks.

'Yes, she did.' Rafe appeals to Finn, 'We might as well tell him.'

'Nora threatened to reveal our condition,' Finn admits. 'And she was a little rough with Rafe.'

'You might have told me,' Owen says.

'I thought Nora would have told you.'

'No. She didn't. But Clovis did, the same day she told me about helping Miss Martin. This means ...' Owen pauses. 'I think this woman's confession could be true. All this time I thought ...' But he has no more words. He pictures the kerb, and Nora's mangled body beside it.

'What are we going to do?' Rafe asks.

'Nothing. I suggest we do nothing right now,' Finn shakes his head.

'We could imprison her again.'

Finn pales. 'She didn't break last time. I don't want to go through that again.'

'You're right. We have to be patient and think about this.'

'What about Jonesy? Do you think she's responsible?' Rafe asks.

Finn heaves a sigh 'I don't know. Probably.'

'She really is the monster I always thought.' Rafe's face is bitter.

'We should go home. I don't want to raise any suspicions.'

'Go home? We can't live in the same house with her, Finn.'

'We have no choice until we sort out what to do. And there's Willa to think of. And the phials – she won't give them back to us. We can't just move out. Not yet—'

'Rafe,' Owen interrupts. 'You're sweating. And it's not hot in here.'

Rafe looks from Owen to Finn. They both move towards him, astounded to see him so quickly drenched.

'Stay away from me, Owen.'

Surprised at the rebuke, Owen backs off immediately.

'You can't tell her. Either of you.' Rafe's clothes cling to him.

'Of course not. We would never . . .' Finn fumbles. 'We're going to protect you, Rafe.' He nods at Mockett. 'Right, Owen?'

'Of course we are.'

'I'm sorry. I . . . I didn't want anyone to know. I need a half hour on my own and a change of clothes.'

'You can use the spare room,' Owen says. 'You've had fevers all these years?'

'I have. And I've known the consequences since your wife . . . I need to rest. No, don't.' He motions to Owen to stay where he is. 'I know the way.'

Rafe leaves Owen and Finn staring after him.

'You didn't know?' Owen asks Finn.

'Had no idea.'

'I'm sorry about all this. I was trying to help,' Owen says. 'Is he really Clovis's son? It would make more sense to me if he isn't.'

'Please don't pursue this. It's dangerous.'

'Everything to do with Clovis is dangerous. I've never wanted to harm anyone in my life, Finn, but I want to kill her.' He pauses. 'Don't you think Rafe has a right to know if she's his mother? I could run her DNA.'

'You'll put him in danger.'

'How?'

'I can't—"

'You know but you're not going to say. Don't you think I deserve a few answers?'

'You do. Of course you do. But not right now. You have to trust me. We should carry on as normal until we figure out how to deal with this.'

'She ordered the murder of my wife! Nora would have known. She must have felt a hand – the push that sent her into the street. And all these years I thought she'd been careless. God damn your wife.'

'God damn her.'

A half hour later, as if summoned by her damnation, a banging on the door makes them both jump.

'Can it be anyone but her?' Finn asks.

'No. Fuck. No. Stay here. I'll try to get rid of her.'

And there she is, impatience glowering off her, a curt tongue to greet him.

'What's wrong with your intercom? I've been ringing for five minutes.'

'We're just finishing up here, Clovis. I didn't know you were coming by.'

'Where are they? What's going on here?'

'Nothing. Rafe is resting. I took quite a bit of blood this time. And Finn's in the flat with him. Come on through if you like.'

But Finn steps into the laboratory, blocking the doorway.

'Where's Rafe?' she demands.

'He's still resting. Leave him alone, Clovis.'

Before she can sting him with a reply, Rafe appears alongside Finn showing no signs of the fever.

'Those aren't your clothes.'

'They're mine,' Owen injects. 'I covered him in coffee, almost scalded him.'

They feel the heat of her as she fixes her eyes on Owen, then Finn and finally, Rafe.

'Whatever you're hiding . . .'

She has no need to finish, confident as she is in her abilities.

CHAPTER FIFTY-SEVEN

Willa squats in the sitting room, picking up shards of glass from the floor, when Rafe and Finn return from Mockett's. Dried tears streak her face.

'What the bloody hell happened here? Did she hurt you?' Rafe asks.

'I'm all right.'

Willa stands amongst books littered across the floor. A crystal vase and the titles of Britain's most prominent hypnotist have suffered Clovis's temper. Willa picks one up and shows them the smiling, balding cover shot.

'She was watching his TV programme and went berserk. And, well, you can see. She's not taking her anonymity well today. She wants to be famous. She actually said she has so much to offer the world. Then she couldn't reach either of you and that was it.'

'What a fucking day,' Finn says.

'Do you want me to stay until she comes back? Make sure she's calmed down?' Rafe asks Finn.

'Yes!' Willa shouts. 'Yes, you should stay. You always do this. You always run away and leave me here with the mess. Finn locks himself in his conservatory, you go to your studio, and what do I do? I go off to the blasted market where it's either too hot or too cold. Where tourists trample me and thieves jostle me trying to steal my phone or my bag. Where Camden Station vomits people for fifteen hours every day. You don't even know that I have an

425

entirely new thing I'm doing now. And then I have to come home to her. Christ!'

'Willa!' Rafe cries.

'What?' she snaps.

'I think you're becoming assertive.'

'Not amusing.'

A clear and horrible thought grabs Finn. Rafe is right; Willa has changed. And Clovis always feels threatened by change. There's nothing fiercer than a person who finds their voice – except the wrath of his murdering wife, who will want to silence it.

'Finn? You look like you're on another planet,' Willa asks, though she is too weary to care much.

'I need to think,' he says. 'I need to think very carefully.'

At three o'clock in the morning, the sun has crossed the celestial equator and Finn's thoughts come into alignment. He knows what must be done. The weakest of them must grow to be the strongest. He lifts the lid of a round, porcelain container, where in addition to his French letters, he keeps a stash of hand-rolled cigarettes, lights one, and takes a couple of drags before he stamps it out. He silently curses that moderation was forced on him; an irony of their condition. Clovis hasn't come home tonight. She's probably purloined some poor fellow's heart for a few hours. She satisfies her needs without stealth or apology. Finn is more careful these days, more discreet, and generous. He no longer pays for sex, but when he has a little extra cash he goes to King's Cross, where once more the bones of London's dead have been dug up during renovation, and where, behind the city's new attempt at glamour, the women still work the night. He gives them a few quid and walks away. Young women are attracted to him; could be what is left of his swagger, or his indifference, because he won't go with them. He's surprisingly uncomfortable with any woman under forty. Each morning when he shaves and meets his thirty-three-year-old reflection, there's something behind his eyes that pierces him with his true age.

Taking advantage of Clovis's absence tonight, Finn knocks on Willa's door, then Rafe's.

'Sorry to wake you,' he says, when they both stand drowsy in front of him.

'It's no surprise. You've been weird since you two came back from Mockett's. Tea?' Willa asks.

'Let's talk first.' Finn locks the annex door and leads them to the conservatory.

Willa's questioning, sleep-puffed eyes settle on Finn. The blank sky hides its mysteries like the man pacing before her.

'Where do we begin?' Rafe asks Finn.

'Oh no. What is it?' Willa holds her fingers to keep them still.

'Willa, when we were in Millbank – I know you don't like to talk about it and I'm sorry – but this is important,' Finn says.

'Okay, okay, what?'

'Did Clovis ever mention a woman named Henrietta Martin?'

The colour drains from Willa's face.

'How ... how ... do you know about her?' she stammers.

'Mockett received a letter from her ... back then.'

'Mockett? What is he to do with Henrietta Martin?' she asks. 'How did Clovis know her?'

'Matron let Clovis out of our cells at night. She was allowed in the darks. She said Henrietta Martin was a case study. You know, for her hypnosis practice.'

'Well, I'll be fucked,' Finn says.

'She'll kill me if she finds out I told you.'

'Why? What's the secret? If matron let her out ...'

'Matron was following orders.'

'Whose?'

Willa gives him a blank look.

'The governor's?'

'Don't make me say it, Finn.'

When Rafe and Finn relay the contents of Henrietta's letter, Willa's old companion tries to possess her and she closes her eyes and breathes out the impulse to rock. Poor Mrs Mockett. Mrs Mockett who had been so kind to her, who once gave her a pot of ointment for her raw hands. Rotten. Pure rotten.

'There were nights at Millbank that I can't remember,' she says. 'She talked me into such deep sleeps, dead-like, as if I'd been in the long sleep.'

'Willa . . . there's also Jonesy,' Rafe says. 'How he died.'

She nods. 'I think I've always known. Jonesy would have told me if he'd hidden a phial. He would have offered it to me because he was kind to his core and he cared about me.'

'There's more.' Rafe says.

It is just before dawn when Rafe tells Willa the results of the DNA test. Finn is relieved that Willa gives no sign that she was forced to participate in the charade of Rafe's parentage.

'I'm sorry,' she manages. 'It must be difficult for you both.' She is preoccupied with the murderous charges made in the wincing hours of the morning, and this other is no news to her.

'What will we do, Finn?' she asks.

'I've spent hours thinking, and have only been able to devise one plan. It would be dangerous for you, Willa.'

'No! Don't tell me anything more. She will wrench it out of me.'

'She's right, Finn,' Rafe tells him. 'So how do we proceed?'

'Well, obviously we need to focus on finding the phials first. We've been lazy. No phials, no freedom. Willa, I'll tell you as little as possible until you need to know more. Meanwhile, you have to keep working on strengthening your mind against her. Take your time, do whatever you need to do. Do you follow?'

'I'll try.'

'Trying's not good enough. You must do it.'

She nods, swallowing queasy fears.

'We have to be patient. Once we find the phials, whenever that may be, then we can proceed.'

'What can I do?' Rafe asks.

'Don't change your behaviour in any way. Resist the testing like you normally do. We don't want her sensing anything has changed.'

It's seven in the morning when their talk dies down in the sharp, early-autumn air. Dead leaves swish up against the conservatory promising the coming of winter with each brutal kiss against the glass.

'You can do this, Willa,' Rafe encourages her. 'You've managed to keep my fevers a secret from her.'

She nods, worried, and not at all sure she will be strong enough for whatever Finn plans.

Half an hour later Clovis arrives home to a tranquil, domestic scene in the kitchen. Rafe grills bacon while Willa lays the table. Finn looks up from his newspaper when Clovis appears in the doorway and buries his head again.

'Breakfast?' Willa asks her.

Clovis leans against the doorframe, her arms folded as if she's observing a staged play. Her gaze stays with Willa.

The girl is changing and she prefers this version to the snivelling thing she was. She knows Willa tries to break away from her influence, and Clovis enjoys the challenge, it amuses her and relieves her boredom.

Willa feels Clovis's eyes bore into her, and busies herself with making coffee. Do not react. Just make the damn coffee, Willa tells herself.

Clovis leans over Rafe and takes a piece of bacon draining on a kitchen towel. She places her hand on his shoulder.

'Good morning, darling.'

He cannot help but flinch at her touch.

'My, aren't we jumpy this morning.' She chews and studies Rafe.

'Didn't sleep well.' He doesn't meet her gaze.

Hmm.'

Clovis pauses before she leaves them and then climbs the stairs. They hear the thud of her door closing. Rafe scrambles eggs and glances over at Finn whose eyes are glued to his paper.

Willa leaves her breakfast untouched, takes her coffee to her room and climbs into bed with a sketchpad. She guides her pencil and wonders that Clovis didn't silence her long ago. She knows more of Clovis's secrets than anyone. And now she is certain of two more: as deadly and horrific as they can be.

Her pencil moves down the paper and the outline of a young girl's face appears. What was her name? Mary. That was it. Mary at the asylum. Later, she will outline her face with stitches. Long-threading she calls it. Portraits of all the women in her long life, sewn in remembrance. A parentation. Willa knows what she must do. It will be hard, but she will do it because they must avenge. If they do nothing else with their interminable lives, they must avenge their dead.

She sets her sketchpad down and retrieves a volume from her bedside table. Curious that Dr Johnson's dictionary does not seem to include the entry of such an old word, such an ancient, evil deed. She runs her finger down the page. Ah. There it is:

We're going to avenge these appalling acts of mtró, mordre, morðor, murdrum, myrdrian, murder.

LONDON
PRESENT DAY

CHAPTER FIFTY-EIGHT

The skeletons of London are rising. The magnificent city is fitful as machinery peels back the pavements. Layers of soil thirty feet high are crammed rich with the dead. Centuries of forgotten graveyards and emergency burial grounds, representing the whole spectrum of society when death spread like a conflagration, are being disturbed in their overgrown, crowded loneliness. There are digs that are more haunting than others. An axe is found in a woman's skull, and a two-thousand-year old cooking pot with the lid still intact is filled to the top with remains.

Despite the attack on concrete, no archaeological site in London is as big and visible as the Thames foreshore when the tide is out. The relentless action of the tides has for thousands of years proven that sometimes, a thing lost might be found.

Autumn has pushed aside summer this year, with early gusts and an overcast sky that threatens winter storms ahead. Yawning nature, weary from bloom and bursts of growth, prepares for the last note of its nocturne.

It is past lunchtime when Constance stands in Narrow Street. The renaming of the street amuses her; it was much narrower when it was Fore Street. How small the houses seem; the rooms felt enormous when they were children. Constance's spirits lift to see the terrace exquisitely restored. Fast and furious memories flood her and she turns away before she is completely overtaken on what may well be her last visit to this street.

As the afternoon loses its warmth she makes for the tranquil cobblestoned streets of Wapping. Her cape flaps with each breeze as she strides past a mammoth tourist coach. Its long, wide body looks like a threatening alien on the slim, ancient street. Tourists queue at the door of a heavily visited riverside pub. While they pile in, eager for their authentic experience, Constance descends a set of algae-covered wooden steps to the foreshore. The river, swift and grey in the dying afternoon, laps and roars.

Ominous bits of jagged glass, crockery and rusty iron lie at her feet. The spoils are never the same twice; the next time the river retreats it will deposit different offerings. Constance is here to visit the river, not its swag. It may be the last time she ever sees it, too.

The sisters were given long life and now they must make an offering, perhaps a sacrifice. If they fail, and are unable to return, Constance wishes for something of herself to remain. What better recipient of her memento mori than the river that has defined their lives. She removes a red-velvet pouch from her bag from which she withdraws a gold locket. An eighteenth-birthday gift from Verity, it contains two locks of hair, one from each of them. It is no use offering a gift that does not strike deep chords. She steps closer to the water's edge and tosses it in.

Navigating the flotsam and jetsam, just as she turns her back to the river towards the stairs, her gaze falls on a tarnished, golden object. Is it the locket I just cast? she asks herself, disorientated. Has Father Thames spat it back at me? Her fingers join the grit and pebbles, animal bones and wrappers, to rescue the locket. Only when she wipes it clean does she see the shamrock engraved on the casing. Fascinated, she stops to prise it open. She reads it once, shakes her head, reads it thrice.

Grá buan
Averil & Francis
Love forever

Constance drops to her knees on the foreshore's unkind surface. Her first thought is of Verity who will think this treasure is God's miracle. Constance would disagree. The miracle is time.

'Passports.'
    'Check, such as they are.'
    'Empty plastic travel bottles.'
    'Check.'
    'Pouches.'
    'Pouches?'
    'For the phials and bottles.'
    'I forgot.'
    'Oh, Verity.'
    'I'm nervous. I can't think.'
    'Run to the market and buy those Chinese-silk pouches. Purchase several, we'll place other things in them as well so that it seems like we're women with travel phobias.'
    'Honestly, I don't know what you're talking about, travel phobias.'
    'Oh, just do it please.'

It's been a week of sleepless nights since Constance found their mother's locket. An urgent and most distressing request from Benedikt arrived in their safety letterbox two weeks ago. There has been some relief from the crisis that has hovered over them for two years. The supply of the phials' liquid is available once again, though limited. Of course it is good news, which they celebrated until they read on. The new problem is the logistics of the next delivery. There is no one available to travel. The letter maps out instructions for the sisters' journey from London Heathrow to Keflavík International. Further details followed.

Constance and Verity accepted without hesitation. They are willing to flirt with danger if it means helping Rafe, for they assume that wherever he is, he too needs the phials. And perhaps, just perhaps, this sacrifice will take them one step closer to him.

Camden Market is at its mid-September phase. Schools are in session and people are gearing up for the heavy work period before the Christmas break. After she makes her purchases, Verity is captured within a flux of Japanese tourists in the warrens of the food stalls. Escaping to the outer food courtyard, she considers what she'll take home for dinner when she hears the incredulity in a young woman's voice.

'Mrs Fitzgerald?'

Verity freezes at the stranger's call.

'Mrs Fitzgerald, is that you?'

Sometimes Verity will search faces on the streets of London and think that she recognizes them; over the years she must have seen the same faces many times. But this girl staring at her now with her mouth agape, she does not immediately recognize. What an odd girl she is, too. With a cone of chips in one hand, the other waves at her in a wild, frantic sweep. People inadvertently stand in her way as the young woman circumvents them towards Verity.

Slowly backing away from the young woman, Verity turns a corner and wends through the stalls and out of sight. She hurries along Parkway until she's sure she's not been followed, and then it hits her.

Rushing through the gate and into the house, she tosses her coat on the floor.

'Constance!'

She climbs the steps and finds her sister packing a carry-on.

'You won't believe it. You won't believe who I just saw at the market. I couldn't place her at first. I can't believe it.'

'Slow down.'

'Oh, what's her name ... Clovis Fowler's girl. What's her name, Constance?'

'Willa? You saw Willa? Are you sure?'

'Oh yes. I am now. She called out to me. And she looked like she'd seen a ghost. I wish I'd recognized her. She must know about Rafe.'

'Yes, she must. Was she on her own?'

'I'm not sure. Should I go back?'

'There's no time. When we return we'll comb the market. Did she look the same?'

'In age, yes, but not in any other way. I remembered her as frightened, cowering, a nervous girl. There's a remarkable difference. It's probably why I didn't recognize her right away.'

'We must find her, sister.'

ICELAND
PRESENT DAY

CHAPTER FIFTY-NINE

Benedikt arrives just before nightfall. The cottage rests on a quiet, peaceful plot of land that sits in The Golden Circle, near a national park in the geothermally active valley of Haukadalur. Tourists have been visiting this area of Iceland since the eighteenth century, and now holiday cottages sparsely dot the landscape, from which a constant flow of twenty-first century tourists marvel at the erupting geysers, giant waterfalls, hot springs, mud pots and steaming fumaroles. They will get themselves in all kinds of trouble. Tough men cry like babies when they watch their tents explode in the wind and learn the meaning of inhospitable. The elements wage an unforgiving perpetual war. Calamity is a commonplace certainty. Tourist hikers have been known to have mental breakdowns. When a blizzard comes on fast and unexpectedly, they give up, lie down and prepare to die in this magical, devastatingly beautiful and savage land.

Benedikt places his bag down in a cottage that gleams with glass and polished wood – strikingly different from the turf walls and dried sheep's bladder windows of his childhood. He peers into the powerful telescope that faces the expanse of the surrounding vicinity, checking for intruders, or at best, lost travellers who may interrupt him. Satisfied, he promptly closes the blinds and the curtains. The Aurora Borealis will soon beckon tourists in rented cottages to their terraces, or bid them to sit indoors by their fires to gaze in wonder at the green and blue lights billowing across the sky. It's a clear night in the season; the chances are good. Benedikt cannot risk their glancing his way.

He builds and lights a fire and then makes his way into the bedroom where he locks the door. Benedikt's hair, long-ish on his forehead, falls into his eyes as he removes his knitted cap. He needs a haircut.

He begins to undress slowly, methodically. First he slips out of his jacket, then a wool jumper, a shirt, and a cotton vest. Then he unwraps the binding around his torso to reveal breasts that have been sheathed for months at a time over a period of one hundred and eighty-five years. Elísabet looks into the mirror. Her arms are slender, yet incredibly muscular and strong. Her breasts are still firm, her face is unlined, and yet her eyes, wise with age stare back at her.

A long scar runs from her right shoulder, midway down her arm, a reminder of the knife fight between the first two would-be abductors. The first men she had killed. There were others – men and women who came too close to the truth, all of whom threatened to harm her son, to harm them all.

Elísabet and Stefán had entered the most elaborate and painstakingly devised plan. She trained her body and her mind the first six months of her baby's life, almost to destruction. Forever adjusting, living through the years like a streak of quiet lightning, constantly responding to legions of alerts, and training, always more training to remain a step ahead, to be stronger and rise to the impossible demand to occupy several places at once. The physical pain she could endure. The emotional pain nearly broke her. The only semblance of peace she possessed during her long saga of protection was the nine years Rafe lived with the sisters Fitzgerald. And even those years, when her son was cradled in love and devotion, the Copenhagen enemies nearly snatched him away. Everything turned black after Clovis reclaimed Rafe from Constance and Verity Fitzgerald.

When she received the sisters Fitzgerald's letter that confirmed her suspicion of the cruelty her young son suffered, she became a machine. She no longer knew herself and was determined to end the whole charade. Stefán talked her out if it, reminding her that if the Falk family ever captured Rafe he would suffer far worse.

Then the intricate system of retrieving and delivering the pool's resources almost collapsed. Ever since the 2010 eruptions of the volcano, *Eyjafjallajökull,* and the subsequent ash clouds that disrupted air space across western and northern Europe; its effect on the pool that holds the life-giving water has been devastating. It has been nearly dry for six years. Though Stefán and the others had prepared for such circumstances, the supplies grew low as their population increased. A few more innocents have stumbled upon the pool in much the same way Elísabet and Jon had. Stefán now regrets the extra phials he'd released to appease and occupy Clovis. He was never in any fear that the liquid or Rafe's sweat could be replicated, but he agonizes that he has been wasteful.

It is long after midnight. The sky-watchers have grown weary from waiting for a multi-coloured sky that never appears. A four-wheel-drive jeep pulls up to the cottage. Elísabet hears Stefán's keys in the locks.

'Elísabet!'

'In here.'

Stefán embraces her.

'I don't like putting the Fitzgeralds in danger, so many things could go wrong, but I think it's the right decision. I can't safely make the journey back to London if my long sleep is on schedule.'

Stefán does not respond, and Elísabet pulls back from him.

'What is it? What's wrong?' she asks him.

'Ask me what's right. Ask me what has finally happened to make things right.'

'I love you, but I'm tired, and in no mood for riddles.'

Stefán embraces her again. He's warm, slightly fevered.

'I'm just back from Copenhagen.' He holds her firmly at arm's length, as if he expects her to collapse. 'Elísabet, there are no more Falks.'

'No more Falks . . .' she repeats, as if in a trance.

'They have completely died out.'

Now it registers and her knees buckle.

'Here, sit down, Elísabet.'

'How do you know?'

He laughs. 'How do I know? I've only been tracking them for almost two hundred years.'

'I can't believe it. We knew they were slowly dying out, but I thought . . . aren't there two young cousins? Do you know what happened to them?' She reasons breathlessly.

'Iceland drowned them. There were four cousins, the photos . . . they were hunting in the east. Reindeer.'

'Trophy hunting? You're kidding.'

'I'm not. And apparently, according to ICE-SAR, either one or two of them fell into a pool at the bottom of a deep ravine. SAR thinks that the other two died trying to rescue them. All four corpses were recovered and identified.'

'And you're positive they were the last of the line? What about any who've gone completely underground? There are no women?'

'It's possible, but no, none that we've discovered.' He brushes her hair from her eyes. 'We'll need to remain vigilant for a while longer, and of course I'll continue to search.'

'Does this mean . . .' She begins to pace. 'Can I allow myself to think that . . .'

'Yes, darling Elísabet. Yes. But first, we must deal with Clovis.'

There is no time for lovemaking tonight. Elísabet and Stefán begin making calls to the others in their group. Now it is time to unravel past deeds, time to shift whatever goodness is left in the world to those who deserve it.

LONDON & ICELAND
PRESENT DAY

CHAPTER SIXTY

Ava Fitzgerald eases out of the small driveway at Lawless House.

'You really don't need to come with us,' Constance says. 'It will ruin you if we're caught travelling with fake passports.'

'I will not allow my favourite aunts to go on such a mission alone. And anyway, yours are fake, not mine.'

'Don't you trust us?'

'I trust you, but not the circumstances. Let's go over the questions. What is our reason for visiting?'

'We're on holiday,' the sisters answer, simultaneously.

'Right. And how long are we staying?'

'Ava. Everything is in hand. It will be all right.' Constance puts on a show of confidence.

As the Audi hums down the M4, the sisters can't quite believe they and their niece are leaving the country. Though they know the inevitable outcome, the sisters have formed a deep attachment to the long line of Fitzgeralds who have looked after them. With each of their deaths has come the brutal reminder that a natural lifespan is breathtakingly short. They are observers with a prison-like view, from where they repeatedly witness the life cycle of those they love, with all its promise, its countless choices and decisions, until one day, half a life is gone. There is something special about Ava. In the succession of male Fitzgeralds who had cared for them through the years no one had ever asked them what it was like to live for so long. Perhaps they were frightened, or even secretly repelled by the sisters' reality. Not Ava. They had the distinct feeling that Ava would leap at the chance and embrace the condition if given a choice. They cannot bear to think of her impermanence. The sisters often speak of it in midnight whispers.

At check-in, the ticket agent asks Verity to remove her sunglasses, which rattles her a bit, but after she complies the first hurdle is completed without a hitch and the three women relax somewhat.

After they board, the sisters are quiet, disorientated by their first experience of air travel. The roar of the engines that will transport them to another country in merely hours flusters them. They hold hands like two children, noses to the window, drawn to the blanket of clouds and their first view of the earth from above.

Just over three hours later they arrive at passport control at Keflavík International Airport. They wheel their carry-on luggage to the Kaffitár coffee kiosk, where they are due to meet their contact. No sooner have they parked themselves near the kiosk when an attractive middle-aged woman walks towards them in an unassuming manner. With a pointed and friendly smile, she offers her hand.

'My name is Margrét. Welcome to Iceland.'

As they walk to the car park, Margrét asks, 'Any problems travelling? Any at all?'

'No. None. Thank goodness,' Ava answers.

'You were not followed at any time?'

'Not that we're aware.'

Less than a five-minute drive later they arrive at one of the airport hotels.

Margrét leads them to a large suite in which she has already checked in.

'Please. Make yourselves comfortable. I'll order coffee and something to eat. You must be famished now that the first leg of your journey is complete.'

While they revive with strong coffee, a selection of smoked fish and bread and butter, Margrét explains that the package will be delivered to the room soon. It is the first mention of it.

Constance will go on to remember clearly the moment she heard the hotel room door's lock click open.

A man and a woman enter the room. The woman removes her knitted cap.

'Oh heavens. It's you!' Constance gasps.

The woman smiles at them.

'Who, Constance?' Verity asks.

'Benedikt.'

Elísabet begins to speak, but Constance rises from her chair and shakes her head in disbelief.

'It was you, wasn't it?' Constance says. 'Under the water . . . swimming . . .?'

'Yes.' Her eyes brim with warmth. 'My name is Elísabet. Thank you for taking such great care of my son.'

'Your son? I don't understand,' Verity is confused.

'Oh yes, sister,' Constance says. 'I see it so clearly now. I think I recognized it that terrible day at the Serpentine.'

Elísabet clasps Constance's hands. 'I can never repay you for what you did for him. What you both have done for him.'

Constance is studying Elísabet's face. 'You're . . . her sister . . . aren't you? Clovis Fowler is your sister.'

Elísabet nods.

'You are much more beautiful than her,' Constance says.

'That villainous woman,' Verity says.

'And the Fowlers? They're unaware that you and Benedikt are one and the same?' Constance asks.

'Yes. And they mustn't know, yet.'

'My God. All these years . . .'

'Tell us. Please. Is he safe?' Verity asks.

'You must know where he is . . .' Constance can scarcely breathe.

'I do, and as of three days ago he was working long hours in his studio, for which I have again to thank you. You nurtured and saved his spirit from the long years he faced, many in misery.'

'How? How could you possible stay your distance all this time?' Verity asks.

'For his safety. Isn't it the driving force behind motherhood? To always protect them?'

'Extraordinary,' Constance says. 'Nothing short of extraordinary.'

'I'm sure you have many questions,' Elísabet continues. 'And you will see Rafe soon, but plans are laid and we must continue to protect him for a while longer.'

In the remaining hours of the afternoon there are moments when Constance and Verity feel they have stepped into a surreal world. Here they are in Iceland, of all places, as they listen to Elísabet, Stefán and Margrét's astonishing histories. Ava sits between them, her presence a calming influence. Honoured that she is included, and while cognizant of all that is being spoken, of all plans laid, another part of Ava twists a persistent thought: might Stefán one day lead her to the pool? For she is certain now. Her desire is solid.

Too soon it is time to return to London. The sisters learn that their old friend Owen Mockett is still alive and soon to fall prey to the long sleep with no phial to use upon waking, hence the urgency.

'I apologize to have put you in harm's way, but the sleep will overtake me any minute now and I cannot travel,' Elísabet says.

'None of us is able,' Stefán adds. 'If it's any consolation, we've never had any issue or problem with our passports. They are each created by the same person.'

'One day soon we will meet on less stressful terms.' Elísabet has held her emotions in check, but falters for a moment at the sisters' departure.

Once again at check-in, Ava arranges their return flight. The ticket agent studies their passports.

'But you've just arrived?' he comments.

'Yes, that's right. But unfortunately, my aunts have just been informed of a family emergency.'

The ticket agent looks past Ava to the two women dabbing their noses with tissues, genuinely struggling with their emotions.

'I'm very sorry,' he says. 'Let's get you on the next flight to London.'

They hardly speak on the flight home. There is much to assimilate, and they agreed that there isn't enough privacy to confer safely. Every so often the three women turn their heads on the headrests and smile at each other with utter joy, touched by their unbelievable turn in fortune.

Late that night at Lawless House, Constance sorts through the day's mail.

'What's this then?' She reads quickly. 'Good lord! It's a personal invitation to Tate Britain and it's handwritten and signed by Willa Robinson! An invitation to a private viewing of a new exhibit.'

'How very odd. So it *was* Willa I saw at the market,' Verity says.

'The young woman you mentioned today in our meeting?' Ava asks.

'Yes, I suppose so, though I never knew her surname,' Constance says.

'How extraordinary. May I go along?' Ava asks.

'Yes of course, we shall all go. It will be a nice distraction while we wait for Elísabet and Stefán to implement their plans.'

'Well, as I'm the only practising Catholic in this house, I'm going upstairs to offer prayers of praise and thanks,' Verity says.

Constance and Ava exchange smiles.

'Are you staying the night, Ava? You know you're always welcome.'

'No, thank you Aunt Verity, I have work to do in chambers.'

'You work too much.' Verity trails up the stairs.

'You look worried,' Ava says to Constance.

'I am.'

'Elísabet and Stefán ... They're extraordinarily organized and well resourced. And they're extremely cautious. My tuppence, but I don't think you should worry,' Ava offers.

'Yes, all true, but there is an element to their plan that is an impossible wild card. You have no idea, Ava.'

'What's that?'

'Clovis Fowler.'

CHAPTER SIXTY-ONE

It occurs during a stroke of serendipity; Finn insists that an auspicious pull of December's gibbous moon grants anything that yearns to be aligned a single, perfect moment to do so.

Willa arrives home late after a long, cold day at Camden Market and a further three hours spent at her current studies. Night courses are her purlieus, where she slowly builds her endurance. If her long life has afforded her anything, it has been time to catch up, to have a better understanding of her own strengths and weaknesses. She might have benefited from seeing a counsellor, but the perils of revealing any one of her many secrets was too great; a slip of a century would court ruin. And there was another danger, that of placing herself in the hands of yet another stranger. Although a therapist may be completely trustworthy and lack any ambition of dominance, the risk was one she would not take. And so the short courses, in rooms in which she sat with anonymous others, were her painstakingly trodden paths to strength.

One course after another, lacing around the night rooms of London, she puts herself back together until finally she can remember the face of her father again. Small things, like the shadows that darkened his eyes, and the gap from a missing incisor. Then the pang of remembrances hit her full force – how much she had been loved and valued, and the bitter circumstances in which her ailing father had no choice but to leave her in Lambeth. The memory of loss became almost unbearable when she allowed it to emerge, until, after nights of silent weeping, she began to feel better, stronger, and yet lighter, relieved of a heavy yoke.

At her current six-week course she probes the psychology of criminals, to understand why people commit the crimes they do. It's hard for her to sit still in class because her mind explodes with revelations and insights. Criminals, no matter how cunning and precise, make mistakes. It may take years, but eventually a crack will appear, she learns. Never before now has she dared hope that Clovis Fowler's tight skin of invulnerability might be broken, nor entertained the idea that one day, Clovis Fowler might make the slimmest error.

Willa towel-dries her hair as she wends her way through the hallway on the first floor to the separate stairs that lead to her attic room. She passes the alcove, where a glass and wooden display case sits beneath a small round window. Soft, recessed lighting falls on the shelves inside the case, where a selection of Jonesy's puppets is displayed. She notices that the head of one of the puppets is ever so slightly off-centre. Her pulse quickens. She remembers when Jonesy carved the wolf in man's clothing; a menacing grin spreads from his exaggerated, red-painted mouth. She hears someone coming up the steps and quickly moves on to her room with her heart seemingly thumping out of her chest.

She and Finn have checked the puppets before, in fact, several times. But of course that means nothing. They're certain that Clovis constantly rotates her hiding places because after all, a house is a limited space. She dares not check the puppets again until Clovis is safely away from the house. And she mustn't get her hopes up. Maybe she knocked it loose when dusting. But oh mighty hell, could this be the error, the little slip?

The rain wakes her after only three hours of sleep. It beats against the window as if it is telling her a fast, furious story. There's no way she's going to the market today. Downstairs, Clovis is slamming the portafilter against the steel basket, emptying the thing with enough force to kill a small animal.

'Willa! Come down here and fix this.'

'Be right down.' She clenches her jaw.

Downstairs, Clovis stands at the kitchen window that offers a dark clouded view onto the small patio garden.

'I cannot believe I have to go out in this. Finn, why can't you take the car?'

'I have a big auction today. A heap of money at stake,' he mumbles.

'You can do that from anywhere.'

'Not from the driver's seat, I can't.'

'Willa!' Clovis calls again.

'I'm here. I'm here.'

Willa first cleans up Clovis's mess, and then fills the portafilter with coffee. Clovis pulls on her Wellies.

'Will you be at the market today?' Clovis asks.

'No. I'm working here.'

'Come along with me to have the tyres rotated and the oil changed.'

'I can't, I'm working on something new and ...'

'It can wait. I'd really like to do some shopping.'

Willa places the espresso cup and saucer on the table.

'I really can't.' She says firmly. *Let this be the beginning.*

Finn looks up from his papers, but Willa won't meet his eyes, frightened she may give away too much. He retreats to his conservatory with no desire to enter the fray.

'Very well. Perhaps we should review your commitments outside the home. You may be taking on too much. It disappoints me that you can't fulfil your duties to me today.'

Ah, there is that hateful 'Mistress voice' again. Willa scrubs the counter, willing herself not to display any reaction, to remain calm and patient. She focuses on the toast crumbs and the grounds of coffee that Clovis has carelessly flung about. She waits for the blissful moment when Clovis and her wellies are finally out of the door.

When the car speeds away Willa watches the clock for a full five minutes. Then she runs upstairs, opens the display-case doors and carefully lifts the wolf puppet off the shelf. Sitting on the floor she removes the head and probes the small opening of the torso. Her fingers feel glass. She wants to scream, to call for help, to shout that she cannot do it. But instead, she takes a deep breath and lifts the phial out of Jonesy's puppet. There is another.

'Finn! Finn! Come quick. Finn! Hurry!'

All the puppets are filled with phials.

Less than a minute later, which feels like an eternity, Finn is bounding up the stairs, phone in hand.

'I'm on the phone with a client, what the hell do you—"

Willa sits with her legs crossed, her arms raised at her sides, palms up, with a phial in each hand, like a Tibetan monk chanting for world peace.

Finn drops his phone.

They look at each other, astonished, for an achingly long moment until Finn Fowler erupts with an enormous, strange cacophony of sounds.

'I don't believe it,' he manages to say.

Willa never expected this day to arrive, and now that it has she is surprised that she feels quite calm.

'Phone Rafe. Don't let on or he may have an accident trying to get here, but tell him to come at once,' she says.

'Yes, yes. Quite fucking right.' He does an odd little jig.

They have very little time. The plan they have honed over the years, turning it over and over in their heads, is now unbelievably in action. The chore of replacing all the phials with a liquid that perfectly resembles the authentic liquid is painstaking. Years ago, Mockett recreated the exact colour, with a tinge of iridescence. His experiments weren't all for naught.

When Rafe arrives he is of no use to them. He's shaking so badly he can't be trusted with the delicate glass. Finn suggests that he keeps watch for Clovis to return. She shouldn't be back for at least a couple of hours, but it has long been her habit to return early to try to catch them off guard.

Now Willa works quickly to put the puppets back together. Placing them exactly as they were is of monumental importance, she tilts the fox's head perfectly.

'Rafe, take the phials to your studio. Can you find a good hiding place where they'll be safe?'

'Of course. Don't worry.'

'Okay. Time to be brave, Willa,' Finn says.

'I feel I'm ready. I really do. Will you call Mockett?' she asks.

'Yes, exactly right. Will do. And of course Benedikt, I'll write to him immediately and post it in his box when Clovis is next out of the house. Rafe, you should go now. Your big evening is nearly here. Are you ready?'

'I am. I'm nervous, but I'm ready.'

'Good. I'm damned sorry that London won't see your name.'

'I'm happy lurking around in the shadows. Honestly. It's where I'm most comfortable.'

'I wish that Jonesy could be here now,' Willa says.

'We all do. Well done, Willa. I'm sorry I bit your head off,' Finn tells her.

'Never mind, I'm . . . I'm so happy!'

Then Rafe and Finn witness something remarkably rare – Willa's face brightening the room with her smile.

CHAPTER SIXTY-TWO

'Goodness. How smart you both look,' Ava tells them.

The sisters are without disguises tonight. Constance sports a deep lavender, velvet trouser-suit. Her hair, which she wears long and loose, shines strikingly white. Slight touches of make-up enhance her refined features.

Verity's lapis-blue, pleated sheath dress accentuates her willowy figure. Her hair is short again, lending her an androgynous look that serves her needs.

'If your mother could see what a beautiful, sophisticated woman you have become. Your father spoke of her often and shared his photos of her. You have her colouring; the same dark hair and sea-green eyes.' Constance says to Ava.

'Sometimes I can't remember the details of her face.'

'You were so young,' Constance tells her. 'I wish we could have met her. It's difficult, not meeting the rest of the family. But then we are grateful for you, Ava, and all of your family who have helped us.'

'Our family,' Ava corrects her. 'You are our family.'

In the warmth of the car a chatty driver who won't take the strong hint that they wish to watch the snow flurries in silence, finally turns his attention to his satnav.

'I actually don't know why we're doing this,' Constance muses. 'You know I've not been back to Millbank since . . .' she glances at the driver, 'well, not for a long time.'

'I forgot about tonight. I can think of nothing but our meeting with Elísabet.' Verity says.

'I'm just happy to be away from chambers. London is beautiful when it snows,' Ava says.

'London is always beautiful,' the sisters echo.

The last of the day's visitors are making their way out the doors of the museum while others are just arriving for one of the Tate's special evenings of free events. Constance pauses on the steps that lead to the sprawling, historic building with its cold and stony Edwardian character, conscious that a temple to art replaced the site of abject misery.

The women enter the glazed door to the vestibule where a striking spiral staircase sweeps down from the floor below them in the centre of the rotunda. There, standing alone, is Willa Robinson.

'I promised myself I wouldn't cry,' she says to the women.

The sisters take her hands, a sensation with which Willa is not entirely comfortable, but she resists drawing away.

'Dear, dear girl,' Constance says. 'How very well you look.'

'Willa Robinson.' Verity takes a step back. 'Astonishing.'

'Please, let me introduce you to our niece, Ava Fitzgerald.' Constance turns to the young woman standing beside her.

'Pleasure to meet you. Are you ... changed as well?' Willa asks.

'No, no I'm not. It's lovely to meet you.' Ava struggles to keep her voice even. A shock courses through her at the girl's youthful appearance. And then another, at the depth behind the eyes in her young face.

There is so much to say, but now is not the time.

'I've invited you here for a very special exhibition.' Willa is exceptionally composed. 'It's not open to the public yet. It's sort of a preview before the preview. Please, follow me.'

Willa leads them through the grand corridor on the main floor and then stops at one of the exhibition rooms. On the side of the doorway a simple sign reads: THE SISTER SAINTS.

A thick, pink light permeates the room like the thickest Limehouse fog.

'Come.' Willa motions to the three women.

They follow her into the exhibition room to a scene that staggers them.

Ava gasps. 'Oh my God. It's ... it's ... both of you. You're ... everywhere.'

They stand encircled by the paintings that hang on the walls. There are more suspended from the ceiling. Paintings that explode with the vibrancy of deep, thick reds and luscious pinks. Rings of yellow, and gold circles of light dance above the heads of the two women in the paintings, the same women in each rendition. In several paintings, shards of silver protrude from thick layers of paint. On closer scrutiny they are discovered to be delicate silver crucifixes. The glistening silver reflects the sisters' white hair.

The effect is so powerful that Constance and Verity are left speechless and confused. They inch forward to the centre, where the largest of seventy paintings hangs on the wall in a majestic, gilded frame. The sisters are portrayed in profile, facing each other, and clearly, a tear streams from the corner of each of their eyes. Old tears, profuse with layered paint, give the impression of active tears, still falling. Above the sisters' heads their aureoles are also thickly layered and finished with moon gold, a gold leaf that gives the golden shade a hint of pinkish brown – and will never tarnish. There are no crucifixes in this painting; instead, three-hoop fede rings extend from various points in the aureoles. They shine so finely.

The paintings are emotive, striking at the heart with pathos while at the same time offering hope with the sisters' smiles, glimmering through their tears.

'Happy tears.' A man's voice whispers behind them.

'Auntie Connie. Auntie Very,' he says.

The sisters turn. He stands in the pink fog, his dark-red hair shimmers in soft streaks of light. Eyes filled with emotion, he smiles.

'I thought I would never see you again. So I painted you over and over.'

The sisters feel his arms around them. Constance places her hand on his rose-gold chain. Time stops completely, and now, in his embrace, their soft sobs contain a world of joy.

Ava and Willa, who have discreetly stepped out of the gallery, have lost any awkwardness.

'You have made my aunts . . . God, I can't talk. Wait a minute.' Ava blinks. 'You've made them so happy, Willa.'

'They deserve to be happy. So does he.'

'You must care a great deal for him.'

'Yes, I do.' She adds, 'Like I would care for a dear brother.'

'I see,' says Ava, a flush of pink in her cheeks.' Is this the first time you've been to the Tate since . . . well, since it was the penitentiary?'

Willa nods. 'It's strange to think you know about that. I don't even know if I should be embarrassed. I really wasn't guilty of anything.'

'Of course not! I apologize. I don't mean to pry. I handle all of Aunt Constance and Aunt Verity's affairs now, and I would never break their trust. I'm the only living member of our family who knows. We've had a system in place since, well, since my aunts changed. Those of us who have known have always adhered to a strong familial duty.' Suddenly pensive, she adds. 'And love.'

'Then you know that while Rafe was with your aunts I was here, right on these premises, in this swamp.'

'Yes. I'm sorry. I don't know how you've managed to survive it. Mentally, I mean.'

'I almost came back to watch them knock it down. But I didn't have as much freedom then.'

'It is quite amazing that Rafe is showing here. His identity isn't known, is it? Not to anyone at the museum?'

'God no. They think they have a Banksy,' says Willa.

*　　*　　*

It doesn't seem at all strange to sit by the fire on a snowy night in December with the boy, who by some miracle has grown into a sane, talented man. The sisters and Rafe don't attempt to catch up, but rather allow their shared memories to lead them where they may. There is talk of the cries of monkeys, and the sweat of fevers, shared tears for Bertie, and missed opportunities without blame. There are things left unsaid for now, the haunt of the want of suicide, the cruelty of one woman, and the gnawing aches when they could not find the arms of comfort. As they promised Elísabet, the sisters hold tight to their recent enlightenment. It is not yet time for another long-overdue reunion.

Two hours pass in a flash. Willa and Ava, who have been talking in the kitchen peek their heads into the sitting room to offer tea. Yes, please, comes the response, they are famished.

'Oh forgive me, Ava! We've been so selfish,' Verity says. 'Please come in and meet Rafe.'

Ava steps forward to him. 'I hardly know what to say,' she says. '"It's a pleasure to meet you" sounds so ridiculous when I've heard so much about you. But it is. A pleasure. A great pleasure.' She wonders why she rattles on.

Rafe stands and takes her hand, half shaking it, half holding it, embarrassed by his awkwardness.

'I am pleased to meet you, too. Thank you for being so attentive to them.'

Willa arrives with a heaving tray of food.

'I just robbed your fridge,' she says.

They nibble on cheese, pâté, smoked meats and fish, olives, bread and chutneys and salad. There's cake, chocolate tarts, and tea, pots and pots of tea. Every few minutes the Fitzgerald sisters catch each other's eye, and what passes between them is an acknowledgement that they stayed the course, the course of love – a long-tested, aged love. Lawless House is effervescent with love tonight. Its very walls throb with it. The fire spits out flames of love.

They talk late into the night. The old clock in the sitting room that once belonged to Averil Lawless strikes midnight, and the night turns over to the 17th of December. For the first time in many a long year the sisters will not take that fraught walk to St Martin's Gardens later in the day. Their boy is home.

CHAPTER SIXTY-THREE

Early in the morning, a few days after the reunion, Willa folds laundry in the kitchen. The snow has cleared, leaving damp patches on the patio's flagstones. She has chosen this hour to begin the ruse, while Clovis is still lazy and cross with sleep. Here she comes, wrapped in her cashmere dressing gown.

'It's cold. Turn the heat on, Willa.'

'Here's your coffee. And pastries.'

'Aren't I lucky that I can still eat croissants and never gain any weight?'

'Yes. Lucky, that.' Willa folds more towels, then says, 'You know, the strangest thing happened at the market a few weeks ago.'

'I'm sure. All things are strange to you.'

'I thought I saw one of the Fitzgerald ladies.'

Clovis doesn't miss a beat. 'Ha! That *is* strange, considering they've been dead for over a hundred years.'

'Hmm. Yes.' Willa pauses and scratches her head as if she's thinking very hard. 'At the time, you said you read about their deaths in the paper. Which paper was that, do you remember?'

Now she has Clovis's full attention.

'I think it was *The Times*, or maybe it was *The Illustrated London News*, or maybe . . .' Clovis pauses, her voice takes on that familiar edge when she is taut and defensive. 'Maybe I read it in one of the hundreds of London's papers at the time.'

'Well, I only ask because I searched through many of the London news publications during that year, that month exactly. It is amazing how many papers are archived at the British Library,' Willa shakes her head in wonderment, 'just amazing. And I found no record for those sisters. Isn't that odd?'

'Indeed. Amazing. But not surprising.'

'And even more amazing is that there is no record of their death. What do you think of that Clovis?'

'Not much.'

'Oh, and did you see this?'

Willa holds up *The Guardian*'s culture section. One of Rafe's paintings is splashed across the front page with the headline: *An Anonymous Success*.

'He brings danger to us with that egotistic display.'

And with that Willa nearly falters. Her mission is for Clovis to be threatened by her, not Rafe.

'No, he doesn't. He covers his tracks and he's good at it, too. They'll never trace the works back to him.'

'They had better not.'

'After I saw – or thought I saw – one of the Fitzgerald sisters, it kind of jarred my brain, you know? Kind of set things off. I started thinking about poor Mrs Mockett – what was her name now? Nora, that's it.'

Clovis brushes the crumbs off her lap and noisily scoots her chair back. She walks to the window, where she stands with folded arms.

'I always thought her death was so, oh I don't know, strange, I guess,' Willa continues. 'She was such a careful and precise lady. How many times had she crossed Commercial Road by then – I don't know, hundreds? Thousands? I wondered at the time, and whenever I think of her, I still wonder if she might have been pushed.'

Clovis blinks as the black crow on the patio looks for its breakfast, poking its head in moss-covered cracks.

'Don't be ridiculous.'

'Oh, I know, I know, stupid of me. Silly, dumb Willa.' She picks up the stack of laundry just as Finn enters the kitchen, murmurs a good morning and retreats upstairs. Then she waits, she waits an eternity for Clovis to knock on her door. But Clovis doesn't come. Finn goes back to his conservatory and she can hear the presence of Clovis's silence in the kitchen, digesting her innuendos.

While Willa packs her bag for a day at the market, Clovis finally climbs the stairs, but she doesn't even pause at Willa's door. Anxiety, Willa's old, unwanted friend, crawls into her gut. She sits on her bed and rocks. How will I ever perform the next phase if I can't even wait patiently? She remembers to breathe slowly and deeply, and eventually the rocking stops.

She wraps up in her coat and a fur hat, grabs her things and prepares to leave for the day, none the wiser as to the effect of her performance. Just as she opens the front door, Clovis calls her name and comes downstairs again, still in her dressing gown.

'It's been a while since our last session. Perhaps tonight? You look as if you could use a little de-stressing.'

Willa heaves her bag higher on her shoulder and summons an even voice, 'It's late night at the market, Christmas shopping hours, I won't be home till midnight.'

'Oh, all right, some other time,' Clovis says, equally measured.

Willa nods and makes to go, then stops and turns around.

'I'm not at the market tomorrow. What about tomorrow night?'

Clovis shrugs. 'Sure.'

Willa waits until she has turned the corner to Tooley Street before she texts Finn. When he acknowledges her message, just for good measure, and because every moment for the next twenty-four hours must be played perfectly, she tears her mobile apart and throws it in a bin.

CHAPTER SIXTY-FOUR

Willa closes her eyes at the first notes of the glass armonica. She thinks of knobs on taps and mentally turns them to the off position. The music in her head stops. She evokes images of samples of her new work, replacing the tones that once held her captive. She imagines sewing shadows on their faces, thick eyebrows and dark lashes, embroidering them into recognizable women on fine silk, muslin and cotton organdie. They are the women of her life: the girls from the orphan asylum, the female prisoners in Millbank, the working women of Limehouse, London's lost prostitutes found on every corner, the women in her study courses. She will never run short of subjects. She calls upon them now to help her.

She places the jade cicada in her pocket so that when Clovis finds it she will feel secure that Willa is still the same superstitious girl with no mind of her own.

Downstairs in the sitting room Clovis continues to play as Willa takes the first steps down to the reckoning.

'Sit down, Willa.'

Clovis lowers her voice to a perfect, peaceful pitch.

'Close your eyes, allow the music to relax you.'

Clovis plays for a few minutes longer, taking more time than usual before she quietly stands. She places a chair in front of her subject, spreads her legs a bit and places them around Willa's knees.

'Relax your forehead. Let it go, Willa. Take a deep breath and let your shoulders drop. Good. Let the chair support your weight. Excellent.'

Willa feels the heat of Clovis's hands as she makes passes over her head. Then she slips her hand into her pocket and holds the cicada in her sweaty fingers. She can almost feel Clovis's attention move to her pocket.

'There is nowhere you need to be, nothing required of you.' Her voice is softly soothing and more coaxing than ever before. 'You can totally and completely relax. And sleep. Sleep deeply.'

Willa's head drops forward.

'Willa, can you hear my voice?'

A pause.

'Yes.'

'I want you to relax even more deeply. And sleep very, very soundly. But you will still hear my voice and follow my instructions. Do you understand?'

'Yes.'

'Good. Lift your right arm.'

Willa takes her hand out of her pocket and raises her arm high over her head. Clovis glances at the old ship's clock on the wall. She won't give another instruction until Willa is in excruciating pain. She waits. Minutes pass.

Willa's arm trembles.

'Now, lower your arm.'

Her arm floats down.

'Stand, Willa.'

The chair creaks as Willa slowly leans forward and comes to standing.

'Raise your right arm.'

She does.

'Good. You're doing so well. Now stand on one leg, your right.'

She easily balances on her right leg.

'Listen carefully, Willa, there's a pole in front of you. It stands securely and is much taller than you. I would like you to dance for me. Just like girls do in the films. Hear the music, see the strobe lights, reach out to the pole and dance.'

Willa tilts her head like she's listening for music. She squints and then she nods to a beat. Her shoulders sway, followed by her hips and pelvis. She reaches out and grabs an imaginary pole and swings around it slowly, in rhythm to the music. She has nothing to lean against, nothing to take her weight, but her body adjusts as she wraps her arms around an imaginary pole. Her back arches, she lifts a leg and slides it down, making the impossible seem possible. Then Willa gyrates more suggestively. Her head tilts back and she moans as if in ecstasy.

Satisfied that Willa isn't faking a trance, Clovis stops her.

'Very good, Willa. Sit down again.'

Willa gropes for the chair with her eyes still closed.

'Take a moment to relax even deeper.'

Willa's breathing returns to normal.

'Tell me, did you see one of the sisters Fitzgerald?'

'Oh, yes, mistress,' Willa's voice regresses fully, returning to that of a young servant.

'Good. And tell me also, did you tell anyone other than me that you thought you recognized one of the Fitzgeralds?'

'No, mistress.'

'No one? Not a soul? Not Rafe? Or Finn?'

'No, mistress, not a soul.'

'Why not, Willa?'

''Twas embarrassed, mistress.'

'Why, Willa?'

'They might think I was a bit barmy.'

'And tell me, do you really believe it was a Fitzgerald?'

'Oh, yes, mistress. I'm certain of it. She's alive and well.'

'Good.'

Clovis places a pen in Willa's hand and a notebook on her lap with a sheet of letter-sized paper on top.

'Just two more things to do, Willa, before you'll wake refreshed. I'd like you to sign this piece of paper.'

'Yes, mistress.'

Guided by Clovis, Willa scrawls her signature.

'There. Good girl. We're almost finished.'

Clovis takes a phial out of her pocket.

'I'm going to give you a few drops of medicine now. You're to drink it all up. Do you understand?'

'Yes, mistress. Drink it all up.'

'That's right.'

Clovis removes the top of the phial and places it in Willa's hand. Slowly, she raises the phial to her lips and then tilts the glass and drinks until all the liquid is gone.

Clovis sits perfectly still, waiting for a reaction.

Willa's body goes slack, then she begins to slip from the chair. Clovis makes a move to catch her, but stops and allows Willa's body to fall to the floor with a loud thud.

Clovis kneels down to take her pulse, which, in Willa's favour, is naturally weak-feeling. She plans to move Willa into her bedroom revealing a case of suicide, supported by the signed note. Easy. Simple.

The sound of the door opening catches Clovis off guard. Finn is not due home for hours. And yet here he stands in the doorway with Owen Mockett at his side.

'Thank god you're here. She's just collapsed. I found her like this. Look, the phial is empty.' Clovis thinks on her feet.

Finn and Owen hold out their hands for Clovis to see the phials in their palms. Then they open them and toss them back like shots of whisky.

For one wild moment Clovis thinks they too have committed suicide. Then Willa sits up. Clovis looks from Willa to Finn and Owen who are still standing, angry and accusing.

'What ... what is going on here?' she spits.

'Willa, all right?' Finn asks.

'Alive and well.' She snatches the letter from Clovis.

'Perhaps you'd like to read them my forged suicide note?' Willa asks Clovis.

Clovis's knees buckle, the chair catches her.

Finn and Owen form a barricade in front of the door.

'Your night has only just begun,' Finn snarls at Clovis.

'Mockett,' she entreats him.' Owen. What are you doing?'

Owen throws a copy of Henrietta Martin's letter at Clovis's feet.

'What is this?' he says.

Clovis snatches it up. 'Oh, this again?' She laughs as she reads the letter, a strange and unsettling laugh that will remain memorable to everyone in the room, the way a terrible nightmare is recalled with a slice of terror, until finally it fades away.

The sound of footsteps at the door interrupts Clovis's hysteria.

Grim and determined, Stefán and Margrét enter the room.

'Oh. You,' Clovis says with rancour. 'The Lord of Iceland and his hag servant, Margrét the Lonely. Yes, I saw it in your eyes the night you brought the boy to me. Lonely as an assassin. Get out of my house.'

Clovis tries to part the group but falters as a shadow darkens the doorway. She attempts to conceal her confusion but the face of the woman who runs her fingers through her short hair, and steps forward in front of the group, is like a punch to the gut. That no one else is surprised is not lost on Clovis and in a quick stroke she recovers.

'Elísabet. How lovely of you to come undisguised.' Her delivery is chilling.

Elísabet looks into her sister's eyes with an equal coldness.

'There is one missing,' Clovis says. 'Where is the magical boy?'

'You will never see my son again,' Elísabet says evenly.

'What a display of self-control.'

Clovis inches closer as if to threaten Elísabet, and both Stefán and Finn move to restrain her.

'It's all right,' Elísabet assures them. 'She's not that kind of fighter.'

'I have married your lover and I have raised your son. Those are facts that will never change,' Clovis hisses. 'You're a coward. You have always been a coward. Content on a stinking sheep farm; a small patch of shitty frozen land. And so pleased to be praised for your knitting. Knitting for God's sake.' Clovis, aware of her audience, pauses for effect. 'But there was eventually a crack, an imperfection at last. You were quick to open your legs for a lusty foreigner.' She laughs at her memory. 'The result of that went wrong, didn't it? So elegantly discarded on your hands and knees.'

Elísabet conceals her reaction, but Clovis is quick to see the change in her sister's face and rolls her eyes.

'Oh how tedious of you Elísabet! Of course it was me,' Clovis says.

Puzzled, Finn glares at Clovis. 'What are you talking about?'

Clovis ignores him, inching closer to Elísabet. Her voice is even and chilling, 'I could not let you free yourself from that life and leave me there. You did not deserve rescuing. So I left you, and I took him. And it was easy, so easy. Even pregnant with his child, he forgot you. Didn't you Finn?'

The taste for violence rises in the acid in Finn's gut. He is willing to go through another hellish redemption if he could have one good go at her with a knife and cut her fucking tongue out. Mockett is tugging at him, whispering for him to gain his composure.

Clovis moves on to the crux of the matter.

'It was . . . interesting . . . to watch your son cry himself to sleep.' She laughs unnervingly again. 'You must have known – you must have seen. To think of your daily pain while you were ridiculously disguised will be . . . quite comforting. You will not hinder me now, Elísabet. None of you will stand in my way.'

Clovis swaggers towards the door.

Stefán pushes her down into the chair.

'Take your hands off me.'

'Silence!' Stefán roars. Then he nods to Elísabet.

'Clovis Fowler, formerly known as Koldís Ingólfsdóttir,' Elísabet begins. 'For the murder of Nora Mockett, for the murder of Jonesy Ling, for the attempted murder of Willa Robinson and for the abuse of Rafe Jónsson, there is a strong consensus amongst several of our people that you should be put to death. However, it is decided that you will be taken from your home and this country with no more than the clothes on your back and you will be escorted to Iceland . . .'

'You are quite mad . . .'

Elísabet talks over her. '. . . where you will remain under our auspices, a prisoner of our people. We are spread far and wide across the country. Stripped of all your rights, you will be moved from one remote place to another, never knowing when or how the transport will occur. You will work at menial tasks in the most isolated areas of our country. If anyone should ever show you any kindness, or the slightest sympathy, or should you be successful at manipulating your keeper, you will be removed to a new location. You will have no access to any form of outside communication. Any clothing, or personal items that you need to remain clean and healthy you must earn or make yourself. The only relief you will have from your punishment is the four weeks a year that you fall into your sleep.

When you reach your first location you will be given a phial. The choice you removed from others for so long will always be offered to you. If you wish to take your own life, you may do so at any time. For someone like you, Iceland will be an unbearably lonely place. One way or the other, you will die in a remote valley in the country that sits at the top of the world.'

CHAPTER SIXTY-FIVE

'She's here!' Verity whispers to Constance. 'I'll go out and open the gate.'

'Who is it, Auntie Very?' Rafe asks.

'Someone who has been waiting a very long time to meet you,' Constance tells him.

Rafe stands at the windows where the garden of his childhood extends, redolent of a lush valley. Two enormous, marble sea-dragons guard three tiered terraces, connected by stone and wooden steps. His old swing still hangs from the massive London plane at the heart of the garden. A turkey oak, a soaring beech, tree ferns, and palms deaden traffic noise. Agaves cast a blue glow. Water splashes down stepped ponds. Beyond the legacy of the canal wall at the bottom half of the garden, the sisters have sown a wild flower meadow. A square pool by the kitchen window reflects light from the cream-coloured walls of the house. A variety of seating options hide in their own secluded nooks including the old stone bench from where his aunties read aloud to him on warm summer evenings when the light was kind. The garden speaks to him. They have been here all this time, it says. They have waited for you.

'Rafe,' Constance says gently behind him.

He turns to see his aunts' arms entwined around the waist of a beautiful woman. Her face is familiar. Her hand goes to her heart. She searches his face and then nods her head. Yes, I am here now. Here with you.

One look at her face and he knows.

'Mother?'

'Yes, son.'

Constance and Verity steal away, quietly shutting the doors. In the kitchen they work silently with their own thoughts between them as they cut and slice, brew and stir.

After some time, the sisters find their voices again.

'I'm so happy for them,' Verity says.

'It's wonderful.'

'The other one. Is she gone now?'

'Yes. This morning.'

'Good.'

The sound of the gate opening has them scurrying to the door.

'Ava. I'll head her off so she doesn't go barging into the sitting room,' Constance says.

A few moments later they put Ava to work with them in the kitchen and update her on all the latest events.

'Willa must have been terrified. I don't think I could have done it,' Ava says.

'We should do something for her, sister.'

'Yes, we must, Verity. Surely she won't want to stay in that house.'

'Perhaps some sort of property for her work and a nice flat.'

'Ava, would you make some enquiries?'

'Of course, after you ask her permission to change her life.' She smiles.

'Do you think it's all right to go in now?' Verity asks.

'Let's give them a little more time,' Constance says.

'Oh, please, I'm like a child at Christmas hiding in here. I want to see them happy and laughing. Ava, pop your head in and offer tea. Sister, let's have champagne. Just a wee glass.'

Ava knocks softly on the doors to the sitting room.

'Yes, do come,' Rafe says, expecting his aunts.

Ava opens the doors.

'Oh, it's you,' he says. 'Hello again!' He finds that he can't stop smiling at her.

'Hello again.'

'Mother, this is the woman I told you about. This is Ava.'

'You did?' Ava asks.

'He did.' Elísabet smiles at her warmly and beckons her to come near.

CHAPTER SIXTY-SIX

At dusk Stefán collects the water from the pool behind the waterfall. The liquid has no preference – glass, wood, plastic, it performs its inexplicable work sloshing in any sort of carrier. He rides Glossi today, forsaking his car for the innate intelligence of his eternally beautiful horse. He bows his elegant neck down towards the pool, but does not drink. The drops sustain him as well.

His old friend makes an appearance this evening. Long arms droop from his shoulders, his fingertips reach his knees. A lean torso and the alarming length of his legs create a rail for his homespun clothing.

'Stefán, son of Hilmar. The day may come when a foreigner drinks from the pool.'

Stefán smiles. 'You mean a tourist? Perhaps, though they like the west of our country best of all. Tourists pass here but rarely stop.'

'My point is that there must be no complacency. Especially now that you are to become a father again.'

'I won't ask you how you know.'

'There are those who still believe in the old people's existence. Remain watchful.'

The man's serious tone cuts Stefán. 'We will. It takes only one. How well I know that now.'

'You, Stefán, will become the Watcher one day. You alone will judge the stranger who stumbles on this pool. You will decide who should be given instruction and who should not. And on that day, you will see me no more.'

The tall man stretches his legs. Another year has passed in a blink of his eye.

Finn Fowler and Owen Mockett sit at a table in a riverside pub with a window view of the Thames. It is rare that they would miss an evening out in ever-sprawling London. They speak of business and the weather. They don't speak of her. Perhaps they will one day, but for now, the topic is too raw.

Finn destroyed all of her belongings. He removed the keys from her chatelaine before he destroyed her talisman of their imprison-ment. One item, however, was curiously missing. The small picture frame on her dressing table is empty of their faded images of 1914. The photograph had always made him uncomfortable, but the thought of her concealing it in Iceland sends a shiver through him.

Finn and Mockett share a half-pint, their daily allowance, while they wait for their food. Often on these nights the same unspoken thoughts join them for dinner. They think how damned lucky they are to have survived. The fearsome Icelandic men who took her away and escorted her to her punishment scared the bejesus out of them. Finn and Owen were unable to form a defence to present to their accusers, who were also their judiciary. When they were pardoned for their culpability, Willa said that she had never heard men weep like that before.

No one in the pub pays much attention to them. They seem to meld into the polished woodwork; their voices mingle with the screen announcing the football scores.

The odd ship and barge pass their view in the rising tide.

Ancient waste will return to the Thames's anaerobic mud, and its

power to tell of the past is buried once more, until the moon releases
its pull again.
Iceland.
England.
Perhaps elsewhere.

ACKNOWLEDGEMENTS

My thanks for the support, energy, creativity and not least, the patience of my brilliant agent, Oli Munson. Thanks to all at A.M. Heath, including Florence Rees and Jennifer Custer. And a special mention for Becky Brown, for early reading and suggestions.

Great appreciation and respect for my editor, the stellar Jenny Parrott, whose care and attention coaxed more out of me than I thought possible, and whose close work helped bring the manuscript to more vibrancy. She did all that with amazingly good humour. Thanks to Paul Nash and all the dynamic team at Point Blank/ Oneworld including the wizard Mark Rusher, and James Jones, Margot Weale, Thanhmai Bui-Van, Cailin Neal, Kate Bland and James Magniac. Kudos to my copyeditor, Emily Thomas, whose eagle-eyed, thoughtful and face-saving (mine) attention to detail was remarkable.

Warm thanks for her encouragement and expertise to Denise Stewart, who kindly and generously drew upon her impressive, vast experience to steer me away from pitfalls.

How fortunate and grateful I was for the facilities and staff of the British Library, the Wellcome Library, the Camden Local Studies and Archives Centre, and to the London Metropolitan Archives. For their particular help with other aspects of research I am grateful to Neil Handley, curator of the British Optical Assocation Museum, Michael Ridpath and Brian Parsons. Paul Talling and his Derelict London guided walks in Limehouse and Wapping opened my eyes and spurred my imagination. Thanks, Paul.

For friendship, hospitality and wise counsel thanks to Kate Colquhoun, Lisa Highton, Britt Berge, and Jason Hewitt, for communing over bottomless cups of tea and coffee. To the gracious Eveline Carn, thank you for allowing a stranger to visit your home. Admiration for and thanks to the taxi driver, who, when I said, 'Follow that taxi!' did not hesitate or ask questions.

Finally, heartfelt thanks to Malcolm for his unwavering support and understanding.

After KATE MAYFIELD was born she was taken directly to a funeral home. Her father, an undertaker, set up shop in a small town in southern Kentucky where the family resided in his funeral home for thirteen years. This is the setting of her memoir, *The Undertaker's Daughter*. Kate attended Western Kentucky University before moving to Manhattan where she graduated from the American Academy of Dramatic Arts. After living in New York and Los Angeles, she now makes London her home.